D1525039

CONTENTS

RAGE

Her Monsters Book One

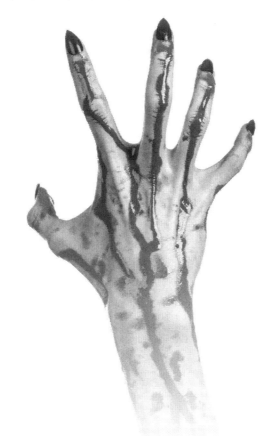

K.A. KNIGHT

Copyright © 2019 K.A. Knight, all rights reserved

Written by K.A. Knight
Rage (Her Monsters Book One)
This is a work of fiction. Any resemblance to places, events or real people
are entirely coincidental.

Edited By Jess from Elemental Editing and Proofreading & Kaila Duff
Formatted by Kaila Duff of Duffette Literary Services

Dedication

For my three-way girls, I never knew you could find your soulmates in friends before you.

Author's Note

Please be aware that this book contains scenes that some may find triggering.

If you have any concerns, please skip to the last page of the book, where I've given a more specific warning that does contain some spoilers.

CHAPTER I

I hate my husband. If I could, I would take this lingerie and choke him to death with it. Eying the newest addition of horrible gifts he's given me, I frown at myself in the mirror. I've gotten skinny, well, skinnier, probably due to his constant fucking need to control what I eat. He says I'm too chunky, that no one will love me if I'm fat. Eying myself now, I feel like a stranger. I loved my curves, the dip in my hips, my rounded stomach, my thick thighs, and ass. Just another thing I've lost in my life because of him. Don't get me wrong, I chose this, well at first I did. He was charming, dressed to the nines in suits and expensive shoes. He spoilt me, taking me to all these fancy restaurants and showing me off. I should have known then that behind that charming facade hid a monster. I never questioned the money, or the lifestyle, not even when the ridiculous gifts started turning up.

It was little things at first, like clothing. I'd felt flattered, but then I realised he was trying to control what I wore, and they were always a size too small. When I asked, he told me I would have to lose weight to fit into them. That was a big no for me, I might be poor, but I knew who I was—well, I used to. I tried to get away, I really did. I stopped texting him back and answering his calls. It only seemed to enrage him, and I'd finally got a glimpse of what he'd hid under that glossy surface.

He started turning up at my apartment in the middle of the night in a rage. In my fear, I'd rung the police. My second mistake. He had them in his pockets, well, more like his boss did. They escorted me somewhere 'safe,' only to pass me over to him. He locked me in the penthouse apartment he called home for three weeks after that.

I'd lost my job, my friends. They thought I didn't want them in my life anymore—nothing could have been further from the truth. I was so alone, so scared. He pictured himself as my savior.

A new plan formed, I went along with it all, but my escape was always lingering in my mind. Waiting for him to slip up, to trust me, and he did. When he fell asleep one night after getting blackout drunk, I snuck out with nothing but the clothes on my back. I had slept on the streets before, I could do it again. Get somewhere safe, away from him.

I lasted a week before his men found me. It was the first time he attacked me. I soon learnt my lesson and he broke my spirit. Time and time again, my body was his to do with what he wanted, even though a small part of me had rebelled at his control, hated him, but I knew I had to bide my time. Be smart, play the perfect girl-friend—sorry, wife.

About a month ago, I woke up tied to a chair with a wedding ring on my finger and a bored looking man ordaining our marriage. He touched me softly that night, telling me he loved me. That I was his everything, he was so happy that I had agreed to marry him. When he fell asleep, I'd crept into the bathroom, the one he took the door off of, and cried. I thought about ending my life, there was no escape from him. His men were everywhere and the police were under his control. I was nothing, just a poor girl from a small town who came to the city to try and make a better life. Even my friends had been more like acquaintances, people to ride out the boring with.

I'd even picked up his razor blade, but I couldn't do it. I'd wait years if I had to—but I would be free of him.

I hear him moving in the other room and it brings me back to myself. The lingerie he's given me is disgusting. It frames my now too skinny body, highlighting my large breasts and plump arse. I look like a fucking sex doll. The red lace frames my pale skin and the bruises marring it.

"Are you ready? You know how I hate waiting?" he calls, his voice already slurring from the whiskey he's drinking.

I know that means it's going to be a bad night. Blowing out a breath, I step into the bedroom to see him lounging on the bed in his suit, scrolling through his phone. The one thing he is more obsessed with than me.

"Tim, I can't-" I flinch when his hard eyes look me over.

"What did we discuss last night?" His hard voice holds a warning and I tilt my head down, pretending to be submissive even as I fight myself to not look into his eyes and spit.

"Sorry, *sir*, I can't wear this in front of your men," I say softly, hoping he will let me change.

He slides from the bed and stalks towards me, stopping when his breath hits my face, making me crinkle my nose. "And why not?" he asks.

Think fast. Placing my hand gently on his chest, I shiver at the disgust crawling along my skin, even as he groans and grips my hips, thinking I want him. "Surely, sir, you don't want your men to be able to look at what is yours?" I lower my voice, trying to be seductive.

Fluttering the fake eyelashes he makes me wear, I watch him carefully in case he snaps.

He hardens against my hand and I know it was the wrong move. "You dare question me? You question your husband?" he screams the questions in my face, and my heart stutters. Later he will blame the whiskey, he will cry and hold my broken body as he begs for my forgiveness, but for now, he is the monster I know and hate.

"I wouldn- I just-" My words cut off in a scream, as he rips one of the dangling diamond earring he demanded I wear from my ear. Pain shoots through my body, but I've had worse. I can feel the blood dripping down my neck and splashing on my heaving breasts. The sight only seems to spur him on.

"You will do what you are told." He grips my chin and makes me look at him, his eyes are blown with lust, and I have to force myself not to cry. A knock at the door distracts him and I am eternally grateful, every time he fucks me it's like I lose a piece of myself. My body isn't my own.

"What the fuck do you want?" he yells, still gripping my chin hard enough to leave a bruise.

The door cracks open and one of his henchmen sticks his head around the door. He looks me over, appreciation filling his gaze before it quickly snaps back to Tim, as if not to be caught. "Sorry for the interruption sir, but they are here." He retreats but throws me a smoldering look. I just stare blankly at him as the door shuts.

Grunting, Tim lets go of my chin and seems to forget I'm even there. Striding to the table next to his—*our*—bed, he downs his whiskey before shrugging into his black jacket and slipping his phone into the pocket.

He turns and looks me over. "You will do." With that, he grips my arm and drags me from the room, and I know I am nothing more than an ornament tonight, a thing for him to show off. To flaunt his wealth and power.

Sitting on Tim's knee as he laughs and jokes with his men, I look around in disgust. The penthouse is buzzing with activity. Butlers and servers rushing about, the women looking uneasy as the men taunt them and touch them, but none would dare question it. Not here, not now. These men are powerful, they run the city from the darkness like puppeteers. Police? They own them. Mayor? He is one of them. I can feel the eyes running down my body, undressing me and fucking me in their mind. I have to swallow my bile, even as it seems to please Tim.

"Wife, get me a drink," he demands, pushing me from his knee and smacking my ass. The group of men we sit with eye me hungrily, and I know if they got the chance they would fuck me.

"Yes, sir," I grit out and march away. I hear them congratulating him on landing such a well behaved slave. Fucking arseholes.

When I reach the bar, a man blocks my way. He's big, his eyes are sharp and filled with anger, and his body almost vibrates with hate—for who I don't know and I don't want to.

I sidestep him and he mirrors my movement, blocking me again. Without speaking to me, he reaches forward and fondles my breast. I step back, wanting to murder him, and he just laughs and wanders away. Fuck it, his drink can wait. I'll pay for it later, but I need a moment or I will explode.

Striding away, I slip around the corner and into the bathroom in the hallway, hiding for a moment.

I swipe at the useless tears tracking down my face and hang my head, looking down at the sink. How I wish I could go back in there, steal one of the guns they're all packing and just kill them all. I was once a good girl, I did as I was told, I followed the law—fuck, I didn't even speed. I enjoyed sex and men, but who doesn't. Now? The darkness is almost overtaking me, I would do anything—*be anything*—if it meant they got to pay for their sins.

The door opens and I freeze, swinging my head around to face the wide-eyed waiter. Shit, did I not lock the door? Stupid, Dawn, real stupid. Straightening, I try to pretend he didn't just witness me having a breakdown, but I see his eyes soften and his face fill with concern. He slips inside and shuts the door gently, holding his hands up when I step back and meet the wall.

"Hey, I'm not going to hurt you. Are you okay?" He steps forward again, his young face filled with determination and concern. I wonder what it's like to be that innocent. "I saw you earlier and I can see the bruises, do you need me to help you?"

"You should go before someone sees you," I say softly, not wanting to be responsible for another man's death. Because if he's caught in here, that's what it will mean—hell, he killed a man for looking at me funny once.

"I can help you," he urges, lowering his voice like I'm cornered animal.

"Please, leave!" I beg, looking around desperately. I can't, I can't have anyone else's blood on my hands.

The door opens just then and my heart sinks. He hears it and spins, standing in front of me like he can defend me. Tim's man from before looks from me to the waiter with a grin. "Well, well princess, lookie what I found. He's going to be so mad, I wonder if he will let me punish you again."

The waiter puffs up in indignation at his words, even as I go numb. "You can't just talk-" His words cut off in a gurgle as Tim's man darts forward and cuts off his air.

"You are coming with me. I can't wait to see what he does to you." The man laughs and drags the choking waiter from the bathroom. I hesitate before following, each step pounding into my head with finality. When I reach the living room, I spot Tim standing with a frown. When he sees the waiter in his man's hand, and me lingering behind, his face turns molten. He excuses himself from the conversation and strides towards us.

He doesn't stop until he grips my arm, hard. "Bring him with us," he growls before dragging me down the corridor and throwing me into the bedroom. I fly onto the floor before quickly getting to my knees. A thump sounds next to me and I turn to see the gasping waiter his face purple, is on the floor next to me. Looking over my shoulder, I spot the door closing as another of Tim's men slips inside and stands in front of it with the first. I'm trapped, and I have a bad fucking feeling.

"Sir, I-" My words are cut off as he backhands me, sending me sprawling to the carpet. I hear his men laugh, even as I spot the waiter trying to get to his feet, anger still seeping to his expression. This kid really doesn't give up, you've got to admire him for it.

"Stay down and you might live," I whisper, knowing it's a lie. They will kill him, they have to.

I slowly get up, standing on my wobbly legs and face Tim. His eyes are dark and filled with hate, his chest is heaving. I have seen him mad many times, but this... this is fury and he isn't in control anymore. That scares me more than anything.

"Sir-" I try one more time, determined to at least try and save the kid's life, but he doesn't let me finish the sentence. I'm thrown onto the bed, gasping. He's on me in a minute, hovering over me as his fists hammer into my skin. I try to protect my head by raising my arms, but one of his men steps in and ties them to the headboard. Looking up, I spot my death in his eyes and tonight is the night I know he won't stop.

I lose count of the hits, my body is just one big pulsing mass of agony. I feel my ribs crack and my skin tear. Blood drips steadily down my face as he finally climbs off, allowing me to see the pale faced waiter staring at me in horror.

Tim pulls his gun and fires a shot in each of the waiter's legs. The kid screams in pain as tears drip down his face. Only when he looks up again does Tim shoot him in the head. I watch the kid's lifeless body drop to the floor as blood starts to pool around him.

He tucks the gun back in his pants and turns to me, hatred contorting his face. "You think I would let him touch you? You. Are. Mine!" he screams, flying at me again.

Tears stream unchecked down my face, as my breathing saws in and out of my damaged chest. I can feel my body breaking and I grin. At least I can escape him in death. My smile seems to spur him on. He yells, screaming nonsense as he grabs a knife and starts cutting. I feel each slice, each cut, and it blurs into all the other pain. My focus narrows down to my breathing as I watch him above me, killing me.

With a scream he buries the knife in my stomach, and looking down, I spot the blood pumping from the wound, and I know it's a killing blow. All my other pale skin is covered in blood, and in places, I can see my muscle showing.

My head falls back as my heart stutters, my breathing becomes harder and darkness edges my vision. I could fight it, but what's the point? My only regret is not being able to make him and his men pay for what they have done to me.

"Fuck!" he screams, obviously coming back to himself, seeing what he has done.

He yanks out the blade, a stupid mistake, and tries to staunch the flow of blood. When he realises it's futile, he freezes on top of me. I feel myself going cold and my breathing becomes erratic.

"Might as well have one last fuck with her," he jokes, but I can hear the pain underneath and his men leave the room. I retreat back into the darkness, not wanting to witness this. Even when I'm dead I can't catch a break, the last thing my dying body will experience is that pig rutting into me. It sends a stab of fury and hatred right through me, if only I could make him pay. Make him scared like I am, watch him die horrifically. It's my last thought before the darkness takes me.

Am I fucking dead yet? It's the only thing I can think of as I feel myself being carried, before I question further, the feeling fades to nothingness.

I manage to fight against the darkness again, only to realise I'm literally in darkness, something is moving and I'm banging about. I'm in the fucking boot of a car. I fade again.

Something cold and wet lands on my face, and my body is too heavy to move away from it as more lands on me. The sound of a shovel ringing out has me panicking, is he burying me? I fade again.

It's harder to fight the darkness this time, it clings to my body, dragging me back with a wordless promise of happiness and love, but I don't want that. I want revenge, I want pain and blood. The thought helps me fight through the dark shroud until my mouth opens with a gasp, and my eyes fly open to see nothing but more darkness. I feel insects and bugs crawling on me, and I have to breathe through the panic. That motherfucker killed and buried me.

Wait, I felt myself die... how am I alive?

Chapter 2

Nos

Something calls for me across the forest, which is my home. The trees move for me, the ground welcomes me, and the animals flock to me, but this is something else. Something dark, primal, and filled with power. It curls around me, restarting my cold dead heart, and yanks on the lifeless muscle. I don't bother changing back to human, I can't even remember the last time I was in that constricting form. I prefer the solitude of the wild where I can be me. I venture into the modern world every now and again. I read the stories they write about me, the tales and scriptures. They have it all wrong, but it is amusing, humans are such fragile creatures. They are born, and then they live for a few years, slowly rotting away. They cause wars, they use words instead of weapons. It all seems so... contrived. They won't last, if only they knew what lingered in their world. Monsters, like me, walking in the dark, the nightmares they whisper about and the stories they use to scare themselves.

The tug comes again, harder this time, bringing me out of my thoughts. It has been so long since I felt anything but numbness, so I must admit, I am curious. What creature could call me? They would have to be powerful. I have spent the last thousand years gaining so much power, I am almost untouchable, practically the boogeyman even amongst monsters. It's the intrigue that gets me moving, leaving my cave and following the feeling. I resist it for a moment, just to see what the power will do, and pain ripples through my body, like a vice tightening around me, making me grunt. Strong indeed.

Even the pain is better than this indifference. As I wander through the woods seeking the call, I debate my life. I could be like the other ancients, I could retreat from the world they no longer understand nor rule. Hide away and remember the good days, let my feelings rot me from the inside out like a diseased tree, but something always kept me tied here. The thought of leaving it causes an almost physical ache, and I never understood why.

I have to duck under a low hanging branch so my antlers don't get caught, as a rabbit hops out from behind a tree, freezing when it notices the bigger predator. Even the wolves in the woods hesitate to venture near me, sensing the power. Yet I am at one with the forest, even if I don't blend in wearing my true form.

The feeling stops suddenly as I reach the edge of a small break in the trees, and linger in the shadows. Blending with the dark, I watch and wait. My nose twitches at the smell of burnt rubber and smoke as a car rumbles away, speeding as if being chased. Silly human. My eyes rove the ground, noticing the upturned soil and sensing the disturbance in the air. Someone has defiled my land.

I freeze when a pale hand shoots from the ground, its long slender fingers tipped with red nail polish and adorned with rings that sparkle in the night. It is too delicate to be anything other than human, but for it to be buried, it must be dead.

Interest gets the better of me and I stalk across the clearing, silencing the animals close by. Leaning down, I capture the wiggling hand and pull. The soil parts for me and I send a tiny drop of power to help it.

A head and body breaks through the earth and I let go, stepping back and watching in rapt interest. The human is naked and female. No, wait, not human. Dragging air into my lungs, I try to work through the smells assaulting my senses. It is other, something I can't identify. I don't know whether it is the comforting aroma of death, but I find myself taking a step closer, only to still when another scent hits me, stronger than before, sending a bolt of lust and longing to my black heart, and hardening my cock. It smells like the forest, like nature itself. Floral but strong, fresh like the air after a storm.

The creature lifts its head, long golden, bloodstained hair covers its face, but I can still see the beauty. *Her* beauty. She sits back on her heels, unashamed even naked and covered in her own blood as she is. Her eyes watch me, not in horror like everyone else, but calm and filled with... lust?

Gracefully, I lower myself into my crossed legged position and tilt my head to watch her. She mirrors my pose, her rose coloured nipples peeking through her curtain of hair. She is pale, paler than the moon's rays shining down on us. Her lips and nipples are the same colour red. Her beauty is timeless, striking and breathtaking. In my early days, they would have written songs about her, they would have worshipped her beauty and begged for a taste. Even I am not unaffected, my long since dormant need rises to the surface with a vengeance, screaming at me to take this creature, to make her mine, and fuck her in a way only a divine creature of lust, fertility, animals, and the underworld can. I have been called many things, god, monster, even savior, but I would go by any name this creature in front of me whispers from those red plump lips. I wonder if she sounds as enchanting as she looks. I have the insane urge to converse with her, just to see if it is true, but my voice is rough and my throat does not seem to want to utter words, so long unused that the concept is foreign.

While I have been watching her, she has been watching me, and instead of flinching away from my appearance, she seems curious.

"What are you?"

Three words, I savor them, running her velvety voice through my head as they burrow into me, claiming parts of me I didn't know existed anymore.

"A monster," I reply, my raspy, unused voice like the darkness around us, powerful and all-encompassing, my power leaking out like I am a young shifter, not one a thousand years old. What is it about this creature that fascinates me so and causes me to lose my infamous control?

"You are beautiful," she says softly, running her eyes over me again.

Frowning, I look down at myself. I have been called many things in this form, horrifying, too powerful to behold, a creature of nightmares, but never... beautiful. Her mind must have been warped from the trauma of her mortal body dying. Yes, that must be it. Now if she had seen my human body, I could agree with her, that form is pleasing to the human eye and hides my monstrous side, while allowing me to walk among the humans, even if I can't blend in. Humans can sense the power. Besides, an almost seven foot man does not fit in well.

I still when she crawls towards me, that body moving in a mesmerising way before she sits close enough to touch, a soft delicate hand flutters over my left arm, my eyes snap to the creature, as I realize she has shifted closer to me, her petal soft hand touching me. I have killed beings for less, but I find myself leaning into her touch, seeing what she will do.

"What are they?" she muses, running her hand along my torcs which I have tied to my arms, tired of holding them. I don't answer, too busy watching her pale fingers against my dark skin. Where I am the shade of wet soil at harvest, she is the color of white sandy beaches. Her hand runs up my shoulder and along my face, trailing a sensual path until she reaches my head and then circles my antlers, making me shiver. More torcs hang from them but she seems more interested in touching my antlers.

"They are like a deer's," she murmurs to herself before her fingers run back down my forehead and circle my eye. "So bright, like the moon has been trapped in them, there isn't even any pupil, they're just... white."

I sit completely still as she discovers my body, not wanting to break the spell in case she runs screaming, or worse, pulls away. My body likes the feel of her touching me, leaning into her like the flower does to the sun. Her fingers run along the cool metal of my ornate neck ring and down my wide chest, circling the golden markings on my skin. Her fingers stop and she sits back, and I find myself missing the heat of her skin. She touched me so delicately, like I am something precious.

"Is this your form? Like I am human? You must be something else," she asks, crossing her legs until our knees touch. I find myself craving that touch more than I should, maybe it has been too long since another being touched me. Yes, that must be it.

"Yes and no," I reply, not apologising for the rough, harsh quality of my voice, but she doesn't seem to care if the shiver of her body and tightening of her nipples are anything to go by. Interesting, it has been a long time since I had a human, but the unmistakable waft of desire from her has me clenching my fingers into the dirt, anchoring me.

"You have more than one?" she says, those lips curving up into a smile, which I can't seem to look away from. I would do anything for her to bestow another on me. I wonder if I would be lost if I heard her laugh. Would it wrap around me, weaving me in its spell? Maybe she is a witch, or a siren.

"Yes," I reply.

She doesn't seem to care about my abrupt answer. "Can I see them?" she asks, her eyes burning with excitement.

"You would not like one of my other forms," I warn, knowing it would cause this delicate creature to scream in terror and flee, and I don't want that to happen just yet.

"What about the other?" she asks.

"Human." I lower my head and watch her body, my eyes unable to look away even if I wanted to.

"Humans are so boring, I think I prefer this one," she says and a tinkle of a laughter escapes, like the birds on the wind, the beauty unparalleled.

"Humans crave beauty, you would prefer me in that form," I find myself saying.

She shakes her head. "Humans may be beautiful on the outside, but underneath there is only rot and hatred, it corrupts them and all that beauty is pointless." Without waiting for me to reply she carries on, "What is your name?"

"Names have power," I caution, knowing it was once used

against me and I will not make the same mistake again, not even for this bewitching creature.

"I'm Dawn," she says with a soft smile, as if trying to comfort a scared animal, is that what I am to her?

"The second most beautiful time of the day, when the sun burns through the sky, alighting the darkness and signaling another night survived." I don't know why the words slip out, but I don't take them back.

"I always preferred the night," she replies with a laugh, she looks at her lap and sighs. "How am I alive and why am I not panicking more over the fact that I awoke in my own grave with a creature of the night pulling me from the soil?" she muses like she is talking to herself, and I do not have the answers so I don't reply. I don't know how she is alive, or what she is.

"You are not human," I summarise, my ears twitching at the animal sneaking closer, obviously as curious about Dawn as I am.

She blows out a breath, making her cheeks round adorably. "I figured as much, humans can't survive being gutted. Do you know what I am?" she asks, looking at me for help. Like a punch to my stomach, I find myself wanting to give her comforting words that other creatures seem to seek, but I will not lie to her. "I do not know. I have never met another like you, that feels or smells like you."

"Well, at least you don't bullshit me," she grins, her eyes focusing on the snake curling itself up my arm and around my shoulder to stare at her.

"It will not hurt you, it is curious," I say, stroking its scaly skin.

"It's beautiful," she whispers, watching it. I look down and I have to agree, its scales are an iridescent green that seems to shine in the light, and its eyes are the colour of gold.

"Most deadly things are quite beautiful. Their beauty used to entice their prey," I murmur as it slinks down my arms and curls in my lap, watching her as if bewitched as I am.

She watches the snake as I watch her, a frown tugging at those lips and crinkles appearing in her forehead. "I can't remember how I died, or how I got here. Every time I try, a shard digs into my brain."

"Of course, your mind is trying to protect you from the truth. It is a human sentiment," I add, and unable to help myself I stroke the snake, catching the softness of her leg as I do.

"I want to remember." Her voice tightens with anger.

"Why?" I ask, curious.

"Would you not? Someone killed me and buried me in the forest, they betrayed and hurt me. Would you not want to know if you had enemies?"

I nod, my antlers ringing in the wind. "I can help, if you wish," the offer slips out.

"You can?" She eyes me curiously, her hand raising and petting the snake between us, stopping as it covers my hand there. I jolt from the feeling, like my very soul is clambering to get to her. I see the same truth in her eyes, she feels it too. This connection, this feeling of need.

"Close your eyes, this might hurt," I warn, and leaning forward, I suck in some more of her addicting scent, while touching my fingertip lightly to her forehead, letting my magic curl through me to her, and pushing away the darkness shrouding her memories until she can see everything. Her eyes snap open, filled with pain, fury, and sadness. Mourning for the life and innocence she lost. I see the memories clashing in her mind as I watch her being betrayed by the human who vowed to love her.

Her mouth opens and a scream of terror and agony pours out, rolling through the forest and into the world like a plea, as she relives her own death. It seems to echo into the night, calling to the darkness in me, and begging for the monsters of the night to save her.

CHAPTER 3

DUME

My chains slither across the floor as I tug, pulling taut from the steel cylinders they are wrapped around. There are six altogether. One per hand and foot. One around my neck and one around my middle. The only reason I haven't broken free from them is because they are enchanted. Not even the strongest metal could contain an animal like me, I am the monster of the Labyrinth that the humans crafted stories about, the terrifying creature they fear above all others. No maze, no human, not even the gods could enslave me... but working together?

I can't remember how long I have been locked down here, left to rot, forgotten like a relic of the past. My animal half takes over my mind more each day as it bellows for freedom, for a taste of blood from the people who betrayed him. The ones who chained him, imprisoned him, and left him.

I let my animalistic side take over long ago, not in body, of course, the chains won't allow me to shift. Instead, I've retreated into the darkness of my beast's mind. It is better than my human mind, which is going crazy from the unending solitude and absolute darkness. I have only my hearing to rely on down here in the cata-combs, hidden beneath the city with only one way in or out. I was left in a pit, a hole in the ground with walls so high they reach the floor of the city, surrounded by steel structures erected to contain me. I tug on the chains again and they tighten with a hiss, the magic bubbling as if it fights my strength. I have been testing them for years, probably around four hundred though it is hard to count, they have started to weaken, cracks appearing in the magic and steel. Magic is not made to last forever, it needs to be reapplied. They will be back soon—they can sense when the cracks occur—to contain me once again, not wanting to risk their nightmarish creation escaping into the world.

I feel the blood running freely from my many wounds caused by the chains, which only enrages my bull further. He roars for their blood, for every drop we lose he thirsts for a pint of theirs. Soon, I remind him, begging for his patience. I sense a change in the air, something is coming and with it, so will my freedom and the ability to kill once more. I will seek revenge on those who betrayed us, who imprisoned us. I will not stop until my horns and hooves are covered in their traitorous blood and gore—a gruesome aftermath of their murders, which I will commit when I avenge my captors. They will remember.

The monster always wins.

My bull perks up, quieting down for once, his roaring stopping in my head. *What do you sense?* I ask, receiving no answer as he paces inside of it, nudging to be let out. *What?* I question again, only to receive a prod for my words.

Then I feel it.

A call.

Not just any call, *her* call.

It wraps around me, cooing at both my beast and me, restarting my heart and kicking my emotions into overdrive. My body hardens, my cock with it, and everything comes back with snap. The colours, the sounds, like I have been living in the grey—and now I am whole.

I let it wrap around me, cradling my magic. It begs for me, so filled with pain and horror that my beast pushes through my body, something which hasn't happened since the beginning when I was a young calf. He doesn't wait for me to call him, instead, he pulls through my body, changing me. Once my shift is complete, my head falls back and I let out a roar of anguish.

She needs me.

Uncaring of the pain or magic, I rip free from the chains, a feat only a bond could attain. I feel the steel rip through skin and fur, trying to contain me, but it can't. Not anymore. I have a new purpose.

Once free, I waste no time, following the tugging in my soul, which leads me up and out. My beast allows me to shift my legs back once more and I begin climbing the walls. I huff in anger, anger that she is alone and in pain, while I wasted away down here. Smoke bellows from my snout, the black tendrils curling around the stone, eroding it. My horns scratch into the stone as I climb and my golden armband squeezes into my chained muscles, reminding me of what I am—a monster.

When I reach the top, I shift my legs back and charge through the winding hallways, leading me up to my freedom. I ram into a gate and roar again as it stops me, halting my progress. Not for long. Letting the call fuel me, I rip the twisted metal and the magic binding it, and then I smell freedom for the first time in over half a millennia.

I let loose a deep bellow into the night, causing the animals around to halt their calls and the humans to shiver in their homes, but it is for her. To let her know I am coming. Anyone who has hurt her will feel the wrath of my monster.

CHAPTER 4

ASKA

The deep darkness of my eternal slumber falters for a moment. I ignore the tug and retreat into the comforting nothingness, but it comes again. Snorting, I roll over, which traps my wings uncomfortably beneath me. I retract the leathery appendages back into my body, returning to my human form, and snuggle back into my nest to sleep. It comes again. Groaning at the irritant, I slit open one eye and glance around my cave to see what has disturbed me, I picked this isolated spot for a reason. To retreat from a world I no longer understand, high up in the mountains where no one can find me. I am hidden away in nature, forgotten... so what woke me?

The tug is persistent, pulling at my magic and soul. I open my other eye and jump to my feet, the muscles collapsing after weeks and months of disuse. I wonder how long I have been asleep. The smells around me are familiar but other than that, everything feels foreign, like the very world I had existed in is gone.

My dragon responds when the tug comes again, tumbling into the rock wall, fighting the change, unsure why, after so long, my dragon would force the change. It huffs at me as I take back control. Enraged, he roars in my mind. Relenting, I shift until I am my monster once again. Lifting my muzzle to the air, I sift through the multitude of scents, but I cannot detect anything amiss. Tilting my head to the side, I allow the glow of my purple eyes to light the darkness of my cave. If the cobwebs and growth are anything to go by, it has been years since I was last awake.

The tug comes again, stronger this time, wrapping around me both inside and out, like a comforting hug, familiar and yet so strange that I halt. I know what that is, my dragon huffs out a laugh at my stupidity, obviously already recognizing the call.

Once it connects with my magic, I let out a powerful roar which shakes the mountain, agony and pain race through my body, trapped within that call. They dare hurt her? I will rip their souls from their bodies and eat them alive. My dragon agrees, opening my mouth wide in warning, the darkness contained within me flows from my mouth, seeking a soul to eat.

The tug happens again and this time I follow it. Shuffling to the edge of my cave I release my wings, and bellow out a roar as I jump from the top of the mountain, soaring through the air. After being cooped up for decades in my cave, the feel of the wind beneath my wings is freeing. Soon, I find my rhythm of flying again, my wings beat through the air as I follow the call. Trees and land whiz by beneath me, but I pay it no mind, I have no inclination to explore this new world. My only focus is getting to her.

The Devourer, The Soul Eater, The Monster of Nightmares once again soars through the skies on a hunt.

CHAPTER 5

GRIFFIN

The human cums with a disgusting sound that makes me crinkle my nose, he sounds like a cow. He pushes the girl away as he slumps back against the brick wall. She falls back, slamming her barely covered ass onto the cold, wet concrete. Her dress has been ripped down the front to show her still young tits. Her cheeks are red with embarrassment, and even from here I can see the tears gathering in her eyes. She rights her dress and stands up on those ridiculous heels, teetering from side to side. The man doesn't even bother catching her, instead, he taps white powder onto his hand and snorts it back, his eyes closing as he shakes in bliss. Sighing, he drops his head back and narrows his eyes once he finds the girl shaking in the cold.

"Why the fuck are you still here?" he demands, and I roll my eyes.

I can't wait for this job to be over, these fucking humans are the scum of the Earth. They call us monsters, evil, but I have seen more evil while watching them in the last week than ever before.

They care for nothing and no one. Trafficking their own people, hurting children. Stealing innocents and corrupting their own land. At least us monsters are honest. We kill, we hunt, and we fuck, but we never try to hide that. Most of us would never hurt a child and our women are protected. Not used and tossed aside like this young one standing in the shady alley behind a nightclub, cum running from her mouth and tears streaming down her face. I should feel sorry for her, and I guess some part of me does. The part that still retains some semblance of normalcy, but I'm too far gone to care enough to stop it. She made her own choice, she has to live with that.

Some call me a monster, others call me a freak. Something that was never meant to exist, even amongst monsters, I am unwelcome. Fuck them, they still come to me when they need something done. They ask me to do their dirty work, relying on my skills and lack of a moral compass.

Something pushes at my shield, making me frown, and I look around at the dark damp rooftop I'm perched on that overlooks the alley. Below, the human tucks in his now flaccid cock and downs his drink. The tug comes again. Frowning, I let my shielding down, only to be forced to grab onto the ledge as I gasp. *No. Fuck no.*

But it's too late, the call wraps around me, tugging at me, begging for me to help. The pain and agony becoming my own as I gasp through it, fighting the need to find her. No, not fucking now. Not fucking ever. It's like cutting my own soul but I push away the call, slamming my shields tightly in place. I can't afford to be distracted, not now. This job is important and if I don't complete it, the council won't hesitate to kill me, I will have outlived my purpose.

I still feel it circling me, looking for a way to penetrate my control. Gritting my teeth, I look back at the alley and swear, just as I see the human slip back into the club. Fuck, I missed my chance and all because of her.

My wings shoot out behind me, I know no one can see them, the darkness of them blending into the night as I swoop down on feathery wings into the now empty alley. Pulling them back into my body, I push back my black hood and stride to the door. I guess I'll be hunting tonight, behind on my plan and having to roll with the punches. All because of the call.

Who the fuck would have thought a mistake like me would ever have received one?

CHAPTER 6

DAWN

I fall backwards, my memories tumbling with me, streaming through my mind like a taunting laugh. Reminding me of everything I lost, of my death, and now my rebirth. My eyes flash open and connect with those bright, shining orbs of the creature before me, that's what he is after all—a creature.

More monster than man, his face animal and still hauntingly beautiful. I'm betting he's the same in his human form, beautiful yet dangerous. Yet, I find myself leaning towards him, seeking the warmth of his skin and the tingle that runs through me when we touch. Yes, I bet he is beautiful as a human, but as a monster? He's powerful, terrifying, and downright addictive.

Most hide away their darkness, letting it twist them, he wears it on his skin for all to see. Claiming it, owning it, his power brushing the very ground he walks on. I should be terrified, I should be horrified, but I'm not. His monster calls to mine, a power pulsing inside of me waiting to be set free, the one that clawed me from death and dug me from the ground.

With a scream, all that power flows out of me, twisting around the horror and pain still running through my body as the memories finally settle. Like a lock turning or a jigsaw finally clicking together, but I can't stop the power. It seems to run through me, from me, into me, flowing out into the world until finally, it stops, and I slump to the side breathing heavy.

My eyes open slowly to see the creature is doing pretty much the same, I should stay and see if he's okay, but something in me tells me I won't want to leave then, and I need to leave. I need to make Tim pay. If killing me and then defiling me once more wasn't enough, he hid my body like a dirty little secret. Hate and fury twist inside me, branding me as its own. No, he must pay. I will make him beg for his life before I end it. I will destroy everything he holds dear. His job. His money. His standing. Then his life.

Seems dying freed something more than just the power in me—my evil side too.

Standing, I smile softly down at the creature who's struggling into a crossed legged sitting position. "I'm sorry, I have to go. I have people to kill," I say, before blowing him a kiss and turning to the forest. It's like I know exactly where to go, something guiding me through the trees. Every footstep is light and cushioned by the earth, it's welcoming me and urging me on. No branches hit me, or animals attack me. I'm safe here, it calls to me, but I can't stay.

I pick up sounds of traffic and I speed up, even as I feel something hunting me, but my body twists towards the darkness and I can see the shining eyes there. I'm not afraid, he won't hurt me even if he is hunting me. I grin and turn back to the sound of cars. Reaching the tree line, I linger in the dark for a moment, before stepping out on the concrete.

The road is quiet at the moment, making me groan. Just my luck. Tilting my head, I hear a car coming. Stepping out onto the road, I wait in the middle, my feet apart and my arms by my side. I'm still naked, but I can't seem to care. My body feels right for once and when I look down, I realise I have my curves back.

The car comes around the corner a moment later, the lights shining on the cat's eyes at the side of the road and penetrating into the darkness of the forest, before lighting up where I am.

The car screeches to a halt, burning rubber as it stops before me. My eyesight is that good now, where I can pick out the man driving behind the wheel as he grips it tightly and tries to calm down from his near miss, and yet I still casually stand here. I see the moment his eyes land on me, they bloom with confusion and lust. How typical, he almost runs me down in the middle of the road, but he's more distracted about the fact my tits are swaying in the wind. *Men.*

He keeps the lights on as the stumbles from the car, his hands shaking as he rounds the hood and stares at me. "Are you okay, miss?"

He looks me over, his eyes widening in horror at the blood and soil coating my skin. Shaking my head, I step closer, and when he doesn't retreat, I swallow my grin.

"Can I get a lift?" I ask calmly, and his cheeks heat as his eyes snap back to me.

"Of-of course!" Something sweet wafts to me on the wind and I swallow it down, wondering what on earth it is. "Here… you can have my shirt." He strips off his button-down and passes it over, revealing a wife beater underneath. I take it from him, my fingers accidentally touching his in the process, and I have to swallow my snarl at the images running through his mind. It seems my new powers allow me to see into people thoughts, and his are full of images of me on my knees in front of him, his cock in my mouth.

Lovely, but I can work with lust. At least he doesn't seem to be asking too many questions. Shimmying into the shirt I do up the buttons, before moving around the car and climbing into the passenger seat. He seems frozen for a moment before he rounds the car and slips back inside, giving me a strange look before starting the car with a rumble.

Looking out the window, I blow the creature from the woods a kiss, even as the male starts to talk. "Do you need me to take you to the police station?" he asks, pulling away slowly.

Looking back to him, I see his eyes dropping to my legs and all the skin on display, making me roll my eyes. "No, take me to the Red House Apartments."

I see his eyes widen again at the name, after all, it is one of the most expensive apartments in all of the city. He speeds up as I stare out of the window, watching the trees pass. We must be in the forest district, a national park which runs around half of the city and extends for miles upon miles. It's easy to see why Tim buried me here. I spot something moving in the woods, faster than humans and even most animals, almost blending into the darkness. It seems I still have my monster stalker, the thought only comforts me.

I can almost hear the man in the driver's seat as his brain whirrs while he peeks over at me, his face heating and eyes shining with lust. I see the tent in his pants from here and I know that it spells trouble. Great, just what I need. Not that I have things to do or anything.

I'll give him one chance, if not, maybe I'll try out my newfound powers on him. "You can pull outside and I'll get you payment for your help," I offer nicely, and I see the war in his eyes as he tries to fight his need. His hands turn white on the wheel when, with a swear, he turns down a dirt path into the forest, hiding us from sight. I'm guessing his lust won, poor him, but I grin. I guess it would be good to test out my new body, just not in the way he's thinking.

He shuts off the car, breathing heavily, obviously building himself up to attacking me. I just sit in my seat and wait. When he doesn't move, I get bored, opening my door and sliding from the car, I round the front until I stand with the forest to my back.

He swears again and slides out, pursuing me, this time determination lining his face. He doesn't stop until he grabs my arms and thrusts me onto the hood of the car, following me down as his mouth smashes into mine. My eyes remain open as he grinds on me, really? I don't have fucking time for this.

The power running through my body hums as his mouth connects with mine, and before I know it my mouth automatically opens, I try to pull away but it's like we're stuck. Something burns inside of me, begging for him—begging to be filled. My hands come up and hold him to me even as he tries to pull away. Our lips fused together and mouths open in a strange kiss. He starts to fight and I wrap my legs around his waist, running on instinct, and then I start to suck. Not physically, but as if something inside me is drawing him in, his very essence... his soul.

It takes mere minutes before I feel like I'm overflowing, ready to burst. I yank my mouth away and lean back with a groan, the feeling of when you've eaten too much coming to mind. I unwrap my legs and he falls to the floor, gasping.

When I look down at him, I freeze in horror. *What the fuck?* He looks like he's been sucked dry, like a puffy skeleton, his eyes are roving in his head as his mouth stays open on a cry. He doesn't even resemble a human anymore. Sliding off the hood I step away, my nose crinkles in disgust. Well, at least I sort of know what I can do.

Turning away I freeze when boney fingers dig into my ankle, the male dragging himself along the floor towards me. I try to kick him off but his grip is too tight. A noise has my head snapping up as I see the creature from the forest come roaring out. He flies at the male, picking him up and breaking his grip like he weighs nothing. He rips him in two, blood and other body parts spraying me in the face. Blinking through the blood, I watch as he drops the now in two pieces male to the floor and stares at me as he breathes heavily.

"Thanks," I say, probably not the reaction he's looking for though.

I frown down at my shirt, now covered in blood and sigh. I look back at the creature and only then do I realise he looks different. Tilting my head, I step forward and he steps back. He's bigger, growing to over eight feet with even more muscle on his body. His torcs hang and everything else is much the same, apart from his face. He told me I wouldn't like his other form, but he's really wrong. He is a masterpiece. He looks like the old drawings of gods and demons you see in museums. Where before his face was more animal, his forehead different and his eyes tilted up at the side, his nose wider and his lips fuller. Now all I can see are those plump lips. A skull, obviously from an animal, covers the entire top half of his face.

He steps back again, trying to blend into the darkness, and I step forward and lay my hand on his chest, stilling his retreat from me. I stare at him in awe. "You are magnificent," I admit honestly. I mean, I just sucked someone's soul from their body, I can't exactly be worried about blood, death, and animal skulls.

I can't stop myself, I'm enchanted. I need to touch him, to taste him. I don't know if it's my power still ruling me and I don't care. I wanted him before, and I want him now.

"What are you doing, little monster?" he asks, those eyes I loved so much no longer there. Instead, there is a crushing darkness in the skull, which I find weirdly attractive, I guess I'm fucked up.

"Kissing you," I state, standing on my tiptoes, but even then there is no way I'll reach those lips. I wait there, letting him decide. He's hesitant, like I'm hunting him this time, and maybe I am.

"I want to taste you," I confess freely, and he groans, the sounds moving his chest against my hand. I understand the hesitation, he did just see me suck the soul from a man with only my lips, but even as I think that he lowers his head, gentle, like I'm breakable, and covers my lips with his.

I don't want sweet, I don't want hesitant. I want the monster who just ripped someone apart with his bare hands. I pull away and he frowns, stepping back from me with a self-loathing twist of his lips. He thinks I don't want him, it's the complete opposite.

I jump at him, and he catches me with his hand splayed under my arse. Wrapping my legs around his waist, I claw at his shoulders and drag his head down to mine. I rip at his lips, drinking from him. He growls against me, yanking me closer and returning the kiss with equal fervor. We fight each other, the blood dripping into my mouth only spurring me on.

We spin and my back meets a tree, hard, cutting into my skin, and I feel the blood trickle down it. The pain and pleasure mix together until I'm grinding against him. I felt nothing with that human, my body didn't even respond to the hate, but this... fuck.

He tries to pull away but I won't let him. I want everything he has to offer, he makes my body and new powers sing. My hands rise and wrap around his antlers, the wood rough against my palms and he roars into my mouth, making me grin. I forget everything else. My need for revenge, my new unknown creature status... everything.

He thrusts against me hard, throwing me back into the bark. Fuck yes. He drags his mouth away from me, one of his hands wrapping around my throat to anchor me to the tree, stopping my desperate jerk for his lips. He cuts off my breathing, holding me there with a growl that runs through my body and straight to my pussy. His head lowers but freezes, with a night silencing deadly grunt.

"Smells like him." His voice is guttural, more animal than man. I blink in confusion, his hand on my throat keeping me still, even as I have to fight the need to pass out. Without giving me a warning he rips away the shirt, leaving me bare for him. "Better," he grunts.

My breathing is coming out in little gasps as he lowers his head, his antlers pushing at my arms, and licks a path through the blood on my chest, circling my nipple before licking back up. He lets go of my neck just as I feel like I'm about to pass out and I slump, but he holds me to the tree with one hand while he explores me with the other, seeming fascinated by my body. One of his arms bands over my middle and he drops to his knees suddenly, tilting his head back so I can see into the darkness of the skull.

"What do I call you?" I ask, my voice harsh and rough from his hold on my throat.

"I have many names," he replies, his fingers running up my thighs.

"I didn't ask your many names, I asked what you wanted to be called," I retort, knowing that him giving me his name means power, but I can't keep calling him creature in my mind.

His head tilts down, the cold, rough texture of the skull meeting my pelvis as he licks a line up my wet pussy. "Nos," he answers, before diving in. The skull smacks into me and I have to hold onto his antlers as he devours me like I devoured him.

"Fuck, you taste like life and death," he murmurs, as I push my pussy onto his face.

My head smacks back into the tree as I wiggle, but his arm across my stomach is like steel and keeps me still. He doesn't tease me or proceed gently, he sucks on my clit, nibbles on it, all the while his fingers dig into my thigh hard.

"More," I demand.

He lets go of my thigh and thrusts two fingers into me without warning, the bite of pain making me buck against him. His arm across my middle moves and I fall forward. He catches me and throws me to the ground, my back meeting it with a thump and he jumps onto me, thrusting my legs apart and forcing his head into my pussy. Gripping onto his antlers, I watch as those black holes watch me. Fuck. His fingers thrust back into me, his tongue rolls around my clit. My breasts are neglected so I reach up and tweak my nipples, but stop when I hear a noise. Tilting my head back I spot the snake from earlier, he slithers through the grass stopping at Nos's side. He tilts his head towards it, like he's talking to it even with his tongue deep in my cunt. The snake nods and turns to me, slithering back through the grass.

"Hands above your head," Nos murmurs, before diving back in. I do as I'm told, for once.

The snake coils around them, binding them together, making me gasp with the feeling of the cool scales against my skin.

"I am the god of animals," he mutters, and I frown in confusion before he lifts his head and his tongue darts out. It looks normal, but then it splits down the middle, forked like a snake. *Oh fuck.*

He grins and leans back down, and I gasp at the first feel of it. Shit, shit, shit. Writhing against the floor, I'm helpless as he fucks me with his tongue and fingers.

I pant and then moan when his tongue licks me from the top of my pussy down to my ass. He circles that hole, making me push against his face. He presses the cold edge of the skull against my clit, his fingers thrusting in and out of me hard as his forked tongue darts into my hole. It sends me careening over the edge. I scream into the night, pushing against my monster as he rides me through my orgasm.

I still feel edgy in my skin, but it relieved some tension I didn't know I was carrying. He pulls away and I lay back on the ground, smiling into the night sky. The snake uncoils from my hands and slithers away as Nos climbs up my body.

"What else can you do?" I murmur, and he chuckles against me.

"I guess you will have to find out, little monster." He kisses my nose before nudging my face to the side. I turn my head and spot the dead body of the man, it should bother me that I just got finger fucked next to a dead man, but it doesn't. Nos kisses my neck gently before pulling away again.

"Night is nearly over," he comments and I sigh.

"Yes, which means I need to get back before they all wake up," I reply, stroking his skull.

"What will you do?" he asks, curiosity lacing his voice.

"Make them pay," I reply sweetly. His lips turn up into a grin and I smirk back.

Little monster indeed.

CHAPTER 7

NOS

I have an idea of what she might be, but I can't tell her just yet. Not until I am sure. She thinks I am letting her go, but she couldn't be more wrong. She is mine and the taste of her on my tongue only cements that. For her, my little monster, I will go back into the human world. I will hunt her through the city, and she will be mine before her hunt for vengeance is through.

She blows me a kiss like I am a child, and climbs into the car of the man she sucked the soul from, the remains of his body scattered around the clearing. I watch from the darkness as she backs away, turning the lights on and illuminating my position before leaving the forest, and driving back to the road, taking my cold heart with her.

The tugging starts immediately, calling me to follow her. Soon it will become painful to be away from her but before then, I have jobs to do to keep my mate safe. Then the hunt is on and she will be mine.

I follow alongside her for as long as the forest will allow, moving through the trees as fast as I can. I see her lips quirk as she sees me, before speeding up. I do the same until I reach the curve in the forest. The road arcs away and I watch as she leaves me behind. A roar leaves my lips unbidden, my animal wanting to destroy every-thing in my way to get to her. I hold it back, just. Gripping onto the tree, my fingers break through the bark, and blood-red sap crawls along my hand.

With more restraint than I realised I had, I turn away and slip away, back into the forest and the night. My focus on getting every-thing ready as fast as I can, to meet her in the city. The thought of chasing her has me licking my lips. She makes the best kind of prize. The image of her spread out beneath me, those lush tits pointing into the night sky as she pulls my fully shifted face closer to her wet pussy has me rock hard again.

I slip through the forest as fast as I can, my changed legs making it easier until I reach my cave. I force the shift back and stride in, nude and human. I pack up quickly and send out a warning message to the animals that I am leaving, my magic, which has satu-rated into the forest, will protect it and them while I am gone.

Grimacing, I slip into the restrictive clothing humans love so much and those feet coverings that cut off the feel of nature beneath my toes. Grabbing the bag, I make my way to the cave entrance and the sheet covered bike hidden there. I found it aban-doned over five years ago, it still runs smoothly and it is the only human treasure I allow myself to enjoy. I might not enjoy the cities and their restrictive feeling, but being on the back of that beast roaring through nature does have its perks.

Ripping back the sheet, I pat my steel baby and climb aboard. Time to hunt my mate.

CHAPTER 8

DAWN

Driving away from the forest, and Nos, has my heart pounding and a dull ache starting in the bottom of my stomach, but I grip the wheel tighter and carry on. I lose control of the car as shooting pains start down my whole body. Screaming in agony, I pull over and fall from the car. My body is shaking and breaking. Something feels like it's trying to break free from my skin, like I'm bursting. I don't know how long I lie there in agony, but when I finally open my eyes again, I groan. Fuck, that hurt. My eyes rove over the sun starting to rise, shit, I need to get back before then.

Racing through the empty roads as first light chases me, I manage to work my way through the city before it fully hits the sky, the dark still clinging to the day. Pulling up outside, I toss the keys on the ground and make my way into the building. The receptionist, Ryan I think his name is, a cute younger lad gapes at me in horror and I remember I'm covered in blood and not wearing pants. Awkward. He stumbles from the desk, still wide-eyed and open-mouthed.

"Are- you- are you okay?" he rushes out, his eyes running down me before his cheeks heat and he looks away. Huh, I'm guessing he's shy. Poor kid. "Do you live here?" he asks, obviously remembering his job, but really.

He stares at me every time I come down here, which admittedly has been less and less frequent, but even then, he should recognise me. Am I really that dirty? I spot the bathroom at the edge and sigh. "Be right back," I say and dart inside, getting ready to be horrified by my appearance.

The harsh lighting has me blinking as I spot the sinks and make my way over, and when I lean in to see myself in the mirror I freeze, a little scream erupting from my mouth. I slap my hand over the strange, unfamiliar lips and stare wide-eyed. What the fuck? Leaning closer I move from side to side and the person in the reflection does the same. I pinch my skin next before slapping myself. Okay, ouch. I look back at the mirror and gulp. No wonder the poor boy stared.

I'm a dude, not in a dramatic sense. I am an actual man. Not just a random man either, I'm the spitting image of the man lying dead in pieces in the forest.

Okay, don't freak out. Breathing deeply I push my panic down and curiosity gets the better of me. Lifting the tails of the shirt I poke the flaccid cock between my legs. Yep, I have a dick. My eyes jerking to the rest of the room I grin, I have always wondered...

Wrapping my hands around the soft cock I give it a pump or two, and it starts to harden. I watch it in wonder as I pump until it is hard. Well shit. Is it weird if I jerk myself off as the guy I just sucked to death? Probably. Ah, I bet the poor guy was wondering why I wandered in with my Percy the Pirate swinging in the wind and covered in blood.

I'm more worried about why I'm a guy, but beggars can't be choosers. The door opens and I hide my hard cock against the cold sink, jerking at the feeling as a man stops at the door and throws me a weird look. His waiter uniform crinkles as he shakes his head and kicks open a stall. What an ass, ain't he ever seen a dude who is really a girl pulling his ding dong before? Please. Letting go of my dick I grip onto the sink as that same agony from before runs through me, oh shit! I clamp my mouth shut and hold on tight. I manage to stay on my feet this time, but I'm exhausted, like bone weary.

Checking in the mirror, I see my own reflection grinning back at me. Well at least that's one thing. I hear the toilet flush and busy myself cleaning up in the sink the best I can. The guy struts back out but freezes when he spots me. He stares at me in confusion before looking around the toilet.

"Fuck, I gotta stop drinking on the job," he mutters, too low for any human to pick up, but I do. Hiding my smile, I wait until he leaves before shutting off the sink and strutting back out. The same poor receptionist kid is gawking at me, obviously as confused as the waiter, but I just wink and stroll to the elevator like I own the joint.

He doesn't stop me, probably wondering if he was seeing things when I first walked in. Slipping into the private wooden and gold elevator, I hit penthouse and enter the code. Humming along to the elevator music I debate my next step. First, I need pants. Now, I hate pants as much as the next person, but I'm starting to get strange looks with my lady jane hanging out, plus it's super breezy.

The elevator stops with a jerk and the ding sounds, and the golden-mirrored doors open up straight into the penthouse. I peek out of them, but when I spot the mess left behind, I snort. Typical.

People are passed out everywhere, waiters, servers, men, and prostitutes. Lingerie is flung around, as are other assortments of clothes. The leftover food covers every surface, as does empty bottles and glasses. Looks like they had one hell of a party after hiding my dead body.

Strolling through I grab a half drank bottle of vodka and start swigging. I tilt my head and grin, as I grab a bag Tim keeps in the hallway cupboard. I begin to gather up all the weapons I can find as well as clothes, because why the fuck not? I woke up naked, so should they.

Leaving my stash by the front door, I make my way down the hallway humming to myself. Our, no, *his* bedroom door is open so I slip inside. Well shit, I grin and snap a picture. How adorable. Tim is cuddled around two of his men, don't get me wrong I like a bit of man on man at the best of times, but he's obviously hiding it for a reason and you never know when it will come in handy.

I quickly pack up as much shit as I can and sneak out before they wake up. Tim's office doors stands open and I hesitate for a moment before shooting back the vodka and pushing my way in.

I stroll around, running my hand over the spines of books until I accidentally catch one and it falls out, and something matte black hides behind it. Well, well, well what do we have here? I carefully remove the others and stack them on the side, grinning when I spot the hidden safe. What a shit place to hide it, it's like the first place people look.

I press random numbers, guessing them, but it keeps blinking red. Shit. I need to get out of here before they all wake up and come up with a plan, but I really want to know what's so important he feels the need to hide it in his protected penthouse apartment.

I look at my hand on the safe and grin, I do seem to have more strength than before. Hell, I held that guy up without breaking a sweat...I wonder.

Gripping the lever I yank with all my strength and go flying on my ass, with the door clutched in my hand. I can't help the laugh that bubbles out, I could get used to this shit. Throwing it to the side I jump to my feet, grinning.

"My precious," I murmur, and stick my head into the safe. "Well, well, well what do we have here?"

I stack up the money and jewels, planning to take them, but the folders and paperwork I flip through catch my attention. My smile growing as I look at each one.

"Oh, you have been a bad boy Timmy."

I grab it all and humming my way through the apartment, I shove it into my bags at the door. Now, I need to figure out somewhere to stay while I plan my next step. A plan forms in my head as I grab my bags and ride the elevator down to the reception floor. I slip into the bathroom and shimmy into a short black dress with a jewel collar and sheer shirt. I need a shower, but that will have to wait. Time to work.

Plan Kill the Bastard is underway.

CHAPTER 9

DUME

Smashing through the forest, I let my roar warn other predators of my approach and to get out of my way, I don't have the patience to fuck around with anyone today. My nose ring jangles as I charge and I manage to cover five miles in about ten minutes. Lingering on the outskirts of the little village, I force the change back into my human form and stand there naked, watching.

Tilting my head back, I suck in a breath and roar when I smell witches. The cloying stink of their tainted magic swirls through my nose. My eyes focus on a woman walking into a cottage away from the rest of the village. She smells like the enemy and the truck sitting outside gives me the excuse I need. Striding through the night, I reach her cottage and kick down the door.

The woman turns, already whispering under her breath as an ice ball hits where I just was. Speeding through the room with a roar, I ram into her before she can finish her incantations. Slamming her into the wall, I pin her there, allowing the change to come over me slowly. I see the anger drain from her eyes, replaced with terror, as she realises who I am.

"No, we trapped you," she whispers, her voice shaking. I throw back my head and roar before lowering it slowly, huffing into her face.

"Not anymore." Pushing forward, I impale her on my horns and twist, ripping her insides as she screams. It serves her right, they all need to pay for what they did to me...what they did to all of us. Traitors. Killers. Violators. The words run through my head as I shred her to pieces. When my anger retreats and she is nothing but a bloody mess on the floor, I change back and step away.

I shower here, washing away the blood before searching the house, and finding a stash of her partner's clothes. They are a bit tight but they will do. I grab the car keys and her money on the way out, and slip inside her truck.

Flipping open her phone, I dial the number I was once told a long time ago. It rings through straight away. "Carmichael, your pain is our pleasure," comes a deep voice, rumbling over the speaker as I pull away from the house.

"You once told me you owed me a favour, Mike." I keep my eyes on the road and grin when there is a deep inhale over the speaker.

"Well fuck, I thought they killed your crazy ass." Carmichael laughs, making me huff.

"They couldn't even if they wanted to, I am calling in my favour," I point out, speeding up, the tug becoming more demanding.

"Of course, the outcasts are at your service," he answers immediately. I knew there was a reason I didn't kill him all those years ago, bloody slimy vampire.

"I need a plane and I need one now. I have the mate call and she is in danger," I grit out, even saying the words seems like treason. A minotaur with a mate? They will kill us both. Gripping the wheel tighter, I try to ignore the tension running through my body at being away from her.

"It will be done." I hear him talking to someone in the background before he types on the computer. I don't bother filling the silence. "Got your location, head north to an old abandoned airstrip called Reinlor, my men will meet you there. And Dume? Congratulations, no monster deserves it more," he replies honestly.

I end the call and concentrate on the road, imagining what my mate might look like, not that I really care as long as she is fierce.

A warrior, like me. I hope she is, or we have no chance of surviving this world.

Warrior, kneel. The voice floats in my mind and I throw both swords into the sand, kneeling so low my horns ram into the floor, my golden armor shining in the light, even covered in blood as it is.

I hear the crowd roar, stomping their feet at the bloodshed held for their amusement. I am the best, The Beast of Cornacadia. The queen's own personal monster, one created just for her. Even as they worship me, they fear me. I can smell it on the air, feel it in my bones. They flinch when they look at me, talk like I am not there.

"The Beast of Cornacadia!" the queen shouts, standing on the dais and soaking in the worship, her witch guards spread around her with their hoods up. Fucking scum, they are the reason I am not truly free. I was born with three shifts, yet I am locked into this one. Never to walk as a man again. I was seduced, I was tricked, and it cost me everything. My beast pulls at his chains, wanting to slaughter them all, even though he cannot disobey his queen.

Her eyes find mine like she can feel my anger and hatred, the same eyes that once gazed at my mortal form with longing and love, even as her husband glared at me from his deathbed. I lower my head once again, looking at the blood in the sands—another massacre at my hands. Another battle won, but how many until my beast decides he has enough of servitude and breaks free? The last cost me a form, what would this cost me?

Slamming my hand into the wheel and denting it, I push back the horrors of my past, choosing to try and ignore my regret. I know what it cost, it cost me my freedom, but at least I got some payback before I was bound and forgotten. I force myself to concentrate on driving, something I experienced only through Carmichael's memories when I fed him. He was thrown into my pit as punishment not five years ago. Instead of killing him, I allowed him to feed. He shared his memories of the world and taught me much. He tried to free me, but could not. In the end, I told him to leave, hope once again abandoning me. It seems the fates had a plan after all.

CHAPTER 10

GRIFFIN

G runting against the pain in my soul, I jump from the ledge and let my wings spread, the black feathers blending into the inky blackness of the night sky. The wind flows through my body, as does the adrenaline I always feel when flying. Swooping overhead, I watch the lights below as I land in an alley, my wings folding in with perfect precision while I keep walking, straight onto the street behind the man I was following. Grabbing him around the throat before his bodyguards even notice, I drag him kicking into the alley.

"Where are you keeping the girls?" I ask silkily, whispering straight into his mind.

He starts to fight me, his body and mind warring as he tries to come to terms with the fact that, in this alley, he isn't the biggest monster.

"What are you?" he demands, trying to stay strong even as his body shakes, and I can smell the fear wafting from him. Smart little sheep, to be afraid of the monster. I don't care about them anymore than I care about the girls he is keeping and selling, but it seems the council does. For some reason, they have taken particular interest in the crime circle that has popped up in this city over last ten years, and I am who they send. It's a punishment no doubt, but it is still an order. One I can't deny unless I wish them to strip my wings...again. The fallen, the damned, halfies...we have many names. The council prefers assassins. Our souls beg to save those in need, a byproduct of my angel father, but my other half, my darker half, wants to hunt, to kill. Half angel, half man. All monster. I know cruelties from both the sheep and supernaturals of this world. No, none of them deserve mercy. Both are evil and filled with the need for power and control. Humans just hide it better.

Yet, here I am. Helping them, hunting them like the vermin they are. At least I can kill on this job, a perk I suppose. The last time I was only allowed to watch and report back. I'm nothing more than a tool for the council, they hold my fate in their hands, a deal I made a long time ago to save someone I loved, not that it did any good.

As soon as the contract breaks, I will rain down heavenly hellfire on those bastards, I don't care if I take this world with me. Something soft wraps around me, as if sensing my spiraling emotions.

Growling, I push it aside, not wanting to deal with the tug still pulling at me. "I will ask once more, where are they?"

"You fucking wanker, you think you can just—" I cut off his threat by placing my forearm on his neck and pushing down, his breath stops as he chokes. I let him hang there, between life and death, before releasing the pressure a bit. He sucks in a breath and starts coughing, clawing at my arms pitifully to try and escape. The terror now rolling off him makes me grin, I feed on it like a vampire does blood, I love the taste on my tongue.

"Where. Are. They?" I whisper out loud this time.

"Please, I can get you money, I—"

I press again, but this time I reach down with my other hand, palming a knife and holding it to his junk. "You have one chance to tell me before I make you a eunuch. You will bleed to death in five minutes exactly. Now, when I remove my arm, you will speak."

He nods and I release the death grip on his throat.

"I'll tell...I'll tell you," he gasps out between coughs and I let him, not moving or saying anything. "And you will let me go?" he begs.

My grin is hidden in my hood. "Yes."

"They are held on the south side, dragon neighbourhood. Warehouse 41." He stumbles away and into the wall, clutching his throat as his eyes dart around the alley, no doubt his bodyguards have noticed his absence, and I'm betting he is thinking they will come and save him.

I walk towards him slowly and his eyes bug out of his head. "You said you would let me go!"

"I lied." I dart forward, blurring to him in my mist form, only to appear right in front of him. "Boo," I whisper and he screams, making me laugh before I rip out his throat with my bare hand.

I hear the noise of a gun and footsteps before a bullet rips through my shoulder. Stupid, I wasn't paying attention, instead watching the light dim in the sheep's eyes and loving it.

I turn to mist again, blurring through the alley and becoming corporeal before the bodyguard on the left. I grab the gun and bend it, throwing the useless weapon at the wall before blurring and appearing behind him.

I slit his throat and blur again, circling the other man. He's sweating now, his arm holding the gun shaking as he swings wildly, trying to spot me.

"I am here," I whisper into the wind and he swallows hard, starting to back away.

Laughing, I appear in front of him, our noses touching. I cut from throat to balls and watch as he gasps and screams, the light slowly leaving his eyes as his insides drop to the dirty alley floor.

Stepping back, I slide my phone from my pocket, walking away without looking. "Clean up, West Side, Street 78 and third. Three sheep dead. Screams heard."

The man on the other side starts swearing as I end the call, before sliding the phone back into my pocket. My wings spread from my back and I take a running start out of the alley, swooping into the sky. The tug is still there and as I head down south of the city it gets strong, almost making me fall from the sky with its intensity. I can't help it. I drop from the sky and stand in an alley.

I don't know how long I stay there, caught between the need to hunt and the need to see her. The sky is lightening and it's early morning when she steps out of the expensive building, home to the rich and powerful and often corrupt of the city.

There she is. She looks around before sliding into a cab and leaving me here, watching her, wanting her.

That glimpse is enough, I am lost.

I am hers.

My mate.

CHAPTER 11

DAWN

Winking at the reception boy on the way out, I step outside to catch the cab a businessman is about to get in. Grabbing the door before he can, I throw my bag in the back. I hear him winding up for an argument and I look over at him and grin. He stutters and steps back with a small smile.

Humming to myself, I slide in and shut the door on the bewildered looking man. "Downtown, please." Picking up the papers I found in the safe, I flick through for something. When I find what I'm looking for I grin. "546 Rosewater Way."

"Nice neighbourhood," the old, chubby man comments as I lean back in my seat.

"True, maybe I'll stay there awhile." He offers me a confused look before pulling away from the curb.

I spend the journey flipping through the documents, my grin only growing. It seems my dear husband has been a naughty, naughty man. Hell, they might even kill him for me if I show them this, but no. I want him to suffer first. First step: love life. Second step: money. Third step: job. Fourth step: kill him. I write it on a bit of paper, underlining the kill him section with an evil looking grin on my face.

Relaxing back in the seat, I close my eyes while we fight through mid-morning traffic. Nos's eyes flash in my mind, starting a burning low in my belly. The heat seems to rise in me, pulling a hunger through my body that scares even me with its intensity.

It feels like I'm burning up, and I start to sweat and my palms turn clammy. My stomach clenches and every flick of air over my skin is pure torture. I don't know how long I'm locked this way until the cabbie interrupts.

"We're here miss, £20 please," he says, looking over his shoulder at me.

Nodding shakily, I throw over the money and slip from the cab on wobbly legs. The hotel stands in front of me. The guy I'm coming to see chooses to stay in hotels for weeks at a time before moving to another, claiming it's safer. It's exactly what I need. Stumbling into the lobby, I ignore the bustling of everyone else and concentrate on the elevator. It just leaves as I get there, and I don't have time to wait for the next one. Leaning my head against the cool metal, I turn to the side to see the stairs. Groaning, I push away, the heat turning up a notch until it feels like my head might explode.

Staggering through the door I throw myself at the stairs, gripping onto the railing and pulling myself up. Panting the whole way, with my vision blurring, I reach a landing as the door opens, and what looks like a room service waiter comes through counting money. I fall into him and we go crashing into the wall.

He looks angry until his eyes lock on me, then they heat quickly and he grins. "Well hello there, you didn't need to fall into my arms to get my attention," he flirts. He's good looking and touching him is cooling my skin.

Something guides me, something I discovered in the forest. It whispers that it will help, tide me over. Willing to try anything to get rid of this inferno, I scale his body, his hands spanning my ass to help me, and cover his lips with mine. He groans into my mouth, fumbling to chase me as he kisses me. It's a good kiss, but still not enough. Pulling away with a pained moan, I kiss down his neck, nipping as I go. Needing more skin, I run my hands under his shirt and onto his chest.

He yanks my head back to his, covering my lips, and it's like something clicks inside me and I know what to do. At the same time, I feel more hands on me, the new ones burning a hole through my body and calming me like nothing else. The heat retreats and the pain leaves as my darkness unfurls inside me, clambering up my throat until I'm sucking from the waiter. He freezes and shakes while I feed on his very soul.

"That's right. Take what you need," a familiar voice murmurs into my ear, as a soft kiss is dropped onto my neck. I shiver in need and push back into a hard body. "Good girl, feed," he murmurs again, and I do. He whispers sweet nothings to me before kissing me again. "Okay, now pull away before you kill him."

I ignore him and snuggle deeper into the human, and the hands on my back grip my sides. "Dawn, stop or you will kill him," he warns, but he doesn't sound too bothered. But the word 'kill' enters my mind, and I drag my mouth away as the hands and hard body disappear from behind me. Stumbling away, I fall onto the steps, out of breath and dizzy from feeding, as Nos called it. Blurrily, I see a tall man standing over the pale-faced, wilting human, with fury like I have never seen emanating from the man. I don't see horns, but I know it's him even if I can't make out much detail, my eyes still foggy. Licking my lips, my head lolls to the side to see Nos step into the man.

"You touched what is mine," he rumbles, as the lights flicker in the hallway. The human shakes and cries, opening and closing his mouth like he can't speak. I see Nos starting to change, getting bigger and thicker as the lights flicker out completely. Those glowing eyes are the only beacon in the dark. I hear a gurgle and then nothing.

"Nos?" My voice is slurred.

A petal soft wet kiss lands on my forehead. "I am here, Little Monster. Be good." Then the warmth disappears.

Slowly, the lights flicker back on and I lean my head back as my eyes start to finally clear. Blinking, I stare at the bloody scene before me. Looks like my monster had some fun—I grin. I should care but I don't. I'm done pretending to be something I'm not.

There on the floor, in a crumpled pile, is the dead waiter, his eyes open and unseeing, and not two feet away is his bloody heart. Around it is a crudely drawn blood heart.

I giggle, snorting as I stare at it. Nos is crazy but it warms something inside me, something I thought was too broken to work again. Pulling myself to my feet, something starts to move in my body. Ugh, not again. Grabbing my bag, I pull myself up the stairs to the floor I need and stagger out, falling into walls as I try to stop the change. A trolley rams into me, sending me sprawling and I see the waiter run from around it, an apology on his lips, but I can't talk. He pulls me to my feet and I grab the lid covering from the trolley and smash it into his head, knocking him out. Looking around, I spot no one—shit, that was sloppy. The service elevator he came from is still open and I quickly push him inside. Tying him up with the covering from the trolley, I shove a roast potato in his mouth so he doesn't scream when he wakes up. I strip fast as the change comes over me. I writhe on the floor, but the process is quicker this time and when I push myself to my feet and look in the mirror on the back wall of the elevator wall, I spot the dead waiter from the hallway. Well, I was going to flirt my way in but this works too.

Stripping off the other waiter quickly, I get changed and stuff my dress in my bag, before pressing the hold button on the elevator so they won't find him for a while. Sauntering back out as a man, I wiggle my hips to try and sort out the feeling of a penis between my legs. Damn, how do they walk with thing dangling between their legs? Peeking in my pants, I grin.

"Mazel tov, dude. Nice cock," I whisper as a room door opens. I close my pants and grin at the lady giving me a weird look. I wink and she giggles. Grabbing my bag on the way, I push the trolley down the hall, hunting for the room I need.

Aha, thirty-four. Knocking on the door I wait, shifting to try and jiggle the cock. I really need to try windmilling it, I've seen so many men do it and it looks fun. The door opens to reveal a bored looking man with no shirt on, just black trousers. He glances past me, his hand in his pocket obviously clutching a gun. He nods and gestures me to come in. I push the trolley past him as he shuts the door. He turns to face me and I smack him on the head with the covering. Damn, this thing is handy. He goes down but is still awake, shit.

Diving onto him, I pull the gun from his pocket and pistol whip him. I knock him out and I sit back as the change comes over me again—shit, it lasted longer than last time at least. Crawling to the side, I groan and wiggle as I shift back. Laying on the cream carpet, I pant into it, my body weak and hardly able to move.

I don't know how long I lie there for until my stomach stabs at me, making me curl up into a ball. It comes again but with an accompanying growl this time, and I realise I'm starving. Not just hungry, but actually starving. Crawling to the trolley, I pull myself onto the bed and sit in front of the food. Fuck yeah, steak, pasta, and chips. I don't bother using the knife and fork, I rip into the meat. Demolishing the steak until I fall back on the bed with a sigh. Fuck, I'm still hungry. Grinning, I roll towards the side table and grab the phone, dialing for room service.

"Front desk, how may I help you?"

"Yeah, I'd like a chocolate cake, a full one, with ice cream please. Just put it on my bill. Room thirty-four." I put the phone down and look back at the man. I guess I better do something with him, I could kill him, but he might be useful.

Moaning again, I get up and force myself to move him. I bite my lip as I come up with a plan. Bending over, I brace my hands under his arms and drag him to the bathroom, not even breaking a sweat. Once I'm in there, I lift him up and dump him in the tub before going back to the room. Using two pillowcases I tie his feet and hands to the tub handle, and grabbing the robe from the wardrobe I stick the waist tie in his mouth.

Stepping back to eye my handiwork I nod, perfect. Wait, I shut the shower curtain so no one can see him and saunter away, exploring the rest of the suite.

I'm just shrugging into the robe and slippers when there is a knock at the door, strolling there, I let in the waiter who delivers the cake.

"Fuck yes," I hum as he stands awkwardly, obviously wanting a tip.

"Ah, one sec!" I grin, darting into the bathroom. I take the dude's wallet and pull out some cash. I pocket some, but I give the guy a generous tip and wink.

He grins at me and looks around before walking backwards. "Let me know if you need anything else, anything at all." I smile and sit in front of my cake until the door shuts. Then I grab it and devour it.

Laying back on the bed with chocolate fudge cake smeared around my mouth, I laugh when the man in the bath starts screaming.

Chapter 12

Dawn

The air shifts next to me and I roll from the bed, landing into a crouch, a hiss on my lips as something rushes up inside of me and takes over. It's like before, but there is no shift and no hunger, more like the power, it's defending me.

I spot the man cloaked in darkness, and nothing registers as I push off the floor and leap at him. He catches me mid-air and brings me to his chest, holding me like a clawing kitten, and before I know it, the primal side of me which has taken over is rubbing on him like a cat in heat.

My power retreats and I'm left looking at a beautiful man. There is something familiar about him, the look in his eyes, the hands on my arse, holding me to him.

The eyes are a deep green, not white, and there are no horns, and his body is less animal, but it's him. Long brown and blond streaked wavy hair is parted on either side of his head, his deep emerald eyes are framed by black lashes longer than most women's. High arched cheekbones and a square jaw covered in a stubble frame pink plump lips. He was right, his human side is appealing, but I miss those eyes.

"Little Monster," he rumbles, that same deep voice from the forest.

"Nos," I moan and throw myself forward in his arms. He loses balance and twists mid-air so he falls back onto the bed.

He keeps his arms wrapped around me as we land and still doesn't let me go while I hover over his prone body.

I search his face before slowly reaching out and caressing his cheek. He closes his eyes and sighs. "I'm still tired," I admit, confused.

"You are new to all of this, I keep forgetting. Your body will require twice it's normal sustenance and rest because of your rapid shifts."

"So, basically I need to eat and sleep more," I murmur and his lips turn up in a smile.

"Yes, only for now. When you get stronger the strain will be less."

I nod and keep stroking my way around his face, mapping it.

"Now, Little Monster. Is there a reason a man is tied up in the bathroom? Did he touch you? Do I need to kill him?" His eyes shoot open at the word touch and I feel his body turn solid under me, like a statue, as his eyes flicker between green and white. It makes me lick my lips, remembering his mouth on me and his hands in the stairwell.

He follows the movements, his eyes turning completely white and glowing between us. "No, he didn't touch me. I need him alive for now, when he has outlived his purpose, I will kill him," I purr, rubbing against him from the need blooming in my chest.

He growls and rubs my ass in massaging waves.

"Why do I need you so much? Why am I drawn to you, like I could pick you out in the middle of the city?" I ask, confusion and need whirling inside of me until I'm panting.

"You are mine, I am yours." That's all he says before slamming his mouth to mine. Gripping onto his cheeks, I control the kiss and he thrusts up against me, making me moan into his mouth.

"Yes," I hiss, reaching down and flicking open the button on his jeans, my hand slithers inside and wraps around his rock-hard cock, already coated with pre-cum.

I pump him once, twice, before I'm flipped onto my back. He

grins down at me and rips away our clothes until we are both naked and pressed together. I seek his mouth with a blind need and he returns it, devouring me and only fueling the fire inside me. Like a beast, it roars its need.

"I need you," I cry, my blood heating uncomfortably.

"I am yours," he says softly, almost tenderly, as he reaches down and grabs my thighs, spreading my legs. Reaching between us, he feels my already wet pussy.

His lips meet mine again as he masterfully flicks my clit before slipping one finger inside me, lifting my hips I beg for more, my body feeling like it's about to explode. He doesn't add another and I bite his lip in punishment.

He pulls away, blood dripping down his chin, and I wrap both legs around his waist and spin us.

When he is under me, I waste no time. I'm desperate for him. Reaching down, I line him up and sink onto his massive cock. He stretches me, making me throw my head back and moan as I sink lower, until my ass meets his thighs. His hands reach up and cup my tits, flicking my nipples as I lift up and drop back down again. He groans and his hands tighten painfully.

"Take what you need, Little Monster," he demands, and I do.

I ride him hard and fast, chasing an orgasm and the coolness I know it will somehow provide. I feel like I'm in a haze, nothing but need and pain guiding me as I fuck him.

"Oh god—" I hear a voice from behind us and when I whip my head around, I see the man from the bathroom. He obviously got himself free and he is standing there, gawking at me. Something snaps and I scramble from the bed.

Grabbing the steak knife from my dinner lying nearby, I fly from the bed and jump at the man, and he pales and screams as I slash his throat. Blood spurts all over me, into my mouth and eyes, and onto my bare tits. Each drop seems to soak into my skin until I'm moaning on top of his dying body.

Nos growls and snatches me by my waist, flinging me onto the bed and leaping on top of me.

"Mine," he roars and I groan, arching my head back as he slams inside of me.

"Yes!" I moan, running my hands down my blood covered chest.

He groans and when I open my eyes, he's shaking and I grin. "Stop fighting it, change," I demand, and he growls but obeys.

I moan long and loud as his cock lengthens and thickens inside of me. His horns erupt from his head and his eyes turn bright white. He pulls out of me before slamming back in, the headboard shaking with his strength.

"Fuck, yes. More!" I scream, uncaring about the guests staying here. They could walk in right now and I wouldn't give a fuck, Nos might kill them, but I sure as shit would find it hot. That much is evident.

He growls, lowering his head and sniffing along my neck and chest at the blood, his tongue darting out and licking it while I writhe beneath him. He pulls out and I moan, needy and long, and jump at him again, all teeth and nails, completely primal like he is.

He catches me, but not before I score my nails down his chest and bite his neck, making him roar. He flips me like I weigh nothing and pins my fighting body. Wrapping my hair around his fist, he pulls until my neck is stretched and arched back. It hurts, but it feels so good and I push back, seeking his cock. His head lowers again, his horns scratching the headboard.

"Mine," he grunts, the once seemingly cultured monster of the forest no more, but a creature of need and rage like me.

"Prove it," I gasp out, and he growls against my throat before sinking his teeth there, his cock thrusting into my waiting pussy at the same time, making me scream.

This angle means he is so much deeper than before and I can feel every delicious inch of him. Monster, indeed. He would probably rip a normal human in half.

He releases my throat, and I feel the blood trickling down and onto the bed below. His other hand reaches around and flicks my nipples, and my face is pushed into the duvet as he fucks me hard and fast, sending me into another orgasm, screaming into the covers of the bed.

Shaking beneath him, I gasp when he flips me again and thrusts straight back into my pussy. Barely recovering from my orgasm, I don't fight him as he fucks me. His wide palm circles my throat, those eyes staring at me.

"You will never win against me, you are mine. This body, everything. You can fight me, try to kill me, and I will still win. I will remind you exactly why the humans fear me, do you understand me?" he asks and tightens his hand, making spots appear in my visions and my pussy pulses around him.

When I can breathe again I gasp out a moan. "Yes, fuck, give me everything."

He growls and keeps his hand around my throat. Hiking my leg up, I wrap it around his waist and tilt my hips so he hits deeper again. We both groan and I tighten my pussy, making him growl.

Slamming in, he twists his hips at the same time as he chokes me, and I open my mouth on a wordless scream as I'm thrown into another orgasm. He stills, emptying inside me with a roar that shakes the bed.

He lets go of my throat slowly, but I'm still needy. I need everything. It feels like my body is burning up and only his touch, his come, can calm me. When he pulls out I reach down and grab his wet, soft cock.

"I need you again," I say breathlessly and he groans.

We both freeze at a knock on the door. Swearing, I slide of the bed and stagger on wobbly legs.

I grab a robe and make sure no blood is visible as I stroll to the door. I don't bother doing it up fully, letting out a breath as I open it to the worried looking security guard. He looks nervous and glances around before his eyes drop back to me. His cheeks heat and he keeps his eyes locked on mine.

"Miss, is everything okay? We have had some...er, worrying noise complaints."

I grin. "Oh, sorry about that. It got a bit rough, we were trying out some new positions."

He blushes bright red. "You-you, er, mean you were having sex?"

I lean against the door, the robe fluttering around me. "Fucking, boning, whatever you want to call it." He doesn't look like he believes me so I push off and step closer, fluttering my lashes at him. "Want to see?" I murmur, and he stutters out a response and runs away.

Laughing, I shut the door and turn to see Nos watching me from the bed, completely unashamed in his monster form, covered in blood and come. My nipples tighten and I drop the robe and saunter back. "Seems we were being too loud, you might have to gag me this time," I tease and crawl up the bed.

Reaching his legs, I lick my way through the blood and come, trailing a path right to his already hard cock. "Little Monster," he warns, and I grin against his cock, flicking my tongue out and tasting myself and him. Groaning, I wrap my lips around him and suck him down to the back of my throat.

I glance up and watch his eyes widen as I swallow him farther, his hands scramble in the sheet and his head tosses when I start to hum. Watching this monster at my mercy is one of the hottest things I've ever seen, and I reach down and flick my clit as I bob on his cock to the rhythm of my fingers.

"Faster," he commands and I moan, loving when he takes control, especially when the rest of my life is spiraling out of it—he is the constant.

I do as I'm told, sucking him faster, and I speed up my fingers so when he yells and comes in my mouth, I scream around his cock and come too.

Collapsing, I notice the burning in my veins has disappeared, and now I'm just bone weary. He reaches down and pulls me into his arms gently, cradling me as my eyes shut.

"Sleep, Little Monster. I shall keep watch. Nothing will ever hurt you again." His vow follows me into sleep.

CHAPTER 13

ASKA

The world all looks the same from the sky, but after hours of endless flying, I'm forced to seek shelter so I can rest. Hibernation means I'm not as strong as I once was and it's becoming very apparent. Circling the small town below I land on a hill on the outskirts, the night sky blocking me from view. It wouldn't be good for them to spot me and have reports of a dragon circulating. That would only draw unwanted attention.

Changing back as soon as I land, I make sure to add clothes this time, a perk of being from the long, royal line. Or one of the only ones left, I would say. Shaking out my form, I run my hands down my body to ensure everything is in place before I make my way down the hill and into the town below.

I'll rest and then fly again in the morning. I must make it to my mate before something happens. For her to call me across such distance means she's strong, which also means she will become a target. I need to be by her side where I belong. If the remaining dragons of the council find I have awoken again and not returned, they won't be happy, so I need to keep a low profile. I have no plans to ever return to Klasfor. Not now, not ever.

When I left so long ago in search of a place to sleep, I made my intentions very clear, but dragons are stubborn and they won't believe that I would give up my role as king. Not that easily, but it's a title I never wanted. I was born into it, raised since birth to lead. Except by the time I was crowned, it was a heavy burden. Our kind had been hunted and slaughtered to near extinction, so we retreated and hid our existence. Our isolation resulted in dragons turning on each other, our words became barbs, and we began killing our own. Dragons are not meant to be trapped, yet we are.

I make my way through the almost deserted town, no doubt quiet due to the late hour. When I spot the sign for a hotel I push open the glass door, a bell signaling my entrance, and I pause before the counter, which has seen better days. In fact, the whole room looks like it has, but I'll only be here for one night. All I need is a door and a bed.

When no one comes to greet me, I press down lightly on the little bell, holding it until a sweaty, greasy teenager throws open a door and glares at me. "What the hell, dude?"

"Room," I grunt.

He rolls his eyes but makes his way over, typing on a computer as I stare at him. "We have double, suite.."

"One bed, the room farthest from the main entrance," I reply, nearly swaying on my feet from exhaustion.

He carries on typing. "Okay, cash or card?" He looks up, peering through long hair that covers his forehead.

I didn't think about payment. Hmm. "Please hold," I instruct him and leave again. I had those plastic things when they were first introduced, but they are too easy to trace. Looking around, I spot a sign saying money withdrawals. Marching over, I stare at the weird computer contraption.

"Money," I order.

Nothing happens.

"Money, now," I nearly shout.

"Er, you have to put your card in," comes a rough male voice. Looking down, I spot the homeless man meters away from the machine.

Nodding, I turn back. Waving my hand in front of the screen, I let my magic do the work, computers and magic do not mix so the screen wavers before it asks for the amount. I withdraw the max, holding my hand as the machine spits it out and tells me to have a nice day.

Grabbing the stash I look back at the homeless man, who is wide-eyed and pale. "For your troubles," I say, passing over some notes.

His mouth drops open as he grabs them, wetness gathering at the corner of his eyes. Not wanting to dishonor the man, since feelings should not be shared—it is the dragon way—I head back to the hotel.

When I get through the door, the kid is gone again, so I ring the bell.

"For fuck's sake," he grumbles as he throws open the door again. "Oh, it's you."

"Here." I thrust half the money at him and grab the key waiting on the desk below.

"Hey! You can't just—" He starts counting the money, his words cutting off as I leave the room in search of my bed for the night.

The room number is printed on the key, so I find it easily enough. He did, in fact, give me the room at the end of the place. Outside, the overhead light flickers on and off so I twist the bulb, making it go out completely. I feel instantly better in the darkness and it might give me the few seconds I need to escape if there is an attack. Sliding the card key into the door, I try to open it only for it to blink red.

"Stupid human contraptions," I growl, as I ram it into the reader again and again until it finally blinks green. What happened to a good old key?

I don't bother flicking on the lights. I can hear the humming of them in the background, and my eyes see even better in the dark than they do in the light. It would be stupid to turn them on like a beacon when I don't need them. Kicking the door shut behind me, I grab the wooden chair from under the window and ram it under the door handle.

The few seconds it will take for someone to break down the door will act as an alarm. Running my eyes over the room, my mouth twists in disgust. I've slept in some worse places for sure, but my body itches from being trapped inside. It would rather find a nice cave somewhere to crash in, but I need to shower and integrate myself back into society.

Rolling my shoulders to try and relieve the tension, I take in the ugly, flowered bed sheets and the rickety table under the window by the door, which I'm currently backed against. An older TV with a silver antenna on the top sits upon a dresser against the opposite wall of the bed. A depressing painting of a sad looking flower in a field takes up the wall across from me and a door sits next to it, obviously leading to the bathroom.

I check around the room for other openings, apart from the tiny bathroom window, which only a midget would be able to climb through, the door is the only way in or out. It relaxes me enough to go and sit on the bed. Scooting back until my head meets the backboard, I rub my forehead where a pounding has started, a sure sign I need to rest.

Sitting here allows my mind to wander, and when it does I start to notice the yelling of someone in another room, the hum of the lights, the sound of cars and street noise. The more I try to ignore it, the louder it gets until I can't dismiss any of it. I forgot how loud the world is, and I'm clearly not equipped or used to it.

Groaning, I reach over and grab the small black remote. Pushing random buttons, I shoot it at the TV. Eventually, the picture flickers to life. I leave it on whatever channel it's on, but turn up the volume until all I hear is the man talking about who is or isn't the father.

Frowning, I lean forward and watch in awe as the man reads out that he isn't the father. Chaos ensues and my eyes widen at the screaming as the 'not the father' yells at a shocked looking woman. Where is the gold that they're fighting over? It is like a behind the scenes look at every dragon family ever.

Sitting crossed-legged, I concentrate on the show until my eyes are sliding shut. Burrowing down in the bed, I pull the covers over me and make my own little nest underneath. Ironic, I know, but it's where dragons feel the safest, especially with everything changing.

Finally shutting my eyes, I let sleep take me.

I hold my hands out in front of my face and frown at the see-through quality. It has been a long time since I was able to enter another's dreams or minds. It only happens with mates or close family. Since all my family is dead, this must be my mysterious mate's head.

It's a constant irritation that we can't master this during wakefulness, but it seems the only time the mind wanders enough to achieve a full connection, especially across distances, is during sleep when you are vulnerable.

Dropping my hands, I look around at the dream she is obviously having. A woman sits on the edge of a body of water with her back towards me.

She's small, probably half my height, with long blonde hair curling down her shapely back. I can't make out much else so I walk closer, stopping when I'm next to her. She looks up at me, she doesn't seem surprised or scared. Her eyes are the deepest blue I have ever seen, like the fire stones we keep in our homeland. Her lush mouth quirk up, drawing my eyes.

She's gorgeous, all sensuality and beauty. It radiates from her.

"Who are you?" she asks, her voice low and velvety.

"My name is Aska, yours?" I sit next to her and she keeps her eyes on me.

"Dawn, I like your hair," she replies, her eyes locked on the short, pastel purple waves that sit unruly on the top of my head. "Your eyes too."

I grin at that, if only she saw them when I used my powers, they would glow black and purple and she would be terrified.

"Thank you, Neriso," I say automatically, the dragon word which roughly means 'mated or mine' slipping from my tongue.

She tilts her head at that. "It's beautiful, say it again."

"Neriso." My accent changes, using my dragon tongue and dialect, and her eyes light up.

"What does it mean?" she inquires.

"I will tell you when I see you," I reply with a chuckle.

"See me? I'm guessing you don't mean in wherever we are right now?" She leans back, her body rippling with the movement. I swallow hard and draw my eyes back to her face, trying to ignore the curvaceous body of my mate.

"Yes. I am coming to you," I mumble.

"Why?" she questions with an innocence in her words that stops me.

"What are you, Neriso?" I query.

"I don't know, I thought I was human until I died." She looks back at the water, calm.

"You died?" I roar, getting to my feet as my fists clench, and scales emerge on my skin.

She looks back and must notice them because her mouth drops open and she jumps to her feet. "You're a dragon?" she asks in awe.

"Yes, you died? Who? When?" I growl rapidly.

She grins, shaking her head as she reaches out and touches the iridescent scales covering my arm. If I was in full dragon form they would be black as night, but for some reason, in this half shift, they are always iridescent purple and greens.

"The colours are beautiful, what do you look like when you shift?"

"I shall show you later, now answer me," I demand, agitated. My monster wanting to burst out of my skin, grab her, and fly away.

"My husband," she answers distractedly, stroking my arm still. I try to ignore the tingles it sends down my body, even as my dragon preens at her touch. Then her words penetrate the fog in my brain that her touch is causing.

"Husband?" My words drip with malice at someone claiming the creature before me.

"I guess it would be ex-husband now. Don't worry, I plan to get my revenge." She grins up at me, her eyes lighting up with an intensity and anger that staggers me as it sends my cock and emotions into overdrive. I expected a fragile mate I would need to protect, but the unknown creature before me, stroking my dragon as she speaks of murder, is anything but.

She tilts her head, her eyes unfocused before they come back to me sadly. "I think I'm waking up. Will I see you again, Dragon?" she asks.

"Would you like to?"

"Yes."

"Then you shall. I will be here waiting until I can meet you in the flesh, Neriso," I reply automatically. She already has my dragon wrapped around her little finger, he lets out a huff when she stops touching me and steps back. Fading from view with a smile and a small wave. After she's left, her dream space starts to collapse, brick after bricking until I am flung back into my own body.

I sit up with a huff, the warm feeling of her skin still lingering on my arm, proving it really happened. My mate is a mystery, one I plan on untangling as soon as I can.

CHAPTER 14

GRIFFIN

I lean back against the wall of the coffee shop I'm in, grimacing at the noise. Humans are so loud. Sipping my overpriced coffee, I watch for the man I'm hunting for. He arrives here like clockwork every day, and today is the day I confront him. I need the access he has. It seems he runs the security system surrounding the warehouse the girls are being held in. I need to get in and out without being seen. Now, I could use my powers, but I also want to take a look at the security footage and see what I'm dealing with. I might also keep it as insurance against the council.

Something tugs on my arm, and looking down with an angry frown, I stare into the round eyes of the sticky human child next to me.

"Shoo," I order, extracting my arm, gently, from its grip.

It gargles something at me, and I glare at it. "Be gone, sheep child," I command in my deadliest voice. It laughs and tries to clamber into my lap when a haggard looking, middle-aged woman rushes over with an apology on her lips as she grabs it.

"Sorry, so sorry. I turned my back for one second. I really am sorry!" she calls as she starts talking to the child, walking away with it in her arms. It giggles, waving at me over her shoulder. Rolling my eyes, I wave back.

Just then my phone rings, pulling it from my jean pocket I swear at the caller ID. Swiping to answer, I put it to my ear as anger already pools in my stomach. There is only one reason they call, and it's never good.

"You are requested," the cold, dark voice says before they hang up.

Fucking rude bastards. I suppose they get away with it being the council and all. Downing the lukewarm coffee, I stand from my table. Looks like all of my plans are out the window today, because when the council calls. You answer.

CHAPTER 15

DAWN

I wake up warm, and when I crack open my eyes I smile, spotting Nos' snoring face above me from where I'm curled up on his chest. We are both still covered in blood, sweat, and come, and it's starting to itch. Slipping from the bed, not wanting to disturb my horned god, I tiptoe around the body lying on the floor in a pool of blood, which is soaking into the carpet, reminding me to sort that out later.

The bathroom is a mess as well, obviously from his escape attempt. Kicking the towel I used to gag him to the side, I flip on the shower. Cranking it as hot as it goes, I step inside and sigh in bliss when the water feels like the fires of hell against my body. Scrubbing at my skin, I watch the water turn red as it circles the drain at my feet.

I have to wash my hair three times—no one ever mentions how hard it is to get crusted blood out of blonde hair and let me tell you, it's not fun.

By the time I'm dry, I walk out of the bathroom expecting Nos to be awake, but he's still dead to the world. Striding to my bag of stolen goods, I slip into one of the dresses. It's midnight blue with little golden buttons down the front and flares at the middle. I add some black heels and stolen jewelry, and pack all the other stuff back up, making sure to keep Tim's paperwork close by.

Looking back at the bed, I debate my options, but now that my urgency and tiredness have left my determination to bring him to justice is back. Writing a quick message for Nos, I slip out of the room with my bags thrown over my shoulders.

Time for part one of the plan: love life.

With the meeting scheduled later tonight, I have time to head back to his apartment building and tail Tim. I'm not sure how I'm going to destroy his love life yet, but I'll think of something. About an hour of waiting later, he walks out of the front door, his security posse and fuck buddies in tow.

When they don't take a cab or the car, I keep to my side of the street, secretly watching them as they walk to wherever the hell the bastard goes during the day when he wasn't tormenting me.

He walks for over ten minutes before striding into a posh looking restaurant. I watch through the front window as he meets a blonde at a table near the window and kisses her, hard. This bitch. He never brought me to places like this, not that this is the issue here, but they do nice looking burgers and that bastard knew I loved them.

Throwing my hair over my shoulder, I do what any good dead ex-wife would do. Make a scene.

I push open the door to the restaurant and ignoring the maître d', I head to the back corridor and wait. It doesn't take long before he gets up and heads my way. Hiding until he goes to the men's room, I block the door with a plant pot, which I'm guessing you aren't supposed to be able to move by the weight of it.

Straightening my dress, I saunter over to his table where the woman waits, sipping on some coffee. Sliding into his empty seat, I cross my legs and meet her startled gaze.

"Hello, love. Don't mind me joining, do you?" I purr.

"Erm, sorry?" she asks, all timid and a fucking blush covering her cheeks as she lowers her eyes. Fucking hell, he's going to eat her up and spit her out.

"Don't be, but he will be," I murmur, leaning over and grabbing his coffee to sip it as I watch her over the rim of the mug. Her bright blue eyes are wide and confused as she watches me. Her blonde hair is straight and in a short bob, framing her cute face. She looks so sweet and innocent that I sigh and put the coffee down. "What's your name, cutie?" I inquire softly.

She swallows, her eyes darting to the corridor Tim went down. "Don't worry, he's busy. It's just you and me."

"Stacey, who are you?" she retorts, fiddling with her cup nervously. I spot the red marks on her wrist and frown. She notices my gaze and pulls the sleeve of her dress down to cover it self-consciously.

"Don't worry, I'm used to that. Makeup works best if you can get the right colour match, but it doesn't stop it from hurting, am I right?"

She sucks in a breath and leans back as I lean in. "Listen up Stacey. I've been where you were. He says sorry the next day, he brings presents to make up for it, swearing it won't happen again." Her breathing nearly stop while I talk and I notice the shame in her eyes, she knows I'm right. "I should know, he did it to me. I don't want that to happen to anyone again because, love? He won't ever stop. He feels the need to dominate everything and to hurt others because he can. It's a mechanism. He will never change no matter how many times you tell yourself that, or how many excuses you make for his behaviour. Right now, you're staring down the barrel of a gun without even realising it. Do you stand there and wait for him to pull the trigger, or do you run?"

"He did this to you?" she whispers, leaning in and dropping her voice so no one else can hear.

"Yup, but much worse. I didn't get out," I reply, my voice low and dangerous, thinking about the hell he put me through.

"What happened?" she questions, searching my face for answers like I'm her savior.

"He killed me. Well, he thought he did after he forced me to marry him and kept me like his fucking pet," I spit.

She sucks in a breath, tears gathering in her eyes. "I don't know how to get out. I tried to get away, but he knows where I live and he keeps turning up." She looks down and I lift her chin with my finger.

"Do you want to be free of him? Are you willing to help yourself? That's the only way this works. I can get you away so he will never find you again, but if you don't want to escape then this is all pointless," I finish, the truth flowing from my mouth. I came to destroy his life, but I'll try and save this innocent girl if I can. Stop him in a way no one ever did for me. I see her despite her broken heart and the bruises covering her body. I see her, and with that comes the need to save her. If she will let me.

"Yes," she responds, desperate. Her voice is strong even if her body isn't. She means what she says, she wants to be free, but she didn't know how.

"I'm going to give you some money. You are going to get on the next flight out of here, do you have anywhere to go? Anywhere he won't know where to find you?"

She thinks hard, nibbling on her bottom lip before her eyes clear. "My family, they own a farm up north, I've never told him about it," she says quickly, and I know it's the truth. The adrenaline is pumping through her body now that she sees the light at the end of the tunnel, and I wish I could have found that escape with her too.

"Good, go there. Start fresh. Never come back, I mean it." I reach down for the small clutch I brought and pull out a wad of his money and pass it over. "Stacey, you're free, now get out before it's too late, because there is a death coming for him and I would hate for you to get caught up in it."

I lean back and down the rest of his coffee, leaving a lipstick mark on the rim.

She grabs the money and holds it to her chest like the lifeline it is. Tears drip down her face as she smiles at me, the first one I've seen out of her. It will take a long time for her to heal, maybe she never fully will, but at least she has a shot.

She nods and grabs her stuff before getting to her feet and beginning to walk away. I watch her go but she stops and turns back to me, rushing towards me and embracing me. "Thank you, thank you so much," she whispers before pulling away. "What about you? Why don't you come with me?"

I shake my head sadly. "It's too late for me, go." I push her softly and she nods. Looking around, she grabs a napkin and pulls a pen from her bag, scribbling something on it before passing it back to me. "Here, if you ever change your mind, there's a safe place for you here. We aren't...conventional people, but I offer you safe passage." She nods, turns, and leaves. I frown at her strange wording as I watch her go. It's like watching what I could have been. I was offered an out a few times and I always took it with one hand, never two. What would have happened to me if I was like her and got away?

It doesn't matter now, this is my life. Slipping the napkin into my bag I decide to have my fun, it's the only thing I can do now. Get revenge, let this power inside of me out until it eats at the dead flesh of this city I once loved.

Uncrossing my legs I stand up, and I pull down my dress as I make my way to the corridor. I hear him banging and swearing as he tries to get out of the bathroom. Smirking, I kick the plant over and open the door, stepping inside as he steps back warily. When he spots me, his mouth drops open and his eyes round. I can see his pulse hammering at his neck, and almost taste the confusion and fear on the air.

"Hello husband," I purr as I step inside and shut the door behind me.

"You're dead," he mutters dumbly, shaking his head as he backs away and hits the stall door.

"Very smart of you to notice, thank you for that, by the way. I appreciated the mud facial you gave me. Really smoothed out my skin as I crawled from it," I comment casually, stepping forward slowly.

His hand grabs the gun I know he keeps tucked in his jacket, his hands shaking as his face pales. What a pussy. "I saw you die," he repeats like a broken record.

"Dude, we just covered that. Keep up, will you?" I taunt and dart forward, making him jump as I step back and laugh.

He points the gun at me and I roll my eyes.

Rushing forward, I twist and pull and turn it in my hands until it's aimed at him. He freezes, his breaths wheezing as I step closer and push it into his privates. "Now, I know it's hard for you to listen with all the cocks in your mouth, but I'm going to need you to concentrate for a couple of seconds, okay?"

When he doesn't answer me, I dig the gun in and he yelps and nods desperately, sweat appearing on his forehead.

"Good boy." I tap his cock with the barrel of the pistol. "Now, little Stacey out there has disappeared and you won't try to follow her, or I will become your own little poltergeist every time you try and get your disgusting little woodpecker wet, whether that be in one of your girls or your security team."

He sputters at that and I grin.

"Oh yes, darling. I have pictures, pictures I'm sure you would hate to get out, seeing as you're one of the biggest homophobes in the fucking city. So you will leave her alone, as well as any other girls you are beating on."

He nods, his Adam's apple bobbing as he swallows hard. "Anything else?"

I lean forward, digging the gun in as I whisper in his ear. "I'll be seeing you soon husband—game on."

I drop the gun and turn, leaving as casually as I can. I hear him muttering about too much drugs and drinking behind me, no doubt his tiny little mind is trying to protect him from the fact that the wife he killed has come back from the dead with her sights set on him. Whatever helps him cope, because I'm only just getting started, and I can't wait to have my fun. Whistling to myself, I leave the restaurant and head to the designer shops down the road. I'm going to put a dent in his cards. Laughing, I pull out the wallet I slipped from his pocket while he was distracted. Let's see how much I can buy before the meeting later. Time for a pretty woman moment...apart from the fact that I'm not a prostitute and he's definitely no Edward Lewis.

Let me tell you, money opens a lot of doors. I didn't grow up poor per se, but I wasn't rich, and it's crazy how flashing some black cards and cash can change a person's attitude towards you. I could probably finger myself on the black, leather sofa I'm sitting on in the middle of the ladies section and they wouldn't give a fuck, only ask if I needed any refreshments.

The two women who are serving me bustle back and forth bagging up clothes, hats, shoes, and more as they bring additional items over for me to try on. I have no plans to wear this shit at all— well, maybe some of it, the rest I'm going to donate. See, I can be a good person...sometimes.

"Miss, would you like another drink?" the pretty blonde, who informed me her name was Sarah, asks with a sneer of her lips that she doesn't think I catch. Her pencil skirt and blouse are pressed perfectly, and probably worth than my old apartment. I nod as I lean back and she brings me a fresh glass of champagne.

It's way too perfect in here, it makes me want to fuck some shit up just because I can. Kicking off my heels, I curl my legs under me on the sofa. Her eyes widen before she schools her expression. Bringing the glass to my lips I block my smile with it.

"Sarah, be a doll. Run and get me a pizza, would you? I'm starving." I tell her, just to see if she will. Call it curiosity. The dead have to have a few perks, right?

"Erm, I'm afraid we have a no eating policy," she counters,

looking around as if hoping someone else will appear and take me away. If it wasn't for the card on the sofa next to me, she would have kicked me out an hour ago.

"Okay, bag all this stuff up apart from those jeans, the red dress, that black number, and those golden heels. Here is the two address of where to send the rest." I pass over a sheet of paper. Written there is a homeless shelter's number and the other number is Stacy's. I figured Stacey deserves some of that dickwad's money as well.

She nods and scurries away, no doubt happy to be rid of me. Pulling out the new phone I bought, I check the time. I still have a couple of hours to kill before the meeting. I wonder if Nos is still at the hotel? Probably not, he wouldn't want to be caught with the body. Not that he would care, but he's probably out here lurking somewhere, stalking me. The thought sends a thrill through me as I sip the overpriced champagne, an evil thought coming to mind. He could definitely help me pass the time if I can find him.

Game on monster, and this time, I'm the hunter.

CHAPTER 16

DUME

The plane is waiting for me like Mike said it would be, I guess the vampire can be good for something. Pulling the stolen truck over at the open hangar on the small, private runway, I get out and leave the keys inside. I slam the door behind me, and cover the distance between the car and the plane in four big strides. The man, who is clearly waiting for me, cowers before me. I take a big sniff and realise he is human—what was Mike thinking? He looks like he is about to piss himself.

"Mister, er..." He looks down at his phone, making me narrow my eyes. I don't have time for this.

"Dume," I grit out, my nose ring heating from the steam, which is almost pouring from my nose at this point. My need to get to my mate so extreme, it's all that's driving my beast and me.

"Erm, yes Mr. Dume. Do you need me to get your bags? We can be in the air within the next thirty minutes, all pre-flight checks—"

"Stop talking," I order as I push past him, and climb up the stairs and into the plane. It's posh, I'll give the bastard that. Business must be good.

It has six plush seats spread out along its length, two of them facing the front and the other four facing each other. All in accents of cream and gold. There is even a mini bar at the back with a door, no doubt leading to the bathroom. Choosing a seat farthest in the back and away from the humans, I slide into it grimacing as the seat creaks under my weight. It's not comfortable, not for a guy my size, but it will do. I've had a lot worse, that is for sure, I can handle this. I can handle anything as long as it gets me to her.

"Mr. Dume, Mr. Tireno said you would want this," the out of breath man addresses me as he drags a large, black bag down the aisle. Panting, he drops it at my feet with a thud. I incline my head and he runs back to the front of the plane, shutting the door and heading to the cockpit, giving me the privacy and silence I so desperately want.

Going from imprisonment to all the smells, sounds, and sights of this world is taking its toll. My head is pounding, my skin feels tight, and my beast wants out—to explore.

Rolling my shoulders, I crack my neck before leaning down and unzipping the bag. I grin when I spot my weapons—the only things I have ever owned—laying in wait for me. Not bad, blood sucker. I will have to remind myself to thank him, since not just anybody could have gotten these for me. No doubt the witches took them and hid them away. I stroke the stained and tarnished pummels of my two dadao swords. The gold was inlaid by the very best, a gift from my queen for winning every match. A matched pair, like she called her and me. One of the only times she gave me anything of meaning, not just more nightmares and scars.

"Here, my warrior. I got you something," she murmurs, sliding from the silk sheets and tying the long, blood-red robe closed at the middle. It gapes at the top, showing off her ample chest. Something I know she is doing on purpose. The sight should arouse me, but I am nothing but a bull for her. Something to fuck, her walk on the dark side. To get out all her base impulses. At first I was flattered, but she soon made it clear she thought of me as nothing but an animal. Another toy for her to fuck, and then kill in front of her people. The anger and resentment burning through me is treacherous, something I can never let out, not with the bindings on me. Instead, I show her through my fucking how much I hate her. How easily I could kill her if not for her witches. She loved every second of it. No doubt putting on a show for her husband lying in the next room. Everything is a game to my queen and she is the fucking best at it.

She returns with a black felt cloth, obviously wrapped around something heavy as she struggles before laying it on the bottom of the bed. Sitting up slowly,

I let the sheet pool at my hips and her eyes dart down and she licks her lips, the image sending a bolt of disgust through me, making me scrunch up my nose even as I lean forward and open the present. I learned the hard way what turning my nose up at her would do.

Inside are two beautiful dadao swords. The pummels gold with threads tied around, my ancestors' symbols painted there. The steel is strong and sure, and when I run my finger down one of the edges it cuts through my skin like butter, something no weapon should be able to do.

"Do you like them? I got them from one of your kind. He didn't want to part with them, called them heirlooms of his forgotten people, but he had no choice." She claps like it's the greatest thing in the world that she just told me about the slaughter of one of my kind, like that was a gift to me. I nod in agreement, I learned to just agree, even as the control chafes against me. "You are supposed to say 'yes, my queen.' Now, kiss me in thanks. Show me exactly how gratefully you are for your presents," she orders, her chest already rising and falling faster in desire as her lips part on a pant. Dropping the sword carefully, I wrap them back up before sitting up on my knees, the sheet leaving me completely bare as I move before her, grab her hair, and pull it tight. The pain makes her eyes widen as a needy moan slips out. Oh yes, my queen likes my hate and punishment. She drinks it up and tonight, I am going to show her exactly how fucking much I hate her. How her touch makes my skin crawl even as her magic forced me to do her bidding.

These swords have stood with me through it all. Through the rise and fall of kingdoms, through the slaughter of my people. They have tasted blood throughout the centuries, my queen's, my enemies', innocents'. All in the name of staying alive, and they will taste it yet again if anyone touches what is mine. I fought like a beast when it was ordered—imagine what I will do when it comes to something I love.

CHAPTER 17

ASKA

F irst light hits the road behind me as I leave civilisation once again and head into the trees. The vision of my mate, Dawn, has only made me more determined than ever to find her. Her beauty was without compare, but it was the spirit, the determination in her gaze as she held mine that keeps running through my head. Even as a child, people bowed their eyes to me. I have a feeling she never will, and the thought excites me and challenges my dragon. He wants to know what it would take for her to kneel at my feet. I want to kneel at hers. Partners. Equals.

That is what we will be, when I find her at least. I can almost feel the danger closing in, circling her. Drawn to her like I am. Her strength, her unique tasting power, calling to us all until we are with her. Until they eat her up and destroy her. Not that I will ever let them, they will never touch her again. She has been hurt too much for any one lifetime.

My fists clench when I recall what she told me of her life, but I know it hasn't broken her. In fact, it only seems to have made her stronger.

Walking through the trees, I let nature soothe me until I step out onto the hill. The sun chasing me at my back and warming my skin, but never touching the darkness that is a pit inside me. Where the souls of the lost and the damned reside.

I wonder what her soul would taste like, would she give it all to me? Would she stare into the darkness in my heart and accept it? I hope so, because I am not giving her any other choice.

Letting the change run through me, the pain pulls at my body like an old friend until, with a muted roar, my wings burst from my back, spreading across the clearing with the wide wingspan. My lineage afforded me a large dragon form even if my powers, as my father called them, weren't traditional. He called me an omen. The only dragon to ever eat souls, to blow darkness from my snout, not fire. The darkness from beyond coming to either save, or kill us, for our deeds. I guess he finally got to see which when we fell.

Raising my muzzle to the sky, I suck in the air, tasting the wind as I push off and soar into the cloud above. Darkness once again walks the earth—will I save or will I destroy this time? Only time will tell.

Straddling my Harley, I pull on my helmet. I could have taken my car but I prefer the freedom of the bike, and I can almost burst from it at a moment's notice if there is an attack. It offers a quick getaway, something you need around the council. The engine rumbles beneath me as I head through the city and onto the road leading through the surrounding forest.

The council chose to live alone, out here, secluded. They say it's for safety, but I think they retreated from this world. Choosing to send out their minions like me to do their work for them, while they sit in their castle, moving around pawns like the world is a chessboard.

I let the air soothe my nerves, which are clambering with every mile closer I get to their dominion. At least in the city I am free from their prying eyes in a way, but here I have no choice except to play their games.

When I drive up outside the wrought iron gates, I pull off my helmet and stare into the camera as the scanner reads my blood work and processes it. With a click, the gates slowly open and I pull through. Not bothering with parking or heading to the garage, I leave my bike at the bottom of the steps leading to the monstrosity that is their base.

A fountain sputters to life behind me as I face the big, double cream doors, two pillars frame it on either side. A mix between castle and mansion, it has two turrets on each side of the massive sixty room house. With two council meeting rooms, a dungeon, a gym, a training center, and much more. For most it's a haven, a place they dream of coming. Of getting a job within our ruling body. For monsters like me it's a trap, a nightmare of softly spoken barbs and punishments.

The doors open and Yoln, the council's bitch, steps out. His sour face pursed in disgust as he takes me in from top to bottom.

"You are late," he scolds, before turning and marching back inside.

This should be fucking fun, let's hope they haven't decided to finally kill me. I would hate to get blood on my new boots.

CHAPTER 18

NOS

Walking through the city, I let our bond guide me. Our mating link has only gotten stronger with each touch, kiss, and shared power transfusion—something I don't think she even knows she is doing. This morning I had planned to tell her what she was, but when I woke she had already left. I didn't hear her, a testament to how much power and energy she took from me last night during our lovemaking.

Leaving the body of the man whom the room belonged to on the floor, I double-checked to make sure there was nothing left behind to link us to his death. Not that they would find us anyway. She is dead and I don't exist, but blood and hair can be used for far worse reasons. Not to mention if the humans tested it, it would create panic. Some know we live among them, but we have a treaty of sorts, a protection. We stay out of the light and out of trouble, and they pretend we don't exist.

When the room was clean, well, apart from the dead man, I left in search of her. She needs to know what she is so she can tackle the growing and hunger pangs, which will result from her new form. It's been a long time since I have even heard anyone mention of her new form, so this is new to me. From what I remember, they are powerful, but with that power comes the need to draw energy from others, which can occur through a mate bond, including kissing and sex, or from a person...not voluntarily.

I catch her power residue outside an upscale restaurant, but the trail is old. Following the tugging sensation in my chest, which happens whenever she isn't around, I head inside a clothing shop. It is stronger in here, but also confusing, like she is everywhere.

I scan the store and ignore the gawking sales women who watch me with desire and moneybags in their eyes, and head upstairs in search of my little monster. I wonder what trouble she is creating now.

I reach a section of dresses and scantily clad mannequins, and I know I am getting close. Wandering around aimlessly, I search the shoppers for a sign of her bright blonde hair. I am just passing a changing room built into the back of the shop when a pale arm darts out, grabs my hand, and tugs me inside.

Without waiting, she is on me and I react instantly. There is nothing like the feel of my mate in my arms. She wraps her legs around my waist as I fall back into the changing room wall, and her mouth meets mine as she kisses me hard before pulling away. A smile curls up those lips of hers as her eyes slowly bleed to black. I don't think she even realises that her hunger and the mating instinct is guiding her right now, and I have no intention of telling her, not yet.

First, my little monster will take everything and anything from me that she wants. I am hers, mind, body, and soul. She could suck every drop of energy from me and I wouldn't die, but I would gladly let her do it.

"Little Monster," I rasp as she hops down.

My eyes narrow as she moves away from me, but she grabs me and pushes me onto the sofa in the corner of the spacious changing room. I sprawl back, watching her hungrily as she strips off her little dress to show me the lacey, almost see-through, white bra and thong covering her body. A mirror placed on the wall behind her shows me that perky little ass of hers as she struts towards me on high heels, and the sight makes my mouth dry and it's hard to speak.

She is perfection wrapped up in a small, dangerous package.

When she straddles me, my hands go to her hips, but she grabs them and pins them to the sofa above of me. If she wants control, she can have it. She can have everything.

DAWN

That same heat and hunger courses through my body again, pulling me towards Nos as I rub my panty-clad pussy over the hard bulge in his jeans. I sensed him when he entered the store and I laid in wait, knowing he would find me. I set a trap for my monster, but he doesn't seem to care. Instead, he watches me with such hunger that I moan and throw my head back, rubbing against him. Needing everything he has.

Anyone could walk in, anyone could find us, and I don't think they would appreciate us fucking inside their changing rooms, but it only makes me hotter. The idea of someone watching has me reaching up and undoing my new bra, before letting it drop to the floor next to us.

He keeps his hands above his head, and his eyes turn bright white in an instant as he takes in my body. His jaw clenches as he grinds his teeth, no doubt from the pressure to remain still, to not touch me. I know because I feel it too. The need to mark his body with mine, to touch every inch until no skin remains that I haven't claimed.

"Little Monster," he says in warning when I just continue to rub against him.

Grinning, I lean down until our mouths nearly touch. "Feeling desperate, my horned god?" I whisper against his lips before I kiss him.

Our tongues tangle as I continue to rock against his jeans. I can feel the tension in his body and I decide to stop teasing us both. Leaning back, I break our kiss and lift myself up so I can kick off my panties. Bare before him, I almost whimper when his eyes greedily take in all my flesh as he sinks his teeth into his lower lip, making blood well from the force.

I lean forward at the sight and lick it away. "Only I get to make you bleed," I scold as I lean back, and lift myself so I'm hovering over him. Reaching between us, I flick open his jeans and push them down. He raises his hips and wiggles until the fabric lies tangled around his feet. I groan when I notice he's commando, his hard cock begging and pulsing for me already.

Licking my lips, I watch him as I run my hands down my own body, tweaking my nipples as I go before I reach my already dripping wet pussy. I spread my knees farther and run my fingers down my pussy lips, making him groan.

"Show me, Little Monster," he orders, still trying to control me even though he lies helpless below me.

I spread my thighs wider, almost painfully so, as I open myself to him. His eyes drop to my fingers playing with my pussy and he groans again, the sound long and loud, reverberating around the room. Dipping my fingers into my empty pussy, I fuck myself on them before pulling out and rubbing my clit, while my hips rock as I watch him.

His hands grip the top of the sofa, and I don't think he's even noticed his nails have changed into claws and are ripping holes in the material while he keeps himself still below me. Moving my hands away from my pussy, I circle my nipples with my wetness and he follows the movements with his eyes and I moan, dropping my head back while I play with my own body.

Panting now, with sweat dripping down my skin, I look back at him. "Taste me," I command breathlessly, needing his mouth on me.

He leans up greedily as he sucks my nipple into his mouth,

tasting myself on it, as he groans and sucks harder. Throwing my head back again, I grip his hair, holding him against me as I rub my pussy on his hard cock. He thrusts up, making me gasp as he switches to the other nipple and gives it the same treatment.

When he's licked me clean he pulls away, drawing a whimper from my mouth. With his eyes on mine, he reaches between us and runs his fingers down my wet pussy, circling my hole but never touching me where I need him to before he comes back up and paints my wetness along my chest again. Leaning forward, he follows the path with his tongue, then nips at the underside of my breast.

I reach down and grab his hard cock, and line up him at my entrance before sinking slowly onto him, his length stretching me as I writhe on top of him. When he's buried deep, he pulls out and thrusts back in, sucking my hard nipple into his mouth at the same time.

Gripping his shoulders, I dig my nails into his skin and draw blood, trying to hold on as we rock together. He bites down hard on my nipple, making me nearly scream.

Nos pulls away and I see his teeth imprint around my poor, abused nipple, but I don't have time to complain because his hands grab my hips and he helps me move. He lifts and drops me faster and harder as he thrusts up into me at the same time. The couch creaks dangerously from our combined weight, but I ignore it, keeping my eyes on his as his claws pierce my skin. I love the mix of pain and pleasure when we are together, and when I feel my blood dripping down my hips I groan and rock faster, chasing my release.

Lifting myself, I drop down hard, grinding my pussy on his cock before leaning up and dropping again. We are both panting, sweaty messes, with blood running from his shoulders and my hips.

"Little Monster," he groans, his voice tight.

"Yes," I cry out when he reaches down and presses hard on my clit at the same time as he thrusts up, throwing me over the edge. I come with a scream, uncaring that people can hear me, as I shake on top of him while he keeps fucking in and out of my clamping pussy until he comes too. Darting forward, he bites my shoulder to muffle his yell as he holds me to him, his cock pumping his cum inside of me.

We both ride it out before slumping against each other, breathing heavily while we come back down from the bliss.

"You were following me?" I ask, grinning at him even though my voice is breathless.

He lays back and pulls me down on top of him, making us both groan before he slips from inside of me. "Yes."

"Why?" I press, not that I'm bothered.

"I know what you are, Little Monster," he offers.

A noise outside the curtain has me scrambling from his lap as we both get dressed. I just manage to get the top of my dress over my head before the curtain is pulled back, revealing a shocked shopper.

"Sorry!" she sputters as she shuts it again, but I hear her retreat, no doubt to go tell a store assistant.

"We need to go," I murmur, turning to him and dropping a kiss on his lips as I pull my phone from my pocket. "Fuck, I've got somewhere to be and I need to go alone. Can we meet later, and then you can tell me?" I inquire and he nods, as his hands come up and frame my face.

"Later, Little Monster, meet me in the park. Try not to leave any bodies behind this time," he jokes, and I kiss him again before grabbing my bag and running from the changing room. I need to get to that meeting. I wouldn't miss it for the world.

CHAPTER 19

DUME

The hushed tones of the pilot and the air hostess have me cracking open my eyes, and leaning out into the aisle to watch them. They are gesturing back and forth and I roll my eyes, do they really not realise I can hear them? Humans.

"What's wrong?" I shout and they all jump, looking guiltily between themselves then back to me. They nod, and the man from before stands and comes towards me with a nervous look on his face and his hands twisting together before him.

"Sir, there has been an attack on master Tireno," he rushes out, his eyes darting to mine for a split second before he looks down at the floor again.

Gritting my teeth, I lean forward. "By who?" I demand, bristling.

"Er, I'm not sure, but they're asking to speak to you," he says nervously, and I stand in a rush, which makes him squeal as he falls back. Eyeing him as I push past him, I move into the cockpit where the pilots await. The one on the left holds out a tiny headset to me, but before I can grab it he opens his mouth, and comments, "They have my friends, just a warning." I narrow my eyes as I sniff the air. He definitely isn't supernatural, but I can smell bloodsucker on him, probably a lifelong feeder. A pet, but he clearly cares about Mike so I nod and grab the delicate piece of technology and hold it to my head. He flicks a button and nods at me.

85

"Speak," I growl down the line.

"We have your friends, Beast of Cornacadia, did you really think you could ever escape us. That you could run from us?" The woman laughs down the phone and her sultry voice is soaked in magic, but it does nothing to me. "They will pay for helping you," she finishes.

"I'm not running, but you should be," I bark, before nodding at the pilot. He cuts off the communication, and his face is pale but his eyes are hard.

"Take me to them," I order, before turning around and returning to my seat. It seems like the witches have found Mike. I might not consider him a friend, but he has helped me, and I can't let him and his outcasts be butchered for my escape. It looks like I will have a little detour on the way.

Grabbing my swords, I whisper the words of rites to them, and they glow golden, the glyphs lighting up and seeking the blood of enemies who dare to hurt me and mine.

Soon, I whisper to them, leaning back in my seat as the plane banks to the side.

Time for a witch hunt, and I won't be stopping until they are all dead.

Chapter 20

ASKA

Soaring through the air, I fly high enough to avoid detection on the ground and any restricted air space. With only a basic location to go on, and being on the opposite side of the world, it's taking longer than I would like to find her.

I'm tiring again. I have flown all day and partway into the night. I'm hoping to reach an old house of mine and regroup there for a day or two. I need to get some supplies and I'm thinking now that I am above the right country, it might be easier to drive than fly, even if I hate the idea of being cooped up in a metal tin can for so long.

I fly for a few more hours before I use my last spurt of energy to cover the distance when I spot the landmarks I am searching for. With a relieved snort, I descend through the clouds and swoop down across the land, as the night shields me from prying eyes. The house is built into the side of a mountain, typical, I know, but us dragons like to be high up and it means I can see any enemies coming. It also means humans are less likely to get curious or step onto my property.

I did put some human staff in place to maintain the home and my finances before I retreated from the world, so I hope they have passed it on through the generations like requested. Of course, they are paid handsomely for this.

Circling the mountain, I flap my wings to slow myself down as I reach the landing spot built into the side of my house. I set down gently and let the change move through my body. When I'm human again, I stride towards the glass door that leads into the living room. It opens easily, always unlocked for me.

When I get inside I don't flick on the lights out of habit, but I take in everything around me. Nothing has changed except that they had it updated, and they have obviously kept it clean. Nodding in approval, I walk towards the fire and quickly get it started knowing it is going to get cold soon and I would prefer to lay in front of it instead of in the master bedroom at the back.

When the fire is roaring, I lean back onto my haunches and roll out my sore shoulders. A fur rug spreads out below the huge fireplace, which dominates this side of the room. A new wide and long leather sofa sits in the middle of the room, dividing it from the modern kitchen they obviously had installed. My bookshelves still run on the wall—leading to the glass door and garden—filled with limited editions, first editions, and so much more precious texts. Standing once more, I roam around my house, checking it over.

They upgraded my bed as well, and the new one is big enough to fit a dragon. The walk-in closet is fully stocked and the ensuite has been updated too, with a large jacuzzi tub and rainforest shower.

They left my favourite part of my house untouched, though, and for that I am grateful. The pool, which is attached to my bedroom through a dipping point, overlooks the mountain with a glass bottom to see it all. It was my sanctuary for a long time, surveying the world, but even then I grew tired of that, but with my mate's touch running through me I can appreciate the beauty once again. I might even bring her here, show her my home and solace. I can just imagine her blonde hair laid over the edge of the pool as she looks down on the world below.

Stripping off, I slip into the cool water and wade in until I can lean against the edge and watch the world. I don't know how long I lay there, content to let the water soothe my muscles, but when I spot headlights cutting through the dirt road that leads to my home, I narrow my eyes as my dragon roars to the forefront of my mind.

Jumping from the water, I get dressed quickly. No one should be here.

It could be the humans I entrusted to look after this place, but logically I know they wouldn't come so late in the night. That only leaves two set of people, neither are friendly.

Dragons—searching for me after feeling me awaken—to either kill me or bring me back to the throne.

Or worse yet, human hunters. I don't know how they would have found me and so quickly, unless they were monitoring the house, which means the location is compromised.

None of it matters though. Whoever it is will die for stepping foot on my soil. It seems there will be no rest for me tonight.

No, tonight I teach them why everyone fears the dragon.

I let out a roar that shakes the very mountain I'm on in warning, as I grab some weapons from my stash. I won't change unless I need to.

Moving back to the living room, I stand by the fire with an axe held in each hand, waiting for them.

I hear more than one car stop and boots crunching as they get out, their hushed whispers loud in the silence as an adrenaline filled smile curves my face. Maybe this is a good thing and I can practice my fighting. I don't want to be rusty when meeting my mate after all.

The door blows off its hinges as men and women in black, strapped with every type of gun and weapon available, stream through the door and into my home.

"You fucked with the wrong dragon!" I laugh as I raise my axes and jump into their masses, their yells following after me.

CHAPTER 21

DAWN

L eaving the department store, I head to a café and use their bathroom to quickly change into the new black dress and heels I just bought.

The silky black material hugs my curves and is skin-tight, ending at mid-thigh. The spaghetti straps cross in the back, showing off my pale skin. The five inch golden heels glitter in the light. I fell in love with them instantly, plus I figured worse comes to worst, I can always stab someone with them.

I also made sure to change the time and date of the meeting for Tim. So he thinks it's tomorrow instead. It will give me some time to snoop on the man he was meeting and see what sort of trouble I can get him into.

Stuffing my other clothes into my shopping bags, I unlock the door to see a granny waiting outside giving me a dirty look, and she eyes my dress with disgust. Snobby old bastard. Why do old people always think they can get away with being bitchy? I nearly died too, doesn't make me a cunt.

"Don't stress, saggy tits. I'm sure you can still piss and hold your nose in the air at the same time." I salute her when her mouth drops open and her face changes to a funny red and purple. Before she can get whatever insult that's floating around in her head out, I walk past humming as I make my way through the coffee shop.

"Toilets are for customers, not working girls giving their hooch a clean!" she yells after me, and the few tables that are full gape at me.

Did this old bitch just call me a prostitute? Motherfucker, just because her vagina claps dust when it opens doesn't mean she can be a bitch.

Turning back to face her, I wink at her instead. "Don't worry, I'll make sure to call an ambulance just in case the next time your husband calls me."

She sputters as I laugh and leave the shop. Still grinning, way too happy with myself, I hail a taxi and slip inside the back seat, the leather crinkling under my bare legs.

"Downtown, 45th and West. Armios Restaurant please," I say politely, fluttering my lashes at the woman driver.

The woman smiles at me in mirror. "You got it." As she pulls away from the curb I relax back into my seat and watch as the city starts to come alive.

I always loved it here. After growing up in a small town, I always wanted to run away to the city and I guess I did. I love the way it lights up during the day, with smells and sounds, and so many different cultures and places to explore, but at night it really comes alive. Music pours from bars in the district, delicious food smells waft through the air from all the restaurants, and the streets are so busy you can hardly move.

I guess a monster does always love the night.

The restaurant they are holding the meeting at is posh, which I should have guessed. When I step inside I'm instantly handed a glass of wine and asked for my reservation. When I tell them I'm here for a meeting being held in the Rower Suite, which I gleaned from the paperwork in Tim's place, the man's smile inches up a notch and they become extra nice.

I'm led through the crowded and candle lit restaurant to a corridor at the back. He holds open the door and as I slip through them, I'm guided all the way to the end where a gold-plated door proudly declares the room 'Rower Suite' in fancy script.

He knocks on the door before stepping back. "Have a good evening miss, and do not hesitate to call for one of us if you need anything." He bows my way before he turns and leaves me waiting in the corridor.

The door opens a few seconds later just when I was about to kick the fucker down. I'm not exactly a patient person. The guy who opens it is clearly security of some kind. In a black suit with a gun bulging at his hip, he screams protection. His boring brown eyes narrow on me as he takes me in from head to sparkling, golden toe.

"We didn't order a stripper," he grumbles and goes to shut the door.

This bitch. What the hell is it about this dress that makes people think I fuck or strip for money? I look down at it in disgust. "As if you could afford me," I taunt, before kicking my new shoe forward and holding the door open even as he tries to shut it on me.

"Listen up airhead, I'm here for the meeting. Now let me in to see Marco or I'll take these stripper shoes and shove them so far up your ass, you'll be spitting out golden sparkles like some kind of fucked up unicorn. Deal?" I order.

He pales but refuses to open the door, his eyes darting around as if not sure what to do.

"Let her in," comes a heavy accented voice from inside the room.

I lean forward and pat the man's chest. "You heard him, let me in," I purr.

He nods, before stepping back and swinging the door open. I pat his chest again on the way in. "Good boy, heel."

His eyes narrow on me in anger and his hand drops to his gun.

"Do it, I dare you," I jeer.

"Red, that's enough," the accented voice orders again, and only when Red drops his hand from his gun do I look at the rest of the room, searching out the man who spoke. He must be Marco.

The room is dark compared to rest of the restaurant. Two large candelabras with flickering flames light it, and there is some dimmed lighting spread throughout. A large, white-clothed table sits in the middle of the room, with eight dark cherry chairs circling it. Only one is taken. My heels sink into the deep red carpet as the flames reflect off the wooden paneled walls. He must see me staring because he flickers a look at them.

"Sound proofed," he replies, and I nod before taking him in. He isn't what I expected, that's for sure. Even from his voice.

He's young, probably around my age. Whiskey coloured eyes meet mine with interest. He's handsome as hell. Pitch-black stubble covers his chin and jaw, highlighting his high cheekbones. Thick black eyebrows are arched my way as he sips on a tumbler of some kind. His short, black hair is wavy and styled to perfection, and from what I can see of his outfit, it looks to be a hand-tailored, dark grey suit.

No, definitely not what I was expecting, but even as I can admit that he's attractive, he doesn't come close to my horned god in his ripped jeans and bare feet.

"Marco, I presume?" I ask, and he nods as he takes me in like I did him.

"Please, take a seat. May I ask who I have the pleasure of dining with?" he inquires.

I pull out the seat opposite him and slide into it. "Dawn," I reply.

His eyebrow flies up and drops his glass to the table, watching me like I'm fascinating.

"Dawn, what can I do for you? You clearly know me, but I'm afraid I don't know you, something we must rectify." His words are teasing, but I see the hardness in his gaze. He is a powerful man, he relies on knowledge, and right now he doesn't appreciate being in the dark. It makes him weak.

"You know my ex-husband. In fact he was supposed to meet you tonight. I, however might have accidentally changed the appointment in his phone. Silly me," I murmur the last and he grins.

"I wasn't aware Timmy boy was married." He leans back, looking at me in a new light.

"It was a...fast marriage, if you will," I reply as a glass of wine is dropped in front of me. I nod at the waiter and wait for him to the leave the room before relaxing back with the glass my hand. "But it did benefit me now, I guess."

"And how is that?" he presses. I can feel him starting to get annoyed with my games.

"Because it offered me information. That's what you thrive on, is it not? It seems little old Tim had some greedy hands and I have the proof."

I let that absorb in as I take a sip of the fruity and expensive wine.

"You can prove that the accountant is stealing from us?" he asks, leaning forward with a gleam in his eye. This isn't new information for him, that's for sure.

"Yes, but I have conditions," I state, sitting forward and matching his posture.

"Name them," he orders.

"I get to kill the bastard, he's mine. You can do whatever you like to his body afterward and the money, I want none of it. I'll even give you the guys who helped him."

"All you want is him? Why?" he questions curiously.

"I'm going to make him suffer and then I'm going to kill him," I answer with a flirty grin, sipping the wine again.

He laughs, sitting back. "A woman after my own heart, but you see, I'm afraid I can't let you do that. He helps me, brings me the money while he gets a cut. So as you can understand, I wouldn't be okay with you killing my monkey."

"You're a silent partner," I murmur, dropping the glass to the table as a numb feeling starts to spread through my body.

"Yes. I've been stealing from Valkov for years. I was the one who convinced the new accountant, your husband, to help me. He really is very easy to manipulate. So, that leaves me with you. You know too much, so you're a complication. What to do?" He taps his chin in thought as I gasp.

My tongue has gone numb and it feels like I can't swallow. My head starts to spin. "You drugged me?" I gasp.

"'Fraid so. Something you should learn about our business, Dawn. Don't trust anyone." He grins, tipping his glass at me.

I'm pissed as hell and I can't even speak anymore, trapped in my own body. The bastard drugged me. I can't wait to fucking kill him. It's my last thought before I tumble from the chair and everything goes black.

Chapter 22

Nos

Something is wrong.

The sun set two hours ago and there is still no sign of my little monster. Pacing in the darkness in front of the fountain at the park, I look at the moon for the hundredth time that hour, praying it gives me strength. When I find her, I am going to smack her arse raw, and if anyone has touched her, I am going to rip them limb from limb and offer their souls to her.

The jittery feeling coursing through my blood doesn't go away. In fact, it is getting worse. I can barely feel her, the connection is dimmed. My body is fighting me, wanting to change and tear through the city until I find her, but I have to be smart about this. I can't rely on our connection to get me to her. Instead, I will have to retrace her footsteps, because nothing hides from me in the dark.

Especially not my mate.

CHAPTER 23

Dawn

I wake up slowly and my head hurts, but the rest of my body feels okay. I check all my limbs to make sure no one has cut any off. Hey, I've watched CSI, people do weird things. Opening my eyes sluggishly, I'm greeted with nothing but darkness. I raise my hand and feel along my head, until I notice a large lump on my skull, and it's on the same side I fell out of the chair. The bastards didn't even catch me.

I flop onto my back and feel along the cold, hard floor until my hand meets something metal. Stroking upwards, I realise it's a bar. I'm in a fucking cage.

Sitting up, I growl when a chain jangles with the movement. My eyes have finally started to adjust to the blackness and I can make out the silver chain tied to a hoop in the floor and linked around my ankle. I blow out a breath and push my messy hair back behind my ears, before checking I still have on underwear. Yay for me, I do.

I get to my feet and begin to explore the cage. It's not very big, barely big enough to lay down flat in. Tilting my head, I scent the air but all I can smell is mould and salty air.

"Hey pricks!" I yell, because no way am I waiting for them to be all dramatic and keep me waiting, I have a date with Nos.

"Shh," comes a small voice.

"Someone else here?" I ask loudly.

"Shut up, you're going to make them come back," another voice hisses, almost feminine.

"How many of you are there?" I inquire quietly this time, sensing their panic.

"Ten, you were brought in a couple of hours ago, making us eleven," a softer voice answers to my right.

I can barely make out the other cages in here, it's that dark. "What have they been doing to you?" I question, my anger resurfacing.

"There were twenty of us to begin with. Five were sold, like we'll soon be. Five were taken below," the same voice answers.

"Below?" I echo, curious.

"Whatever they do down there to you, you don't come back," another sad sounding voice responds.

"Shut the fuck up, will you? Do you really want them to come back?" comes a hiss again, but their fear wafts in the air.

"Yes, yes I do," I answer honestly.

"Why?" the other voice asks, as I hear rustling of movement.

"Because the quicker they come back, the quicker I can kill them all and get free, and the quicker I can get back for my date." I laugh.

"She's fucking crazy," someone mutters.

"That I am, but I'm going to save your sane asses so be nice," I reply before cupping my mouth. "Hey pencil dicks, wanna play? I'm booooooreddd. Helllooooo?" I shout loudly, and it reverberates around the large, empty space. From the echo, it sounds like we are in a big, empty room somewhere.

I hear footsteps before a door flies open somewhere on the other side of the room, hitting the wall. Someone swears before they flick on the lights. Buzzing starts overhead as the lights slowly turn on, illuminating the warehouse we are in—because that's what it is.

Boxes and crates sit to one side in a corner, and a truck is parked to my left with a big roll up door in front of it. We are in a row in the middle of the warehouse, ten cages on each side, twenty in total. Only ten are full though. I catch my first glimpse of the girls being held here and only one word comes to mine—haggard. They have all been beaten and abused in some way. One even flinches from the light, curling into her barely clad body and crying out, and whimpers slip from her mouth as she rocks back and forth.

Dragging my eyes from her, I spot the studio setup behind the cages. It's a white background with big light stands against the back wall, and numerous cameras aimed that way. No doubt that's how they showcase and sell the girls. The thought makes me sick, but also angry. I can deal with anger, it's mostly what kept me going since I clawed my way back from the dead.

I meet the dead eyes of the woman opposite me—nothing lives there. No fear, no anger...they are just empty. It sends a shiver down my spine. It's the look of acceptance. Her brown hair is cut in different lengths and is greasy, but there is a pink highlight standing out, which tells me at some point this woman did care.

Her face is gaunt and smudged with dirt and blood, and her bottom lip is split and one of her eyes is black. She is wearing nothing but a white tank top and some black panties with a rip at the top. Her tanned, long legs are covered in bruises and hand marks, and when I meet her eyes again, I let her see the fury there at her treatment and hopefully their death.

She steps back, her hands dropping from the bars as she stands in the middle of the cage and waits for the boots I hear approaching to get closer.

"I warned you," she whispers sadly.

The boots get closer and I get my first glimpse of our captors. He's dressed in all black, like nearly every bad guy you see. Black cargo pants are tucked into black military style boots, and he wears a tight black t-shirt with guns strapped across his chest and thighs. He's an opposing man, for a human.

Tattoo's cover his neck—a moth with its wings open, curling up and around his jaw. A teardrop is inked under one eye, only making the darkness and cruelty I see in those brown orbs seem more intense. His hair is buzzed close to his head and he walks like a soldier. All stiff, upright, and his eyes are scanning everything. Maybe a merc? It means these guys are the best, well organised, and this wasn't a rushed job. They are trading in humans and doing something much worse to them, if what the girls in the cages are saying is true.

He walks down the aisle in the middle of the cages, looking in each one. Every girl flinches, scurrying away from him until they rest at the back of the cage. The look in their eyes, the tightness of their bodies, shows he has definitely hurt them before, maybe even violated them.

Leaning casually against the bars, I wait for him to get to me. This little impromptu kidnapping is ruining all my plans. One of the girls on my row, two cages down, makes a noise when he passes and he smacks the bars with his fist, laughing when she flinches. Screw plans. I'm going to have some fun.

He stops in front of my cage, eyeing me with interest. "So you're the new piece of ass they brought in?" He leers at me, his eyes running down my body. "The new ones are so much fun to break in."

"I'll admit, I do have a good ass. Why don't you come and find out for yourself? But I'll warn you. I bite." I grin, stepping back from the bars and into the middle of my cage, waiting for him.

His eyes waver for a moment, looking around before he comes to a decision, his need outweighing his survival instincts. "That's what these are for." He unclips a gun and aims it at my stomach as he fiddles with the lock on my cage.

I don't know if I can survive a gunshot, but I guess we're going to find out. I wait, unmoving, until he unlocks it and swings the door open. He edges in, his eyes pinning me as he steps through and clangs it shut behind him, but I know it's unlocked. I'm betting he's expecting the gun to stop me, or scare me. Idiot.

"Make it easy on yourself, don't fight me. Or do, I love it when you break. The first time you realize it doesn't matter what you do." He licks his lips, his eyes burning with excitement. Oh, he likes the fight alright, and I'm going to give him one.

"I like it rough, what can I say?" I laugh when I hear a snort and a laugh from one of the other cells. I grin at the man as he narrows his eyes.

"On your knees," he orders.

"Yeah, I'm going to pass. How about you get on yours?" I purr.

"On your fucking knees!" he shouts, his finger tightening on the trigger.

Rolling my eyes, I strut towards him until I can run my finger down his chest. His eyes watch me, waiting for me to make a wrong move. Trailing my touch down his hard crotch, I watch his mouth open as his eyes heat. Idiot. Circling my finger, I run it back up his chest until I can curl my hand around his throat. I squeezed hard suddenly and he yells, his finger slipping on the trigger.

The shot throws me stumbling back and I lose my hold on him. Wide-eyed, I look down at the blood blossoming on my stomach and the hole through my dress.

"This was a new dress you bastard!" I yell as he gulps, his eyes round as he falls back.

"Wh-what are you?" he stutters.

"You fucking shot me!" I shout, and with a growl I fling myself towards him.

He howls and turns, trying to get the cage door open as I land on his back and wrap my body around him.

Yanking his head to the side, I sink my teeth into his neck until I taste blood. He screams and falls back. I release his neck and jump down and spin until I'm in front of him. Blood streams steadily down his neck as he watches me, his face frozen in terror as he backs away from me.

I saunter towards him, licking his blood from my lips with a hum. He swallows hard and I'm on him again in an instant. I knock him back to the floor and pin him there, then I lean down and lap up the trail of blood before looking back at him.

"Now, be a good boy and tell me what you do with the women you take below," I purr, stroking around the bite wound. When he doesn't answer me I press my finger inside it, widening the cut and he screams.

"Tell me," I demand. "I have somewhere to be and I'm getting bored with you."

"They-they aren't human," he whispers, and his eyes dart to the side.

"Well, shit," I mutter. "You hunting the non-humans?"

"No, no, no! They steal and take girls to sell, we get our fun and well, erm, they tend to out themselves when we touch them. Like you did. Usually, though, they don't have a clue until that moment and their powers are weak."

"What do you do with them?" I ask, leaning closer.

"They, not we. We just take them down there. I think they experiment on them, try to bring their powers out further. If they can't, they are resold or if they are too broken, they kill them," he rushes out, with sweating dripping down his forehead.

"If you can bring them out?" I press, sitting back.

"They sell them, I don't know who to. They are some mysterious weird people. They claim they are their people, and they buy them all and we never see them again. I swear, that's all I know!" he pleads.

"Well, that's boring. If that's all you know, what use are you to me?" I query, tapping my chin dramatically.

His eyes widen and his breathing stutters. "I can get you out of here, without me you won't get through the doors, there are hand scanners!" he shouts, bucking up against me, but I just brace my legs and keep us there, my new strength coming in handy.

"Oh, I don't need you alive for that," I say softly as I lean back down. "Don't worry, it won't hurt—much." I laugh.

He opens his mouth to scream and I latch on, my mouth covering his as my powers roars to life, sucking down his energy and life. He kicks and fights beneath me while I keep him pinned, holding his face with both hands in a vice-like grip, our mouths fused against each other.

I feel him weakening with every pull, and his legs slow down and his hands stop their beating until they drop to his side, useless. Opening my eyes, I meet his as they start to dim, his whole face going gaunt like I'm sucking the life from him—which I guess I am.

When he's nothing more than a husk, I pull away and lick my dry lips. I throw my head back and groan at the full feeling—you know, the one where you go to an all-you-can-eat buffet and you over stuff yourself? Yeah, that. It feels like I might burst. Luckily, I know what's coming when the shivers start to rack my body, and this time I try to speed them up.

Calling inside of me, I search for that power that flows up and over my skin, changing it. Closing my eyes through the pain, I breathe deeply and let it change me. My body extends and my muscles harden.

It's faster this time, and in under thirty seconds I open my eyes and look down at my body to see that of the guard. I even have his clothes on, but no guns. That will be a dead giveaway.

I stand up and freeze when I hear the whispers of the other girls, forgetting for a moment I had an audience.

"What the fuck?" one mutters, her voice shaking in fear.

Turning around to look at the other cages, I see that they are all looking at me in fear, apart from the girl in the cage opposite me. She stares with a small smile curving her lips, and it's the closest thing to life I've ever seen enter her eyes. "Well shit, you were right." She laughs.

I grin back at her and she grimaces. "It's weird, I know it's you, but all I can see is that bastard."

"Try growing a cock, that shit is weird," I reply with a wink, as I turn back and unstrap the dead man's weapons and slide them onto my body. Spinning back around, I face her and hold my arms out.

"Everything look the same?" I ask.

She runs her eyes down me, and wraps her hands around her middle in an attempt to keep herself warm. "Yes, apart from the blood on your chin, they will question where it came from."

Nodding in thanks, I wipe my chin and when I face her again she nods. Turning back, I quickly search his body for anything useful. I find the keys in his front pocket and I hang them from one finger as I kick his body into the corner of the cell. He lets out a ripping fart and I crinkle my nose, even in death he's an ass.

Slipping from my open cage, I head across the row and open hers first. She nods but waits until I step away to slip through the open door, I guess my new face is throwing her off. No doubt she endured his hands and personal form of 'breaking in' that he planned for me. I turn to the others but they all cower away from me as I unlock their cells. Stepping back, I hold my hands up to show them I mean them no harm.

"You're free, I'll open the door and get you guys to the front so you can go on your way," I say, trying to soften my voice I don't scare them.

"What about you?" the talkative one asks, stopping near me but not near enough to touch.

"I'm heading below," I reply, my hands turning into fists and inciting a whimper from one of the girls.

"You can't go alone, you heard what he said. He only goes down there to take the person who they believe is...not human. If you go alone, it will raise suspicion," she points out and I swear, knowing she's right.

She sighs, rubbing the back of her head. "Fuck. You can take me down there, but you have to promise you will get me out."

I nod and she sighs again. "Good enough. They haven't seen me so it should work. Come on, before someone comes to see what's happening."

She straightens her back and life returns to her expression with a fierceness I wasn't expecting from her. Sweeping my eyes over the others, I walk in front in case anyone comes in. When we get to the door I scan my hand, like the guard mentioned, on a pad at the side. I have to wait an annoyingly long time before it pings green and the door opens.

Swinging it open, I step through confidently and scan the hallway. When I don't see anyone, I gesture for them to follow me. They scurry out and I lean back in, and flick the lights off. It might buy us some time if someone goes to investigate.

"Does anyone know which way?" I inquire softly, looking from left to right.

A corridor leads either way and I was knocked out when I was dragged in, so I don't know which way is out.

"Left is the way down, right is the way out," Talker mutters. Where the others hide behind me like a shield, she lingers next to me. Even as her body shakes and her eyes give away her nerves and fear, she stands straight.

"How do you know?" I ask, curious, and she throws me a scathing look.

"I was awake when they brought me in and I've watched enough girls being dragged out and downstairs from my cage," she replies harshly and I nod again, that must have been hard.

"What's your name, I can't keep calling you Big Balls in my head," I joke, trying to break the tension as we start down the corridor on the right, ready to get the other girls out first.

She laughs, the sound rough, like she isn't sure how to do it anymore. "It doesn't matter, the name belongs to the old me, the me before this place. I do like Big Balls though." She smiles over at me and I return it before concentrating back on our task.

"BB it is then," I finish, holding my arm out for them to stop and get back to the wall as we come to a sharp corner.

I stick my head around and sigh when I spot no one there, kind of disappointing to be honest. I wanted to try this new body out. I can feel the strength running through it and when I handled those guns, this body knew exactly what to do. Like riding a bike or fucking.

"Come on," I urge softly, stepping out around the corridor just as two more guards round the corner at the other end. Fuck.

Grabbing BB's arm, I drag her to my side. I look down at her with a warning and she goes limp, her eyes downcast as her hair hides her face, playing the part of the good slave.

The two guards notice me and stop halfway down. "There you bloody are. We were just coming to see what the hold up was, Rick has just dealt the next hand," the bigger one on the left calls. He's bigger than this body, but not by much. He has the same buzz cut and a flat-looking face. Square almost, with greenish eyes staring into mine. His friend to his right is smaller, skinner, but something about him unnerves me instantly. Where the big guy seems to welcome me, or the guard I should say, this other one eyes me suspiciously.

"Had to get my dick wet, was trying out the new bitch when this one," I throw BB forward and she stumbles and falls to the floor with a whimper, "Decided to show herself," I finish, laughing as BB struggles to her feet.

"No fucking shit? Figured if she was one of those freaks it would have come out long before now." Big guy laughs, thrusting his hips at BB and making her cringe back.

"What did she do?" skinny guy asks, eyeing her then me.

I open my mouth to say I don't know what, when big guy nudges him. "What's it matter man, that's another one! Boss Man will be really happy!"

The skinner one grunts but seems to accept it. "Want me to take her down?" he questions, his eyes turning greedy as he looks at her body. I feel her shake against me and I know this is the man she fears the most. When she looks up at me, her eyes are pooling with tears and beg me not to let him get her. He must be seriously fucked up to make this cold woman cry.

The smart thing to do would be to leave them to it, let them get back to their game, but I can't. Not knowing he hurt these girls. It could have been me, they could have been me, and now I have the strength to help and make it stop. Am I going to walk away? Am I? Fuck no.

Let the killing party begin.

CHAPTER 24

GRIFFIN

While watching the warehouse from the shadows, I frown when the tugging comes again, stronger than ever before. I push it away and lean farther back into the shadows as a car pulls away from outside, the same posh Ferrari that pulled up earlier. I had watched as they grabbed something from the boot and dragged it inside, with the man in the suit watching with a smile before he followed them in.

My guess is that he's one of the men in charge so when he leaves, I relax a little. I don't want to go for management yet. It's more fun to make them sweat it out, plus after the council meeting today, I know I need to make this job last as long as I can.

Grinding my teeth, I ignore their warnings and laughter. They had decided that after this job they wanted to bring me back to the fold. They wanted to cage me more like.

So I will take the warehouse down tonight and let the bosses sweat it a bit before I hunt them too, because I'm betting this runs high up. To have this sort of money and security, it must.

Watching for an hour or so longer I decide to make my move, there is no use in me just sitting up here all night. It's time to have some fun.

Dawn

Bending down, I draw a gun, hiding my movement behind BB's body. I grab her arm with my other hand, letting them see my harsh grip. She starts to fight me and I lean down farther. "Get behind the wall," I warn, before hauling her to her feet. I throw her and she falls behind the wall as I take aim and pull the trigger. I hit the big guy right between the eyes and he goes down hard, with blood blooming from the hole, but the skinny guy must have suspected something because he dodges to the side and the bullet goes through his arm.

Swearing, I shoot again, raining down hell, but he slides behind the corner and before I know it my gun clicks and it's empty. I toss it at the wall and grab the other one at my hip and wait, standing with my legs parted as I keep aim at the corner he's hiding behind.

"What the fuck are you doing?" he shouts and I hear more yells, obviously other guards coming to see what the shots were about. I need to end this quickly. Striding around the corner, I come face to face with him and he yells and pulls the trigger. The bullet rips through my thigh as I squeeze the trigger, my bullet hitting home and going straight through his chest. He gasps and slumps over as blood starts to pool underneath him.

Guards flood the hallway, all with guns aimed my way. I hold mine to the side and drop it to the floor. "Calm down!" I yell.

"What the fuck happened?" one of them shouts, his eyes darting from me to the dead man at my feet.

Think, Dawn, think.

"They were letting the girls escape. I have nine back here with me. I caught them smuggling them out when I was taking one down below. When I questioned them, they told me they were going to sell them for themselves and invited me to join in."

I stand completely still as they debate my words, and just then the other girls round the corner and I see the men relax, obviously believing my lie.

"Damn it, I knew I didn't trust those two. Marco just had to bring in some greedy nobodies." The man drops his gun, as does everyone else. "Good job Derrick. Get them back to their cells and take the one down like you were, we'll clean up here."

I nod and grab two of the girls' arms, ignoring their gasp, and drag them back around the corner. The others rush after me and only when we're back outside the cell room door do we relax.

"Well, now what do we do?" BB mutters, flickering her gaze back to the corner.

Blowing out a breath I open the door. "Get in." I gesture at the others. They look at me, horrified. "I'll be back, I'm not putting you in the cages, just get in until I can get those out downstairs first, then I'll pick you lot up on our way out." I pass them over the stolen guns. "Know how to shoot?" One of the girls nods and I hand it to her. "Just in case, but please don't shoot me, it's not fun."

They bob their heads and shuffle through the door before I shut it in their faces and lock it. Turning to BB I grab her arm. "You ready to put on another performance?"

"Let's get this shit over with," she agrees, as we set off back down the corridor, the other way this time. I feel bad leaving the other girls behind, but it would raise suspicions if I brought them with me.

The hallway is quiet, and when we get to the end I spot the door leading to the staircase. It has another scanner, so I let go of BB and lay my hand on it, and let it read me until it pings green again and the door unlocks. Pulling it open, I check out the empty stairwell before jerking my head at BB.

She slips through and with one last look back at the empty

hallway and the closed door of the cells, I shut the stairwell and start down the steps with BB at my back.

"So, what are you?" BB asks from behind me, sounding out of breath. I'm betting it's been a while since she was out of that cage and it doesn't look like they feed her much.

"Honestly, I don't know. I have some guesses, but I have a friend who thinks he knows. I was supposed to be meeting him tonight for a dick appointment, and show and tell so we need to get this shit done," I reply and she stumbles at dick appointment. I look back at her to see her leaning against the banister, laughing quietly.

"Erm, you okay? Like you deserve a mental breakdown, but could it wait until we escape?" I request, looking around to make sure no one is just going to pop up.

"Dick appointment," she wheezes through her laughter, and I stare awkwardly as tears start to run down her dirty cheeks. "Damn, I can't remember the last time I laughed like that."

"How long have you been here?" I inquire softly and she sighs, her laughter stopping.

"What month is it?" she asks sadly.

"September."

Her eyes widen in shock. "Four months," she whispers almost to herself and I wince. Four months is a long time. Four months stuck here in a cage as the guards' entertainment? It's a surprise she's still walking, never mind functioning.

"You're seriously fucking strong," I admit freely, observing her in a new light. She eyes me like I might be lying to her, but when I don't add anything else she smiles sadly.

"I had no choice but to be."

I nod, looking back down the stairs. "You got somewhere to go after this?"

She looks down at the stairs. "No, my dad sold me to the bastards to cover his gaming debt."

"Fucking prick. Want me to cut off his balls and use them for target practice?"

She laughs again. "Yup."

"Look BB, there's a shelter not far from here. It would be a good place to start."

She frowns and looks away. "I don't want people to think I'm broken, I don't want their fucking sympathy. I want to make a new life. I want the bastards to pay."

I grin. "What did I tell you? Big fucking balls."

We hear a noise up top and our bonding moment is over. I start back down the stairs with her on my heels.

When we reach the bottom I frown at the steel door. It looks like a prison, not a basement. There's a small slot at the top of the door, covered in three bars. The door itself looks like it could withstand a nuclear blast and it's an awful blue colour, with the paint peeling in places and rusting in others.

"You ready?" I inquire, knowing whatever we find down here won't be good.

She nods and I grab her arm and drag her to my side. I can feel myself tiring, my body wanting to change back, so I need to get in and out. Scanning my palm, I wait but it blinks red. I swear and hammer my fists on the door and wait with bated breath. Every second it takes seems to make me even more tired, the effort of staying in this form is draining me.

Eventually, the door swings open to show me a bulky guy in a lab coat. He looks like he should be bench pressing cars, not taking blood and experimenting on women. His blue eyes leave mine and when they center on BB something akin to hunger enters his eyes, except it's not for her body but what he thinks it holds.

"Another one? Great, bring her through." He gestures, and I walk past him and let him shut the door before he carries on. "What can she do? Or do we know what she is?" he asks excitedly, before clearing his throat and starting to walk, but he keeps throwing BB looks every now and again, making her cower into my side.

"Not sure, one of the others asked me to bring her down. She royally fucked him up though." I grin at him, pretending to love this as much as him, when in fact I want to gouge out his eyeballs and make them into earrings.

I make sure to keep my looking around discreet, nodding along as he talks while I observe where we are. It's one long hallway with a few rooms going off of it, but they look like cell doors. At the end, the hallway seems to open up and that's where he's leading us. When he walks into the open room, he heads straight to a clipboard as I gawk.

It's dark, musty, and depressing as hell. The room is a giant square with a command hub in the middle filled with computers, paperwork, and monitoring equipment. He's the only man in here at the moment.

To the left and right are what look like more cells, but this time they have a glass front and I spot two women cowering in each, trying to blend into the dark stone walls at the back of the cell.

On the other end of the room is a glass separator. In the room beyond sits what looks like a dentist chair, but with straps for restraints on it. Medical equipment, x-rays, tools, tables, micro-scopes, and much more line the walls and cabinets behind it, and I have to swallow hard. What the hell are they doing down here to bring out their 'freak?'

"Okay, put her in the chair. We have a gap in the schedule at the moment because Ki had to run upstairs and help with something," he mutters, staring at the clipboard with crazy intensity.

Nodding, I walk BB through the glass door and to the chair, then I push her gently. She sucks in a breath but slowly clambers into the chair, her face pale and worried and her eyes darting every-where. Once there, with my back to the man, I smile and raise my finger to my lips. She nods and it seems to settle her a little.

I pretend to do up the restraints, but I leave them undone in case she needs to escape quickly. I won't get her hurt anymore than she already has been. Stepping back, I grimace when the guy comes in and I spot the blood on the right side of his lab coat that was previously hidden from me.

"You get any sells today?" I ask. I know I'm pushing my luck, but I need to know who's buying these people. If they are like me, surely someone should be stopping this? Monsters just can't be roaming the earth with no government or justice system, right?

He eyes me strangely as he goes over to the cabinet, and starts pulling stuff down and adding it to a tray. "What, you grunts got bored fucking the freaks? Now you wanna talk?"

Well shit.

"Just fucking curious," I mutter and he rolls his eyes, grumbling to himself about idiot help.

He grabs a roller and adds the tray to the top, and moves it over to the chair. I spot a needle and what looks like some pliers and a scalpel. The rest I have no idea what it is.

"Hold her, will you? We don't know what she can do and they never react well to the blood the first time." He jerks his head and I walk over and grip her legs, watching her.

"I've always wondered, who buys them anyway?" I mumble, and grin down at BB for good measure.

I can feel him staring at me so I reach down and push on the cut on her arm, making her yelp.

"Some rich fucking exclusive cult if you ask me, or maybe some of the freaks' fucking owners. Hell, it could even be more freaks."

He lines up the needle at her arm after adding a tourniquet. When he punctures the skin, her legs come up automatically and he looks down with a frown to see them not strapped in.

"What the—" He starts, looking back at me just as an alarm blares overhead.

Using the noise and flashing red light as a distraction, I grab the needle and hold it to his neck. He freezes and stares at me wide-eyed.

"You're going to tell me everything. BB, get out of the chair and go see if you can let the others out," I order.

She slips from the chair on wobbly legs and I grab him and lay him in it, strapping him in as I press the needle to him again.

"Now, start at the beginning and don't take all day," I command, my control on this form slipping until I nearly stagger into him.

"Now!" I shout, but it comes out slurred.

My head spins as the needle drops from my unresponsive grip. I fall back from the chair with a groan and land on the floor, hard, while my body contorts as the change comes back over me.

My mouth opens in a silent scream, my body arches from the floor, and the lights fade from my vision as everything blurs together.

CHAPTER 25

GRIFFIN

I t was all too easy to carve a bloodstained path through the humans. They were unprepared, and I can smell the alcohol and sex on most of them, leaving them slower than they should be. Instead of going in covertly, I went for kicking down the front door.

Four men rushed from the hallway beyond and started firing, so I turned into mist to avoid their bullets and popped up behind them. I shot one, and then broke one's neck before turning and gutting the other two.

I made my way farther into the facility, dispatching the guards quickly as I went, following the stench of blood, tears, and fear. The warehouse is a maze of hallways until I find one with a hand scanned doorway. Leaning against it, I hear the whispering and terror behind the door of at least nine women.

Looks like I found my holding, though I thought there would have been more. I obviously just missed a sale or an order. I punch through the scanner and quickly hack the door, and it unlocks.

Cocking my head, I sift through the scents to figure out how many guards are inside. When all I smell is the women and the scent of gunpowder, I frown. I knock on the door to be polite and wait there until it swings open, and a small, bruised face peers out with a gun held in her grasp, her hands wavering.

"Who-who are you? Are you with her?" She jerks her head at a doorway at the end of the corridor.

Arching my brow in confusion, I look behind her at the other girls crowded there. I can just make out cages and a studio before she closes the door slightly. "Yes," I reply.

She sighs and the door opens a bit farther as the weapon drops. I grab it quickly and chuck it down the hall as her and the other woman gasp and fall back with a scream. Rolling my eyes, I open the door and stride in. "You should be more careful who you trust, never drop your weapon unless you are a hundred percent sure," I order, trying to impart some wisdom on the sheep.

"Where are the rest?" I ask, when no one replies to me. They dart a look at each other nervously while I look around at the twenty empty cages behind them. I notice a dead body of a naked male in one and it piques my interest as I glance back at the sheep, who might not be as stupid as they look.

"She, I don't know her name, was brought in last night. She-she attacked one of the guards and, erm, then she changed into him?" the one who held the gun says, her voice shaking, but I can smell the truth in her words. Interesting, a skinwalker? Here? What are these humans up to?

"Yeah, then she got us all out but she killed two guards on the way and the others got suspicious, so she stuck us here and went below with another girl to try and get the freaks out," another rushes out, nodding emphatically.

"Freaks? Below?" I query.

"The humans, they erm, they hurt us and if any sort of...freakiness or otherness comes out, they take us down below to experiment or kill us, I don't know. If we don't show any signs, they sell us after they've had their fun."

I rub my head then hold my hand up to stop their nervous chattering. "Okay, she went below? There are others down there, other women with powers that your slavers are selling?" When they nod, I growl out, "To who?"

They back away slightly, cringing at my obvious power and I sigh. I need to remember they are innocent and have been hurt by males, but my tolerance and patience are wearing thin. This was supposed to be an easy job, and a skinwalker complicates things. As does the fact humans here know about supes and seem to be selling them.

"We don't know, they will below," the original woman who held the gun answers, and I nod and turn away, intending to leave.

"Hey, what about us? She told us to stay here," she cries.

"You can leave, everyone outside this door is dead," I reply, as I sweep through the door and head to the one at the end of the hallway.

They don't move for a while, but eventually I hear them cry out before they rush from the room and away from me. Sheep.

There's another hand scanner at this door, and with a roll of my eyes, I disable it the same way I did the other one. The door unlocks with a click and I barge it open. Stairs lead down, and I jump over the railing and land on the landing at the bottom outside—yes, you guessed it—another locked door. Whatever they are doing down here makes them very paranoid.

Forgoing the scanner, I decide to just kick this door open. Something tugs deep inside me, making me growl as I raise my leg and bust open the door. It flies inwards, smashing into the wall. I expect to hear yelling or screaming, but other than the siren going, which started when they first saw me, it's deadly silent.

The tugging comes again, and I grit my teeth as I follow it into the basement. It's dark and smells horrible down here. Wrinkling my nose I peer at the doors as I pass. I can sense movements behind a few but I'll come back. First, I need to find out why the tugging of my mate is leading me farther into this human slaver's basement.

The hallway opens up into a large circular room with computers and other shit in the middle. Two glass cages sit on either side and when I look in, the two women are too busy looking at the other side of the room to notice me. Their eyes are locked on something beyond.

Circling around, I gape at what I find.

There, on the floor, writhing, her body flickering between man and woman, is my mate.

Her mouth is open in a silent scream, and her bones are stretching and snapping with a wet-sounding, pained noise. Like a ghost is superimposed over the man's body, I can see her true form flickering in and out of view.

The change.

My mate is a skinwalker.

A woman I didn't notice before turns with a roar, pointing a gun at me. Her hand doesn't wobble at all, and when I sniff I realise she is human.

"Don't fucking come closer, I will shoot you scum!" she shouts, and when I hear a muffled yell I look behind her to see a doctor strapped into what looks like an operating chair with a gag over his mouth as he stares at me wide-eyed.

I look back at the woman and frown until I realise she thinks I'm part of the guards, probably due to all the black I'm wearing.

"Don't point your toy at me sheep, not when you stand between me and my mate," I sneer and she scowls, before glancing at the woman still changing on the floor and back to me.

"We'll wait until she's finished, and if she doesn't know you, you're dead," she shouts, her voice sure. When she looked at the changing mate of mine, she didn't even flinch or seem surprised. So she has seen it before, yet the dirt, blood, and lack of clothing on her shows her as one of the humans' captured women. How long has my mate been here?

If any of these sheep touched my mate, hurt her, experimented on her, I will burn them all to the ground before ripping out their souls.

I stand casually with the gun aimed at me, my eyes locked on my mate, as all of us wait for her to ride it out. Eventually, the writhing and noises stop, and she's slumped against the floor, breathing heavily. Long, blonde hair obscures her face from me.

She's still and the sheep looks from me to her, obviously nervous until my mate groans and starts to push herself up.

"Fucking hell, that bastard hurt. Seriously, growing a cock is fun and all, but when it goes back up, not so much," my mate moans, getting to her knees with a sigh. She has a grimace on her face as she looks at the human woman before she follows her gun to me.

Her mouth pops open, and those eyes of hers are still black from her change as she watches me.

"Name's Griffin, sweetheart," I taunt, my asshole side coming out. I never wanted a mate, yet here she kneels, and she is fucking beautiful and powerful. It shrouds around her until I'm almost choking on it.

She gets to her feet and ignoring me completely, she turns back to the man in the chair. "Well, Griffin Sweetheart, why don't you make yourself fucking useful and go and open the cells if you're here to help. If not, get the fuck out before BB here shoots you or I rip you to pieces." With that, she grabs a scalpel and grins at the human male who visibly cowers before her.

"Now, where were we?" she purrs, the sound sending a bolt of lust straight to my already hard cock.

CHAPTER 26

DAWN

I gnoring the newcomer, Griffin, I smile down at the doctor. That
change really took a lot out of me, I think it was because of how
long I held that form. I'm almost sagging from exhaustion, my body
is obviously burnt out, but I can't let them see that. Especially Griffin, since something tells me he's watching me very carefully. It
doesn't help that I can't tell what he is. He isn't human, that's for
sure, but he doesn't feel like Nos. He's hot as hell though, and my
tired lady bits even perked up when I saw him. That attitude is a
huge turn off though, so I ignore him and concentrate on what I
came down here to do—the faster I do it, the faster I can leave to
rest.

BB, with wary eyes still flickering between the doctor and Griffin, comes to stand on the opposite side of the chair.

"Now, you were going to tell me who you're selling the women
to. Weren't you?" I say softly, leaning closer with the scalpel and
running it lightly across his cheek. He flinches to the side before
freezing, his eyes staring at me as he breathes around the gag. "If I
take this gag out and the first words out of your mouth are not the
address or name, I will cut you. Understood?"

He breathes faster as I cut away the gag, his mouth moving hard
as he swallows. "Fuck you," he spits out and I grin.

"I was hoping you would say that." Darting forward, I cut his cheek and he cries out as the scalpel slices through his flesh faster and deeper than I thought.

"Tell me," I demand and he shakes his head. "BB, pass me that full syringe from the side, will you?" I ask sweetly and he swears, starting to struggle in the chair.

BB turns and passes it over, and I uncap it and hold it to his neck, his pulse jumps there as he freezes again.

"Now, I'm no expert and I don't know what's in this syringe, but by the look on your face, you do. One more time, who are you selling them to?"

His eyes dart around the room desperately before coming to rest on me again. "I don't know, I swear. I was just brought in to test and experiment on their...unique natures, and get them to manifest as fast as possible. I just get them from above and then they're taken away again. I don't have any part of it!" he rushes out and I sigh.

"Well, that's disappointing. I don't need you then," I mutter and sigh dramatically.

"No! Wait! I know who will know though!" he screams, watching the needle.

"Who's that?" I whisper, leaning down so we're almost touching.

"Marco," he gasps.

My face twists in a scowl. "That prick, tell me where to find him."

"You know him?" he asks, looking confused.

"We've met, it ended in me being drugged and waking in a cage," I respond with a laugh.

I hear a growl, and when I look over Griffin is scowling, his hands are clenched into fists at his sides, and murder is written in every line of his body. "Who drugged you?"

Ignoring him, I turn back to the doctor. "Where?"

"I, erm, he owns a club. I know he visits there often. It's called The Clubhouse," he gushes.

"Good boy," I purr, tapping his chest as I straighten. He visibly relaxes so I lunge down and inject him in the neck.

He screams and thrashes in the restraints. "You! You fucking bitch, you've fucking killed me!"

Throwing the syringe at the wall, I grin. "Good. Now, stay."

I look back at BB. "Watch him."

She nods, throwing a look at Griffin. Turning to face him, I see him still silently fuming. "Who. Drugged. You?" he grits out, his voice deadly. Rolling my eyes, I step past him and pat his shoulder.

"Don't you worry, I take care of myself, Griffin Sweetheart." Whistling to myself, I wander over to the glass cages. I ignore the man I can feel prowling after me and gesture for the woman inside to step back. She nods and retreats to press herself against the wall, and her skin changes when she touches it so she blends in with the brick. Cool, a human chameleon.

Winding my fist back, I punch through the glass. It shatters, cracking along the wall before it all falls to the ground in pieces.

"What the fuck? I could have done that!" Griffin yells, rushing to my side and grabbing my hand as he eyes the blood and cut skin. It heals before our eyes, the glass embedded there pushing out and dropping to the floor with a tinkle as the skin heals. He watches it hard before brushing the blood away with his thumb to see the smooth, unblemished skin.

"I don't need you to, like I said, I can take care of myself. Now, if you want to help go and open the other cells." I pull back my hand and try to ignore the tingle his touch ignited. I could feel his touch throughout my whole body and that was only from him holding my hand. My blood is burning, pulsing again, wanting him like it wants Nos, but I step away and ignore it. Turning my back on him, I give the other glass cell the same treatment. Both women stay inside, watching us warily.

I step back and hold my hands out to the sides. "I don't want to hurt you, you're free. If you go out of the door at the end and up the stairs, you can go wherever you want. I would advise not going back to your normal life though, since they might find you. If you need any help, there's a shelter run by someone I trust just down the road." I rattle off the address and with another look at me, they both spring from their cells and race down the hallway and through the busted open basement door.

"Woman, come here!" Griffin yells from down there.

"Woman? Are you fucking serious?" I fume, stomping over to him.

He looks down at me from where he's standing outside a cell door. "Well, you never fucking told me your name. What else do you want me to call you? Sugar tits?"

Grumbling, I sigh. "Dawn, my name is Dawn."

He smirks at me. "Dawn, I like it. Now, sugar tits, what would your majesty like me to do about this?" He jerks his thumb towards the open slot in the door, allowing you to see inwards.

Pushing past him, I peer inside and try to ignore him when he pushes up behind me, his body hard and filled with power. I can feel the steel running through it and the breath he blows on the back of my head.

Breathing out, I concentrate on what's inside, not how he feels pushed up behind me. When I spot what he was talking about, I smirk. Well, fucking shit. A bloody wolf is prowling the back of the small, closed in cell. Claw marks line the walls and when it spots me, it growls, throwing itself against the door before retreating again.

"Werewolf?" I ask, beyond happy. It makes sense that they exist too.

"Looks like, it's feral though. If we let it out it, it will attack us and then I will have to kill her," he muses, stepping back and letting me move away.

"Feral?" I question.

He eyes me. "Means when a werewolf has given over to their baser instincts. They have let their animal take over. You can't bring them back, the nicest thing to do is put them down. Now, why don't you know that? Unless you were raised in the middle of butt fuck nowhere?"

"I'm new to this whole world," I reply distractedly, frowning at the wolf. Poor woman, they pushed her past her breaking point, forced her to shift into a wolf, probably for the first time, and now they want to put her down for it? No.

"What does that mean?" he growls, and it makes the wolf howl and throw itself at the steel door again, rattling it.

"It means it's a long fucking story and if you haven't noticed, sweetheart, I'm kind of busy. Why don't you go stand in the corner looking all brooding if you aren't going to help?" I quip before pushing past him and making my way back to the room with BB and the doctor.

When I get there, I see him sweating profusely. "Doc, listen up. The wolf, how do we turn her back?"

"Gi-give me the antidote and I will," he cries shakily, and I follow his gaze to another syringe waiting on the side.

"Deal, but you tell me how first," I demand.

"You can't help her," Griffin adds, and I throw him a dirty look where he leans against the wall, almost blending in with the dark there.

I grab the syringe, ignoring him, and face the doctor again. "Tell me."

He must realise he has no options now, and he's desperate, especially when blood starts to drip from his nose. I raise my eyebrow at that. What the hell was in that vial?

"There's a convocation, in the left drawer. Labelled Moon. It forces shifters into their form and keeps them trapped there until you administer the vial next to it labelled Bain," he gasps out, with blood dripping from his mouth. It starts to come from his eyes too, like tears. "Please, please give me the antidote," he yells, the last word turning into a scream that rattles the room.

Leaning down, I stick it in his neck like I did the first one. Within a few seconds he slumps in the chair. His face is less red and the blood coming from everywhere seems to be slowing down.

I step back and turn to the cupboards, and root around until I find the bottle labeled Bain.

"What are you going to do? Throw it through the slat?" Griffin jokes, but he frowns at the same time. To be honest, I hadn't even thought about it.

Shrugging, I head back down the hallway until I stand outside the werewolf's door. "If she bites me, I won't turn into, one will I?" I ask, curious more than anything. I have enough going on with changing my skin, I don't need to go full animal mode.

"No, but it can kill certain supes," he warns. Brilliant. Here goes nothing.

Unlatching the cell, I suck in a deep breath as I prepare to open the door. I can feel Griffin watching, but he doesn't say anything or offer to help. "You want to do it?" I joke.

"You want to save it, you do it. Don't worry though, I'll protect your pretty ass if it gets too close," he replies. Wow, that fills me with confidence...hey, does that mean he's been staring at my ass? What a creep. Total creep, not hot at all.

I poke my head through and eye the growling she-wolf, who's backed against the wall, her paws parted and fur on edge. She's beautiful. All white fur apart from a heart-shaped patch just above her nose on her muzzle.

"Hey there, beautiful. I'm Dawn. I'm a friend. I'm here to help," I coo, stepping slowly through the door. When she growls again, flashing sharp canines, I stop and show her the syringe. She snaps before darting back to the wall again.

"Shh, I'm not here to hurt you. This will help you change back." I wait for her to stop growling before I step closer again. You are probably supposed to drop your eyes, but I'm too alpha now for that and I want her to see the sincerity in mine.

When she growls again, I stop in the middle of the room. Okay this isn't working, now that I've got closer she's snapping her jaws at me. Blowing out an exasperated breath, I make a reckless decision —let's just hope Griffin isn't lying about protecting my ass.

"Stop!" I yell, narrowing my eyes at her and holding our gaze. Her growling stops and turns into a whimper as her eyes drop to the floor and she drops to her belly, her rump in the air with her tail downcast.

"Come here," I order, and when she tries to fight back I add a little more oomph to my order. "Now." She cowers again, whimpering in the back of her throat as she crawls on her belly until she lays at my feet. "Good girl," I coo and she rolls onto her back, exposing her belly.

Crouching down, I pat it, stroking her as she vibrates. Distracting her, I speak to her in hushed tones as I line the injection up at her flank. This is going to have to be fast. Wincing, I push it through her fur hard and push it in quickly before jumping back with my arms in the air.

She jumps to her feet, growling and snapping before spinning and licking at the injection point. "Shh, you're okay," I soothe and she stumbles to the side, the drugs obviously taking effect.

She staggers again before her legs give out, a whine escaping as her head drops to the floor, and her eyes slide shut even as she seems to fight it. Her body folds in on itself. I can hear bones snapping and reforming as the fur retreats and skin flows over her body. It's not smooth, in fact, it looks downright painful and only thirty seconds later, a naked woman is curled up where the wolf was. Blood and white liquid cover her skin as she lifts her head.

Short, spiky, grey hair covers her head, and her eyes are the same deep grey with flecks of orange inside. She eyes me tiredly, not even trying to move. "Thank you." Her voice cracks, obviously from disuse, and I back away.

"You're welcome, I'm going to set everyone else free. When you're ready, you can leave," I say softly and leave the cell.

Griffin is waiting outside and he claps when I emerge. He has a proud look on his face before he masks it into cool indifference again. "Now what?" he asks, leaning there casually. I hadn't even noticed the siren had cut off, leaving just the flashing lights, until I noticed he wasn't shouting anymore.

"We get everyone out, then I go to that club and hunt down that slimy bastard who drugged my wine. Who would ruin good wine like that?" I shiver in disgust and his eyebrow quirks up.

"No, I will go to the club and hunt him down. You will go home," he grits out, his eyes narrowing on me as his nostrils flare.

Snorting a laugh, I tap his chest as I head back down to BB and the doctor. "Sure thing, Griffin Sweetheart."

"I mean it, *vasculo*, you will go back to that swanky hotel," he growls behind me and I freeze. Turning slowly, I eye him in a new light.

Who the hell is this man? Has he been stalking me?

He must realise his mistake or see the accusation in my eyes because he rolls his. "Don't flatter yourself, I saw you coming out of one of the sheep's apartments and figured I would follow you in case you turned out to be important." He starts to walk past but stops at my side and leans in and whispers, "You weren't."

He walks away then and I spin, fury rolling through my entire body. Who is this man to decide my worth? He thinks he can just dismiss me and leave like that? No, Marco is my next victim whether this pig-headed man 'allows' it or not.

Ignoring him—it's either that or kill him—I stride past him disregarding his mocking laughter that follows me, and walk back into the room to see the doctor still strapped in but back to his normal colour. BB nods at me from her perch.

"Okay, let's go. The others we'll let out on the sweep back through, but they will realise something is wrong soon."

She nods and leaves the room and I turn to follow her, but I stop when the doctor cries out. "Wait, please! What about me?"

Grinning over my shoulder at him, I reply, "Just because I stopped you from bleeding to death doesn't mean I won't kill you. Some people don't deserve to live, an eye for an eye, isn't that the old saying?" I muse, before stepping back as he starts to struggle.

I laugh and saunter down the corridor, releasing the rest of the girls. They fly from their cells with a mixture of anger, hurt, and wariness. "Ladies, you are free to go, but if you want revenge like I imagine, then there happens to be a certain someone tied up down that corridor behind you." Smiling, I leave them to their decision. I won't kill him outright, but he sentenced himself to his own demise when he hurt those women.

As I climb the stairs with BB and Griffin, the sound of his screams reach me and I can't help the grin that breaks out across my face—that would have been my choice too.

Once we are back upstairs, I check the cell room but Griffin informs me in a snotty tone that he let them out so they could leave. I nod and go back to ignoring him as BB and I leave the warehouse. The hallways on the way to the exit are covered in blood and bodies, and it only makes me look at Griffin in a new light.

The man definitely isn't human, so what is he?

The front door to the warehouse stands open and off its hinges, and I throw Griffin another look but he ignores it, stalking over to a computer system and starting to type. I roll my eyes and make my way outside, sucking in the clean, city air as opposed to the dirty, blood-filled atmosphere left in the warehouse behind us.

"Thank you," BB says softly, her voice carrying on the night's air. I nod and turn to her to see her wrapping her arms around herself.

We must be in the industrial district, since only other ware-houses and empty factories stretch as far as the eye can see. The one we are in is surrounded by a chain-link face and the car park is nearly empty. A perfect place to hide a slave trade.

"Where will you go?" I inquire, needing to know she will be okay. I won't ever be some fucking hero or any of that bullshit, but that woman stuck her own neck out to help me.

"Home. They won't scare me away, but I will take precautions." She looks around, a new light in her face, one I don't doubt speaks of change—going through something like that changes a person. You see the depths of depravity and greed of the human soul and you don't come out untainted.

"Don't you want to leave?" I question, genuinely curious.

"No." She smiles slightly before looking at the city around us. "This is my home. It might be corrupt, we might have more ghettos than we have posh apartment buildings, but I wouldn't trade it for the world. I was born here, I grew up here. They can't take that away from me."

"Touching, truly it is, but we need to get going," Griffin grumbles, breaking the moment.

Throwing him a glare, I look back at BB with a sad smile. "Good luck."

"Who needs luck when I have my own guardian angel?" she teases, as she turns and starts walking away.

Griffin snorts and I turn to him, already glaring. "Shouldn't you help her get home?" I growl.

"She's not my concern. I will drop you off and then go to the club." He crosses his arms, staring me down.

"Nope. You're going to make sure she gets home. I'll take myself," I retort snottily.

He rolls his eyes up to the sky with a sigh. "Why would I do that?"

I step closer, lowering my voice as it turns into a silky purr. "Because for some reason you're following me." I hold up my hand to stop his denial. "Cut the shit, I don't know why or how but if you ever, and I mean ever, want to get onto my good side then you're going to take BB home."

We stare each other down, and his jaw works while his eyes flash sparks at me. "Fine, how will you get home?" Each word is harsh, like a whip hitting my skin with near physical intensity.

"By car of course." I grin, holding up the car keys I stole from the doctor's coat pocket. When I click 'unlock,' a silver BMW near the door beeps and I grin.

He looks from me to it before stepping back. "Home," he orders, shaking out his shoulders. I frown at him but it turns into a gasp when two large, black wings emerge from behind him.

I just gape, and he winks at me before turning and with a running jump swoops into the air. He holds his wings out at his side as he swoops down on BB and grabs her. I hear her scream and him swear before they are lost in the darkness of the night.

Shaking my head, I block out the craziness. If I think about it all then I'll lose my mind, and I have too much to do tonight for that. Time to go get pretty, then go clubbing. Who said the life of a dead woman wasn't fun?

CHAPTER 27

DUME

We land on what the pilot tells me is Carmicheal's private airstrip. He gives me directions to the house where they were attacked, and I nod before strapping on my weapons. When I am done, I turn to face them. Their faces are pale and I can smell their fear, it only makes me smile.

Leaving the plane without a word, I set off in the direction of the trees that edge the small airstrip. The pilot told me it was the fastest way and there is a path cutting through nature if you know where to look, which leads right to the back of the house.

I guess it is time for this minotaur to be back in the battle again, and I will start with the witches who dare threaten me.

Once in the trees, I can see the path he meant and I follow it at a slow jog, stretching my body and forcing it back into motion again after so long of being immobile. The flat forest slopes down and I can start to make out a mansion in the distance. It's no fucking house, that is for sure.

When I reach the treeline bordering onto the backyard of the property I stop, letting the shadows conceal me as I take it all in. Beyond the forest lies a large backyard. A pool is to the left, and to the right is a whole garden filled with large trees, plants, and even a statue. The mansion towers over it all with a large balcony and stone railing, which looks over the backyard. Three doors lead into different sections of the house and large, arched windows show me it is at least three stories high.

On the roof above the balcony is a flat section, obviously for stargazing. Looks like the outcasts are doing well for themselves. Tilting my head, I push my senses out farther until I can see the spell cast around the property like a tripwire. It's not quite a containment spell, they obviously didn't have enough power or witches for that—no, it's a simple tripwire laid in a crisscross pattern around the house to alert them of anyone approaching.

The doors and windows are also spelled with a locking charm, the magic flaring in my mind as I look at it. Spending so long around magic, witches, and cruel queens, taught me to notice the way magic flares. Most supes can't see it unless they are really concentrating hard, and even then, some can't. It takes a special type of supe and a powerful one at that, to see past the illusion magic throws up.

It also means if you can see it, you can most likely break it. Not the tripwire, they would notice that, but breaking an illusion on a window? It wouldn't even ping back if I do it properly.

It's getting to the window that will be a problem. Searching around, I spot the answer among the trees. I can move around until I am to the right, the treeline is closer there and all I will need to do is take a running jump and make it to the roof.

I move through the darkness quickly, making sure to pick my feet up and advance as silently as I can so as not draw attention to myself. When I reach the spot I picked out, I sling my swords from my front so they are swiveled onto the very base of my spine—this way they won't make a noise when I hit the roof. Backing up, I lean down and take a couple of deep breaths before pushing off and sprinting to the edge of the treeline.

When the light hits the edge I jump, flinging myself through the air, with my hands outstretched to grasp the lip of the roof, which overhangs the grey, wooden slats of the house.

The feeling of being weightless hits me, but I don't look down. I concentrate on my goal until the lip slaps my hands. Grabbing it, I stop my fall into the wall with my feet, remaining still and breathing, waiting in case anyone heard me.

When no one comes to investigate I pull myself up onto the roof and crouch there. I sneak across the slate tiles and steady myself with my hand. I'm a big guy and we aren't meant for sneaking. I prefer to just kick down doors and kill everybody, but I have no idea what I am walking into and before I never cared if I lived or died, now I have a mate to think of.

When I reach the flat bit in the roof, I drop down to the balcony below, and freeze when my boots make a bang against the floor. Holding my breath, I wait again, but no one so much as looks out the sliding doors leading onto it.

Shuffling my feet instead of walking, I hover my hands over the magic sealing the door shut. It's weak, not like the trip wire or even the downstairs windows and doors. It's obvious they didn't expect anyone to get up here and didn't waste much magic on it. Stupid fucking witches.

Cockiness is always their problem, they think just because they wouldn't come in this way no one else would. It's always their downfall, their egos. They believe in the eyes of their gods. That they were blessed with their gods' powers and that they can wield that magic, even now when most lines seem to be dying out. This makes them believe they are the strongest.

They rely on their magic so heavily that most don't even know how to fight or wield a weapon. Strip them of their magic and they are no better than humans.

Pushing against the magic, I test its bounce back without breaking it. It only bounces slightly, just like I thought—weak.

I close my eyes and concentrate on drawing my power from the witch-charmed torc on my arm. It was given to me by the only witch I never killed on sight, spelled to my arm and mine alone to let me break enchantments. It didn't work with such magic like the ones that held me, but for small things like this, it will.

It flows down my arm and to the magic I am touching, growing across it until it encompasses the magic there, then it squeezes, popping the magic until it falls in glowing tatters to the floor at my feet.

Sliding open the door, I step into the darkened bedroom the balcony leads to. I scan it quickly noting the king-size bed, armoire, rug, fire, and the open bathroom door leading off. I am positive no one is inside, so I walk forward but freeze when my boots make noise against the wooden floor.

Growling quietly to myself I reach down and unlace them and kick them off, placing them side by side at the open sliding door. Now on silent bare feet, I make my way to the closed door that obviously leads out of the room. I hold my hand over it and search for any magic, but when I find none I snort and crack open the door, peering out.

A hallway, with other closed doors, sits beyond with an open landing not too far away, and there is another hallway on this floor at the other end of the landing. Sneaking out, I close the door softly behind me and move towards the other hallway. They would have grouped them together, all the better to watch them, and they must be using magic to control them or bind them.

When I reach the landing I spot the black, twisted wooden banister leading along to curved stairs, which go down to the second floor. The house is deadly quiet, so when I hear a sigh and a door opening behind me, I spin and grab the startled witch before she can loose any magic or warnings.

Covering her mouth, I twist her neck and snap it, and let her drop to the floor quietly. There was no point asking her any questions, her mouth and words would be her weapon. One witch dead, many more to go.

Grinning, I reach behind me and grab both swords, this is going to be fun. It has been too long since I let the beast out to kill, but I let it out now.

The change takes over me, sliding across my body like silk and reforming me into the minotaur.

Chapter 28

ASKA

The hunters scream as I massacre my way through their masses. They manage to get a few good cuts and shots in, but I ignore the pain and the blood, letting my need for their blood, for their death and souls, roar through me until all I can think about is my next swing of the axe.

Ripping the head off one man, I throw it like a ball at the woman behind him with such force, that she flies backwards through the front door with a scream. Something slices down my back, and I turn with a growl, wrenching the knife away from the human who tried to stab me and chopping off his head.

More pour in and my dragon is fighting me for control, wanting free after all these years of sleeping. He can taste the souls on them and the ones lingering from the dead littered at my feet.

I roll my eyes at his huffing and jump over the crowd and back away, dropping my weapons to the floor with a clang as I let him take over.

One second I'm a man, the next I'm a dragon, the change is that swift and sure. Landing on the floor with a roar, I lower my head and grin at them. Their mouths drop open and either they haven't seen a dragon before, or they have never heard the tales and lore of me in my dragon form.

I'm not like the others, no scales of multiple colours cover me. My skin is like leather, a dark shade of black. Not the black of this world or even the night sky, but a complete and utter lack of colour. One that if you stare too much, they say you see death and the beyond itself. My wings have long, sharp talons at the end and look more bat-like than dragon. Huge, black spikes run down my spine leading to my tail, which has a ball at the end with smaller spikes on it.

Those spikes continue onto my head, splitting down each side like horns framing my skull in what dragon lore used to call the royal crown. My snout ends in a point and my teeth are double the size of a normal dragon with venom held inside.

My eyes are a luminous purple, and when I breathe fire it is purple as well, so bright that it is said to be seen through my skin, but it is the black fire they should fear the most. The one that steals and captures the souls of innocents and evils alike, swallowing it whole.

They linger inside me after, and I can use their powers or strengths, sometimes even see their memories. Eventually they fade, and they will never go to whatever waits behind this world. They are destroyed, every scrap of them wiped out from the world like they never existed.

No, it is not my fire they should fear, but what comes after the fire. The reaping.

Breathing in, I let the fire build in my belly. Their fear doubles and in this form I can see each individual sweat droplet as it rolls down their bodies, see the hammering of their pulse, and feel their heartbeats and shaking. It's addictive.

Opening my mouth wide, I blow.

Purple fire rains hell down on them, scorching them and burning them alive as they scream and try to fight it. Swinging my head from left to right I catch them all as they try to flee from me.

When none remain, I shut my mouth before the black smoke starts to leak out, begging and calling me to eat their souls, which hang in the balance, but I don't want that sort of evil and judgment coursing through my body, so instead I watch as each soul floats above their vacant bodies before fading from view.

May hell have mercy on their wretched souls, mercy I did not show.

I spent the last two hours tracking my mate across the city. I found some witnesses that led me to a restaurant. When I...questioned the staff there, they told me she had left with a patron of theirs. I could smell their fear and hate, and that told me all I needed to know. She didn't leave voluntarily.

Back to square one, I focused on our bond again until I finally ended up outside the warehouse that I am staring at now. Over in the industrial district, with litter and run-down factories and buildings, the place looks abandoned, but when I tried the door I found it open.

When I step inside, the smell of death, decay, blood, and unwashed bodies hits me, making me crinkle my nose, but underneath it all? The smell of my mate.

Tracking it through the hallways, ignoring the bodies of men dressed in black, I find myself outside a large room. Inside there are metal cells and video equipment that has me clenching my fists, especially when I scent my mate in one of those cages. The dead, naked man inside gives me pause and makes me grin. Oh yes, she has definitely been here.

I backtrack out of the room and head to the only other door. It leads down, and when I reach the bottom of the stairs I frown at the bloodstains and chains littering the little landing. Stepping into what

I can only describe as a fucked up laboratory, I scan the cells with their open doors.

The smells down here give me pause as I sort through them all. Wolf, naga, witch, demon, and so many more, but the strongest of all is the scent of human, my mate and...is that a fucking Nephilim? I thought the bastards had been killed off by now.

They are untrustworthy psychopaths, usually trained as assassins, and council lap dogs. So why is one here? Unless it was captured like the rest, but that doesn't seem right. The rest of the scents are distinctly feminine and this one is male.

The freshest scent of death leads me down the hallway until I find the half mangled, bloodied body of what I am guessing used to be a doctor. From the equipment and setup, it looks like they were experimenting on supernaturals, but why?

Left with more questions than answers and no sign of Dawn, I head back upstairs and stand in the chaos that is the hallway. What has my little monster gotten herself into and where is she now?

Leaving the warehouse, I tilt my head when I hear a caw from above. I spot the bird and grin at my fortune. Crooking my finger, I hold out my hand and wait as it flies down and lands there, its intelligent eyes locked on mine. Birds make excellent spies.

Stroking its head, I hold its beady gaze and reach across the distance, fusing my mind with its. Memories pour in and I frown as I watch what happened here tonight.

I cut off the flow of information and stroke the bird's head once before throwing it up in the air, letting it fly away. At least I know where my mate is heading, that winged bastard mentioned The Clubhouse and warned her not to go, but if I know my mate at all, his order will only make her want to go even more. She also seemed unhurt, which might just save the city from me decimating it if she had been, but the humans' fates still hangs in the balance. I will wait to pass judgment until I know fully what happened.

Now, it's time to find Dawn.

CHAPTER 29

DAWN

Driving the stolen BMW with a grin, I change gear and speed up, whooping to myself as I race around the empty city corners of the industrial district. I should head back and meet Nos, but I know Griffin will go straight to The Clubhouse without me and I want to make sure I get there first.

Marco drugged me, threw me in a cage, and left me to his humans. He dies and not just by Griffin's hands, I want in on that. I look down at myself and frown, and I doubt they would let me into the club like this. I look like I've been part of a serial killer movie. My dress is torn and covered in...well, I don't even know at this point. I don't know if Nos will be back at the hotel and I don't want to head back to grab my stuff if they are investigating the body I left behind. I really need to come up with a safe place to store my things.

Looks like dress shopping it is. Then Marco. Then Nos. Then I might sleep for a week. It has been a long week and it's only Wednesday. Killing people really takes a lot out of you. I need to be quick so I speed up and pick the closest shop I can find. Pulling up outside the darkened shop I frown again—oh yeah, it's the middle of the night.

Pocketing the money I swiped from the doctor, I step out and lock the car before looking around to make sure no one is around.

It's quiet but it soon won't be. I stride to the shop like I own it, and yank the handle. It snaps and I open the door, freezing in case an alarm goes off. Thank fuck to whatever gods are up there that it doesn't, unless it's a silent one. Rushing inside, I scan the row of clothes before I find a long red number. I grab my size, get undressed, and shimmy into it. Satisfied it fits, I grab my balled up dress and shove it in the trash can under the cash register. It's only a small shop, obviously independently owned, and it makes me feel a tad bad about breaking in.

Oh well. Leaving the wad of cash that will cover the dress and more, I saunter out and quickly slide into my stolen BMW. I lean towards the console in the middle and search for the club on the sat nav. It finds it easily and I press go before reversing into the street and speeding away from the scene of my crime.

I guess I should feel guilty, but I don't. I have too much to worry about without the toll on my soul for stealing, plus I think that ship has long since sailed with my killings. I am morally iffy, that's for fucking sure, but I hope I get points for killing bad guys.

As I drive down the road The Clubhouse is on, I search for somewhere to park. When I don't spot any, I pull up at the side of the road, leave the keys inside, and saunter away. Serves the asshole right, he's probably dead about now anyway, but knowing he will be fined for illegal parking makes me feel good, petty, but good.

The Clubhouse is nothing like I expected. From the name, I kept imagining a biker bar type of deal, but I should have figured, knowing Marco, it would have been the complete opposite. In neon lights, above a large building, the sign proudly declares 'The Clubhouse.'

A queue spreads around the block, where chattering and half-drunk club goers are waiting to get into what looks like an exclusive club. Two bouncers frame the blood-red doors, watching everything with hawk-like eyes.

My shoulders back and my head held high, I strut up to the bouncers and arch my eyebrow as they hold their arms out to block the door.

The big guy on the left grins at me while the one on the right narrows his eyes, jerking his head to the queue.

"Don't think so pumpkin, I'm here to see Marco and we all know he doesn't like being kept waiting." I tap my foot impatiently and stare him down.

Eventually he nods, and after both step back, I open the door and slip inside, blowing out a relieved breath that I didn't have to kill them or something to get inside.

"Coat?" comes a dull, female voice. I turn my head and spot the bored-looking, middle-aged woman in a red vest manning a coat booth.

Smirking, I gesture at my floor-length, deeply cut red dress. "Honey, with a dress like this you don't cover it up with a coat." I wink and walk away.

The hallway opens up at the end and under my feet I feel the music pulsing. My heart races in time to it and I lick my lips as I step out and whistle at the club before me. The place is huge.

Chandeliers, with dancing women, hang low from the ceiling over the wooden dance floor where hundreds of party goers writhe to the music. Two bars, both busy, run on either side of the club with at least a five person line waiting to be served.

The walls are done in black with wood accents, and neon red lights are everywhere. It should look cheap but for some reason it doesn't. I don't spot a VIP area anywhere, but to the left and right are two curved staircases leading up to a floating platform above the dance floor. Guessing that's where it must be, seems right that the rich bastards would be lording over the regular folks. A woman in a tiny black dress and ridiculously high heels totters past with a tray on her arm.

I follow her progress and squint at the booths I didn't see before. Lining the wall on each side of me, almost removed from the rest of the club, are deep red and wooden booths, which are filled with women in scantily clad dresses and men in suits. It looks like a mafia meeting. It probably is.

Stepping forward so I'm not just standing there gawking, I make my way to the dance floor. It'll look strange if I try and head straight upstairs, plus the music is pulling me to dance.

Slipping through the bodies, I wind my way into their mass. The music calls to me until my head is thrown back and I'm losing myself in the rhythm.

"I told you to go home," comes Griffin's annoyed voice right next to my ear.

Grinning, I keep dancing as his hands drop to my hips and tighten, stopping my movements. "Dawn," he growls, the sound sending shivers down my body as he whispers in my ear.

"Yeah, I don't do well with orders," I joke, leaning back into him, his body to calling mine.

"I'm not joking Dawn, go home," he grits out, his voice silky and sending dirty thoughts spiraling through me. His body, against mine with the music in the background, is making me almost pant as I try to stop myself from pushing back against him. I have to remind myself he's a stranger, and an arrogant one at that.

"Neither am I." Turning in his hold, I arch my brow as I lean up and wrap my arms around his neck. His eyes flare before they narrow on me.

"This is none of your business, go home before you get hurt," he demands, as his arms tighten and his eyes flash dangerously. You can feel the power running through his body, one he holds in check so tightly.

"Too late," I whisper, with a disgusted twist of my lips.

He frowns, and his eyes flash faster as his hand tighten again, bruisingly so. "What do you mean?"

I laugh, starting to move to the music so he has no choice but to move with me. "You really think I would be hunting these bastards for fun?" He scowls hard, his eyebrows slanting, and I grin sardonically. "They killed me, drugged me, and threw me in a cell. So, sorry Griffin Sweetheart, not even you can stop me."

I feel the anger racing through his body, and his jaw grinds as he stares at me before he pushes words out through gritted teeth. "You should let this go, some very powerful people want these men and this crime circle dead, and you getting in the way will only draw attention to yourself. Trust me, you don't want to draw their attention."

Rolling my eyes at his threat, I carry on dancing. "That man killed me, the one upstairs imprisoned me and tortured countless women, and then sold them. So no, I won't be letting this go."

He growls, like actually growls. His eyes turn darker, with what looks like smoke or mist twirling faster and faster in their depths. "Dawn," he warns again, but I just turn my back on him and carry on dancing.

I feel him gearing up for an argument when I spot Marco. Zoning Griffin out as he lectures me on safety and bullshit, I watch the bastard who threw me into the cells as he walks through the club like he owns it. To be fair, he does, but he acts like a god. I can't wait to make him fall like one.

He winds through the crowd, accepting handshakes and kisses on cheeks as he smiles and flirts, imposing in his smart suit. To think I actually thought this bastard was attractive but now, looking closer, I can see the evil surrounding him. Maybe I didn't want to see it before, or maybe I wasn't paying attention, but it follows him around like a shadow.

I watch his progress as he stops at a booth where three other suited men are sitting and slides in, with a drink being placed in front of him immediately as he leans back and crosses his leg over his other knee, his arm placed along the back of the booth as his eyes start to scan the club.

Turning, just in case he spots me, I cover Griffin's still moving mouth with my hand. "Shut up, will you? Now, listen and listen good. You do not know me, you do not get to tell me shit. If I wanted to start an orgy right here, you couldn't say a fucking thing, get that through your stupidly thick skull. You can either help, or you can fuck off." His eyes widen in shock, no doubt nobody has ever talked back to him before. I watch in fascination as the shock soon burns away to desire. "Now, I'm going to the toilet and you can get the fuck over it." Leaning closer, I rest my lips on my hand separating our mouths. "Then you can tell me why you are stalking me, what this mate crap means, and everything else." Kissing my own hand I pull away and saunter through the club, with absolutely zero intentions of going to the toilet.

It's time Griffin saw the reason why I don't need his protection, or condescension. He might be beautiful, but he's a fucking asshole. Why does that make me want him more? Maybe because he isn't delicate around me, nor does he censor his mouth or even give a shit. I've been flattered all my life, told my beauty opens doors— hell, it even led me to Tim. So the fact it doesn't seem to bother him, never mind be a factor in how he treats me, is addictive. Doesn't mean I won't kick his fucking ass if he carries on being a wanker though.

Women, we are complicated creatures, and it seems turning into a monster or a skinwalker, as Griffin called me, has only upped my lack of filter and rational thinking. At this point, I'm mainly instincts and wants.

Shrugging away the thoughts for another time, I add an extra sway to my hips as I head across the dance floor, aiming for Marco. I can still feel Griffin's eyes burning into my skin and it makes me want to turn around and put on a show, to push him and see how he would react.

GRIFFIN

I watch, captivated, as Dawn wanders away through the crowd. My eyes track her easily, since she stands out here, even among the masses. I can almost still feel her in my arms, and see her eyes light up as she challenged me.

She is definitely not what I was expecting, and I can't seem to help myself around her. I need to push her, annoy her, see that spark

143

in her eye and feel the pain of her sharp tongue. Even now, when I should be working, all I can think about is my mate.

I watch her progress through the crowd, with my eyes dropping to the hypnotic sway of her ass in that dress. I know she's doing it on purpose, but I also know some of it is just her innate sexuality. It oozes from her like her powers, she is untrained and reckless, but oh so fucking powerful.

With a frown, I watch her turn and begin swearing as I push through the crowd as she makes her way towards the man I spotted getting into the car outside the warehouse.

For fuck's sake, this woman is going to be the death of me and maybe all the fucking sheep in here if he touches her.

CHAPTER 30

DAWN

M arco doesn't notice me coming, since his eyes are watching a fight breaking out over on the other side of the room. It isn't until I'm right before him that his eyes swing my way. Bending over, I place my boobs in his face, hoping it will stop him from looking too intently at me and noticing who I am.

He raises his eyebrow and sips his drinks, his eyes dancing as they rove my body before meeting mine. I hold my breath, waiting for him to alert his guards, but I see no recognition in his eyes. Maybe he drugs girls all the time, but I'm a tiny bit disappointed even if it makes my job easier.

"Can I help you, sweet thing?" he asks, watching me with a knowing look.

"I don't know, can you?" I flirt. He grins and I know I need to catch his attention now or he will get distracted.

Pushing his ankle off his knee with my heel, I lift my leg and straddle his lap. Both of his eyebrows raise and he smirks. I lean forward, ignoring the sick feeling his hands cause when they land on my thighs, and I brush my lips across his cheek to his ear.

"Why don't you see if you can help me?" I purr, licking his lobe before biting it. He groans huskily and I back away, leaving his lap as I smile seductively, crooking my finger for him to follow me before I turn and, swaying my hips, wander away from the table confidently. My shoulders loosen when I hear him trailing after me.

Men.

Leading him down the hallway behind the dance floor, which I'm guessing goes to the toilets, I spot the fire exit at the end of the darkened corridor—perfect. Unfortunately Marco, the handsy bastard, decides he can't wait and pushes me up against the wall roughly, slams his hands next to my head, and kisses me.

Crinkling my nose in disgust, I roll my eyes and wrap my arms around his neck, fake moaning into his mouth as he rubs up against me. Turning him while he's distracted man-handling my breasts, I start backing us down the corridor. When he goes to lift his head I grab both cheeks and kiss him hard until he's grunting and moaning.

When we reach the door, I kick it open and pull back. His eyes are unfocused and I grin as I press both hands to his chest and push so he flies out and hits the alley wall behind the club. I step out, kick the door shut behind me, and look around. Bins line the bottom of the alley, the other end leads to the street, and the lights don't penetrate down here.

He frowns, eyeing the surroundings before shrugging and leaning back with a smirk. "What, you don't like an audience? I wouldn't have guessed from your little display in there." He runs his hand down his suit and flicks open the button on his slacks.

Rolling my eyes again I hold up my hand. "Calm down Marco, you can keep your little friend in your pants. I'm afraid the only thing getting wet tonight will be your eyes. I'm betting you're a crier."

He reaches for his pocket, maybe for his phone or a weapon, but I dart closer and grab both hands, pinning them to the wall next to him like he did to me as I line up our faces, and grin at him. Letting him see the hate and rage in my eyes.

"Remember me yet, or should I let you drug me first?" His eyes widen in recognition.

"You," he sneers.

"Me. The bitch who just killed and took down your whole fucking little warehouse," I taunt.

He narrows his eyes. "Liar," he hisses.

"Oh really? How else do you think I got out? Or how did I release all the 'freaks' from your basement."

"You fucking bitch—"

I backhand him quickly.

"Yes, yes, yes, I'm a bitch. Now, what I want to know is whom you are selling the girls to, both freaks and normals. I also want to know whom you answer to."

He laughs, actually laughs. "Why the fuck would I tell you that?"

Grinning, I lick up his neck to his ear. "Because you smell like prey."

I hear his heart rate speeding up as I pull away, and he puts on a brave face like I can't hear the fear pumping through his blood. "Get the fuck away from me before I decide to deal with you once and for all," he orders.

I laugh, throwing my head back. "It's cute how you think you get to order me around."

I hear the flapping of wings and Marco's eyes dart about, but when they don't widen in alarm I take it to mean Griffin is hidden somewhere. Well then, maybe I can show him and Marco that you don't fuck with me. Two birds, one death...that's the saying, right?

"Get the fuck away from me and I might let you live," he threatens, pushing away from the wall.

"How boring. I was hoping this would be more fun. Now, tell me who you're selling them to," I demand, leaning back against the door with a bored look on my face.

"Go fuck yourself," he fires back, standing and straightening his suit before narrowing his eyes on me. It's easy to see why he's so high up in the organization, even now he's unruffled.

"No thanks, I have someone else to do that with later. Last chance, who were you selling them to?" I inquire slowly, straightening from my position against the door, almost buzzing with the hope that he won't answer.

"Fuck. Off," he replies, grabbing at the gun or phone again.

I grin. "I was hoping you would say that," I purr before jumping at him.

Grabbing the arm going for his pocket I twist, and when I hear a crack and he screams, I yank it behind his back and hold it there with my face pushed against his. Sweat beads at his forehead as he lets out a colourful rant at me.

"Finished?" I ask calmly and he nods, his words eventually cutting off as his eyes meet mine, finally understanding I'm serious.

"You...you're one of them," he gasps, rising higher on his tiptoes to try and alleviate the pain in his arm.

"One of whom?" I ask innocently, fluttering my lashes, wanting to hear him say it.

"Freak," he spits, making me grin.

"Hell yes I am, but the last guy who pissed me off ended up with a ripped out neck, bleeding out on his hotel room floor as I fucked a forest god. So, if I were you, I would get smart real quick," I purr.

He swallows hard, finally nodding, obviously coming to the same conclusion I have. His bodyguards think he's busy fucking, and that gives us an hour, maybe more, depending on how long he usually lasts, but I'm betting he's a pump and dump sort of guy. Nobody knows where he is and he's trapped out here with a hurt arm, and what he calls two 'freaks'—not that he knows Griffin is there.

"I don't know the buyers' names, they came to us," he starts and I narrow my eyes. He gasps, freezes, and I blink hard. "Your eyes—"

"What about them?" I grit out.

"They are black, just black."

Huh, that's new. Although I've never really looked at myself when I use my new powers, so maybe it's not. Something else to think about later on.

"Marco," I warn.

"Sorry, sorry." He gulps, his gaze flickering away before going back to my eyes like he can't stand not to look. "They really did, they must have found out that I was dealing women right under Victor's—shit." He snaps his mouth shut and I arch my eyebrow.

Working his jaw, he shakes his head. "What the fuck does it

matter anyway," he mutters to himself before looking back at me. "Victor Valkov is the man in charge, he hides away in the city, like a puppet pulling the strings. He has too much going on so you can slip some things through him. His rules are simple, they don't deal in people or drugs, but what he doesn't know doesn't hurt him."

Wow, real fucking classy.

"So, myself and a few other guys started this enterprise. It began small but kept getting bigger and bigger until we had a client base and buyers already lined up, putting in their own requests. I had no choice but to bring Tim on board, and he was all too happy to help, getting a split off the profits."

"How did you bring him on board?" I ask, needing to know.

"I found out he was stealing from Victor, skimming the books. I mentioned it might slip out if he was to say...not help us." As he speaks, he straightens haughtily, his power and money appearing once again.

"Anyway, eventually someone calling themselves 'The Others' approached us. It's not unusual for clients to give us fake names or organisations. We didn't think anything of it when they set up a meeting."

Getting bored holding him, I push him back against the wall and cross my arms, his eyes drop to my breasts, making me grunt. "Eyes up top," I warn.

He holds his hands up, wincing as he uses the injured one, before leaning back against the wall like he's here for a business meeting.

"Anyway, at the meeting there was just something weird about these guys. They wanted some very specific things and before I knew it, they had proved that freaks...I mean, people with, erm, powers were real. It all moved really fast from there. They suggested that if we so happened to find these people, they would pay big money for them. They were clear that they didn't want the humans, only the freaks."

I hear a growl float on the wind and I want to agree with Griffin. Someone is going around snatching and buying supes...but why?

"These others, what can you tell me about them? How do they

pick up? What do they look like? Any names?" I step forward. "You must have done some research, you're smart and I'm betting you don't trust easily. You must have had an insurance policy in case it all went wrong."

His eyes dart to the side, a clear indicator that he's going to lie to me. "Truth," I order with power lacing my words. I'm starting to get itchy from all this waiting and talking. All I want to do is kill this bastard and hunt the others down, and fuck and eat.

"You're right. I couldn't find much, they were good. Real fucking good. They obviously have money and power, hell, they even have the cops in their fucking pockets. I did catch one man's name, Veyo."

"Anything else?" I press, needing something else to go on.

He purses his lips. "If I tell you, we need to make a deal, will you let me go?"

Pouting for a moment, I pretend to think about it. "Sure," I agree and he must be desperate to accept that, though I'm not exactly lying.

"I think they were like the women, I think they were freaks," he says, dropping that bombshell.

Griffin growls again, making menace drip down the alley from him above. "What makes you say that?" I question, wanting to pace, but I don't move from my spot in front of him.

"They were...different. They were too strong, too rich, too everything. They knew too much, even for buyers of the freaks. It's like they could sense them without even having to check."

Motherfuckers. I give into my urge and begin pacing back and forth, before I start to mumble to myself. "Why the hell would supes be buying other supes?" I whisper.

"All I know is, freaks and humans aren't that different." I spin on him and he holds one hand up again. "Maybe freaks do it for the same reason we do, money and power. They are big influencers."

How the hell did I get myself wrapped up in this? I just wanted to kill the man who hurt me and now I find myself in the middle of a fucking cattle market with enemies on every side with no idea who to trust. My whole world has been thrown upside down and I'm scrambling to try and stay a float.

"Okay, anything else?" I ask distractedly.

"No, I swear. I can go?" He pleads, his eyes darting to the alley entrance.

I nod and step back, even as Griffin growls again. Marco sighs, holding his injured arm as he sends me another look as if unsure. I grin, waving my hand towards the alley end, but blocking the door.

He starts edging that way, his eyes on me until he passes me, then he turns and starts to run. Giving him a couple seconds head start, I burst into movement just as Griffin takes off from the roof. Increasing my speed, not wanting him to get to him first, I grab the back of Marco's shirt just as he reaches the end of the alley. Turning, I throw him back into the dark and away from safety.

I grin wickeldy as I saunter down the alley and he starts to crawl backwards away from me.

"We made a deal!" he yells looking around for help.

"I let you go, I didn't say I wouldn't come after you," I point out.

"You fucking freak!" he shouts, grabbing a bin lid and flinging it at me.

Plucking it out of the air, I throw it behind me and advance on him as he scuttles back faster and faster. He swears and drags himself to his feet and I pounce, bored with the game of cat and mouse.

He goes down hard, his back hitting the floor and knocking the breath out of him as he cries out. Lunging down, I yank his head to the side and bite his neck. This isn't about feeding, or even changing, this is about killing him.

I rip back and tear through flesh and arteries, pulling a chunk of skin with me. Letting it drop to the floor beside his head, I look back at his pale face and smile, no doubt my mouth and teeth covered in the bright red blood, which is currently pumping from his neck.

He gasps, his eyes wide and filled with fear, and that knowing look people get when they realise they are dying and there's nothing they can do to stop it. They finally understand the fragility of life and how easy it is to snuff out. This man craved power and money, and it won't help him while he bleeds to death in the back alley of his own club.

"Messy, but effective," Griffin drawls, and I look over to see him leaning against the building, watching me as I hover over Marco's cooling body. His breath is rattling now, his body fighting as it dies and decays beneath me.

I don't know whether it's the blood, pain, or even the killing, but it calls to me, making me act on instinct. At the moment, that instinct is geared towards Griffin, a call pulling between us.

His eyes round as I fling myself at him, leaving Marco to die alone. Unlike Nos, he doesn't catch me. He grunts as I hit his body, climb up him, and wrap my arms and legs around him.

"Whoa, Dawn, look at me. This is just the power, death is heady, it brings out our baser instincts for any monster. Just breathe," he says, but his hands slip to my arse and hold me to him.

Licking my lips, I watch him like he is the prey and his eyes narrow dangerously, that mist and smoke reappearing in his gaze. "*Vasculo*," he warns, his voice pained like he's fighting his own instincts, but I don't. It might be stupid, it might be wrong, but they haven't led me awry since my rebirth. Life is fleeting, why not just go with it?

Licking down his neck, leaving a blood trail behind, I taste the sweat and flavour that is just Griffin. It explodes in my mouth like the sweetest wine, making me groan.

"You taste like smoke and magic," I murmur and he groans, the sound rolling through me and making me shiver.

"Dawn." The way he chokes my name out is like a plea, but for mercy or more, I'm not sure.

Trailing my tongue across his cheek, I hover over his lips. He might look like an angel but he tastes like sin, and I'm craving more. I wait there, our breathes mixing as we both freeze.

"Griffin," I murmur and he groans. His hand reaches up and cups the back of my head, his fingers weaving into my hair as he yanks me to him, closing that distance and kissing me.

My lips part and he sweeps his tongue in, the taste of blood mixing with him and making me moan and rub against him. He kisses me hard, dominant, like it's our first and last, and before I know it, he yanks me away and drops me to the ground, backing away from me. His chest heaves, his eyes are dark, and Marco's blood paints his mouth.

I hear a noise behind me and spin, crouching down ready to spring at the encroaching person, but I freeze at the sight of Nos. He's framed by the alley light, watching me with glowing, white eyes, and his body is vibrating with the need to change.

"Little Monster," he growls, and I straighten as he strides towards me, completely ignoring Griffin. Did he see us kissing? Will he care?

He doesn't stop until we are pressed together, his hand touching me gently, almost reverently, as he cups my chin and raises my head until I meet his eyes.

Watching me intently, he sweeps his thumb across my lips and lifts it away, showing me the blood. I swallow hard and watch in rapt fascination as he sucks it into his mouth.

"What have you been up to, Little Monster?" he whispers seductively. He lifts his head and grins when he spots the body of the dead mobster on the alley ground.

Then his eyebrow arches as he looks at Griffin. "Fallen," he greets, nodding his head, but I see his eyes twitch and clench.

Fallen? Like Fallen angel?

I look over at Griffin to see his face wiped clean, his hands by his side in a stance ready to fight as he eyes Nos. It's clear he doesn't know what he is and he doesn't like that, or maybe it's the fact that Nos is touching me, seeing as his eyes keep darting to the hand Nos has on me.

"How do you know what I am?" His tone is threatening as he steps forward, making Nos smirk.

"Fear not Fallen, I mean you no harm. I am just here for my mate." Nos looks back at me with a soft smile before pulling me under his shoulder so we both face Griffin. Pain and confusion flash across Griffin's face before he conceals it so quickly that if I didn't see it for myself, I could have imagined it.

"Mate?" he spits out, throwing me a venomous look.

"Yes, problem?" Nos questions, frowning hard.

Griffin laughs bitterly, throwing his hands in the air. "For fuck's sake! Yes, mate, there is a fucking problem because it seems we both have the same mate."

He sneers the word like it's dirty, the hate and...hope, behind it are confusing. I'm new to this world, I haven't given much thought into being destined for one person, never mind two, but I can't deny the attraction and pull I have for both of them...and the dragon from my dreams.

"Is that common for a person to have more than one mate?" I query, the word feeling strange on my tongue.

Nos taps his chin deep in thought and when it becomes clear Griffin won't answer us, too busy throwing us glares, I turn to face my god.

"The more powerful the person, the more powerful the call is. Your supernatural side knows what you need and it will only call those who can help you, who your very soul was made for. Like missing pieces in a puzzle, you will fit together. It is common for the more powerful or older supernaturals to call more than one mate, but usually over years when your powers develop and you grow with them."

Arching my brow, I cuddle into his side as my need disappears while I think through the ramifications. "So, there are more monsters looking for me?"

"Maybe, probably. With the power it takes to sustain your shifts, I would say yes. Skinwalkers are unbelievably powerful and also unknown. This will all be new and I am guessing different than most other mate calls. There has only ever been a few, and they didn't last long once the council realised what they could do," Nos replies, and I realise he knew what I was.

"You knew what I was and what do you mean?" I ask and Griffin scoffs. I throw him a glare, back to being annoyed by his attitude.

Nos frowns at him before turning his intense eyes on me. The white is slowly fading the more we talk, until they are back to being his human colour. "You can change into anyone you want, think of the ramifications. You could infiltrate the council itself. It means they fear you and what they fear, they destroy. They made skin-walkers into the undesirables. People call them vessels, face stealers, or changers." He stops, wincing at the names people call what I am.

Are we really that bad? Thinking back over the last few days since I woke up as a skinwalker, I guess I'm not a great case against all those slurs but fuck. "Wonderful," I comment.

"But you seem to be more than that," Griffin adds and Nos sighs.

I look between them, and then finally settle on Nos. "What? What does he mean?"

He shifts from foot to foot before sighing again. "You didn't notice, but I did. Your eyes, they went white when I came down the alley and when you killed the man in the hotel."

I gasp. "Like yours?"

He smiles at that. "Yes, it seems when you connect or feed from your mate, you gain some of their power. Makes sense when you are essentially feeding from it. Everything I know about skinwalkers are myths, lore, and stories passed down through time, so I am afraid we are all learning as we go."

Griffin scoffs again. "Yep, our mate, the fucking unicorn of the shifter world."

Ignoring his attitude I ask Nos, "Are there unicorns?"

He shivers before nodding. "Yes. I love all creatures, it's part of being an animal and forest god, but they even creep me out."

"Erm, are we talking about the same creatures? The ones with horns and shoot rainbows?" I muse, confused.

"Fucking hell, she knows nothing about this world, lucky fucking me," Griffin adds, but at this point I'm just ignoring him.

"They are nothing like the stories told to human children. They are dark creatures, their horn is coated in a poison, and they are moody, evil bastards who control the elements and can move through space at will. They tend to be very primal and they do not take well to others, human or supe alike, interrupting their land."

Well fuck. "Okaaay, so no unicorns. They sound fucking horrifying."

"Just you wait, *vasculo*, this world is dark and filled with monsters. Monsters who will all want you," Griffin sneers, and I glare over at him.

"What the hell is your problem? It isn't my fault I called you or whatever!" I throw my hands in the air in exasperation and he stalks forward until we are nose to nose.

"I do not want, or need, a fucking mate. You are nothing but a complication, one I will be rid of soon," he drawls, and each word is like a blow or a knife to the gut.

I don't let the hurt show, since he's right, he didn't ask for this, but neither did I. I might not know him well, but he is still buried inside me with my new skinwalker and powers wanting him. "I didn't ask for this either. I didn't ask to be beat, raped, and murdered and buried in a shallow grave in the fucking forest!" I scream, letting out all my excess emotions, it's been a long night after all.

He flinches like I slapped him, regret and...caring enters his eyes before Nos interrupts.

"We should leave, Little Monster. People will start to investigate soon." He nods at the body.

Sucking in some deep breaths, I back away from Griffin and nod at Nos. "Where are we going? We can't go back to the hotel," I inquire, wanting nothing more than a shower and a bed to curl up in with my monster at my back.

"Fucking brilliant," Griffin mutters, and when I swing him a look he grabs a phone from his pocket. He doesn't look at me as he thumbs in a number and hits dial.

"Clean up, no witnesses. The Clubhouse, downtown," he snaps before ending the call and sliding the phone away.

"You two are bloody useless—a new skinwalker with no impulse control and a fucking mystical old god with no place to go." He rolls his eyes to the sky before sighing. "You can stay with me for one night, one fucking night, and you will tell me everything about your involvement in my case," he orders.

I look at Nos with an arched eyebrow but he waits for me to decide, and right then and there, I fall a little bit more for my god.

He should be mad, he should be jealous. Hell, I can feel it running through him, but he lets me make the decision. He doesn't bark out orders or demands. Instead, he waits, his eyes telling me that whatever I decide, he will go through it with me.

Mate. I can understand that word now. I just don't know what it means for a messed up person like me, but I know if I say no, if I walk away from Griffin now, that will be it. He will shut down, he will lock me out and curl up in his hate and anger. His mind twisting so all he knows is that beast. He might not want a mate, he might deny it, but he needs me and I obviously need him if my power makes any kind of sense.

Fate brought him to me for a reason, another monster from the dark waiting for me. His hands and future are in my hands. Do I walk away and leave him to crumble and fade away like mist?

"Okay," I agree, my decision made. The world speeds up again, the power in me settles like I made the right decision, but that remains to be seen because the same danger I sense in Nos, I sense in Griffin, and he seems like a different kind of monster altogether.

CHAPTER 31

DUME

Witches' blood covers me from ear to hoof. Roaring again, I watch the witches cast spell after spell, their magic running low from such a long assault. I dodge the spells and ignore the ones that hit me, and charge them. I impale one on my horn before flinging her across the room.

The next I rip in half, and it goes on and on, until the walls and floors are painted with the blood of my enemies as I work my way through the house. There were more than I thought, and when I reached the landing they were ready, obviously hearing my massacre upstairs.

"Monster!" one calls out, from the circle of her coven in the middle of the room. She insults me from safety, they always do. They think they are so untouchable, so immortal. I'm about to show this witch what it means it be mortal.

"Witch," I spit, and the words are a mix of a huff and a growl in my shifted form's mouth. My nose ring jangles as I stomp my hoof, my torcs moving with me as well while I tower in the entrance of what looks like a ballroom. Wooden floors line the level with high ceilings above us and there, behind the witches in a cage of magic, are the outcasts and at the very front—Carmichael.

"My ancestors should have killed you when they had the chance. It's a pity, but I will rectify their mistakes today," she yells, her red hair floating in the breeze of the suffocating magic in the room.

I huff at her monologuing and charge. She didn't expect that, none of them did. They all expected me to hesitate long enough for them to chain me. Not happening, not today, not ever again.

Tearing through their masses, breaking their protective circle, I roar as I rip them limb from limb. I lose all track of time, until nothing or no one stands alive around me. Just a circle of dead witches and their blood.

I snort, huffing at them. "Who's dead now, bitch?" I spit and laughter starts up from the outcasts. The cage must have broken when the witches fell, because they are standing at the back of the room watching me. Most in thanks, some in disgust, but nearly all in fear.

Carmichael steps forward, clapping dramatically. "Bravo, my friend. I guess thanks is owed for the rescue? Come, I will find you some clothes and somewhere without body parts to change." He steps over the red-haired witch's head with a twist of his lips, and gestures for me to go first.

Inclining my head slightly, I walk side by side with the vamp as he leads me through his house, which is silent except for the whispering downstairs in the ballroom.

"Forgive them, most have never seen a minotaur in the flesh, you are the stuff of legends after all," he adds.

I don't feel the need to answer and he soon stops trying to speak to me. He leads me to an empty room and grabs some clothes from the dresser. "They might be tight but, well, you are massive and most here are not. The shower is through there. Go wash up and change, sleep if you need to, and we shall talk after." He goes to leave and I force the words out, I still find it strange conversing after being alone this long.

"I am leaving again later, I have my mate to find."

He nods, those eyes of his filled with amusement. "Of course, I will call the plane and make sure it is prepped." He places his hand on the door before sighing. "She is a lucky woman, but maybe leave the dismembered bodies until after the first meeting, eh?" he jokes, before sweeping from the room.

Waiting until he is gone, I take the clothes to the bathroom and close the door behind me. I keep my swords with me, placing them on the rim of the bath as I flick on the water.

Steam starts to fill the room as I look into the lit up mirror above the basic white sink. My monster half reflects back. Scars crisscross my fur, most old, ancient even. Turning away, I force the change and stagger from shifting and killing so much in a short amount of time.

Dragging my tired body into the shower, I scrub all the blood away and get out, not bothering to linger. I will stay long enough to ensure they have their wards and protection back up again, and that the witches are truly gone. Then I am leaving, I have wasted enough time.

I need my mate.

CHAPTER 32

ASKA

Standing before the still lit fire, my naked skin bathed in blood and soot, I watch as the flames dance, entrancing me. The hunters' bodies lie behind me and it hasn't even been an hour since I killed them all. My dragon is sleeping soundly, happy after his little spree—for now, until he starts calling for his mate again. The reprieve is nice, allowing me to breathe and think through my next steps.

Clearly, the hunters are looking for me and that means I need to be careful. I do not want to lead them to my mate or expose myself to the world and the remaining dragons. It means I need to be smart about this. It is fair enough to say my cars here have probably already been compromised. Either with a tracking beacon or bug.

That means I need to find another form of transport, and flying is out for obvious reasons. Leaving the flames behind, I walk down my hall and back to my bedroom, heading straight into the welcoming pool. I don't know when I will be back, so for tonight I will enjoy the feel of home, dispose of the bodies, and rest.

Tomorrow, I will leave again.

Submerging myself in the water, I let it wash away the blood and scent of death before staring out across the mountain, letting the cool air and nature soothe me. I sigh, knowing time is ticking away, so I slide from the water, leaving myself to air dry as I make my way back through the halls to the bodies.

Standing above them, I cross my arms while I think. Now, what to do with them? Before, I have tossed one or two off the side of the mountain. I have also burned one previously in the fireplace. One I let the helpers clean up, but this large amount?

It will require a cleaning crew. Sighing, I head over to the counter and the phone sitting there. I dial the one number I have that always puts me in contact with a member of the Sinclair family —the humans I trust—and I wait as it rings. I suppose it is in the middle of the night, but exhaustion is pulling at me now, making me irritable.

Eventually, someone picks up the other end as a tired sounding, heavily accented voice answers, "Yes?"

"Dragoliou Sinclair," I address, speaking the words of our bond throughout the ages.

There is silence on the other end, then he responds, "Monsieur, how may I assist you? I am so sorry for my rude greeting. Are you back? Do you require food or supplies?" He speaks quickly now, with excitement in his voice. No doubt when this fell to him from his father or mother, he never expected to be called to service.

"I need a clean-up crew at the mountain estate in the morning, make it discreet, we have eyes. I also want a full sweep for tracking devices or bugs," I demand, and I hear him scribbling on the other end, good. Hopefully he might get it right. The Sinclairs are nothing if not prompt and reliable.

"Anything else, sir?" he asks, eager to please.

"I am leaving for a while and I will need a car, clothes, and money sent to the mountain estate by morning. I shall also need the ring from West Bank. You have the key to the deposit box, yes?" I inquire, and there is a heavy pause.

"Of course sir, does this mean—I am sorry, that is rude," he backpedals, making me smile even as I lean against the wall and my muscles scream at me.

"One thing you will learn, never feel the need to hold your tongue with me. Edgar didn't, and that is why I trusted him above all else in the world," I comment.

"Yes sir, thank you. I just wished to know if this meant you had finally found your mate? I have read the journals day after day and the only mention of the ring is between yourself and my great-great-great grandfather when you said it was a present, one only meant for your true mate. Your call," he gushes, making my smile turn full-blown. He is intelligent, I shall give him that, and it is clear he knows the history.

"Yes, she called me from my slumber. I am seeking her tomorrow," I reply.

"How amazing! I will include your family journals, presents, the call gifts, and everything you will need for your future mate." He sounds distracted again, no doubt his brain is whirring as he makes plans, but it is good he thought of all of that because I certainly did not.

"Thank you..." I trail off, realising I never asked his name.

"Jean Paul, sir. You may call me whatever you want. I will program my number and any others I think you need into the cell, which will be with your belongings in your car at the estate by nine AM sharp. Anything else, sir?"

"That is all for now. I must rest, it has been a trying day. Goodnight, Jean Paul," I conclude, as a yawn cracks my jaw.

"Goodnight, sir, and may I say it is good to have you back," he comments, and I laugh as I hang up the phone.

It is good to be back.

Unlocking the door of my house, the only occupied one on the block, I internally kick myself. This is a bad fucking idea. I have never invited anyone here, it is my space. My safe zone. Not even the council knows about it.

It's my retreat, my armory, and here is my mate exploring it with curious eyes, her fucking mate wandering behind her.

Of course I would get a mate, only for her to have another. She has barely looked at me since he turned up. I can feel the power flowing off of him from here and I know he's concealing it as well, he isn't even trying, he's just that fucking old and powerful.

It isn't hard to figure out who he is from the way he spoke of the creatures—a fucking god of old. One that they spoke of in myths, even at my birth, and we have the same mate.

I glare at her from my perch in the corner as she goes from room to room, not giving a fuck about my privacy as she explores everything, exposing every secret. It feels like she's ripping me open and examining me, causing me to take in my house with fresh eyes, so I look around to try and see what she sees.

It's not cramped or cluttered, it's not even dark. There are no shadows here, I don't need them. Photographs, which were taken over my long life, fill the wall in the living room, all in greyscale.

Two black, pincushioned sofas take up the rest of the room with a flat-screen TV hanging on the wall, and a mantelpiece with a fire-place underneath it. Steel-plated blinds hang on the window with blackout curtains behind them for privacy.

The kitchen is modern and I handmade the table, counters, and doors myself over the years—each has little hand carvings in them, depicting my life and my story. Just something to leave behind in case I never come back.

My armory is down here with a safe door on it, which is standing open. A huge, silver table lies in the middle with a gun already displayed. Just because I don't like them doesn't mean I don't have them. All the three walls are covered in every weapon you could imagine, from both past and present. Some I stole, some I bought, and some were passed down. All are mine now.

She touches them reverently, like they speak my secrets to her. Frowning, I follow her up the stairs as she goes. All of us trooping behind as she explores the spare bathroom, which is sparse and utilitarian, before she reaches my bedroom.

I suck in a breath and she pauses with her hand on the doorknob, before looking back at me for permission. I don't know why, but I nod. She smiles and swings the door open and creeps inside.

My bed, made with black satin sheets, is unmade and I almost blush. My furniture all matches—more handmade pieces I'd made over the years, an old hobby from my childhood that I took up when I couldn't sleep. If she had looked hard enough downstairs she would have found the basement door. Down there is a home gym and my woodworking center. I even have a firing range.

My bedroom is sparse as well, and the only personal touches are the little ornaments lining the corner bookcase, which I carved whenever I finished a mission. A matching black, pincushioned recliner sits next to it underneath the window, showing me the rain splashing down on the city.

She runs her finger above all of them, counting, and when she eyes me they are full of sadness. Why, I am not sure. Before I can get angry or snipe, she leaves the room and swings open the other door on the floor that leads up to the empty bedroom.

I'm not sure why I got this two-bedroom house, it just...felt right, and with her ass sashaying up the stairs at the moment, maybe now I can admit I got it for a reason, I just didn't know it then.

The room opens up and runs the full length of the house. An old, unused, four-poster bed, upon a raised dais, sits in the middle of the room and the carved headboard I made rests in the archway. Two windows sit on either side. One with a seat and cushions. This room also has a fire, the chimney connecting to the one from downstairs, with a huge rug in front of it. Bits and bobs that I couldn't store anywhere else cover one corner of the room, draped in a protective cloth.

She tilts her head back with her mouth parted, and my heart thumps and my cock hardens. I keep trying not to look at her...or smell her. She's fucking beautiful and powerful, I can't forget that. More so than I thought, she proved herself in that alley and it only twisted me up inside. I have never wanted another person so badly

—the man's blood on her mouth incited images of my cock ramming there, with the blood of her enemies still in her mouth. I am fucking sick, but it seems like she is also.

As if sensing my thoughts, her eyes move to me and she grins that naughty fucking smile as her eyes dance. Her eyes had been black in the alley, the deep black of the night I hide in. It had sent shivers of desire through me while my chest filled with the feeling of rightness and home.

Breaking our stare, I follow her gaze to see that she was staring at the exposed wood beams of the high, arched roof.

That's when I realise no one has spoken since we arrived and I wince. I am not good at this interacting shit. Never have been. I'm a loner and I like it that way, but she makes me want to speak. To ask her anything and everything just to hear that fucking sensual voice again.

Shit, say something, anything.

"You can stay here for the night," I comment, and she raises her eyebrows.

Wow, good going.

"I'm going to make food." Okay, again not what I was going for. That stupid god is looking at me like I'm an idiot.

Blowing out a breath, I scratch my arm like I always do when I am nervous, a bad habit I haven't had in years. "Would you like some?" I force out.

I might not be fully down with this mate bullshit, but it doesn't mean I'm stupid enough to turn her away, and whenever I hurt her, it's like hurting myself. Doesn't mean I will stop being an asshole though, she will just have to fucking deal with it.

"Love some," she replies, and I turn without another word and flee downstairs, the smell of her on me chases after me, mocking me.

Fucking skinwalker.

CHAPTER 33

DAWN

W ith Griffin storming off, I turn back to Nos. He watches me, his face completely blank.

"Are you mad?" I ask.

He shakes his head, leaning against the window.

"Are you...hungry?" I purr, sauntering until I can place my hand on his chest.

He grins now. "For you, Little Monster, always for you."

I smile and a giggle tumbles out. He's fucking crazy. Sighing, I keep eye contact as I stroke his chest. "Are you bothered about Griffin being my mate?"

He sighs as well before covering my hand, his eyes turning distant. "At first, I was. Mainly because I am selfish and I want you all to myself, but I can see he fulfills something in you, something I can't. I also know your call wouldn't do what it isn't supposed to. There is a reason for everything, Little Monster. There is a reason for Griffin, why he was brought to you, why you are mated. The world doesn't revolve without them, I just wish I knew what it was."

I nod and he smiles at me, those lush lips curling up. "Are you bothered about Griffin being your mate?" he inquires, parroting my question back to me.

"Well, he's not exactly a fucking ray of sunshine...but no. Something in me is drawn to him and I think underneath all that surly there is something real, and I have a feeling by the end of this, we are going to need him."

He wraps his arms around me, bringing me in for a hug, his chin resting on my head. I love how big he is, I could hide in his arms forever, my own perfect hideaway. Safe.

"What do you mean? I still don't know what happened," he growls, his chest rumbling with it.

"It's a long story, I promise I'll tell you, but I learned that the human crime ring, the very one Griffin is hunting, is selling women. Not just any women, but women like me. Women with powers. They are torturing people, and when their powers come out to save them, they sell them to these people called The Others, who the man I killed thinks are like us as well," I finish off, stroking his arm as he hums.

"Then you are right, we need him. I am good, I am powerful, but I haven't really been a part of this city and life for a long time. It is clear he has been and he is a skilled fighter. He knows what we are up against."

Looking up, I grin at his words. "We?"

He arches his eyebrow at me, kissing my forehead as he lays his against mine, creating our own little world. "We, Little Monster. Wherever that takes us, always we. From now on we do everything together. You want to kill your husband and you want the people who hurt you to pay. You want to hunt these bastards selling super-natural creatures. I will follow you through it all. We," he concludes, and I grin before leaning up and kissing him hard.

How did I get so fucking lucky? Maybe my death was a good thing, it brought me to him after all.

I kicked off my shoes and left them upstairs as I make my way to the kitchen. Griffin's house is a surprise. I expected the armoury, but what I didn't expect was the photos and all the handmade carvings everywhere. I'm really intrigued, but the closed off look on his face lets me know he won't answer any questions I throw his way. So instead, I sit at the table, running my fingers over the wood and watching as he moves around the kitchen. Nos follows me in and picks me up, before dropping me in his lap. Grinning, I still watch Griffin, wanting to learn more about my angel, or fallen as Nos said, mate.

I could be doing things, I could be hunting Tim and his men, hell, even The Others or Victor, but right now I don't want to be anywhere but where I am with my mates. Tomorrow, it can all wait until tomorrow.

"What are we having?" I ask.

His shoulders tense as he keeps moving, banging down a pan onto the stove and grabbing ingredients from the fridge. "Stir fry," he replies, the words sharp and short.

I tilt my head and watch as he starts chopping the veg, his movements quick and refined. It's obvious he knows his way around the kitchen. It must get lonely though, always cooking for yourself, living with yourself, hunting...by yourself.

"So, you work for the council? What do they do?" I inquire, leaning back into Nos' arms.

"They govern all the races," he says snottily, with an applied 'duh' tacked on the end. Rolling my eyes, I turn and straddle Nos' lap, ignoring the grumpy man cooking behind me.

"Okay, tell me about the council," I address Nos, smiling at him as he leans back and his hands come up and frame my hips.

"Like the Fallen said, they govern all the races. They are a mixture of species and tend to be the strongest of all. Each race also has their own ruling body, but all must answer to the council. They rule everything, well, in this country at least. There are three councils in total. The eastern council, the western council..."

"And the other?" I press.

"Pray you never meet the other," Griffin mutters, making me throw him a look over my shoulder.

169

"Why?"

"They are the sleeping council, they rule over all. Each council member was voted into one of the five seats of the lords. Their word is law. Only one is ever awake at a time, the rest sleep, saving their powers until their reign. They are the stuff of nightmares and lore. Even older than Griffin and me combined. They have seen the rise and fall of empires, and they endure. They make sure our world, our lives, remain hidden. Even the other two councils must answer to them," Nos explains.

"Okay, but you're old. Older than I can probably even guess, and I can feel the power running through you, you are a god, for fuck's sake. Why aren't you part of the council?"

Griffin snorts and the sound of sizzling reaches my ears as a tasty aroma of fried chicken and veg makes my stomach growl.

"I have been asked before," Nos comments, as his hands find the bare skin of my thighs where my dress has ridden up and stroking, making me shiver. Will there ever be a moment I don't crave this monster? I'm constantly drawn to him, aware when he's near and when we touch...it's like fireworks.

"You turned them down?" I ask, tilting my head in confusion. The way Nos and Griffin spoke makes it seem like they wouldn't be the type of people to take rejection well.

"Yes, in a sense. I am a different kind of monster. I am not merely a shifter or a made creature like vamps, or born of nature like the fae...I am other."

"Fate Chosen," Griffin spits, making Nos sigh and nod.

"I was chosen, it is true. They call us mystics, where only one of us occur in the world. For example, the gods or monsters you read about are Fate Chosen. For there is only one of us, ever. Therefore, I simply could not sit on the council. It would not be proper, I have no people to govern and I never wanted to. I hate politics, it's why I live in nature. It might be brutal and bloody, but it is consistent and honest."

I guess I could understand that. Leaning forward, I peck his lips in thanks for explaining. "So the council?" I prompt, getting back on track.

"Are not people you want to fuck with, *vasculo*. Every legacy, lore, and monster in this world is theirs to call and control. They are the law and you do not fuck with them, ever. To deny them..." Griffin shakes his head and I turn in Nos' lap to see him.

His shoulders are tense again. "Like you did," Nos points out and Griffin freezes, then the room turns icy and it's like the light is being sucked into the fallen. Shadows swirl and stretch out of him, filled with rage and hate, before he sucks in a breath and they disappear just as easily as they came, but I shiver from the memory.

"You denied them?" I question, which is probably not the smartest move, but I don't fear Griffin, even as much as he would like me to.

"All fallen have, that is why they are fallen," Nos comments and Griffin spins, and his eyes flash as his bares his teeth, with a knife held in his hand and pointing at Nos.

Moving to block his view of my god, I draw his anger to me. "What are you? Angel?" I inquire softly.

"Nephilim," he snarls, turning back to the food and giving us his back once again.

"Half human, half angel?" I muse, trying to remember the term from stories I've read and see in films.

"Sort of," Nos murmurs in my ear, and I watch Griffin as he speaks. He ignores us completely, like he doesn't care what we say, but I know that isn't true. "Angels are naturally occurring species, and contrary to popular belief, nephilim are not the natural mix of humans and angels. They can't biologically have children, but a long time ago one angel—"

"A crazy fucking bastard," Griffin adds and Nos nods.

"A crazy angel, heartbroken after losing child after child, came up with a plan. He took it to the council who turned him down. He retreated to the wilderness of Siberia and built a compound there. The council thought nothing of it and left him alone in his grief and madness, but he didn't stop his vision. He kidnapped human women from all around the world with a naturally occurring gene that he deemed necessary to carry an angel baby to term. He recruited...some angels, shall we say, and they experimented. By the time the council found out what they were doing, it was too late. Hundreds, if not thousands, of women had died in child labour but the crazy angel had done it. With help from science and some stolen fae magic, he managed to create half human, half angel babies, the nephilim. He had them of all ages, and he was training and raising them to be an army. They were brutal, unforgivable killing machines. Assassins. Warriors. All of the darkness, none of the light."

Nos stops again and I'm entrapped in the tale. "The council raided the compounds, and they had a vamp wipe the memories of the humans they could save, and then they sent them on their way. The angels involved were sentenced to death, including the man who started it all—Gabriel."

I suck in a breath. "What happened to the children? They were innocent," I defend and he sighs again.

"They were, but the council still deemed them unreliable and...well, monsters. Abominations against the creator's and fate's vision for our lives. They were offered a choice, death or a life of slavery. Those who chose to live...they were forced into servitude under the council. Nothing more than their pet assassins and the shadows of the monsters. They are hunters. The council found a way to make them toe the line. They found that nephilim wings can be stripped and they will grow back, but it is a horrendous act, so vile most of the species balk at it. It usually strips them of their sanity and their powers until they regrow, but even then, the nephilim is never the same again...they are fallen."

My heart skips a beat as I look at my other mate, Nos' words still ringing in my head. They stripped him of his wings? Rage like no other bursts to life inside me and this time I feel my eyes change. They dare to hurt my mate?

"It is said, because they are not of nature, nephilim do not have mates," Nos whispers, and it all makes sense now.

No wonder Griffin is such an asshole, he should be. He has been told his whole life that he is no more than a monster, an abomination, forced to do the bidding of others with no chance of freedom, no chance of happiness. Trying to suppress this unparalleled rage, I look around the house he brought us to. Yet, he brought us, the mate he should have never had and her other mate to his safe place. His haven.

"Dinner is ready," he growls out, grabbing three plates and banging them onto the table without glancing at us, before grabbing the wok off the stove and laying it on the towel in the middle of the table. Only then does he look up, and he freezes when he meets my eyes.

Standing from Nos' lap, I run my hand across the wood of the table as I walk, until I stand before Griffin, with my eyes locked on his. "I don't pity you, you survived it. You are alive, they are not," I say and his eyes flash in shock. "Pity is for the dead and broken, and you are neither." I let him see the truth behind my words. I don't think less of him for his past, in fact, I think more of him. We are alike, although he sure as hell has been through a lot more than me. He inclines his head slightly and I turn back to the table, staring at a proud looking Nos. "It smells delicious, let's eat," I declare.

CHAPTER 34

DAWN

It's quiet while we eat, with Nos and myself on one side and Griffin on the other, concentrating on his plate. The food is delicious, but the atmosphere is frosty and that's all my fault.

As soon as he's finished, Griffin disappears upstairs and I hear his bedroom door shut. Sighing, I clear my plate before taking all the dirty pots to the sink. Nos drops a supportive kiss on my head and as I wash them, he dries.

"Come on, Little Monster. You need to rest." He grabs my hand and I nod, following him upstairs to the room Griffin said we could stay in. When I pass his room, I pause but I don't bother knocking. He clearly needs some space, and that's okay. I'm not forcing him to be my mate, and I'll walk away if it's easier for him.

Following Nos up the stairs, I stand in the middle of the room with my arms crossed as I study the space. I must look as lost as I feel, because Nos comes and stands before me. "Everything will work out, but that is tomorrow's problem. Tonight, tonight is about you and me." He kisses me softly before walking over to the fire. He crouches down and gets it going, the flames licking across the wood as he stands back up and walks over to me.

The firelight dances around the room, throwing shadows across his beautiful face as he grabs my crossed arms and drops them to my side. His fingers graze the side of my arms gently, raising goose-bumps in their wake.

Circling me, he moves my hair to my other shoulder and drops a gentle kiss on the base of my neck, making me shiver again. Need pulses through me, this isn't fast and primal. He is seducing me, showing me. My mate...he's laying claim to me.

He grabs the zip and pulls it down gently, and the back of the dress gapes, letting in a cool breeze as he moves to face me again. Grabbing my hands in his, he lifts them in the air, and no words spoken between us.

Keeping them there, I watch as he grabs the straps of my dress and tugs them down before the fabric slides down my body, pooling on the floor around my feet. His mouth opens as his eyes watch me hungrily.

Standing there in just my tattered lace, I watch my god as he watches me. Tonight I'm all his, and it's clear from the hunger and possession in his eyes that he intends to keep me.

His hands circle my throat and tilt my head up. Leaning down, he kisses me, hard and strong, before pulling away. He strokes down my chest, circling my waist, until he runs his hands around and cups my arse, exploring me. His warm touch makes me dart my tongue out to moisten my lips. He follows the movement, and with a groan hoists me up, holding me to the front of his body as he turns and lays me down in the middle of the big bed.

I look up at him as he stands there, just watching me, with his eyes running across every inch of my bare skin, and I start to get impatient. Cupping my own lace-covered breasts, I moan, arching into my own touch as I roll my nipples between my fingers.

My eyes fly open and I gasp when he grabs them, stilling my movements. Sucking in breaths, I watch him as he kneels on the bed next to me.

"That's not how it's going this time, Little Monster," he growls, his eyes sliding to white as he watches me.

"No?" I tease, arching up, rubbing against his hands and making him growl again.

"No."

Releasing my hands, he pulls off his shirt before grabbing them again. He yanks me up the bed and ties them together, binding them to the headboard and testing the restraint before sitting back, happy with himself.

Struggling, I pull on them. They are tight, biting into my wrists, but I could get free if I wanted to. I settle down and lay my thighs open, observing my monster.

He looks like the god he is right now, with flames dancing across his golden skin. Each line and muscle are defined, rippling as he moves over me. Lying between my parted legs, he licks up my stomach to the valley between my breasts. He circles the lace with his tongue before covering my hard nipple and sucks. The lace and his warm, wet mouth make me groan as I arch into his touch. Forgetting about my tied hands, I try to reach him to keep him clasped to me, but I can't reach.

He lets go with a pop and moves to the other, as the now wet material sticks to my nipple while he gives the other the same treatment, before letting go and taking in his handiwork.

Stroking down my belly, he runs his hand lightly over my pussy before moving to my thigh, and stroking down my leg until he reaches my ankle. He grabs it and pulls it over his shoulder and onto his back.

Leaving wet, trailing kisses up my belly, his bottom lip catches on my skin as he lifts his head. "Did you know that in the old stories, skinwalkers take powers from blood?" he whispers and I groan again, my eyes widening as a bolt of pure lust and power shoot through me, straight to my pussy.

"They did?" I ask, breathless, my eyes locked on my god.

"Yes, you obviously feed through sex and energy, but I wonder..." He murmurs as an evil grin overtakes his face while he watches me squirm. The thought turns me on until I'm rubbing myself against his hard body for relief.

"I'll take that as a yes." He laughs.

"Nos," I warn, narrowing my eyes on him.

He moves up my body as his lips hover over mine. "Did you know your eyes are a mix of black and white right now? Like a star shooting through the night?" he whispers before kissing me hard, and sweeping his tongue in my mouth.

Groaning into his mouth, I chase him and when he pulls back I nip his bottom lip with my teeth in punishment, but something else guides me and I bite down until blood bursts into my mouth.

He moans, reaches out, and holds my head still. I pull back and lick my lips, enjoying the taste of copper in my mouth...and he was right, the taste of power. It tingles across my tongue.

"Blood is used in many rituals, bindings..." He whispers.

"Bindings?" I gasp.

"Not to worry, Little Monster. You are already bound to me, heart, body, and soul." He grins again.

Raising my other leg, I wrap it around his waist and rub against him. "Change for me," I beg.

"No," he growls, reaching out and clenching his hand around my neck, making me gasp as my breathing is cut off. He holds me there, between pain and pleasure, while he watches me and I watch him, letting him do whatever he wants. "Not this time. This time, I am going to fuck you as a human. If you can still move after, I will change for you and you can have your monster between your thighs."

He lets go of my neck, no doubt leaving a mark behind, but he didn't even use a fraction of his strength, just reminding me what he's capable of. He might be sweet, he might be my safe haven, but he's a fucking god after all. I want it all, his sweet, his bad, his destruction. I want him to carve a path through my body until nothing's left but blood and power.

Crawling down my body, he places a gentle kiss on my belly before nosing at the edge of my panties. His hand strokes up my thigh and I watch in fascination as he holds his fingers up, and my eyes widen as I watch them transform into claws. He swipes away the lace, ripping through it like paper. One of his razor sharp claws catches my hip bone, drawing blood, and he leans over and laves it with his tongue with his eyes still locked on mine.

"You taste like sex, power, and mine," he growls, before licking across my hip to my pelvis. Groaning, I arch into his mouth as he licks down my pussy, parting my lips with his tongue and fingers.

I tug on my bindings and whimper as he sucks my clit before nipping it, his fingers pushing inside of me brutally with no warning, and stretching me as he pulls them out and slides them back in, curling them inside of me to find my sweet spot.

"Nos," I cry, my thighs locking around his head to keep him there.

Raising his head, his lips parted, my juices and blood covering them and his chin, he watches me as I shake and moan before diving back in. With his fingers fucking me, he devours me with his tongue like he did the first time we met.

When he nips at my clit again I scream, fighting my bonds, as I'm thrown into an orgasm. His name is on my lips like a prayer, and I fall back to the bed as he crawls up my body and kisses me, the taste of me on his tongue.

I swivel my hands in the restraints, testing them experimentally before twisting my body, taking Nos with me. He lands on the bed with me on top of him, grinning down at him, with my hands still tied to the headboard.

"You should know by now, you can't contain me," I warn, leaning down and nipping at his chin before sitting up as much as the ties will let me.

"No," he growls, grabbing my hips and throwing me back on the bed next to him, as both of us fight for control.

Landing between my legs, he yanks them farther apart, lines up his cock, and thrusts in, making me yell as I arch up, unsure if I'm fighting to get closer, or farther away.

His hand hits the headboard when he starts moving, his hips rolling with every hard thrust, showing me how strong he is, but he's still holding back.

"Fuck me, I want it all," I moan.

"You are going to have it, don't say I didn't warn you," he growls, raising one of my legs as he starts to hammer into me. He picks up speed until he is almost a blur and his grip is bruising as he spears me on his big cock.

"Yes!" I yell, pushing down as much as I can to meet his thrusts, my body shaking with every strong touch.

Breasts bouncing with his thrusts, my eyes roll back in my head as he drags the head of his cock over that spot inside of me before bumping my cervix.

"Nos, please," I beg.

Pulling out, he impales me on his cock, his balls slapping my skin as he reaches down and flicks my clit, making me scream again as I'm thrown into a second orgasm and he follows, my pussy milking him as he explodes inside of me.

Whimpering, I toss my head when it gets to be too much, the pleasure still cresting with aftershocks every time we move. With a groan, he lays his sweaty head on my heaving chest.

I tug hard on my restraints and free myself, rolling my shoulders to relieve the tension before twining my fingers in his hair, stroking his head as I try to remember how to breathe, with his cock still hard in my pulsing pussy.

He lifts his head and smiles at me, all soft, his eyes still blazing white. "Little Monster."

Smiling, I lean down and kiss him gently. "Now change for me, I want my monster. I want all of you," I demand and he laughs.

"Such a needy little creature, aren't you?" He grins, thrusting into me slowly and making me gasp.

"You're fucking right I am. Change, now," I order, framing his face with my hands. I don't know why I want his other half so much. I loved what we just did, but now my monster side wants to play and it wants his.

He growls as his body shakes and the change comes over him. Antlers sprout from his head and grow out, his eyes lengthen and turn oval. His face, even under my hands, changes. More pointy, more angular, more monster. He stretches above me, taller and monstrous. It makes me groan when that intensity turns on me. He even lengthens and widens inside me, making me moan as he stretches me impossibly farther. When he's human, he is still his monster, but in this form he looks it and he acts more feral.

He growls, sniffing at me, and those white, glowing eyes light up the space between our faces. "Little Monster."

Covering the distance between us, I kiss him hard, sweeping my tongue in as he rumbles against me. I lick at his lips and pull away, my now black eyes meeting his white ones.

"Fuck me, my monster," I purr.

Grabbing onto his antlers I hold on, his cock having grown and expanded inside of me, as he starts to move. He doesn't go slow at first, no, he pummels into me. Driving into me again and again. The pleasure borders on pain as I arch into him, with my head thrown back, and my eyes closed.

Letting go of his antlers, I moan when he flips us and grabs my hips, yanking my ass in the air as he drives back into me. Holding onto the headboard, my face in the pillows, I push back onto his cock as it impales me.

"Mine," he growls, yanking my head back, and stretching my neck in a tight line as he leans down and bites the soft space between my neck and shoulder.

I moan, the pain only adding to the building pleasure. Panting, I push back as he holds me there, fucking me hard. Then he lets go, and I feel the blood trickling down my shoulder and between my breasts.

His hand releases my head, and I lean back against him with my knees spread as he powers in and out of me. His hand slips in the blood and the power tingles across my skin. Gripping my breasts, hard, he holds me against him.

"Yes, god yes," I moan.

"Your fucking god, not any other," he growls, nipping at my skin in warning.

"Yesss," I gasp out. The blood trickles down my body, still leaving power in its wake. Releasing my body, he brings his arm up and slashes his own wrist open, letting his blood pool in his palm. Pushing my face down with his other hand, I feel every little drop of his blood on my back and each one sizzles with his god powers, making me cry out and writhe on his dick buried deep inside me.

When he starts painting my back with it, I scream, and my body lights up like a storm. His power moves through me, feeding me like he said, while it twines with mine. When I open my eyes I spot the white glow from them.

Looking over my shoulder, I watch the beauty that is my monster. He speeds up his thrusts, each one slamming me forward and his body blurs. His antlers jangle when he throws his head back and roars as I come around his cock, milking him. He thrusts twice more before stilling, holding me close as his come lashes inside me.

My throat is sore from where I obviously screamed my release, and I collapse into the blood and cum covered sheets, my eyes already shutting in exhaustion, even with a satisfied smile curling my lips.

CHAPTER 35

ASK A

As soon as I close my eyes, I reach for her. Searching across the distance for her, it doesn't take long, and when the blackness clears she faces me in a short, almost sheer white dress, her blonde hair dripping in red blood.

She tilts her head to the side as she eyes me, and when I look down I am in nothing but my skin. Her eyes show no sense of hesitance or embarrassment as she takes me all in. I let her, not moving until her eyes meet mine again, filled with a fire that wasn't there before.

Striding across the distance, she meets me halfway and our lips clash in a desperate kiss. I grab her cheeks and hold her to me as I kiss her. Her hands reach up, twisting in my hair as she moans, my tongue sweeping in and tangling with hers.

Slowing the kiss down, she pulls back before swallowing hard, her lips swollen and pink as she searches my eyes. "Mate?" she asks, and I nod.

She licks her lips as we stare at each other, our bodies not touching but close together. "Are you safe?" I question, needing to know.

"Yes." She doesn't elaborate, so I nod.

"I am coming, soon," I promise and she tilts her head again.

"Where are you?" She drops to the floor, sitting crossed-legged.

I follow her down, leaning back on my hands as I watch her.

"Not too far now. It should only take me two weeks to get to you," I add and she grins.

"You didn't answer the question," she teases and I laugh.

"I guess I didn't." Leaning forward, I drop my hands between us. "What are you, neriso?"

She grins and stands, glancing over her shoulder before turning back to me with a twinkle in her eye. "Why don't you come and find out, dragon?" With that she blows a kiss as her body starts to fade from view until I am left alone in the dream space.

My eyes flash open, as I lie in the middle of the bed on my mountain estate while the sun starts to rise, bleeding through the sky and lighting up the room. The water sparkles as I lie here, and I raise my fingers to my lips, capturing the fleeting warmth of my mate's kiss.

I take a moment to center myself before I hear the rumbling of a car heading up the mountain. Sighing, I get up and get dressed, ready to meet Jean Paul and head out.

I wait and look out of the window, but I don't move as the car stops outside and the front door opens.

"Sir?" comes a hesitant voice.

"In here," I call back, sipping my glass of water.

His boots are loud on the floor and I hear him mumble a curse when he almost slips on a body. "Sir?" he squeaks, and when he sees me, I watch his reflection in the window before turning. He isn't what I was expecting.

He still has the family's iconic red hair, but other than that he looks nothing like anyone of his line. His red hair is short and styled up on his head. A plain grey, V-neck shirt hugs his barrel chest and stretches across his tattooed arms. Both are covered in sleeves and I smirk at the dragons, fire, and crown drawings, but upon closer inspection they are the original drawings from the Sinclair journals. I remember the day he showed them to me. He's tall, nowhere near as tall as me, but a good size for a human. He has a fire in him, one I can see from here—a drive, a determination.

He completely ignores the bodies, smart man. He doesn't cower either, also a good sign.

"I have everything ready for you outside. Clean up and sweep crew are going to be here at eleven AM. Would you like some breakfast before you go?" He holds up two fast food containers and my stomach growls loud enough for him to hear.

He smiles. "I'll take that as a yes. I shall grab the plates."

Sitting across from Jean Paul, the pancakes, bacon, and sausage he brought spread out between us, I watch him as he eats. "I am assuming you learned everything from your father?"

He covers his mouth and swallows. "Nope, my mother. She was the first female in the line to take up our sacred mission. She would have loved to meet you..." He looks down and I frown. He is not so old that his mother should not still be here. Unless...

"She died, cancer," he says, his voice sad as he picks at his food. Humans are so fragile and cancer is a horrible disease, one I have seen ravage more than one of my friends. That helplessness still lives on in me and was one of the reasons I retreated. I loved humans, but I couldn't save them and I grew tired of watching them wither and die, not being able to do anything.

"I am truly sorry," I offer and he nods, giving me an understanding look before sitting back, obviously done eating.

He shakes his head and that smile comes back to his face. "What is your mate like? Have you met her?" he inquires, excitement clear on his face.

"I have met her in our dreams, she is very powerful. Very beautiful as well...she makes my heart race and I feel like a babe again whenever she looks at me with those sparkling eyes. No one has ever called me like she does, even across the world she is right here with me."

I stop, blinking at the oversharing on my part. Jean Paul is very easy to talk to.

"That's amazing, I can't wait to meet her. I wish humans had the same experience," he jokes.

"What you have is beautiful in itself, you find one or more person and you chose to spend the rest of your life with them. Sometimes it doesn't work out, sometimes it does, but you love so deeply and so fully. You feel everything. It's a choice, and it's beautiful. Before my mate, it was like living in the grey. Everything was colourless, I was screaming and alone and she walked in and everything came back to life...but for some who never find their true mate or the call...they are doomed to spend their life like that. Always wondering and never experiencing." I pause, gritting my teeth.

"That's horrible," he whispers, looking at me with stricken eyes.

I shrug and lift what he called coffee to my mouth and sip it. "It is the way of life. Now, I must get going. Everything is prepared?" I ask, standing from the table.

He scrambles to follow me, talking as we walk, as he almost runs to keep up with my larger strides. "Yes, sir. Everything is ready for you." He passes over the keys as I open the door and spot the vehicle waiting for me. It's black and sleek.

"What is it?" I question, confused.

"It's a sports car, sir, I figured you wanted fast." He grins and I laugh.

"Take care, Jean Paul. I shall ring if I need anything." I extend my hand and he smiles, shaking it heartily.

"I will wait for your call." I nod and head down the steps towards the car where I can already see the bags waiting for me.

"Good luck with your mate, sir, I hope she is everything you ever dreamed about!" he shouts from the door.

Oh she is, but just wait until she meets her nightmare—me.

CHAPTER 36

DUME

The clothes are tight, so much so that I had to rip the sleeves away from the shirt to make sure it fits. The pants reach my ankles and are pretty much skintight, but they will do until I can find more and obviously before I meet my mate. It won't do to present myself as if I am unable to dress myself.

Leaving the guest bedroom, I head downstairs, ignoring the looks thrown my way. I follow the scent of the dead, not that they smell bad but just...not alive. I find Carmichael sitting in the kitchen, nursing a suspiciously red cup of warm liquid.

Sitting opposite him at the dining nook, I squish into the small chair with my legs spread as I kick back and watch him. I have never been a talker. Keeping my mouth shut kept me alive in the arena and throughout my life more times than I can count. It also serves to unnerve people, like now, when even Carmichael glances away.

"What are your Outcasts?" I rumble. I understand the basics, but I am confused why so many different species are clumping together. Just in this house alone, I can smell over thirty different species. Most hate each other, sticking to their own kind and land, never interacting. It works for the best.

"Exactly what the name says. Outcasts, freaks, the ones the other species don't want. Some are born different, some it's their lifestyle, but all have been rejected by their family or species. With nowhere else to go they became nomads, as was I after our...little meeting. I grew sick of that life, always moving. Always fighting, always watching my own back. I wanted roots and so did a lot of others it seems. So I started my own fucking species, one not limited by what or who you are. As long as you are part of this family, you can be or do whatever the fuck you want. We watch out for each other, we are a true family." He gestures around as he speaks, and I can hear the fondness and truth in his words. I have been a nomad, as he would say, for a long time, the only one of my species to live. My queen slaughtered the others, either in the great wars, the labyrinth, or the arenas. It is all I have ever known, I cannot imagine a life like he has made here, but I am happy if it works for him.

I nod and he laughs.

"Still not a talker, eh? That's fine I can talk enough for the both of us. I'm unsure how the witches got the drop on us, but rest assured they will not again, but brother, you must watch your back. They are after your blood and they won't stop until they have it. This was only the first, a test. You know better than anyone what they are capable of," he warns, serious for once, and I nod before swinging my gaze out of the glass door at the end of the room to the back garden.

He is right, they won't stop. They will get the best of the best, the trackers and summoners, to come after us. One wields demons like pets, the other uses their magic and can find you wherever you go—you are never free and I'm leading them straight to my mate.

But, I have no choice, do I? If they find out she is my mate then they will go for her anyway, and if I am not there I can't protect her. If I go and they didn't know, they would be able to use her as bait.

"I can see that mind of yours turning, do not let them scare you off. You have been waiting too long to find a mate, and it's not something everyone gets. Do not turn away in fear of what could happen. The fates have chosen her for you, she will be stronger than you could ever expect. You need each other, now more than ever. Brother, stay true to the course," he adds, his logic sound for once.

Looking at the table, I blow out a breath. He is right, first I will find my mate. Then I will deal with the witches. I just hope she is strong enough to stand by my side...it is all I have ever wanted.

"Is the plane ready?" is all I say, even though my head is crowded with thoughts.

He grins and claps, getting to his feet. "Of course, go get your girl."

Nodding, I stand and clap him on the back before turning and leaving without looking back. No more of that, everything is about my future now. Everything is about her.

CHAPTER 37

GRIFFIN

Lifting the weight over and over, I yell and throw it at the wall as she screams again. Once they had started going at it for real I retreated to the basement, sticking on my music to cover the noise of him fucking my mate, but it's not working. It's like my brain can't escape it. Half of me wishes it was me, the other half hates them both.

Getting to my feet and ripping off my t-shirt so I'm just in my black mesh shorts, I grab the steel bar and start pulling myself up, faster and faster, concentrating on the burn in my muscles rather than the moans of pleasure still echoing around my head, imprinted there.

I wonder if she would scream like that for me. Shaking my head against the thought, I growl and push myself faster, reminding myself of all the reasons why I don't want a mate, especially a fucking skinwalker with a fucking god for a pet.

No, she's better getting the fuck away from me and fast. Dropping from the bar when it doesn't work either, I head over to the home firing range and grab my ear muffs, hoping it will help.

I lay out an arrangement of different weapons and lose myself in them. From throwing stars to guns, I fire and fire, trying to ignore everything. Especially the scent of my mate, which seems to follow me wherever I go.

Yelling, I throw a star, reliving memories of another woman I cared for dying in my arms. I grab my head and hit it again and again, trying to push the memory away.

The warmth of her blood as she gasped her last breath. The blue of her eyes as she started at me with fear. The pale colour of her skin and the coolness of the floor underneath my feet. The mocking laughter as they came towards me with the hot rods and cleaver for my wings.

Screaming, I hit myself again, trying to make it go away, trying to knock it out of my mind. This, this is why I should never have a mate. They are right. Stripping our wings—it fucks us up. I am far too fucking crazy and messed up for her.

"Grif—" She coughs, her blood coating her lips.

Shouting, I throw myself at the wall, ramming my head into the concrete again and again.

"Griffin."

Bang.

"Griffin!" Her voice blends with another, and when a soft hand comes between my head and the wall I freeze, before turning my head slowly. The blood drips down steadily, almost blinding me.

The artificial light frames her as she frowns at me. Her blonde hair is a mess, floating around her, and she's in a borrowed shirt that smells like Nos. I turn away from her, disgusted with myself. I grit my teeth, of course she would see me when I'm at my worst.

"Grif—"

Breathing deep, I push back the memory, her touch helping even if I will never tell her that. "What the fuck are you doing down here?" I growl.

"I could ask you the same thing," she snarls back, pulling her hand away, and when I turn my back to the wall, she steps in front of me with her arms crossed, obviously trying to look intimidating, but all it does it showcase her rosy nipples poking through the white shirt.

"What the fuck do you want? Taking a break?" I sneer at her, but she just raises her eyebrow at me.

"Griffin," she barks.

Fury bursts through me, how dare she? This is my fucking home and she's my fucking mate! Pushing away from the wall, I advance on her. My powers and emotions are going haywire, so much so that I can't control them.

She caught me at my weakest.

Broken.

Crazy.

"You think you can just go wherever the fuck you like? Walking around here like you're the fucking queen bee? Because what? The hole between your legs? Or the magic you think holds us together?" She doesn't step back, she coolly faces down my anger.

I stop when our noses are touching, both of us breathing heavily as I spit the venomous words at her. "You are nothing. You are a fucking face stealer, a fucking parasite."

Her eyes flash black before the colour bleeds across them, her body vibrating with matching anger. Good, she should be, it's better than her sympathy or worse, pity.

"And you are the parasite's mate," she yells back. Getting in my face.

"I am nothing to you. By morning, you will be gone, out of my fucking life, and I never want to see your fucking face again," I yell.

"Liar!" She pushes my chest and I stumble back a step, not expecting it.

I expected her to cry, cower, or to turn away from me in disgust.

"You are a fucking liar." She pushes me again and I fall back from her strength. "Your words are a fucking weapon, sharper than any down here." She shoves me until I fly backwards and hit the wall, and then she pins me there with her body, all in my face. "You want me, you want the call, but you're scared," she purrs, the black of her eyes reflecting my image.

Growling, I grab her under her arse and spin, before slamming her into the wall. "Who's the liar now? You are the one who wants me, not the other way around." I hold her with my body and grab the shirt, ripping it in two so it hangs in tatters at her shoulder, exposing the valley between her breasts. Reaching my hand under the fabric, I groan when I meet the wet skin of her pussy.

I lean in and whisper against her, "Now who's the fucking liar?" I cup her and she rubs against me even as she growls.

"You're a fucking coward," she spits.

"And you are nothing." Pushing a finger into her, I tighten my hold as her wet heat holds me snugly.

Pulling out, I yank at my shorts and kick them off while she glares at me.

"What, little Griffin got his wings clipped? Big fucking deal, get the fuck over it. It doesn't mean you can be such a prick to everyone. No wonder you're alone," she yells, fighting me as I line up and slam into her.

Her tight, wet pussy clings to me as I gnash my teeth, and pull out before ramming back in, smacking her back into the wall as she wraps her legs around me.

"I will be back to being alone after tomorrow, you're nothing but a quick fuck." I lie, lying to myself and her as I hammer into her.

She grabs the metal bar above her head, stretching her body up, and the shirt flutters around her to show me her nipples peeking out. Leaning in, I bite one and leave an imprint of my teeth. She moans, long and loud, her pussy pulsing around me, making me groan as I pull out and thrust back in, her arse jiggling with the movement.

"Like I would ever accept you as a mate," I sneer, loving it when she gets angry. I need her to be so that she fights me, so that she stays in this moment with me and doesn't let me slide back into the memories. I need her fury, her rage.

Growling, her fingers cut down my back like claws, making me growl and lunge to bite the other nipple, matching the other with a red imprint of my teeth. She yells, her hand yanking my head back as she moves fast, her surprisingly sharp teeth biting into my neck, hard.

I snarl and grip her arse harder, no doubt leaving bruises, and speed up, my hips pistoning again and again as she screams, her pussy clamping around me, milking me.

I feel my balls tightening and my belly clenches as I explode inside her, making her take all of my cum as I still. Both of us are breathing heavily as I stare into her eyes before slipping out and dropping her to her feet. She stumbles, but I yank up my shorts and high tail it out of there. Her mocking laughter following me.

"Coward."

She's right. I am, because she fucking terrifies me. What kind of woman would just accept all my vile and hate, and keep pushing me? Making me spew everything out, all that's in my head? Who is she to pull me from my pain and crazy, and make me feel?

I was so fucking wrong, she is not nothing. She is everything.

CHAPTER 38

DAWN

Leaning back against the wall with wobbly legs, I wince as the door slams shut as he leaves me alone down here. I wrap my arms around my chest and cringe at the liquid dripping between my thighs. What the hell just happened?

I only came down here because I woke up with a horrible feeling in my chest, like he needed me. It pulled me down here and I saw him trying to knock himself out, and it's my fault?

Shaking my head in confusion, I look around and take in the space. I never realised there was a basement, but I don't know how. It's got a fucking firing range for god's sake and a full gym. No wonder he was down here.

I mean, it probably didn't help that Nos and I had loud sex. That couldn't have been fun, but he hadn't shown any real indication he cared. Even as he was spitting those horrible insults and words, his eyes begged for me. It's like he doesn't even know himself or what he wants.

Nos warned me, he told me he might be slightly off the rails because of the wing stripping, but I didn't listen...yet, I wouldn't change what just happened for anything. I loved it, loved his anger, both of us fighting. It was hot as hell and for some reason, the thought that he's crazy only makes me more intrigued.

Maybe I'm the crazy one, not him.

Waddling because, well, after sex is never fun, I climb the stairs and head straight to the spare bathroom. Stripping out of the unsavable shirt, I give myself a whore's bath in the sink, wincing as I graze my sore nipples. That rat bastard, he's left a red mark of his teeth around both, nearly drawing blood.

I flick off the overhead light with a sigh and head onto the landing. Hesitating, I sigh again. I might not like him very much right now, but he's hurting, that much is clear.

"Goodnight, Griffin," I say, loud enough for him to hear. He doesn't respond, not that I expected him to.

I head back to the guest bedroom and crawl into bed and Nos' waiting arms, and close my eyes. The sore twinge between my legs makes me smile, even as I fall asleep.

I wake up warm and content, before turning over with a groan and burying my face in something hard. Cracking open one eye, I spot an expanse of bare skin and follow it up to see Nos already awake and staring at me, with his arm under my head and his free hand stroking the skin of my thigh and side.

"Good morning, Little Monster," he rumbles.

"Ugh, please tell me you aren't a morning person," I mumble, burying my head back in his chest as he shakes with silent laughter.

"More like a mid-morning person, though, you did have a late night," he comments, and I open my eyes again with a suffering sigh and lean back, trying to gauge his mood.

"You knew about that?" I ask, confused.

He grins at me and the worried ball in my stomach disappears. "Little Monster, I have more developed senses than you could ever realise. He is your mate, do not feel guilty. He clearly needed you, but if he ever insults you again, I will rip him limb from limb," he growls, and his eyes flash white, making my pussy pulse.

Goddamn, I am so fucked up.

"Noted. We should probably get up," I suggest and he shakes his head.

"Not yet. First, let me just hold my mate for a while, and good morning." He leans down and sweeps a soft kiss along my lips, making me smile.

"Hmm, you might be able to make me a morning person after all," I joke, making him laugh again.

CHAPTER 39

I had woken up early and decided to get some work in while the house was quiet. Setting up on the kitchen table with a mug of coffee and my laptop, I plug in the USB I had filled with information from the warehouse when Dawn wasn't looking. Thinking of her, I look up at the ceiling before shaking my head and logging into my laptop.

I can't say I'm sorry about what happened last night, even if I should be. I am sorry about how it happened though. I had snapped and gone into one of what the council calls 'madness spirals,' and she had tried to pull me out. Some of the things I had said to her had been disgusting and I'm so ashamed, she deserves better than a mate like me.

Ignoring my self-hate, I open the USB and start clicking through files. Most of it has to do with transactions, videos of girls, and buyer lists. All handy to track down the human monsters, but I'm looking for who is buying the others. Anything, something.

I spend hours trawling through footage, which makes me sick to my stomach, and paperwork, before I hear movement upstairs followed by a giggle.

My hand tightens on the mug in my hand and I growl at myself when I crush it, the pieces cutting into my hand. Standing with a sigh, I throw it in the bin and wash out the cuts before heading back to my laptop to keep searching.

When I hear footsteps on the stairs, I stare at the screen intently, not wanting to see the damnation on either of their faces in the morning light.

"Morning," Nos greets me, way too chipper for the morning as he heads over to the kettle and just makes himself at fucking home.

I nod and go back to the screen, but freeze when Dawn comes to stand over my shoulder. Her smell hits me, all sin and sex as she moves closer, not even flinching when she lays a hand on my shoulder to look closer.

"What are you doing?" she asks and I frown, turning back to the screen.

"Looking at some information I collected from the warehouse," I mutter and she moves away, leaving a warm imprint in my shoulder that I want to reach up and clasp.

"Let me know if you find anything useful. I have a bunch of paperwork upstairs we could go through as well." She smiles and sits down, but she winces and I freeze. She must see it because she rolls her eyes.

"It seems I heal fast, but bites from fallen, not so much." She points at her nipples and I bark out a laugh, looking to her mate to see if he cares. He either ignores it or doesn't care as he brings over two mugs before going back for another, setting it down in front of me. Pissing me off. Why does he have to be so fucking nice when I've been nothing but an asshole to him? It makes me look petty, unless that's why he's doing it.

"I'll go get the paperwork, one sec." She jumps out of her chair and races upstairs, and both Nos and I watch her go.

The nice act drops in a second as he turns to me with a deadly look in his eyes, and I'm reminded of exactly what kind of monster is sitting at my kitchen table.

"You ever talk to my mate, your mate, like that again, and I will rip your fucking tongue from your throat and feed it to the wolves," he warns, his eyes flashing white as his body seems to grow. He leans closer and I arch my eyebrow. "I might not be able to kill you, she likes you too much, but I will make your life hell. You better decide real quick what way you want this to go, because I will take you breaking her heart as a form of hurt as well, are we clear?" he snarls.

"Crystal," I sneer. "You're welcome to her though, I don't want or need a mate," I repeat, the words sounding like a lie, even to myself.

He just snorts, his face and eyes returning to normal. "Whatever you say Fallen, lie to yourself if you have to. It won't make it any easier."

I go to ask what that means when she bounds back into the room with a happy smile on her face as she lays the paperwork between her and me on the table.

"So, what's your plan?" I find myself asking.

She leans back, bringing her knees up and resting her head on them as she looks at the table. "Hmm, well, I was going after my husband—" Nos growls and she rolls her eyes. "Ex-husband, but I've already ruined his love life and sort of his money line now. I'm thinking I might expose him to Victor, and in return for proof of their deceit, ask for me to be able to kill him. Payback and all that. But first, I think we need to figure out who is hunting and buying supes. Especially women."

I raise my eyebrows at the 'we' and the well-thought-out plan. It's obvious she's smart and has been thinking through every step.

"Well, I have paper trails between Marco, Tim, and Victor's money here. We could take that to him." Fuck, why did I say we? She obviously notices the slip because she smiles.

"We, huh?" She grins as Nos laughs.

Fucking skinwalkers.

Dawn

He glares before looking back at his laptop. "As for the others, there isn't much here. Our best bet is to track down other members who were working with Marco and Tim, and getting information from them. If we could track or trace the women as well, that would be good," he murmurs as if talking to himself.

"Sounds great, but breakfast first," I add, my stomach rumbling on cue.

"Fuck's sake," Griffin mutters, but he gets up, goes to the fridge, and starts rummaging around. Letting him have his huff, I start digging through the paperwork and passing some to Nos, planning to look for any indication of who's buying these women or who we could hunt next.

He bangs the pots and pans around, making my lips twitch as I scour the pages. About twenty minutes later, omelettes get pushed onto the table as he goes back to his seat, ignoring us both.

I tuck into the omelette, groaning at the peppers and cheese. He is such a good cook. When I look up, they're both watching me.

"Pervs," I tease as I wipe my plate clean.

Pushing it away, I go back to my paper.

"I think I have something." Griffin breaks the silence and we both scoot closer as I try to look at his screen.

"It seems Marco trusted one man to run the sales of the freaks. His name is Ray Leroy. I can get his address, one second," he murmurs, starting to type on his computer, and when I look over his shoulders I can't even follow what he's doing. I glance at Nos and he shrugs.

"Got it, okay, so we go to him. Squeeze him for information on who's selling the supes. Then you can take your shit to Victor," he grumbles, leaning back and finally looking at me.

"Okay. I'm going to shower and then we can get going." I down the last, cold dregs of my coffee before pushing away from the table and sauntering back upstairs, feeling both of their eyes on me the whole way.

Grinning, I head to the spare bathroom and flick on the shower. Steam soon fills the room and I jump in, sighing in contentment as it washes away the gross feeling on my skin and relaxes my muscles.

I lean against the wall and let the water run down me. It's been a busy week. Between dying and coming back, not to mentioning finding two mates, getting kidnapped and escaping, and being brought into a plot to sell supernaturals, oh and dreaming of a dragon who is also apparently my mate, I'm feeling pretty wrecked, so I just take the moment to relax and breathe.

Opening my eyes, I scrub my body and hair, before flicking off the shower and getting out. I realise my problem straight away. There are no towels, and unless I want to put back on the t-shirt I grabbed this morning, I'm going to have to go out naked.

Fuck it.

Opening the door, I slip into the hallway and run into a hard body. I bounce off and fall into the wall. Growling, I glare at a smirking Griffin.

"Were you just waiting outside the bathroom? Because that's just creepy, dude," I comment, crossing my arms under my breasts. If he thinks he can make me uncomfortable just because I'm naked then he has another thing coming.

Arching his eyebrow, he mirrors my stance and leans back against the other wall, watching me. His eyes drop to my body like he can't help himself, and everywhere they look I feel a red-hot burning, like he's physically touching me. Shivering in desire, I clench my thighs together, which only makes his eyes pull back to mine, and they're filled with knowing and amusement. Ass.

I tilt my head back and return his stare. From the way his eyes tighten and he tries to push himself back, I can tell he isn't used to it and doesn't like it. He's so cocky and sure of himself all the time, but it's obvious that he isn't used to anyone looking past his attitude and anger. He expects people to be scared of him or use him. I see it all, and from the tension in his body, he knows it.

Pushing from the wall, I saunter towards him until my body is plastered against his and I meet his mismatched eyes. "You know, your bullshit might fool some, but it doesn't fool me." Smirking at him, I turn and leave him to it.

I couldn't have two more opposite mates, and I'm finding I love the challenge. I love Nos' sweetness and brutality, and I even like Griffin's take no shit attitude and hardness.

Getting dressed in some skintight leather pants, just to piss Griffin off seeing as though he appears to be obsessed with them, I add a filmy white shirt, matching leather jacket, and some biker boots. I brush my hair and add some red lipstick—thankfully, I had fun on my shopping trip and Nos grabbed all my bags before he left.

Looking in the mirror, I can admit I look hot. Death was good for me. I don't hunch or flinch anymore, and my eyes don't hold a sadness or the expectation of when the other shoe is going to drop again.

No, my shoulders are back and I have a new sensuality and power. It shows in the way I hold myself and the look in my eyes. I might not be good, I might not be pure, but I sure as shit am no victim and that's good enough for me.

Grinning, I head downstairs to see that Griffin, now loaded up in weapons and looking like a walking armoury, is glaring at Nos as he sits on the sofa watching the pacing man. When I come downstairs, however, he stops pacing and both him and Nos look over at me. Their eyes flash as they take in my outfit.

Winking, I grab the front door. "Ready?" I open it and they both rush to follow after me.

CHAPTER 40

DUME

One of Carmichael's family, as he calls them, drives me back to the airstrip. I nod my thanks and watch them drive off before turning back to the plane. Frowning, I eye the dead beast. No lights are on inside, no whirring of the engine, no crew waiting. It looks deserted.

Slipping my swords from the sheath at the base of my spine, I stride up to the aircraft and whatever is waiting inside for me. I should have known the witches would have a backup plan up their sleeves, but they did one thing wrong—got in the way of me and my mate.

I climb the stairs and step into the plane, and sweep my eyes around, my night vision allowing me to see easily. The pilots and flight attendant are tied up in the cockpit and gagged, their eyes are wide and filled with fear as they look beyond me to where the darkness is almost impenetrable at the back of the plane.

Almost, but not quite.

"Demon," I greet and it hisses. The black mist, which occurs when a demon is summoned and contained within a space, swirls and starts to burn as a man breaks through the darkness.

The lights flicker before coming on, remaining dimmed above him as he smirks at me.

"Minotaur," it mocks, its voice distorted for a moment as he flickers back to his true form before settling into that of a middle-aged, attractive male. Probably one of the souls he has killed and kept.

Demons can appear in whatever form they want, depending on how powerful they are. Lower ones can only appear in their hellspawn form, but the more powerful they are the more forms they have. This one is clearly powerful, and it wants me to know it as it steps forward, changing to that of a brown-haired woman in the same breath.

"It seems you have pissed off the witches." It spits the name, no happier than I was to have been trapped by them. Demons live on a different plane, they are content enough to stay there with the odd break through to ours, but witches, the summoners, learned how to harness their powers and actually call them through the breach. The first couple of times the demon killed the summoner and returned to their own world, but the summoners soon got a handle on it and now they are theirs to control. I should know, it was my queen who ordered them to do it.

"It seems you are their slave," I respond, turning so my back is to the cockpit and I brace my legs. Demons are unpredictable, forceful, and a fucking pain to try and kill.

There are only three ways. You break the bindings and sometimes they will let you live. You kill them, which only a magically enchanted blade can do. Or you send them packing back to their world, which only witches or magical beings can do. Seeing that I don't have a blade and I can't send them back. That leaves me with the first option—negotiation. Something I hate on the best of days.

His face morphs back to its true form before settling back into the man, but that flash tells me all I need to know. It hates being trapped and it hates the witches.

Stepping forward, I meet it in the middle. It watches me curiously, its snake-like eyes flickering.

"I'm betting they summoned you and trapped you in their coven, their own fucking monster to kill for them," I say conversationally, and the fire that starts in its eyes lets me know I am right. "I know, because they did the same to me."

"What are you saying?" it asks, tilting its head.

"I am saying, I will break your bindings, but you will not attack me or any on this plane. You will go back to the witches who imprisoned you and kill them all," I offer bluntly and it laughs, throwing its head back as the sound echoes around the space like nails on a chalkboard. I hear the humans cry out and I feel blood drip from my own ears, but I don't move to wipe it away. I let it fall as the demon looks back at me with interest in its eyes.

"You would trust me not to kill everyone on this plane?" It laughs.

"No, I would make a binding with you," I inform it with a snort.

Its eyes widen before they settle and a grin stretches across his face. "You are clever, you know demons."

"I know monsters," I reply and it laughs again.

"I would think so, seeing as though you are one of the greatest, the beast of Cornacadia." It steps back, standing down.

"Do we have a binding?" I growl, sick of games.

"Yes, yes minotaur. I will not kill any of these people or you, and you shall release me so I may return to those doomed witches and kill them all." It changes back to its demon form, licking its lips at the thought of the witches' deaths.

Its black horns are so large they almost meet in the middle, with a ball of flames constantly moving between them both. Its eyes are small and slit like a snake's. It has no eyebrows or nose, and just two small, thin lips. Its ears are pointed and stretches out like a fae, and its skin colour is a mix of black and red.

They don't look like the ones you see in movies or books, they are terrifying, and most humans can't stand to look at them without wanting to claw their own eyes out. Even now, I step between it and the humans to make sure they don't. I can't have a blind pilot, now can I?

I nod and it holds out its hand and I can just about see the glimmering of the magic binding it. I am really hoping this works since I have never tried it before. Gripping my sword, I touch it lightly to the band on my arm before raising it and bringing it down on the magic holding it.

I am thrown backwards as it breaks. Clutching my sword, I

quickly jump to my feet in case it still tries to attack. All it does is rolls its shoulders with a murderous grin on its face before it salutes me, and with a pop and the smell of sulfur, disappears.

The lights come back on and the plane heats up. Shaking out my arms, I sheath my swords and turn to the pilots. I kneel and undo their bindings.

"Let's go," I order, before turning and taking my seat at the back of the plane. I close my eyes as a small smile plays on my face. I can almost hear the screams and pleas of the witches as they die.

CHAPTER 41

DAWN

R ay's house looks like a drug den. For someone who makes so much money from selling and betraying humans, you would think he would live somewhere fancier. I guess it makes it easier though, no one will bother to look and they will ignore the screams.

The outside is dirty and covered in graffiti, and the once white paint of the two story, detached house is fading and rotting. The front garden is overrun and looks like it's never been looked after. The driveway is empty and crumbling.

"Are you sure this is the place?" I ask Griffin.

He's behind me, lurking in the shadows, while Nos stands by my side.

"Yes," he snaps.

Arching my eyebrows, I look over my shoulder at him and give him a warning look, before turning back to the house. I step off the curb, make my way around the dimly lit road, and up the drive. We are on the other side of town, even past the warehouse district, and it's obvious no one cares about anything out here. Maybe that's why he chose it.

With no other options, I knock on the door politely and wait. Nos and Griffin stand at my back, a god and a genetically engineered assassin, I wouldn't open the door either.

Frowning, I raise my fist and knock again.

"Someone is coming," Nos comments, and when I look over at him he taps his ear. "Ears of bat, eyes of an eagle." He winks.

I grin and turn back just as the door opens, revealing the man I'm guessing we are looking for. Blinking, I do a double take. I expected a guy similar to Marco, but this guy is nothing like him at all.

Craning my neck back, I stare at his scarred face. Well, shit. So many scars criss-cross on his face, like he was pushed into a barbed fence, that I give up trying to count them. His left eye is slightly droopy and his lips are pressed in a thin, tight white line. His head is shaved, and a skull tattoo runs all the way around, from what I can see.

His body is similarly as huge, encased in a black, long-sleeve top and jeans, with black army style boots on his feet.

"Ray?" I inquire, because really, he looks like he should be called Blade or some scary ass shit.

"Who's asking?" he demands, his voice rough and deep. He sounds like he smokes ten packs a day.

Looking behind me in confusion, I point at my own chest, playing dumb. "Me, I would be asking." I smile and flutter my lashes, but his eyes only narrow on me, not once sparing a look for the men at my back.

"What the fuck do you want, whore?" he spits out and I blink, taken back.

"How rude, do you kiss your momma with that mouth?" I sass, wanting to lean forward and prove what a little bitch I am. I'm betting he would be faced with my monster side.

He steps forward, right into my space, and smirks. "If you want some cock, fuck your way through the city. So tell me, why the fuck are you at my door, calling me a name not even my brother dares call me?"

Hmm. To cut off his balls or not to cut off his balls? This dude is really pissing me off. If it wasn't for the fact I know I need him alive, I would have already jumped him.

"Listen up fuck face, if you want to measure dicks then do that with your buddies. Now, I suggest you let me in before I get bored and decide to make you," I reply sweetly.

He scoffs, crossing his arms and glares at me.

"My mate has a tendency to rip people apart...or kill them. She's not fussy, so let us in before I get a front row seat to the blood-bath," Nos remarks, and I wink at him over my shoulder. When I look at Griffin, I see that his eyes are locked on my ass, perv.

"You have three seconds to decide, no wait. I'll make it five, you look like you're a slow learner," I taunt. Lifting my left hand, I pop down my thumb. "Four," I count calmly.

He glares, blocking the doorway. I pop down another finger. "Three."

"Two."

He shifts, reaching for the weapon no doubt concealed at his back.

"One," I growl, and fling myself at him.

He stumbles back, trying to avoid me, and trips over the step, going down hard. Crouching over his chest, I let a growl rumble out, certain my eyes are turning black while I grin at him.

"Your eyes! Your, uh, teeth!" he yells, and I sit back on my haunches and look at the guys for clarification.

"You have fangs, Little Monster." Nos winks and shuts the door behind them both.

"Huh, that's new," I reply before jumping up.

Grabbing the guy by his shoulder, I heave and pull him farther into the living room before throwing him on the couch. I circle the couch and press my arm across his neck as I look at Nos and Griffin. Then, I let everything go, going full monster as I lick up the man's face.

"He tastes weak, do you think we could make him scream?" I murmur, and he starts to fight me, but even with all his muscles and strength, I pin him with one arm.

Griffin leans back into the wall, watching me in amusement. "Why don't you try?" he challenges with a grin.

"With pleasure," I purr, and circle back around the sofa until I can straddle Ray's lap.

His eyes fly wide as he searches the room, obviously confused about what's going on. I stroke his face and lean down until our lips are nearly touching. "You are going to tell us whatever we want to know, aren't you, Ray Ray?" I coo and he glares at me, his hands grabbing my hands and squeezing. I don't even wince, instead, I grin.

"Fuck you, crazy," he sneers.

Griffin growls. "Only I get to insult her," he warns and I laugh.

Seems my mate is getting wound up and a part of me wants to push him further. So that's exactly what I do. I lean into Ray and seal our lips together. He tries to fight me, but I grip his cheeks and keep him still while I pull on the light, the soul inside of him. It's tainted and dark and so fucking delicious. Moaning, I writhe on him as I feed. The man's struggling gets weaker and weaker the more I take.

"We need him alive," Griffin points out helpfully, and I lift my head and pout at him where he's now watching from behind the sofa, closer than before. Eyes on his, I drop my lips back to the man's again, and Griffin growls. "*Vasculo,*" he warns. I want to push him, I want to see if he will stop me, what he'll do. He thinks skin-walkers are below him, maybe a little part of me wants to disgust him, or see if I can.

Griffin pushes away from the wall, and the next thing I know he disappears into black mist before appearing behind me. He grabs my head and pulls it back, and the man under me gasps, sucking in breaths and shaking.

Griffin growls and I meet his blue, swirling eyes in the mirror and my own face, with black eyes, reflects there as well. He wraps my hair around his fist and tugs back so my neck is stretched in a thin line, and the pain makes me moan.

"I said no," he growls.

I fight his hold and he swears before reaching down and throwing me over his shoulder. He spins me around and I watch as the man slumps before falling to the floor, throwing me a pale-faced, terrified look as he cries and he tries to crawl away, but Nos blocks his exit.

"Why don't you calm our mate down? I will make sure this parasite doesn't die." I grin at Nos and he blows me a kiss as Griffin strides through the hallway back to a different door. He kicks it in and I only catch a glimpse of a fancy office before I'm thrown onto a wooden desk.

Laying back, my legs parted, I watch as he glares at me. That swirling mist still circles him, obscuring my vision of his legs and arms, and his eyes sparkle blue as he watches me. "I told you, we need him alive," he grits out, his hands slamming on the desk next to me, pinning me in.

I relax into the wood and grin at him. "So?"

"So, you can't fucking kill him! Control your fucking instincts!" he yells, his face red.

"Like you do?" I ask sweetly, and he sucks in a breath before glaring down at me, his face set in a warning.

"*Vasculo*, I mean it. Do not push me, not right now," he growls, his voice guttural, and the next thing I know his wings have burst out of his back. I look at his arms next to my head on the wood to see them shaking.

He's fighting himself, trying to control those instincts that he accused me of giving into, but I was in control all the time. I wanted to see what it took for him to lose it, and it looks like I'm about to find out.

Reaching up, I grip his cheeks and lift his face, wetting my lips at the death and destruction I see in his eyes. It's like the night before, when I found him hurting himself. I can almost taste the madness, and I want more.

He turns his face away as the shadows in the room trying to conceal his face from me and I growl, gripping it harder and turning it back to me.

"Or what?" I grin, showing him how little I care about what he is. I want him, that's all there is to it.

"Dawn," he warns, those eyes like lightning, shooting through the room.

I want to find out what it feels like to be in the middle of his storm.

"Coward," I prod, and it does the trick.

He grabs me from the desk and I gasp as it feels like the whole world is spinning. Looking into his eyes, I see the mist swirling around as he moves us across the room. My back meets the bookcase hard and the mist retreats. His hand darts out, curling around my neck and squeezing as he growls, his eyes completely blue now.

"I warned you." He grins, and jerks his head to the side before looking back at me. Nothing but madness lives in his gaze now, just like last night, but ten times more and I moan, winding my legs around his waist as his wings flutter behind him, blocking all the light and the rest of the room until all I can see is him.

He squeezes harder, cutting off my breathing, and leans in as he licks up my face like I did to the man out there. "You are mine. I wanted to rip the fucking beating heart out of that man for tasting you," he whispers seductively, sounding so sweet as he breathes his madness across me.

Gasping in the little air I can, I close my eyes as he licks my lips before biting down on my lower one. His hand loosens enough for me to suck in air before it tightens again. He licks where he bit, and when I roll my lip in, I can taste my own blood.

"Thought you didn't care and you don't want me, remember?" I tease breathlessly.

"Mine," he growls and bites my neck, making me moan.

I laugh and he grips my throat and smashes my head back, making me grin as he glares at me. Even now, it seems like he's fighting himself on whether he wants me or not.

"Prove it." I grin and reach up to his shoulder, dragging him closer.

Stroking down his back, my hands brush against where his wings meet his skin and I stroke it. He groans, thrusting against me.

"*Vasculo*," he warns.

He squeezes my neck harder and glares at me, while I bring my hand around and skate it down his body until I cup his hard cock in my hand. Dots appear on the edge of my vision as he cuts off my air, thrusting into my hand at the same time. Leaning closer, he bites along my shoulder before growling and reaching out, ripping my shirt down the middle so my bra is exposed.

He grabs one of my breasts and squeezes hard, and my mouth opens, trying to draw in a breath to moan. He yanks down the cup of my bra and sucks one hard nipple into his mouth, laving his tongue over the still sore bite marks from last night.

Swapping to the other side, he sucks that nipple into his mouth before pulling back and blowing on it. My vision is seriously fading, but I refuse to fight him. He wants that, he wants an excuse for me to push him away. Instead, I pull him tighter with my arms and legs.

Even as I can feel myself passing out, I hold on until, with a growl, he rips his hand away and I suck in air, then he smashes his lips to mine. Groaning into his mouth, I inhale his breath as he tangles his tongue with mine. He yanks his mouth away and drops me to the floor, spins me, and pushes me into the bookcase with a bang.

Gripping the shelves on either side of my head, I moan when he kicks my legs open. He reaches around, unbuttons my trousers, and pushes them to my feet before tearing away my panties. Bare before him, I shiver in need. Loving this.

"Yes," I moan, pushing back into him.

He grips my hair again and turns my face so he can see me. "You ever touch him like that again and I will rip his beating heart from his chest," he threatens, and I push back again.

He slams me into the bookcase, the pain mixing with the pleasure as his other hand reaches down and cups my bare pussy. "I mean it."

"I know," I gasp, rubbing against his hand.

"And they say I'm the crazy one," he murmurs, kissing my shoulder lightly as his finger delves inside me, teasing before pulling out. He rubs my clit and has me gasping and moaning in no time, but he pulls away again. Keeping that orgasm out of reach.

He growls and pulls me away from the shelves, and then throws me over his shoulder as he mists across the room. Draping me over the desk, my ass in the air, he grips my hips and drives into me in one smooth move.

Moaning from the pleasure, I grip the edges of the desk and push back, meeting him thrust for thrust as he hammers into me. His hand grips my hair and forces my head up until I notice the window behind the desk. You can clearly see us in the reflection, and I cry out as both of our eyes light it up, our bodies shining as he blurs, fucking me.

Each thrust has me moving forward, the friction rubbing across my breasts, and I soon build back up. He reaches between our bodies and flicks my clit before leaning over me and fitting his body against mine, licking up my spine before biting the base of my neck. I gasp, my eyes nearly closing, but I blink in shock when I spot Nos at the doorway.

His white eyes light up in the reflection, making me cry out as I come, loving that he's watching us. Griffin comes with a yell, his bite getting harder, making me shout out again as I feel him explode inside of me. His thrusts still and his bruising grip on my other hip holds us as close as we can get while we both breathe heavily.

He lets go of my neck and stands up, and I collapse on the desk, watching in the window as he steps back and tucks himself in his jeans before looking over his shoulder. Forcing myself onto wobbly legs, I turn around and almost trip over my leather pants, which I somehow kicked off one leg. I go to bend down to pull them up when Griffin looks back at me. He drops to his knees and taps my leg, so I lift it obediently, and he pulls my jeans back onto it before pulling them up my legs, running his fingers over my skin as he does, making me shiver and my pussy pulse.

He fastens the button before staring up at me with an unreadable expression. Standing, he rights my bra and ties my shirt in a knot to keep it in place before stepping back. He throws me one more look before turning and leaving, and when he reaches Nos' side, he presses my red lacy panties to my god's chest, and then leaves without another word.

My mouth drops open before I giggle. Nos' eyebrow arches as he looks at the panties then at me. "Looks like you two are finally getting on?" he asks.

I shrug and lean back on the desk as he wanders over. He lifts me so I sit fully on the desk and steps between my legs. I reach up and wrap my arms around his neck. "Sort of, we agree on the fucking part."

He shakes his head, a laugh tumbling out. "I can see that. Come on, Little Monster. Time to learn what we came here for." He goes to step away and I frown.

Yanking on his neck, I pull him down and he reluctantly bends his head so I can kiss him softly. He groans, his tongue tangling with mine as he grips the back of my head. I pull back and rest my forehead against his. "I don't know what I would do without you, you pulled me from that grave and haven't left me ever since," I whisper, needing him to know how much he means to me.

"You never have to worry, Little Monster, nothing you ever do will make me leave you. I am at your back at all times," he promises and I smile.

"Promise?" I beg.

"Forever, Little Monster. You will never get away from me." He seals it with a kiss that leaves me breathless before stepping back.

I hop down from the desk and we share a grin, and I watch as he pockets the panties. I don't ask. We twine our fingers together and head back to Ray and Griffin.

215

Chapter 42

GRIFFIN

I ignore Dawn and Nos as they enter the room hand in hand, instead focusing on Ray. Nos had obviously tied him up while I was busy with Dawn, and he's sitting in the middle of the living room now. His hands and legs are bound by rope to a wooden kitchen chair. When I nudge his head up, I smirk at the busted lip and black eye—looks like the god doesn't like others touching his woman either.

"Who are you selling the girls to?" I demand, crouching on the floor in front of him while I play with one of the knives that are stashed on my body.

"Fuck you," he slurs, spitting blood at my feet.

"No thanks, I just fucked her." I jerk my chin at Dawn before swiftly grabbing one of his fingers and pressing my knife under his nail.

"Who?" I ask for the last time, already bored of this game.

The house smells like Dawn and sex, and it's driving me crazy. The quicker we get out of here the better. I don't want to look at her anymore. I gave in a second fucking time. I let her see the madness that lurks within me. I can't let that happen again. I never want her to fear me, even if I don't want her and have no plans on keeping her.

I dig the knife into the bed under his nails and pull up quickly, ripping it away. He screams and his face pales, and I lean back. "Bets on if he passes out?" she says with a laugh, and when I look over, she's sitting on the sofa to the right, watching me intently, with that fucking smile flirting on her lips. I look back at the man when he screams again.

Blood is welling where his nail once was and he's looking at in horror. "I can keep going, eventually you will break. You decide how much torture you go through first," I inform him in a bored voice, twisting my knife in the light to check for blood.

"What-what do you want?" he slurs.

"Keep up, will you? Who do you sell the girls to?" I demand, trying to take shallow breaths as the smell of her seems to intensify. It both calms me and drives me mad, and I don't know how it's fucking possible.

"I don't know, we don't do names. Marco just called them 'The Others'!" he yells, and when I sigh and lean forward he starts fighting in his bonds. "I swear! All I do I is get a text with a drop off location, then they meet me and I take one girl at a time."

I lean back and look over at Dawn and Nos.

"They text you where to meet them?" she clarifies.

"Yes! From a burner phone," he replies, looking at her desperately, like she would save him. He should have learned by now, she's a bigger monster than both of us.

"When's the next one?" She glares.

He stops struggling, throwing us all pleading looks. "Tomorrow night, nine PM, east side docks. One girl."

She gets off the sofa and crouches at my side. I find myself leaning in and sniffing her without meaning to, and almost kick myself.

"Do they know what the girl looks like before?" she asks and I glare, knowing where this is going.

"No, they just know it's a girl, but I have to be there," he adds. Maybe he isn't as stupid as I thought.

"That's not a problem," she purrs, the sound going straight to my cock.

She looks over at me with a smile. "I'll be bait, I can keep him in line and we can see who we're up against."

"No," I say and turn back to the Ray.

She ignores me and keeps talking. "You have a better plan? Know any girls we could use, and then I could go as dickwad here?" She jerks her thumb at Ray who is looking between us, obviously trying to figure out if he's going to die or get tortured some more.

"I say we bring him with us for now while we think over what we need to do. We can tie him up and gag him in your basement," Nos suggests, intervening on the argument brewing between us.

"Fine," I grit out and stand. I reach down automatically and offer her my hand. When I realise what I've done, I swear. She grabs it and I pull her to her feet before letting go, the soft skin of her hand burning a trace where we touched.

"Let's go," I growl.

ASKA

I have been driving for over four hours when I get bored of the open road, not to mention my dragon is roaring inside, hating being trapped in this metal can. Sighing, I pull over to a picnic area and get out of the car to stretch my legs.

No one is around for miles, and the late afternoon sun heats my skin as I reach up to the sky and twist my back to get out all the stiffness from being hunched over the wheel.

Rounding the back of the car, I peek into the boot to see what Jean Paul has packed for me. I didn't look before I left, since I was more bothered about getting on the road and reaching Dawn.

I rifle through the bags and spot the clothes, and even some weapons. Underneath is a wooden chest, protected by the clothes. Running my hands over the carvings on top, I sigh. It has been a long time since I looked inside this box.

I gave it to my human keepers when I had decided to retreat. It holds all of my lineage's heritage and artifacts. The very first ring ever given between the dragon king and his queen, my crown, and so much more. Laying my hand on top, I feel the magic pulsing through the box, calling me to open it.

I hear a car gunning down the road so I quickly cover the box and busy myself in the boot, thinking they will drive past so I can go for a run at least and stretch out my body before I continue on my way. I have calculated it should take at least four or five days to reach Dawn with minimal stops.

But the car doesn't drive past. In fact, I hear them slow down before it pulls onto the gravel behind me. Shutting the boot, I turn around to face them, feeling paranoid, and when I spot the symbol on their chests through the front window, I swear.

How do they keep finding me? I know the car isn't being tracked or bugged, I swept it myself, my paranoia too ingrained to trust Jean Paul completely.

Walking away from the car to give myself some room, I head onto the grass next to the gravel and place the trees at my back as I wait for them to get out of the car. I see them hesitating, obviously expecting to have caught me off guard. They clearly don't know a lot about dragons.

Holding my hands out, I gesture for them to come over with a smile. I wish they would hurry up. Don't they realise I have places to be? Silly hunters.

The doors finally open and four men pour out. Really, four? I am disappointed. I am betting they were only supposed to tail me, but it looks like they are getting brave.

"Just imaging how much pussy and fame we will get if we bring in a dragon!" the driver hisses at the passengers, and I hold up my hand.

They stop, sharing a look, before glaring over at me cockily as they puff out their chests.

"I'm going to stop you there, gentlemen. Yes, I can hear everything you are saying, I can also hear your hearts pounding and smell your fear. This is how it's going to go. You are going to try and attack me, I am going to kill you all. Or, I will let one of you live for messenger purposes. Your choice. I will give you thirty seconds, feel free to discuss." I wave between them as I start to hum, glancing around to give them some form of privacy.

"What do you think?" one of them whispers, not the driver.

"Shut the fuck up Lo, we are killing this cocky fucker!" he shouts, obviously realising I can hear them, no matter what volume they speak.

Looking back at them, I grin as they start coming towards me. They freeze again. "One question, which one is Lo?" I ask conversationally.

The brown-haired, mousy man at the back raises his hand as sweat pours down his head and he glances at the others. "Brilliant, thank you. Proceed," I command.

They are all wearing black—really, what is with the monotone —and the crest of hunters somewhere on their body. I notice each is carrying a gun, and one man has a net and another a knife. I need to kill them before they shoot, being shot isn't fun, and I don't have time to heal, but if they knew they were hunting a dragon they might have altered their bullets to contain Yret—a flower grown in our region, which can be deadly to dragons in certain doses.

I have built up a tolerance, a request made by the council to make sure I could not be poisoned, but it has been a while since I last ingested some and I fear it would slow me down and render me useless for a while. A break I can't afford.

They rush me with a pitiful war cry. Lo and one of the others hangs back, allowing the other two to circle me. One of them spits at my feet and I memorise his face, he will pay for that. No one disrespects a dragon and gets away with it.

Tired of waiting for them to make the first move, I jump the second man and snap his neck easily. As he falls to the ground, I prowl towards the driver.

He glances at the fallen man before glaring at me. "Three way split, no big deal," he bluffs and I grin.

Wagging my finger, I advance as he steps back. "You shouldn't have done that, little boy," I warn and I watch his Adam's apple bob as he gulps.

He steps back without looking and he goes down hard, tripping over a discarded can. Grinning, I leap forward. He scrambles to his feet and I lift him into the air by his neck.

I hear the others moving closer, thinking they are sneaking up on me. I laugh and grab the man's jaw hard with my other hand, wrenching it open. Grabbing his tongue, I look into his eyes and snarl, "Time to teach you some manners, boy." I rip it out and drop it to the ground.

He screams, his eyes bulging out, before he goes limp in my hand. Turning, I throw him at his friends and they shout as they go down under him. "Come on boys, look, I'll even give you a fair chance," I taunt, holding my hands behind my back and waiting for them to get to their feet.

Lo looks at the unconscious man and pales. He glances at me and back to the man, but the other one yells as he rushes forward, and he fires the net gun but I easily dodge it.

He grabs his other gun and aims and fires as he walks, bullet after bullet. I smell the flower, Yret, in the air and sigh. I concentrate on them as they near me and I manage to duck all but one, which embeds in my left arm, sending it to sleep right away, before crawling veins of agony start there. I need to end this now, he just royally pissed me off.

My dragon roars his agreement in my head and I narrow my eyes on the man. "Run. Run now, little human," I warn.

He grapples with the gun, trying to reload, and I sprint at him, too fast for the poor human eye to see. Grabbing the gun out of his shaking hands, I aim it at his crotch and fire, making him scream before I place it to his forehead and shoot him between the eyes.

I drop the gun and turn to Lo who falls to his knees, crying already, and I haven't even touched him. Crouching down, I tilt my head animalistically as I eye him.

"How do you keep finding me?" I growl.

He shakes his head, opening his mouth, but only a high-pitched noise comes out.

"Tell me and I will kill you quickly," I offer.

He lets out a sob but nods, wiping his nose with his hand, obviously realising he isn't getting out of this alive. A dragon always keeps his words, so I will offer him a quick death.

"Th-they are working with some people. People who knew you were back. They have—" He looks around before lowering his voice. "Witches with them, I didn't even know they existed, but they traced you somehow and sent updates to our phones."

Growling, I surge to my feet, making the human whimper and cower in fear. "Who, who are they working with?" I demand.

"I don't know—I swear! Th-they call themselves The Others!" he screams.

I nod with my hands clenched into fists by my side. "Anything else?" I growl.

He recoils closer to the ground. "We are the only team on this side right now, we are normally spread out so it's taking a while for them to recall them to go after you."

I blow out a breath, and smoke curls from my nose and he screams. "Thank you," I growl in a mix between human and dragon, before I reach forward and snap his neck.

Turning around, I spot the other man. He is on his knees with his hands covering his mouth as he tries to scream. I step forward and lift him to his feet by his hair, and once he is standing, I punch my hand through his chest and crush his heart.

Pulling my arm back, I let him drop to the earth before admiring all my hard work. Frowning at the blood and bits of bone covering my arm, I look around and sigh before leaning down and ripping off the rest of the man's shirt. I use the rag to clean my arm before dropping it on top of his corpse.

I walk back to the cars and stop at theirs to do a search. I check two of their phones but like they said, they are burners and not much good. The only other items are fast food wrappers and some weapons. Sighing, I leave their car on the side of the road for their hunter brethren to find as I make my way back to mine.

I was going to head straight to Dawn, but with a witch tracer on me, I can't. First, I need to find a witch I can trust to break it, and fast before the hunters find me again, because this time they will be bringing reinforcements.

CHAPTER 43

I throw the human scum at the pipe in the corner of the basement, before I stomp down after him and quickly tie him up while he's unconscious. On the way back here he'd become mouthy and Nos had knocked him out. Luckily for him, he's still sleeping.

Heading back upstairs, I shut the basement door and walk into the kitchen. Nos and Dawn are already there, the paperwork still spread between them, as she laughs at whatever he just said.

I grab a bottle of Jack from the side and pour myself a glass, then relax in one of the seats at the table. Dawn reaches over and grabs the bottle as Nos gets up and grabs two more glasses, and brings them over. She pours them and they both sip the whiskey as I snort.

"Make yourself at home," I say snidely.

She grins over at me, reclining with the glass in her hand. "I will."

"What do we do about the meeting?" Nos interrupts, probably a good thing since it would have only spiraled into another argument.

Dawn grins at me over her glass before turning back to Nos. "Well, Fallen here thinks he can get us a female stand in, then I can just feed off Ray Ray down there, and change into him. Then we go to the meeting, figure out who the fuck The Others are, and kill them all." She toasts us, and Nos laughs.

"Fucking perfect, *vasculo*, and what about when they figure out you aren't him? Or when they try to take the girl?" I point out.

She reaches over and presses a finger to my lips, shushing me. "We will sort that out when we get to it. Now, can you get us a girl or not?"

Pulling away from her, I lean back from her touch before I do something stupid like bend her over the fucking table. "I can get us a girl. I am a man after all," I tease, trying to get a rise out of her on purpose.

She narrows her eyes on me, and I see jealousy flare there as they flash black before she relaxes in her chair and sips her whiskey. "I'm going to need clothes that will fit me in that body. I'm not wearing his." She shivers in disgust and I growl at her for ignoring my jab.

She finishes off her drink before placing the glass on the table. "I'm going to chill for a bit before the meeting, then I'll look through more paperwork. Griffin, make sure you get the girl for tomorrow." With that order, she gathers the papers and trots away.

Nos throws back his drink, gives me a smug look, and disappears after her. Bastard.

After checking that the sheep isn't dead, I grab my carving gear and go and set up at the table upstairs. I don't want to work with his eyes on me, and I don't want to go upstairs and hear whatever the fuck those two are doing. Spreading out my equipment with gentle hands, I run my fingers over my tools before sitting down and preparing.

I don't know why carving brings me such peace, but I can lose myself in the wood and designs for hours, in the rhythmic work and the tiny details. For that short period, I forget everything but the piece in my hands. I could do with that clarity and peace right now.

I left a message for a sheep I trust, so I set my phone on the side in case he rings back. I'm hoping he has a girl we can use, he should if the payout is worth it.

Gripping the wood, I clear my head as I try to think of what to carve. I sit there for minutes with nothing coming to mind, which is strange. Groaning, I grab my knife and decide to just go with it, hopefully the design will come to me while I work.

Losing myself in it, I let the space around me go and my mind wanders until a voice has me snapping my head up and blinking at my mate. I'm mad at myself for letting her sneak up on me.

"Where did you learn to do that?" she asks, nodding at the wood in my still hands.

"My mother," I reply without thinking.

Her eyes widen as she hesitates in the doorway. "I thought you didn't know your mother."

I sneer at her, clutching the wood in my hands. "Just because I was created doesn't mean I didn't meet the woman who birthed me," I snap.

She holds her hands up but comes farther into the room, ignoring my anger. "Okay, what was she like?" She grabs a chair and sits opposite me.

I glare at her before I go back to carving, ignoring her questions. It's better not to drag those memories up, nothing but pain and madness live there now. Obviously realising she won't get an answer, she reaches across the table and stills my hands.

"I'm sorry, maybe you could teach me one day." With that she stands, grabs a bottle of water, and retreats back upstairs.

Only then do I look down at the carving and swear. It's of her face. It's rough and not finished, but even to my eyes I can see her features there.

Dawn

I leave Griffin to it, seeing the closed look on his face. He had looked so peaceful, so free when I had found him hunched over his carvings that I couldn't help it. I'm learning about him slowly. Stopping in the living room, I look across all the photographs on the wall. His perspectives are beautiful, but the black and white makes every scene depressing, and it's obvious that even in beauty he sees the darkness.

Not wanting him to get pissed and find me staring, I head back upstairs and to Nos. He is laying back on the bed where I left him with his arm under his head, and his chest bare. He looks beautiful and otherworldly, so much so, that I stop for a moment just to admire him.

He truly is a piece of art. I can understand why they made him a god and worshipped him. His lips quirk up and I catch my breath. "Are you just going to stare, or are you coming back to bed, Little Monster?" he teases.

Grinning, I drop the bottle of water on one of the nightstands and climb onto the bed, then snuggle back into his chest. I run my fingers across his bronzed, defined skin and look up at him to see him smiling softly down at me.

"Tell me more about you," I urge. I know a lot, and when you spend so much time with someone, when you kill with someone, you learn things that no words could ever explain, but I know he's old and has lived a long life and I'm curious. What did my mate do before me? Why was he in the forest? Why doesn't he hate humans like Griffin?

"What do you want to know, Little Monster?" he murmurs, sounding relaxed as he plays with my hair. It's the first time we aren't rushing to do something, we're just relaxing. There are no dead bodies or kidnapping, just our words. It's nice.

"Everything, what was your life like? Where did you grow up? Your family?" I ask, and lean up to see that his face has clouded before he shakes his head.

He looks at me and strokes my cheek gently. "I have lived a long life, Little Monster, seen the rise and fall of empires, queens and kings, and more…yet, it all felt like I was waiting…waiting for you. It meant nothing, it was…all grey, until you came along. So I have not purposely kept my life from you, I just don't care about it. I only care about you."

"Motherfucker." I grin and lean down to kiss him. Pulling away, I run my fingers along his face. "I still want to know, talk to me. Tell me some stories."

"Anything for you, Little Monster," he murmurs and we get comfy, his head resting on mine, and our legs entwined as we cuddle.

"I do not know my family. The first thing I can remember is being in the wilderness, I was around four or five then I think. I grew up in nature, it was just my way of life. I learned to talk to the animals before man, I studied their ways, their hierarchies. My powers grew and grew, but I knew nothing else. Then I met the fae, they took me in and taught me of the world, except I was a man by then and fiercely independent, but I was also curious. I ventured out into the world, but more often than not I would return to the wild. It was my home, it was where I was happiest. Around man I had to hide what I was, I didn't there."

Stroking his chest, I think about how lonely that sounds but I don't say that out loud.

"I loved the languages and cultures, enjoyed watching the world develop, so I stayed in touch with the human world while removing myself from it, but I couldn't seem to help myself. I helped where I could and I guess people started to notice, they worshiped me and called me a god. Only when I went to a fae learner, which is what they call their teachers, I learned that was exactly what I was. Over the next fifty or so years, I honed my powers and my story became myth."

I frown and still my movements, but he continues, "All the humans I knew were dying, plague. It was a sad time, it was also when the council found me. They are always aware of a relic's birth, but because I was in nature they did not. It angered them and I was kept there for a while so they could understand what I am and what I can do. Eventually, they realised I would not be kept prisoner and they had no choice but to release me. Every now and again they would venture into my land to try and convince me join them."

"Why didn't you?" I ask.

"I didn't want that life, I just wanted to be left alone. It always felt like I was searching for something, like no matter what I did it wasn't enough," he says sadly, before cupping my chin and raising my head. "That itch went away the night I met you. I finally knew I had found what I had been searching for, for so long. Everything paled in comparison, when you took that first breath it was like I did as well."

I smile and kiss him again before settling down. "Anyways, over the years my land, in what you now call Scotland, was diminishing. Humans were getting bolder and bolder, and cutting and destroying it. One day, I went to the cities to meet with the council. It took a couple of days, and when I came back, it was gone."

Even now I can hear the desolation and devastation in his voice, and it causes a physical pain in my heart so I snuggle closer.

"My whole land was destroyed for them to make houses and roads. They demolished the fae's habitat as well, killing them," he admits, making me gasp.

"They killed them?" I growl.

He sighs, squeezing me closer. "Little Monster, humans are hardwired for it, killing and destroying. They also have love and beauty but I digress, yes, they killed them. They couldn't see them,

229

didn't know they were there thanks to the glamour, but the fae could not escape even if they wanted to, they were surrounded."

"Why would they not want to escape?" I question, confused.

He sighs again, and it hits me just how little I know of this world. "Fae are tied to their land. It is where they get their powers from, and if their land dies then so do they. Many would rather die with it then live without its power or try to recreate it somewhere else."

Sitting up, I swing my leg over so I'm straddling him and I brace my hands on his chest. He grips my hips and his eyes show me how much pain it cost him when they died.

"You loved them?" I ask.

He nods. "They were the only family I really had. They raised me, many were my friends. I had helped birth children, I had played with them, they were my life, Little Monster, they were gone just like that. I went to the grove where they lived and it was horrible. Their broken bloody bodies littered the ground, still clinging to their land even in death."

I part my mouth when he reaches up and captures a tear on his finger, which I didn't even realise I had shed for him. He kisses it before watching me again.

"What did you do?" I inquire, knowing my monster wouldn't let that go and neither would I.

"I am not proud to say that I let my heartache and pain consume me. It was the first time I changed so completely. The skeleton grew across my face, and for once I felt like the god they called me. I made my way through the remaining forest, calling animals to my side. Wolves, bears, everything you can imagine, and together we attacked the town. It was like I couldn't stop myself. The hate and pain was too much, everything was red, and only when I stood in the middle of the massacred town did I realise what I had done. My hands were stained, my body too, with their blood. I killed them all, Little Monster, men, women, children. Innocents. I slaughtered them, killed families. I had become the very thing I hated." He sucks in a breath, his eyes shuttering, and I see the fear there, the fear I will judge him for his actions.

Leaning down, I grab his cheeks and force him to look at me. "I will not forgive you for your actions. You, and only you, can do that, but I know why you did it. I understand the instincts and I'm betting you atoned for that, did you not?" I growl.

He nods, swallowing hard. "I tried, I am still not a good man, Little Monster. I have more blood on my hands than I could explain in two lifetimes. I have killed and destroyed, I let power consume me until I could not see past my own instincts. I am a god, I am a monster, and I will never let you go."

"Good," I purr, kissing him hard. He moans, gripping me as his tongue tangles with mine. Before it can go any further, I break our kiss and sit back. "What did you do after?" I ask, tilting my head to see him. His hands stroke my skin, running up and down my body, nearly distracting me.

"I left. I couldn't stand to be there anymore, the land was tainted. I came here and have been ever since," he admits and I nod. I don't think I could stay either.

"Thank you for telling me," I murmur and he grins.

"Always. I will keep nothing from you. It might not be pretty, but if you ask I will tell," he promises. Smiling, I slip down and curl up against his side again.

"Tell me some more stories?" I press and he laughs.

"What about the time I offended the lord and lady of Herilo and they tried to kill me?" he suggests and I giggle.

"What did you do?" I ask and he settles back.

"Well..."

We spend the next couple of hours laughing and talking. He tells me tales of the world he watches grow, and I gather more information about his life. It seems my god has been alone for a long time. Maybe everything happens for a reason. He clearly needs me and I need him.

CHAPTER 44

NOS

Holding a sleeping Dawn in my arms, I smile into the darkening room. Night is descending, I can feel it. Happiness is like a living creature inside my chest. It felt good to share my life and stories with my mate. She's listening to them all, asking questions here and there, and never once judging me for my choices or lifestyle. I have not told her everything, not yet, but we have plenty of time—a million lifetimes to be exact, if she keeps feeding from me.

Gods are immortal, so therefore their mates are. I probably should tell her that little tidbit at some point. Smelling her scent in the air, I close my eyes and inhale deeply. My heart bursts and there is a smile on my face. That soon melts away at the bad feeling taking up residence in my bones.

Fluttering open my lashes, I search the room before closing my eyes and sinking inside of myself, allowing my power to reach out. As far as I know, no one else can do this, but with my blood sacrifice to my land and the animals there, I have a connection. It allows me to keep watch when I venture into the human world and right now it is tingling in danger.

Following it along, I check my land and search for any invaders, but I can't see anything. Grasping at more connections, I connect with a local wolf pack and whisper in their head. It is more images than anything since they can't understand my words, but it gets my point across. They split up, spreading out over my land, searching for the threat. Even now, their hair stands on end and their howls split the night—a warning.

Pulling back from the pack, I turn to the birds. They are smart creatures and see far more than people give them credit for. I whisper a warning to them and they take flight. Checking the area from the sky. When they find nothing, I whisper to them to keep watch before pulling back and warning the other animals.

With that, I venture deeper into my land, paying close attention this time. It's faint, but I find it. A disturbance, someone has been there, someone looking for something.

Looking for me or my mate.

I growl and pull back on the connections, returning to my body in the city. Sitting up, I meet Dawn's startled gaze. She is sitting at the end of the bed, crossed-legged, watching me in confusion.

"Where did you go?" She shivers. "I couldn't feel you."

I open my arms to her and sigh when she clambers into my lap, all is right again.

"I am sorry, Little Monster, someone trespassed on my land. Someone with great power. I must return to my land and find out who and what they want. I fear we are not safe there any more than we are here."

DUME

I'm not sleeping, but my eyes are closed to deter the questions from the nosey flight attendant, so when the lights flicker and the bing sounds, I crack them open. Leaning out into the aisle, I see the pilots panicking slightly just as the air masks drop from above. Groaning, I get to my feet and make my way to the cockpit —what now?

Bracing myself with hands on either side of the door, I huff, "What?"

The co-pilot glances back at me before concentrating on the sky in front of him again. "Sir, please take your seat," he grits out, while flicking switches.

"What the fuck is going on?" I growl, impatient now.

He doesn't glance over at me again, but he does force out the next sentence between clenched teeth. "A storm, sir, a bad fucking storm. We have no chance but to land if we can find ground."

"What do you mean?" I ask, because that doesn't seem normal.

He looks over at me then, letting me see the fear and confusion in his face as it pales. "This isn't a normal storm, we—our equipment is malfunctioning, like it can't find its way out of the storm, like something is blocking it and it came out of nowhere. One minute clear night sky, the next, one of the biggest, most aggressive storms I've ever seen!" he yells, before turning back around. I tune him and his pilot's conversation out as I peer through the front window to the sky.

Clouds are rolling with lightning and thunder is humming through the plane. I watch the storm, unblinking, and if I look close enough I can almost see outside of it to the clear night sky. It is only surrounding the plane. This isn't a normal storm, it's fucking magic.

Witches. "Take us down, take us down now!" I yell.

They look over at me, confused.

"If you don't, they are going to rip this plane apart and fry us all. Down. Now," I order.

The pilot nods as they both turn back to the controls in front of them, flicking switches and talking into their headsets as I turn back into the aisle. The flight attendant is sitting in the first seat, clutching his seat belt for dear life.

Moving to the seat on the other side, I grab my bag and hold it on my lap as I buckle in. I turn my head and stare out of the window as the clouds boil over. The plane dips and beeps come from the cockpit. Holding on to the seat, I slow my breathing, watching until I see the shimmer of magic.

Above the shouts and beeping in the plane—I hear it.

The chanting of the coven doing this, their voices rising like they are here. Their words are not in any tongue I know while they chant and scream. It all blurs together until I hear an explosion. Turning my head toward the sound, I groan when the door to the plane rips open. The flight attendant screams, looking over at me for help before he is sucked from his seat.

He is suspended there for a moment, his fingers clutching desperately at his chair, his face pale as his eyes meet mine, and then he is gone. Out through the gap where the door once was and flying backwards. I hear the moment he hits the engine of the plane and wince, then we tilt dangerously.

Watching the hole, I know we are fucked. The wall is cracking and ripping away with the pressure, and if we don't land soon, we are all going to be airborne. I don't think even I could survive that sort of drop.

The air masks are down but I don't need it. I just sit and wait, hoping I get to hold my mate once, just once, before I die.

We are dropping steadily now, I can feel it, but the hole the plane is getting wider and wider.

"We are landing now!" screams the pilot over the sound of the air rushing through the cabin.

A noise catches my attention and I turn to look at the opening, where flames are licking the side of the plane. I turn back to the front and refuse to close my eyes. If I am to meet death today, I will do it with my eyes open and a curse on my lips.

We hit something hard, sending me bouncing in my seat, before we touch down again and again. I shoot forward when the brakes are applied and I have to grip my seat to avoid being thrown out. The plane turns to the left, tilting dangerously before we right ourselves.

We slam to a stop and the engines overheat until the whole cabin feels like it is on fire. I rip off my seat belt and jump from my seat, throwing my bag over my shoulder. Striding to the cockpit, I grab both pilots, ignoring their yelling and incredulous noises, and leap from the hole in the plane.

Landing on both feet, I start to run, the sounds of the plane catching fire close behind me. So close I can feel the heat singeing my back before an explosion rocks the air.

I'm thrown forward and I quickly turn so I don't crush the humans. Landing hard on my back, my breath is knocked out of me from the impact and I lay there for a minute trying to breathe before pushing to my feet. The plane is on fire, and its smouldering remains are still shrouded by the storm.

It looks like a boiling cloud around it, with lightning snaking out, and thunder rumbling within it, yet the air and sky everywhere else is clear. It slowly starts to dissipate, and the clouds are sucked back up until nothing but the fire and the corpse of the plane remains.

Glancing over my shoulder, I see both dazed pilots climbing to their feet, with their eyes locked on the fireball that they were inside not seconds before.

"You're welcome. Call Carmichael, tell him to get our location and get me another form of transport," I order.

When they don't move, I step closer with a growl before the one on the left yanks out his phone and starts dialling. Fucking witches. That was close, too close. They are getting brave, first a demon and now a circle? What will they do next?

They will never stop, I know that. They can't, not after I took their queen from them.

CHAPTER 45

ASK A

Putting the phone on speaker, which took me more tries than I would like to admit, I place it on the dash and wait for Jean Paul to pick up. He does, on the fifth ring, sounding out of breath.

"Sir?" he greets.

"I need directions," I say bluntly.

"Erm okay? Where to?" he asks.

"A ship, I need to know where it has made port. It is called The Witch's Delight. It's usually around here somewhere," I growl out.

I had thought I could find it by myself, but after driving for five hours and only getting farther and farther away from my mate, I have given up and enlisted the help of Jean Paul.

"I'll look, let me call you back," he offers, his voice already distracted, and I quickly end the call before looking back at the road I'm on.

I'm hoping the witches who run it are still about, but it should have been passed down through their family at least, and they are the only ones I can think to go to. They have no affiliation with the council or other supes, and their main concern is money. They sell their services to buyers, travelling the world with their wares. They don't even hide what they are and have been around as long as I can remember. All I will need to ensure their loyalty is money and I have plenty of that, but time is running out.

The storm is circling, I can feel it. My mate, the hunters, I'm running out of time.

Not two minutes later, my phone rings again. I answer without looking and Jean Paul's excited voice blasts through the speakers.

"I found it, and I tracked your phone, you aren't far. I will text you the address, simply click on it and it will open in your navigation. Anything else you require, sir?" he asks.

"No, thank you. Be careful, it seems I have more enemies than I thought," I warn, it would be a lot of work to find a new human to serve me and he seems like a nice boy.

"Of course, sir, do not worry about me. I have means to protect myself. Have a good meeting." I hang up again with nothing else left to say. I pull over and horns blare, but I ignore them as Jean Paul's text comes through. He sent me the address and a little dancing man. Staring at the phone in confusion, I watch it move for a while. How did he do that? It is fascinating.

Typing out a text with clumsy fingers, I ask as much.

Aska: How did you trap that man in this phone to dance, is it magic?

I wait for a reply, truly concerned my phone is spelled.

Jean Paul: Noooo, it's an emoji. I will teach you when I see you again, trust me, it's normal and just part of the technology. LOL.

Frowning even harder, I eye the phone wearily before thumbing out a reply.

Aska: Okay, what is the meaning of the word LOL?

I wait impatiently, waving on disgruntled drivers as they overtake me, their impatience sounding in their horns and angry voices.

Jean Paul: This could be a long conversation. Go to your meeting, sir, and I will explain text speak another time, but LOL means laugh out loud.

What the—

Aska: Fine, but that seems stupid. Why would you laugh out loud and why not just type that? Humans.

Clicking on the address like he said, I watch it boot up a navigation app before an angry, female voice blares through the car.

"Navigating. Make a U-turn if safe to do so." Placing it back on the dash, I throw it a narrow-eyed look before pulling out and making a U-turn, further angering drivers.

"You will reach your destination in approximately one hour and eleven minutes."

"Thank you." I nod at the device but it doesn't speak again, how rude.

"I will burn you!" I scream at the phone, gripping the wheel hard.

It had been going smoothly, even if the 'sat nav,' as Jean Paul called it, woman's voice did grate on my nerves, but now she is being purposely difficult. Telling me to turn where there are no turns or taking me to the middle of nowhere.

"Your destination is on your left," she says in that same monotone voice.

"I will eat your soul!" I warn.

"Your destination is on your left."

Grabbing the phone, I glare at the screen. "You lie to me, phone witch! Now you die!"

I roll down my window and go to throw it out when I stop because there, on my right, is a sign pointing to left saying dock. Oops.

Bringing the phone back in I throw it another narrow-eyed look. "You shall live another day, tiny trapped magician," I rage, before throwing it over my shoulder into the back.

Turning, I head and follow the signs, gritting my teeth as the woman continues to mock me. "Your destination is on your left."

"Silence!" I roar, and for once she listens to me as I travel down the twisty road.

"You have reached your destination," she mocks.

"Make it stop!" I scream, banging on the wheel.

Pulling over to the place it says to park, I reach into the back, grab the phone, and stare at the screen before dialling Jean Paul.

"Sir, did you find it?" he asks straight away.

"The woman you sent through the phone with the directions will not shut up and I thought you would be displeased if I broke this device," I growl.

I hear him struggling to breathe on the other end. "Jean Paul? Are you being attacked? Are you choking?" I ask, concerned, and he makes a weird high-pitched sound before laughter flows through the phone.

Pulling it away from my ear, I eye it strangely before bringing it back to hear him trying to control himself. "Sir, that's the sat nav, you just have to click end route," he chokes out.

"Will that make the tiny magician go away?" I question seriously, and he barks out a laugh again—strange, maybe he is watching a humorous film?

"Yes, sir," he eventually tells me.

"Okay." I hang up and eye the screen. I spot the button he mentioned and I press it timidly. The app closes and no more voices come from inside. Sighing in relief, I pocket it.

I look at the dock I have been brought to and roll my eyes. It's busy and surrounded by humans, only witches would be this bold. Leaving the car, I take my keys with me and walk along the path designated for pedestrians. I have to circle the dock a few times, trying to find it.

A spell cloaks the boat, making it look like any other, but I haven't seen it in centuries and they have clearly upgraded the appearance. Instead of the old barge mixed with a pirate ship look the boat used to assume, it now looks like a freighter, including steel boxes on the back of the ship.

Only when I stopped looking for the ship and the name did I notice it. Looking around, I head over to the boarding dock, which is already set up. I walk across and stop when I stand on the hull, letting the magic wash over me. If I was here to kill them or part of the council, the magic would feel that and I would be vaporised, but

I had also seen them do it for fun sometimes. So I stand respectfully and wait.

The tingling of it runs over my skin, and when it finally drops to my feet and back into the deck, I blink my eyes and the ship I remember appears. Striding across the wooden hull, I knock three times on the only door on the whole ship. Magic, it can make strange things.

If you were to wander alone, looking for another escape, you would find yourself lost in a never-ending maze, or maybe in the water. Who knows.

The door swings open by itself, letting out the smell of incense and sulfur. Someone has been summoning. Stepping into the darkened galley, I run eyes around, searching for one of the sisters.

I spot no one so I walk around. Looks like they are playing games today, that never bodes well. I pass trinkets, voodoo dolls, cursed items, and ingredients for spells as I search the room until I find them waiting for me, with a spell brewing behind them.

The three are almost identical, apart from their eyes. These witches have been alive even longer than I can guess—not that I will ever ask them how, it would require a lot of blood magic and death, I imagine. Yet, they still look no older than twenty-five. Their hair is all the same shade of ash, a mix of grey and black, and curled down to their waists, even in the same style. They all wear jeans and boots, but have on different t-shirts.

"Mercy," I greet the first, the one on the left with the green eyes. "Chloe," I address the second with the blue eyes. "Loxley," I acknowledge the last one on the right, with brown eyes.

"Askaliarian, first of his name, the soul eater," they say at once, their voices mixing together.

I incline my head and they all smile at the same time, the effect creepy, before they break away. Mercy walks straight up to me and places her hand on my chest. Chloe circles me until she lays her hand on my arm and Loxley stops at my back, running her hands down it. Gritting my teeth, I stop the growl from leaving my mouth with their hands on me. Before I could endure it for a purpose, but having met my mate and feeling her touch—this feels wrong.

"Witches," I warn and they giggle.

"Wait, sisters," Mercy says, her hand stilling above my heart. Grimacing, I hold still as I feel her magic moving through me. I never quite know what they are capable of. It pulls back and I shiver at the sensation. I will never get used to that.

"I feel something as well," Chloe murmurs, her hand stilling on my arm as her eyes cloud with her magic.

Loxley's hand presses to my back before she hisses and steps away. "He has found his one," she declares, before rejoining her sisters in front of me. "Congratulations are in order dragon, it has been a long search."

All signs of teasing leave their faces and genuine smiles stretch across them. "She will test you, be warned," Mercy adds before Chloe laughs.

"Oh yes, she is trouble indeed. Please bring her to us when you can, I would love to meet her." She licks her lips and I narrow mine with a growl.

They all step back, laughing. "Fear not, we mean you nor your mate no harm, dragon," Loxley promises and my shoulders slump.

"You have seen her?" I can't stop myself from asking.

Loxley nods, stepping forward. "Yes, she will have your need for death and blood," she states, her darkness showing. She always was a lover of death.

Chloe steps forward next, linking her arm with her sister's. "She will be kind and caring," she vows, her obsession with love obvious in her tone.

"She will be one of a kind, a true monster," Mercy declares with a wicked grin. "But that is not why you came to see us, was it?"

"No, it looks like some hunters are working with witches and they have placed a tracer on me," I admit, and then trying to appeal to Chloe, I add, "It is preventing me from going to my mate, I do not want to risk her safety."

They all laugh and I watch them in confusion before Loxley grins at me. "Do not fear dragon, your mate is fraught with danger and she thrives in it."

"But we will help," Chloe interjects with a dreamy looking smile.

"For a price," Mercy finishes, ever the practical sister.

"I have your money, I need the tracer gone," I growl and they nod as one. Their weird quirks and teasing disappear as they all turn and start to work on their spell to break it.

Turning and leaving them to their work, I wander through the room, careful not to touch anything.

"You fear she will reject you," Chloe whispers from behind me, making me jump and spin. I don't know how they do it, sneak up on me, but it is unnerving to say the least.

I say nothing and she smiles sadly. "My love rejected me when he found out..." She trails off, shaking her head. "Yours will not, I have seen inside her heart. She is pure, dark, but pure. She will love you completely, she will endure your wrath, your life, and your dragon."

"Why are you telling me this?" I ask, narrowing my eyes. The witches always require a payment.

"Not for the reason you think, dragon. The world is always such a dark place. Can I not wish well for the love of one I know?" she counters, tilting her head, and Loxley appears next to her.

"Her darkness will match your own. Nothing to fear dragon, she likes it kinky too." She winks as I choke on air.

Mercy appears next. "Come, we are ready." She turns before calling over her shoulder. "Yes, she will be able to take all of your...size." They all giggle and I drop my head back and stare at the ceiling. I really wish they wouldn't use whatever magic they wield to see my fears, but it does settle me a little—though it is a bit concerning that the witches are thinking about my cock.

"Don't flatter yourself dragon, we have our own cocks on hand." Loxley grins, her eyes flashing before she turns and follows her sister.

"Maybe one day, you will meet our death-defying men." Chloe laughs and follows as well.

Witches.

CHAPTER 46

DAWN

Nos disappeared back into himself after that early warning. He told me not to disturb him and kissed me before his eyes closed. When he closed them it felt like his soul left the room and I shivered hard. Watching him sleep, or whatever he's doing, isn't exactly very fun and after an hour or so I get bored. Slipping from the room, I sneak downstairs, and then stop on the landing, unsure what I want to do.

I could go find out some more information from Ray, or even bug Griffin, but when I spot his bedroom door open I grin, knowing exactly what I'm going to be doing. Snooping.

Hey, it has to be okay since we're mates, right? Plus, he's never left his door open before and when it was closed I respected his privacy, it's not my fault he forgot to shut it. Walking towards it, I stick my head inside just in case he's waiting in the shadows like a weirdo or something. Hell, it might even be a trap knowing Griffin.

When I don't spot him, I slip inside, close the door softly, and wait in case he springs out of the shadows and attacks me. When no booby traps or fallens come at me, I relax a little.

His room is nearly barren like the first time I was in here, and the only real decorations are his figurines he carves, which line the shelves in the corner. Walking their way, I admire the craftsmanship and the story they tell. There are so many of them— wings, angels, men with knives, a woman held in a man's arms. Running my hands along the shelves, I grab a book at random and flip through it before pulling out another. Putting them back again, I look around and grin when I spot the bedside table. Do I dare? Of course I fucking do.

Plus, if he catches me, he might hate fuck me again and I'm down for that. Pulling open the drawer, I freeze. All that's in the drawer are different cameras and lenses. So, this is what he uses to take such beautiful pictures? Picking one up delicately, I put the strap around my neck to make sure I don't drop it before switching it on. It boots up, flashing a screen before it goes dark. Lifting it, I look through the lens and move it around the room. Only then do I realise his room is like his photos— colourless.

Turning, my eye still to the lenses, I look about his room but freeze when I get to the door. There, standing with it still open behind him, is an angry looking Griffin. My heart pounds and before I can question myself why, I click and take his photo. Pulling down the camera slightly I stare at him. His mouth is twisted in a snarl and his hands are fisted by his sides. He looks so much bigger framed by the door, impressive and terrifying at the same time.

"Give it to me," he orders.

Grinning, I strut over and pass him the camera. He checks it over and I roll my eyes. Throwing me a glare, he turns his back on me and hunches his shoulders as he clicks through the menu until he can see the last photo taken. When he does, he sucks in a breath.

Peering over his shoulder, I arch my eyebrow. Not bad if I do say so myself. He looks fierce and fucking sexy. "What?" I ask, confused.

"Is this how you see me?" he questions harshly.

Blinking, I lean back as he spins to look at me. "Is. This. How. You. See. Me?" he grits out each word, his face turning red.

"What do you see in the picture?" I counter, baffled.

He glances away and pulls the camera closer before looking back at me. "A monster."

I sigh sadly. "Then no, you do not see yourself the way I do. In that picture you look powerful, sexy as hell, and so bloody other-worldly that my breath catches."

He inhales sharply as his eyes search mine. "You don't see a monster?"

I shake my head. "You might do monstrous things, we might be called monsters but those aren't my thoughts when I look at you. In fact, the first thought I had was 'fuck me,'" I tease, and he barks out a laugh before sobering up.

He lifts the camera towards me and I grin cheekily, posing. He snaps it and looks at the screen. "Beautiful," he whispers, before turning and leaving me in his room, lost for words on whatever just happened.

It's how Nos finds me, watching the space in which Griffin just disappeared, probably looking as confused as I feel. "Little Monster?" he calls, and I snap my gaze to him.

"Come on, we need to talk. Something has happened." He offers me his hand and I grab it. Instead of leading me back upstairs like I figured, he takes me to the kitchen where Griffin is sitting, carving again.

He pulls out a seat and sits then pulls me onto his lap. "We need to talk."

Griffin puts down his carving, hiding it behind his glass, and leans back as he stares at us with a blank face. "Then talk," he snarks.

"Someone has been on my land, searching for either Dawn or me. I have stationed the animals around to make sure they warn me if the person comes back, but from what I could feel...they were powerful. Very powerful. I have arranged a meeting with the fae to see if they felt this, and to ask them to protect it in my absence," Nos explains bluntly, and I snuggle further into him, offering him comfort he doesn't know how to ask for. It's obviously annoying him that someone has threatened his safety and mine.

"And?" Griffin prompts, arching his eyebrow at Nos, and ignoring me completely.

"And," Nos grits out, "I am going to have to go to this meeting, it is in the morning. I do not think I will be back for our plan, so we have a choice to make. Do we leave this threat and wait until after the meeting fae, or do we rearrange with the fae?" he finishes, his voice tired.

"Will the fae rearrange?" I ask, turning so I can look at them both.

"Not likely," Griffin snorts.

"Okay, so it's simple. You go to the fae meeting, take as long as you need. Griffin and I have this meeting covered, and we can meet back up tomorrow night and debrief each other," I suggest and he looks at me sadly. "I'll be fine," I promise.

"Debrief? We are not having a three way," Griffin retorts, and I throw him a narrow-eyed look before turning back to Nos, almost sensing his denial coming.

"Nos, I'll be fine," I point out and hold my breath. I love his protection and worry, but if he gives up on this meeting then I'll know he doesn't trust me to look after myself, and that means a lot to me after being controlled for most of my life.

He nods, leaning in and kissing my forehead before turning to Griffin. "She can protect herself, but if at any time she can't and she doesn't come home without a scratch, I will harm you," he warns, his eyes flashing white.

Griffin inclines his head and Nos stands, grabbing my hand. "Come on, Little Monster, I want to spend the night with you if I am to spend the whole day away from you tomorrow," he murmurs and I nod, leading him away, but not before I throw a smile at Griffin and mouth, "Goodnight."

He smirks before going back to his carving. I lead Nos upstairs and he lights the fire while I sit and watch him from my position on the bed.

"You are going to be okay, aren't you?" I ask, suddenly worried.

He turns and frowns before walking over and getting on the bed. He pulls me into his arms and we sit with my back against his chest. "Little Monster, nothing could keep me from you, but yes, I will be fine. Promise me you will be as well?"

I grin, snuggling back. "Yes, I'll be fine."

He sighs and buries his head in my hair. I sit, happy to be in his arms, and watch the flames dance. Tomorrow he will leave, but I don't know for how long and sadness envelops my chest. Since awakening, he has been my constant. Even when he wasn't there, I knew he was close by.

So tonight I will make the most of him. Turning around in his arms, I straddle his lap. "Fuck me, my monster. Remind me that you are here tonight," I order and he grins, his eyes turning white once more.

He grabs my hips and I smile. Standing from the bed, with me wrapped around him, he walks over to the fire and lays me down on the rug in front of it, stripping off the t-shirt I was wearing as he goes. Lying there, I grin up at him.

"I want to watch the flames dance over your skin while you scream for me," he murmurs, while unbuttoning his pants and pulling down his trousers, his already hard cock springing free.

Groaning, I arch up and grab my breasts, tweaking my nipples as I watch him strip. He rips off his t-shirt and stares down at me as I run my hands down my stomach and part my thighs for his gaze.

Running my fingers down my slick pussy, I tease him until he narrows his eyes and drops down on top of me, pressing me down into the rug with his weight and trapping my hands.

He kisses my cheek, running gentle kisses along my face until he reaches my ear. "Do you want to see what else I can get from my animals?" he asks.

"Yes," I moan, loving it when he goes all monster on me.

He leans up and reaches between our bodies, grabs my hands and presses them into the fur rug above my head, the heat of the fire warming them until I start sweating.

Kissing down the valley between my breasts, he ignores them completely and continues down to my stomach, laving his tongue around my belly button. Rolling his eyes up to me, he hovers over my pussy.

He smirks, his eyes completely white now, before I feel his body vibrate with his power. Then it all stills and he opens his mouth. I've seen him change his tongue before, into that of a snake, but I have no fucking clue what animal it represents now— holy hell. He sticks it out at me, showing me how long and thick it is, and I almost choke on air.

His voice is garbled when it comes out. "Don't move," he orders before laying down between my parted thighs.

He grabs my thighs and throws them over his shoulder, opening me up to his gaze. I can feel it burning across me until I'm panting, and then he touches me. His fingers part me and that tongue darts out, running across me and making me cry out. It's rough, so fucking rough, and the friction is perfect.

He laps at my clit before running it down me again and thrusting it inside with no warning. Arching into him, I roll my head back and look at the flames as he fucks me with it. It's so wide and thick, it feels like a cock inside me, and it reaches so deep that I am seeing fucking stars. Fighting against him, I whimper, but my eyes fly open when it starts to vibrate inside of me. Looking down at him with wide eyes, I watch those white orbs of his.

"Fuck," I cry out, gripping the rug as I push my pussy closer to his face. He keeps me trapped there, not being able to move or get away as it vibrates inside of me, filling me up and keeping me there.

I come with a scream, the orgasm taking me by surprise as it rips through my body all the way from my toes, and yet he doesn't stop. No, he keeps that fucking vibration going even as my pussy clenches around his tongue, until I'm screaming again. A second orgasm pulls from me and my throat becomes sore from screaming until I relax into the rug, my whole body like jelly.

He pulls it out of me, my pussy still pulsing, and wipes his mouth on the back of his hand before crawling up my body. I watch the way his muscles clench and I can't help it, I reach out and grip his shoulders before running my hands down his back to his arse, pulling him against me.

Lifting my head, I kiss him deeply, tasting myself on his mouth. His tongue has gone back to normal and I groan into the hard kiss. Tomorrow is like an impending storm or weight, sitting heavily on us until we are clinging to each other. Like if we pull away, the other will just disappear into nothing.

I wrap my thighs around him, and cry out when he lines up and enters me in one quick thrust. Pulling back from my mouth, he leans his forehead against mine as he fucks me slowly. Each thrust is unhurried and purposeful. Each time he pulls back, he twists his hips, hitting that spot inside of me. This isn't fucking—it's making love.

Holding onto his arse, I urge him to go faster but he growls, his eyes narrowing.

"You will be a good little monster and lay back and let me love you," he orders. My mouth parts on a groan and my eyes are still locked with his, like I daren't look away. "You look so fucking beautiful, laid out beneath me like this. The fire dancing across your soft skin, your pussy gripping me."

His dirty words have me kicking my legs, needing him to speed up, but he keeps moving slowly, prolonging my torture. Each thrust is hard and deliberate, and when he leans down and nips my nipple before sucking it into his mouth again, I come with a groan. Explosions ignite behind my lids, and he groans, stilling as he erupts inside of me.

Panting, I hold him to me, and my eyes flutter open to see him leaning against my chest. "You drive me crazy, Little Monster," he admits and I grin, before unwrapping my legs and he frowns. "Where the fuck do you think you're going? I'm not done with you yet," he growls.

He twists my nipple, shooting a spike of pain through me, before pulling out. I don't have time to catch my breath before he flips me. My face pushes into the fur rug and my eyes are on the flames as he pushes my thighs open and enters me again, his cock already hard.

"Nos," I moan, reaching back and gripping his hair as he starts to move. His thrusts are slow at first, but then he picks up speed, fucking me hard, each thrust bumping my cervix.

"So fucking perfect," he groans. "So fucking wet for me, you're so tight, like a glove wrapped around my cock." I love his fucking dirty mouth.

He grabs my hips, and pulls them into the air as he kneels behind me, and hammers into me. His balls slap against my skin and we moan loudly.

Pushing back into him, we soon find our rhythm. It's fast and hard and perfect after the loving he just gave me.

"Please," I beg, my stomach tight as that impending feeling of an orgasm encroaches again already.

He pulls out, making me growl, but before I can protest he parts my cheeks and presses the thick head of his cock against my other hole and starts slowly pushing in, pushing past the tight ring of my muscle.

He pulls back, before slowly pushing in. Again and again until he's seated in my ass all the way to his balls. Only then does he bend over me, kissing my shoulder as he pulls back and thrusts in.

"Nos, Nos, Nos," I chant his name like a prayer.

"Mine," he growls.

He picks up speed again, his cock filling my ass, until I'm fighting against him, needing him deeper and harder, needing that bite of pain. His fingers reach down, flicking my clit again and again, until I scream into the fire, coming so hard it feels like I can't breathe. Like he just pushed me over the edge of a cliff.

He speeds up, his thrusts violent as he fucks me until, with a roar, he explodes again. Whimpering, I lay on the rug, my breathing erratic. I daren't even try to move, I think he fucked me to death, again.

He relaxes into my back, kissing me gently, and our sweaty skins rubs together as the fire crackles in front of us. "You get ten minutes, and then you are mine again," he whispers softly, and the threat has me grinning.

Oh yes, being a monster has its perks.

CHAPTER 47

NOS

D awn is still sleeping when I get ready for the meeting with the fae. My gaze keeps going back to her. I should let her sleep. Although, she was the one who woke me in the early hours of the morning with her mouth around my cock. By the time we were done again, the sun was starting to rise. I had remained in bed far longer than I probably should have, but I am balking at the idea of leaving her.

If our bond is this strong after barely a week, then what will it be like in a hundred or a thousand years? She has quickly become the center of my world. My little monster. I would do anything for her, kill anyone for her, but I can't protect her from this. I know she is strong, I know she is powerful, but I have lived a long life and seen even the most powerful of people fall. The idea of losing her sends a bolt of panic through my chest and I sit on the edge of the bed, moving a stray curl of blonde hair away from her sleeping face.

Even if death did take her again, I would venture into the underworld and bring her back. She doesn't get away from me that fast, not now, not ever. Nothing in this world or the next will keep us apart.

My heart beating faster, my chest clenching in pain, I force myself to lean down and kiss her rosy lips goodbye. "I love you, Little Monster," I murmur.

Pulling away, I get up before I climb back into bed with her, and turn away. Grabbing my jacket and keys, I close the door softly and head downstairs. I didn't expect Griffin to be up, but when I get downstairs I see him on the sofa with a cup of coffee on the table in front of him, and a camera in his hands. He shuts it off when he hears me and I hesitate before going to sit across from him.

"Didn't sleep?" I ask, curious. I have no issue with my little monster's other mate, not at the moment anyway.

He shrugs and leans back. "Hard to with all the noise," he says bluntly and I grin.

"Don't expect me to apologize," I counter, and he scoffs.

"I wouldn't, shouldn't you be gone by now?"

Always straight to the point, is the fallen. Even now, I can see the hate and madness in his eyes. I don't know what Dawn sees in him, but when they are together she doesn't lessen that, in fact, she seems to call it out in him and revels in it.

Maybe she is his madness and he is hers.

"I am leaving, Fallen." His eyes narrow at the name, and mist curls around his fingers as he grabs the camera closer. "Griffin," I correct. "I know you have...mixed feelings about having a mate, but that woman up there still sleeping? She's my whole fucking world. I have searched every corner of this universe for her and no one will keep her from me. I won't be there today, but you will. Put your feelings aside, because if she gets hurt..." I trail off, letting him see how serious I am.

He grins. "What are you going to do, God?" he mocks.

"I wouldn't kill you, no matter how much you crave it. No, I would keep you alive. I would torture you for centuries until that mind of yours finally falls all the way into madness. Until you are nothing but a fucking animal on a leash. I will make whatever the council and Gabriel did to you seem like a fucking tea party. Griffin, I wouldn't kill you, I would destroy your world and you. Keep her safe, or I promise you to the heavens and back— you will regret it."

Without waiting for his response, I climb to my feet and leave him alone with his thoughts. One day he will regret the way he treated her, but he needs to realise that all on his own. Who knows, maybe he is too broken, too fucking mad to have a mate, but that is not up to me. The fates have a plan for the fallen and somehow it involves Dawn.

Getting on the bike I drove here, I kick it into gear, and with one last look at the window that leads to Dawn, I turn the bike and roar away into the early morning air. The city isn't busy at this time, and I make it through and into the forest roads with ease. Following the winding road, I speed up, loving the feeling. The only way it could be better is if my mate was on the back, with her arms wrapped around me. One day, one day I will show her my land.

When I reach the easily hidden dirt road, I slow and head down the beaten path to my cave. If you didn't know your way, you would easily get lost, and humans are known to perish out here from nature reclaiming them.

I spot the cave up ahead and ride in before turning off the ignition. Leaving the keys there, I strip off my clothes and fold them. You cannot go to the fae in your human form, they wouldn't show you the way or allow you in their sacred places. They seek the truth, even while they find ways to twist it. It is their weakness. They cannot lie, so they expect everyone else to follow that rule, and to them human skins seem like a lie.

Stepping back, I let the change come over me, switching to my full monster form, as they call it. The skull transforms on my face, and my knees widen and bend as hooves climb where my feet once were. I feel my antlers sprout from my head, my bones stretching and elongating as my whole body changes. It is over in seconds, and I crack my head from side to side before leaving the cave.

Making my way through the forest, I greet the animals I pass along the way. The fae lands are connected to mine, and through our friendship they told me to class it as mine as well, but to me it is always their land. Looking up at the sun, I groan. Being late to a fae meeting is never a good start, especially if they are feeling attacked.

I pick up speed and race through the forest. Tree branches move out of my way, and I knew every log, every twist, and turn, so it's easy going and within thirty minutes I have covered the two hour walk.

Slowing back down, I stop at the edge of their territory, the glamour they keep on it still intact before me. To humans and other supernaturals, it would simply look like a broken bridge with no way around it. They would also get the intense feeling to leave, and fear would race through their body as it does mine now— another byproduct of their glamour and wards to keep outsiders away.

Pushing past it all, I step onto the bridge and it all falls away, leaving me back to my normal self. If I was not welcome, I would have been killed or possibly just thrown back depending on the strength. If invaders still made it through, there were fae guard stationed at each entry point to their land. Their strongest warriors were always waiting and ready.

Like now, they drop from the trees and seemingly emerge from the dirt, with their hands and weapons all pointed at me. Grinning, I raise my hands in mock surrender.

"Brother, it is good to see you again," Ashera calls, fading into existence in the middle of the bridge. No doubt called by his fellow warriors upon my entry to their lands.

"Brother." I nod, genuinely happy to see the fae male.

The land on this side of the glamour is so much more than I could ever explain. Colours that do not exist within the human realm are dotted all over, and everything here is alive and powerful. The land itself vibrates under my feet, welcoming me. The trees lean closer to shelter us from the sun, and the flowers open up again.

The same bridge is still here, of sorts. It isn't broken now and it is made of fae metal, the strongest in existence, infused with magic — a crossing to their world and plane. It's also a point where fae can transport themselves to if they have that power.

Beyond the bridge lays their land and their castle. It is a strange place, because it both exists in our world but does not at same time, and the castle looks nothing like any of the human creation. Gothic, and infused with nature, it is said it is possible for the castle to actually move. Transforming into whatever you need, or whatever it wants. it only answers to the royal line and the rightful heirs, which

255

is how they decide who will lead them. If the land does not welcome you, then you do not lead.

"The king is expecting you," Ashera calls, walking closer until he embraces me in a warrior's hug. You do not touch the fae unless they first touch you, or you are invited to. Ashera is tall and willowy like most fae, with distinct pointy ears and cat-like eyes, in a stunning emerald green. His hair is long, blond, and held back with weaved braids. He is strong though, as the king's right-hand man he is one of the strongest fae to be born in centuries.

He steps back, nodding at his guards who fade back into their positions, and I join him as we walk across the bridge, side by side. "Then he knows why I am here?"

Ashera nods but does not speak, which isn't unusual. He only says what he feels must be said, nothing else, and unlike most fae, he does not speak an untruth.

All fae are incapable of lying, but they can twist the truth easily enough. Ashera does not, he believes any twisting is a lie and will not do it—not even for his king. It's one of the many reasons I like the fae man, you get what you see with him and he is honest.

As we step down from the bridge on the other side, I let myself relax with the trees creating a canopy above us, leading us straight to the heart of the castle. There are many myths and stories of the fae themselves. Some are true, some are...exaggerations.

Within their land different courts do exist, but only two. The Night Court, also known as the Winter Court, and the Light Court, also known as the Summer Court, but you are not necessarily born into that court. Your magic decides for you, as does the land. No fae is welcome in both, and strangely enough it creates harmony. Oh, don't get me wrong, they warred for a long time when a terrible queen sat upon the dark throne and a greedy king sat upon the light. It was when I first moved to the land and they both ordered me to pick sides.

The loss of life was great, both courts lost their powers, and the land started dying, sick of all the bloodshed and death. Only then did both leaders realise they were dooming their race by fighting. The humans were already killing enough of their territory, they did not need to do it between themselves. So I stepped in, and together we made a pact, a deal of sorts. One that even today is unknown to most people, a secret buried so deep that I will take it to my grave.

A baby.

Born of both courts, their bloods mixed and welcomed in the light and the dark. Tested by the land and named queen in both. She will one day take the throne, not that she is aware of her heritage. Not yet, it's not time. Only when she comes of age will she unite both of the courts, creating peace. One sought for a thousand years. One girl to save them all...because they are dying. Humans, metal, and magic, leading to less and less babies every year. Their magic is dying out and watering down. It was the only choice.

But that is a matter for a different day—now, we must figure out who was brave enough to step onto my lands, and I must see if they saw anything.

"You are different," Ashera observes, breaking the silence.

Looking over at the man, I notice the difference in him too. Where I once saw a boy, now stands a man with the scars, and a hard stare to prove it. Has it really been that long since I have been here? Maybe I was letting things slip before Dawn came along.

"As are you," I reply.

He nods, his face still serious, no laughter or smile there anymore. Once he would have—what has changed?

"I have found my mate," I confess with a grin, and he stops and looks at me.

"Congratulations, brother," he cheers, embracing me again before stepping back. His face once again stoic.

I incline my head and we continue our walk, the trees opening up as we cross the drawbridge into the castle grounds. There, in the center of the square, or the heart as they call it, is the mother tree. I tap my heart in greeting and step towards it. A branch breaks away and moves through the air towards me. I don't move, I stand still as it wraps around my finger and pricks it, taking my blood.

Everything with the fae includes sacrifice.

I turn and follow Ashera again as he leads me through the

twisting corridors, always seeming to know his way even as they shift right in front of him until we come out into a sitting room.

Ashera breaks away from me and heads over to the wall, fading against it, as a silent protector. Taking the seat opposite the king, I wait for him to speak.

The room is filled with the scent of oranges and flowers dot the walls. The ground is not steel, concrete, or stone, it is hard dirt. Four sofas sit in a square with a table behind one of them and chairs. It is an informal sitting room, which bodes well. Even the room the fae deem to see you in is a choice. If this had been the throne room, or worse, I would have known they were being coy with me, or treating me as a stranger or an enemy. This lets me know I may speak freely.

The king looks up from the book in his hand, pretending to have just noticed me. When most people think king, they think an older man. Now, Bayard is that, at over a thousand years old, but he doesn't look a day over forty. His golden hair falls to his shoulders in waves and his golden crown, with flowers and trees, is wrapped around his head. His eyes are the brightest blue and if he was using his power, would most likely blind or stun someone. He is like looking at the sun itself. Now, it surrounds him, glamoured to hide his true power. That also means he intends no harm. If his power was in use then I would be fucked.

He sits back and crosses his long legs. His body is one humans dream about. "Cernunnos," he greets, the only man to still use my given name.

I smile in greeting, making sure not to show teeth. Another strange tradition, but most creatures have fangs and flashing them is a warning.

"Your Highness," I greet him formally, knowing how to play this game. Even among friends, you must go by the rules or pay the price. If I had addressed him as King Bayard, the bloodied and fertile, I would have been addressing him too formally. Only calling Bayard shows that I am not giving him the proper respect of his title. It's the little things that matter with the fae and where many trip up.

"Please, call me Bayard." He nods, and I relax even further. It's a good sign.

"Then please call me, Nos," I reply in turn.

His eyebrow raises and a wicked grin curves his lips. "Nos?"

I grin back, unable to help myself. "My mate likes it."

He bursts into laughter, and the light catches him like a rainbow as a multitude of colours sparkle from him. Many would be mesmerized but I simply wait for him to finish.

His chuckles die off as the door opens and in sweeps Isla. Her red hair frames her beautiful face, and she has grown as well since I last saw her. Now she is a woman. Her skinny body has filled out and she has curves, but she is still nothing compared to my little monster.

Her maroon dress is tight around her upper body and cascades in waterfalls behind her, and when I hear a quiet inhale, I look over at Ashera. Interesting. He is watching her, his eyes seemingly unable to pull away. Blinking, he drags his gaze away almost reluctantly and meets mine. His face hardens, daring me to mention his perusal of the princess, so I simply wink. I see his lips twitch before I face the king again. I stand and bow.

"Princess Isla, as beautiful as ever," I greet formally and she laughs, the sound similar to her father's.

"Cernunnos, you flatter me. Please, call me Isla, are we not old friends?" she teases before sitting next to her father.

He arches a brow at her and leans over, his finger trailing across her ear and coming away red with blood. She bites her lip as her mismatched eyes—one blue and one green—dance in amusement. "Up to trouble again?" he asks.

"Me? Never father, the very thought," she quips.

When she crossed her leg, flashing skin, like her father I laugh. She has never been a normal Fae lady, in fact, most hate her for her spirit and confidence. She can talk politics with the best and wrap them around her finger, but she is also a warrior. She grew up with a dagger in her hand. Her father indulged it when she was younger because the court found it cute, but as she grew up he ordered for it to stop and, as Isla called it, 'princess lessons' to begin. I remember when I visited during that time of her life, she used to hide her hair, wear baggy clothing, and pretend to be a recruit to take part in the warrior training.

Once Bayard realised it would not stop her, he reluctantly allowed her to do both, much to the chagrin of the fae nobles. In their mind, a princess should be nothing more than a figurehead. In fact, many are wishing for the land to choose another, not that it will ever happen, but they do not know that. They do not know we already tested her, and the connection was even stronger than her father's—at both courts.

A princess, born of two bloods, during a time of great war. It makes sense she should be a warrior.

"Did I miss anything?" she inquires.

"Only that Nos has a mate," Bayard answers, and her eyes widen and swing to mine, showing genuine happiness in her gaze. I had watched this child grow, her father himself named me Uncle. Another thing which annoyed the court, but I still think of her as family, maybe even the child I never had.

"Truly?" she gushes, almost bouncing in her seat.

I nod and a smile breaks out as she laughs again. "It's about time old man, what is she like? She must be amazing to handle such a grumpy man," she teases and I hear Ashera snort.

"Isla," Bayard warns, but you can even hear the amusement in his voice. He has never been able to control her and he never will.

"She's amazing, a skinwalker. Very powerful and a warrior," I boast.

"She fights?" Isla asks, and I can tell she loves her already.

"Of course, in fact I think she could probably beat me. She can be quite scary when she wants to be. That is why I am afraid this meeting must be quick. She is very independent and is currently taking on a crime ring selling women...women both human and supernatural," I say sadly.

They both gasp, sitting back, but when they trade looks I know they aren't as shocked as they should be. "Bayard," I growl, sitting forward.

He sighs, and I truly look at him again. Under the power and sunshine, he looks weary. "What you felt on your land is not the first. Somehow, we do not know how, fae are disappearing, all women. We have tried to hunt the source, but we have been unable to. That is why this meeting is so important, my old friend. Our people are disappearing without a trace, from both courts, and no one can figure out how." I hear the anger in his voice and I sit back in shock.

For someone to get through the glamour and onto their lands, as well as block any sort of fae magic to trace them—they are powerful indeed. This is so much bigger than I could have imagined and that means Dawn has a bigger target on her back.

Standing in a rush I growl, "I must get back. My mate is in danger if what you say is true."

Bayard stands as well. "Please, old friend. One minute of your time then we will take you back to your mate."

My heart is torn in two directions, but I know Dawn has Griffin and I should still be able to make it back before the meeting, so I reluctantly sit. Wishing more than anything that she was by my side again.

"Tell us what you know, and we will do the same," Bayard implores, and I throw a look at the sun in the window. I still have time.

CHAPTER 48

DAWN

I woke up late morning, with the sun already streaming through the window and the bed empty apart from me. When I reach over and feel it's cold, I sigh, knowing Nos left hours ago. I wish he had woken me. Rolling over, I groan at the sore feeling of my whole body. I might be supernatural but it seems even monsters have their limits.

Forcing myself from the bed, I grab some clothes and slink downstairs, and into the bathroom before Griffin spots me. I'm way too tired and sore to be dealing with his dirty looks and remarks. Switching on the tub, I decide to relax and have a bath before the meeting later today. I'm going to need to switch skins as well, which will be tiring, so I'm going to rest for as long as I can and hope I can stay in that skin longer.

There is no bubble bath or anything, so once the tub is full I flick off the tap and sink into the warm water, sighing as it hits my tight muscles. Laying back, I sink in up to my chin and close my eyes.

I float for a while, letting out the cold water and refilling it with warm before the door bursts open. Without opening my eyes, I grin. "Well, good morning to you to Griffin, please do come in," I joke.

The door shuts and I hear moving about. "It's more like after-noon," he grumbles, before sitting on the side of the tub. Cracking open my eyes to look at him, I grin when I find his gaze locked on my body.

"Perv," I tease, before closing my eyes again.

He doesn't speak but I feel his fingers graze my thigh in the water, and I open my eyes to see his focused on me. "Don't forget about the meeting," he mutters, glaring at his hand that touched me like it betrayed him.

"I'll be ready, do we have a girl?" I ask.

He nods, looking away. "A human, I spoke to a sheep I trust. He's lending us one of his hookers for the night."

A mix between a snort and a laugh escapes me. "Hookers?" I parrot, and he throws me a scowl.

"Whatever the fuck you call them," he growls.

"Sex workers," I supply helpfully.

"Fine, sex workers. We will pick her up on the way." He stands up and storms out, making me sigh and sink back into the water.

Every time I think we make progress, he throws another wall up, one step forward and two steps back.

I left the pilots to deal with the human authorities and got in the car that Mike sent. Luckily it came with a driver, because I wouldn't have the fucking first idea how to drive.

Ignoring me completely, which I am happy with, he sits in the front of the black car and I sit in the back. Keeping my eyes moving, I check our surroundings as we drive. There have been too many attacks in such a short space of time, surely the witches will need to regroup soon, and that is my opportunity to disappear.

They clearly have a tracer already on me, not much I can do about that now, but they should be dying any minute now which will break the tracer. If the demon does his job.

"Phone for you, sir." The man in the front passes it back and I grab it with a nod.

"Speak," I rumble into it.

"Really? You had to destroy my plane? And please tell me why one of my blood bags is talking of demons?" Mike sighs, but I hear the interest in his voice.

"There was a demon, now there is not," I say bluntly and he laughs.

"No shit, how did you get rid of it? Usually people just die," he points out.

"I gave it something that it wanted more, the witches' deaths," I grumble, bored with talking. My voice box is sore from it, I never understood the need for words. Actions speak for themselves.

"You fucking genius." He laughs and I hear him telling others what I have told him.

Looking out of the window, I leave him to his conversation before he comes back. "Sorry, okay, my driver will take you where you need to go. Ring me if you need anything else."

"Fine." I hang up but the phone rings again.

Accepting the call, I wait. "That was rude, goodbye." Mike laughs and hangs up. Fucking vamps.

"How long?" I question the driver, handing the phone back.

"It will take us three days with stops," he informs me politely, looking at me in the rearview mirror.

"Don't stop," I growl and sit back, getting comfy. Three days, maybe two, and then I can finally meet my mate.

CHAPTER 49

ASKA

Sitting in the middle of the circle of witches, I close my eyes like they instructed, trusting them not to harm me. I made sure to keep half of the payment back first, it should keep me alive and stop them from cursing me.

Their hands are connected around my head and their voices rise as they chant foreign words. They assured me this would work, so I sit still even as my dragon growls impatiently.

The first brush of their magic reaches me, sifting along my skin, and looking for an opening before I feel the tendril disappear into my ear. My mouth opens on a gasp as more of it restricts around my body, caging me. It grows tighter and tighter as their chanting gets louder, until it cuts off all my breathing. I feel it stretching in my skin, reaching from the top of my head down to my toes.

Refusing to panic, I listen to their voices as they reach the crescendo and the magic breaks around me. Exploding outward and throwing me onto my back on the ship's floor.

My lungs fill with air as my eyes snap open, locking on the witches as they stumble into each other, obviously exhausted from their magic use. Not wanting to be in a weak position, I climb to my feet.

"Is it done?" I growl. My dragon is close to the surface after being kept prisoner in my own skin.

"Yes, dragon, it is done," Mercy says, her voice strained.

I nod and hand over the rest of the payment and turn to leave, but their voices stop me. "It does not mean whoever is hunting you will stop, I have never felt such power before. It was..." Mercy trails off.

"Different," Chloe adds.

"Mixed," Loxley confirms.

Looking at them over my shoulder, I frown. "Mixed, how?"

They share a look before all speaking. "It was not just a witch, it was many different types of magic mixed together."

"Th-they are stronger than you could ever imagine," Mercy declares.

"Tread lightly, dragon. Your mate is what they seek," Loxley advised.

I nod my thanks and quickly get out of there, their words haunting me across the walkway and to my car. The people who are hunting me are after my mate? What does mixed mean, how can the power of a witch be harnessed by others?

One thing is for sure, she is going to need me now more than ever, enemies are closing in on every side. It's time to find Dawn.

CHAPTER 50

NOS

"I have to leave!" I argue, pacing around the confines of the sitting room.

Bayard sighs and leans forward, placing his hands on his knees. We have been talking for hours and it is getting us nowhere, not to mention the longer I spend here the longer Dawn is in danger. I have to warn her, I have to get to her, not discuss politics and untruths.

"Cernunnos—" I growl and he corrects himself. "Nos—"

Turning to him, I narrow my eyes. "My mate is out there, in danger right now. Do not mince your words, Your Highness. Tell me what we need to know so we can make a plan or I shall leave."

"Father, please," Isla begs, throwing him a withering look.

He waves his hand, before sitting back like a sulking child and she smiles. "Here is what we know. Twenty fae nobles, ten from each court, have been taken. All women, all powerful. There were no breaches of our glamour or border, and our guards were...investigated, and no errors were found," she explains. What a nice way to say they were tortured...

"You have said supernatural women are being sold, is it possible more are being taken from other clans and races, and we just don't know because we are all too spread out and do not speak?" she muses, and I incline my head at her logic. "So now, more than ever, we must stick together. We need to find out who is taking them and why, then we can exact our revenge and save our people if we must."

Sighing, I sit down again now that we are getting somewhere. "The council will need to hear of this as well, if they are not already aware. What are your plans to make sure it does not happen again?" I ask, needing to know they will be okay while I leave and find Dawn.

Bayard looks at his daughter and inquires, "What do you think we should do?"

She sucks in a breath, and even I raise my eyebrow at that. He is a very confident king and he is asking her opinion? "We should increase security, rework our defenses and glamour. We should implement a curfew, but father, what we need most is an alliance with the Night Court." He goes red and she interrupts before he can explode. "Yes, I know we don't get along, but their people are missing too, so it's obviously not them behind this."

"Unless that's what they want you to think," Ashera mumbles but she ignores him.

"That means someone is targeting the supernaturals, especially with all the information Nos has supplied. We need to call a truce and work together to defend our people, they are what come first, after all. Nos, you will find your mate and attend this meeting. You work in your world and see what you can find, we shall work in ours. You have the full disposal of our people, and I assume we have you?" she implores, and I smile at her, beyond proud. A true leader.

"Of course, and the council will condone this," I add, and she nods.

"We will meet again in a week to discuss our findings, we also need to start reaching out to other species, see if they have the same problem," she lists, her eyes downcast as she thinks through everything that needs to be done.

"I shall try, I have connections," I assure her.

"Okay, and we will talk to the Night Court. Father, we could use them now more than ever. With our magic combined, we might be able to see something that we couldn't before. Now is time for unity, together we will survive, alone we will die." She sits taller in her seat, looking like the queen she will be.

"And who, exactly, is going to go to the Night Court to suggest this? I cannot, it is forbidden!" he shouts, with fury on his face but also consideration. He is a smart man, he knows what must be done. All of us in this room can see what will happen next.

"Me," Isla answers simply. "I will go."

Ashera steps forward then, his eyes on his king. "If she goes, I go." Isla's eyes widen, as do Bayard's, at the fae warrior having such strong feelings and actually speaking to his king like that.

"Fine, take two more with you. Your best, any more warriors than that, then that bitch will think it is a war party. I will send word of a diplomatic mission. Nos, you will return, yes?" he asks, already standing.

I stand as well. "Of course."

"Good, bring your mate next time," he orders, and sweeps from the room. Isla and Ashera all take a breath and relax.

"I must leave," I say, and Isla frowns but stands, running over and embracing me.

"Be careful, please Uncle Nos?" she begs and I grin at her.

"You know what they say, Izzy? You can't kill a god." I wink and she laughs. I turn to my old friend to see him looking at her. "I must leave, brother, see me to the barrier?"

He looks over at me and leaves the room. I look back at Isla. "Be gentle on him, Izzy, for someone so smart he is blind to the ways of his heart," I warn, before leaning down and kissing her forehead.

"I will," she promises, and I give her one last look before following Ashera.

The fae and I walk in silence back to the bridge, and what I have just found out sits heavily on my shoulders. There is no denying it anymore, someone is hunting us, I just wish I knew who and why.

When we reach the halfway point of the bridge, Ashera stops and I mirror him. "If someone is strong enough to get in and out without us noticing. They are powerful, really powerful," he concludes.

"They are, that makes them dangerous, but one thing I have learned in my life, brother, is that powerful people are the first to fall." We both stare out into the forest lost in our own thoughts.

"Your mate, how did you know?" he finally asks.

"I felt complete, like a piece of me that was missing finally came home. Looking into her eyes didn't make me want to give her the world, it made me want to walk across it by her side. Love is easy, a fleeting thing. There are different types, the one you fight, the one that hurts, and the one that is forever. She is the forever kind." I shrug.

He doesn't say anything, but I see the confusion on his face and clasp his shoulder. "Brother, may I give you some frank advice?"

He nods, turning his eyes to me. "Don't fight it, I saw the way you two looked at each other and I know you well. If it was a fling, you would ignore it, but this goes deeper. You love her. As we are finding out, we are not as immortal as we thought we were, do not waste that time. Love deep and love hard."

He nods. "I'm scared," he admits, and that in itself nearly staggers me.

"Good, that means it's real. Fear means you are alive. The strongest warriors use that fear, they do not let it control them. Even a warrior has a heart, Ashera—make her yours." I pull away, leaving him to his thoughts as I head to the barrier.

"Be safe, brother," he calls.

"And you," I reply, before I step over the magic and back into my own forest.

As soon as my bare feet hit the soil, I am running. The sky is almost dark—I am too late. I can feel it.

Little Monster, I am coming. Hold on.

Chapter 51

Dawn

O nce I'm dressed and my hair is dry, I head downstairs. When I don't spot Griffin anywhere, I open the door to the basement to check down there. When I reach the bottom, I spot him preparing a bag of weapons. Ray is still tied in the corner, with his eyes open and wide as he watches Griffin. I raise my eyebrows at the gag tied over Ray's mouth and walk over to Griffin.

He ignores me, even when I hop up on the gun range table next to him. "Why is he gagged?" I ask curiously.

He grunts but ignores me. "Griffin, why is he gagged?" I repeat, my voice harder.

He sighs, drops the gun he was playing with and looks over at me. "Because he wouldn't shut up and it was either that or cut his tongue out."

"Okay." I shrug and he looks at me in confusion.

"Okay?" he echoes and I nod, swinging my legs back and forth. "Why okay?" he asks slowly, like it might be a trap.

"Well, he's going to die anyway, I don't care what you do to him." I shrug again and I hear Ray struggling in the corner, screaming behind his gag. "Shut up, Ray Ray or I will cut off your balls one at a time and make you eat them," I threaten, before turning back and smiling at Griffin.

"Let's do this, shall we?" I inquire and he nods, watching me intently, and when I jump down he actually jolts.

He follows behind me, throwing me looks every now and again when he thinks I can't see. Kneeling before Ray, I wag my finger. "If I take out the gag, you aren't going to scream, are you?"

He shakes his head, his eyes filled with fear, but I can almost taste the lie, making me tut. "If you do, I will let Griffin cut out your tongue," I say sweetly, and he stops moving, his eyes swinging to Griffin before he swallows and nods his understanding.

Pulling the material from his mouth, I let it drop to his neck. He swallows and licks at his lips as he watches me.

"Now, Ray. I'm going to need to borrow something from you," I tell him kindly, moving closer.

He pulls back, plastering himself against the wall, but his eyes are for Griffin, obviously thinking he will be the one to kill him.

"What?" he asks, his voice rough and wobbly.

"Your skin," I purr.

He turns to me sharply and his mouth opens when I dart in. Holding his head hard, I seal my lips to his. Surely, there has to be a better way than this, but that's a problem for another time.

He starts to struggle against me, his legs kicking out, but I hold his head tighter, pulling his energy from him. This time I don't stop. He's evil and he deserves to die. He was never going to live, not once we had his name—it seems apt that his death is at the hands of a woman they tried to sell.

He stops fighting soon enough and I pull my mouth away. His skin is sunken, his mouth stretched wide, and his eyes are almost popping from his skull. A noise leaves his mouth and I grin. "What was that?" I coo and he whines again, his eyes rolling around.

I feel the change rolling through me and I know what to expect this time, so I fall back to my ass and let it come. It moves over my body, and now that I'm not fighting it as much, it seems easier. There is still pain, and the horrible sensation of skin moving and your body changing, but it's over quicker—quicker than ever before, until I sit in front of Ray as a carbon copy of him.

"Hi, sugar." I laugh, my voice deep like his.

A whine comes from his mouth and his feet are twitching, but I get bored of playing with him. Leaning close I drop a kiss on his forehead. "Have fun in hell." Grabbing him on either side of the head again, I rip.

It's easier than I figured it would be, and I stand with Ray's head held in my hand. Blood drips to the floor as his legs twitch next to me.

Looking down at myself, I frown. "I'm going to need some clothes."

Watching Dawn, Ray, whatever the hell I call her, slip into my boxers and clothes is the weirdest thing I have ever seen, especially when she looks over and winks at me.

Turning away, I grab my bags and get ready. When I turn back she's dressed and ready to go. "Come on," I murmur, shaking my head when she blows me a kiss and stomps back down the stairs and waits for me at the front door.

Leading her to the garage attached to the house, I roll up the door and flick on the light. She whistles when she sees my sports car and I can't help the grin that lights up my face.

"Figured we couldn't fit three people on my bike," I mutter before sliding in. She slips into the passenger seat, having to cramp the big guy's body in.

"I'll never get used to having a cock," she mutters, and I can't help the laugh that falls out.

"And I'll never get used to you having one," I tease, grinning over at her.

273

She winks, running her hand down her body. "Want to try some butt stuff? I love it, personally."

I cringe, throwing her a narrow-eyed look. "I'll stick to your 'butt stuff,'" I warn, before turning on the ignition and pulling from the garage, pressing the button inside the car to make the door roll down.

She laughs as we shoot down the street with the sun setting in my rearview mirror. We are quiet for the rest of the drive, the meeting weighing heavily on us. Gripping the wheel tighter, I watch the road. "Speak as little as possible, less likely for them to catch you out. As soon as you have information, you signal. Tap your chest three times. If you feel in danger, tap your chest five times. We are in and out," I warn.

"Why, Griffin, it sounds like you care," she teases.

Swerving around some cars going too slow for my liking, I ignore her comment. "Dawn," I growl.

She sighs, leaning back in the seat with a frown. "Yes, I under-stand. It's not like I can die twice, right?" she jokes, but it only makes me growl harder.

"Griffin, I'll be okay, plus you have my back," she says softly, well, as soft as she can when she's a man.

Pulling up into the parking lot next to the strip club the sheep I am trusting owns, I wait for the girl he told me would help me out. Turning to face Dawn, I open my mouth, to respond when there is a bang on my window.

I have my knife out in a second and Dawn growls, her eyes going black. When I spot the woman waiting with a bored look on her face, I roll down the window, keeping the blade in my hand just in case. "Crystal?" I ask bluntly.

She nods. "You going to let me in darlin'? It's fucking cold out here."

I unlock the doors and wind up my window as she slips into the back. I turn to face her. "You know your job?" I growl, scrunching my nose up at the fresh scent of cum and sex.

"Yes." She grins. "Play stupid, act helpless, and listen to hottie there." She nods at Dawn and I grin.

"You should see her without her skin," I joke and Dawn laughs, looking over at the girl.

"You're too clean," she murmurs, and the woman laughs.

"Darlin', I've never been clean."

Dawn sighs, shaking her head and looking at me. "She looks too clean for the way they were selling the girls."

Looking back over the woman, I nod my understanding. Although her clothes aren't brand new, they are well cared for—tight blue jeans with holes, a corset top, and leather jacket. She doesn't exactly look like a prisoner.

Dawn leans over the seat, meeting the girl's eyes again. "You mind if I undress you?"

I have to hold in a laugh at the excitement on the woman's face. I'm pretty sure she thinks Dawn, or Ray, is coming on to her.

"Go for it, darlin'," she whispers.

Dawn grins, climbing over the seat and putting her butt in my face, and joins the woman in the back. I watch through the mirror as she makes the woman giggle while she half undoes the corset and actually takes the woman's jeans off. Sitting back, she nods, looking at me for confirmation.

"Better," I add, she does look like a slave now.

Dawn pats the woman's head, who pouts, as Dawn climbs back over the center console and into the passenger seat. The sex worker leans forward and places her hand on my shoulder, making me look at it in disgust.

"What about you hottie, you want to undress me too?" she asks.

Looking at her over my shoulder, I let her see my cold, uninterested gaze. "No," I growl, before gripping her hand and removing it from my shoulder. She sits back in her seat with a weird smile on her face.

Turning back to the wheel, I start the car and head to the meeting point, listing all the possible ways this could go wrong in my head.

Twenty-five, if you were wondering.

CHAPTER 52

DAWN

By the time we get to the meeting place at the docks, we only have five minutes to go.

"Better hide your car and yourself," I murmur to him, as I grab the handle and slide out. He leans across the seat, stopping me as I'm closing the door.

"I will be watching the whole time, remember, tap your heart three times," he orders. Leaning in closer to him, I grin.

"Such a worrier," I tease, before shutting the door in his face. I open the back door for the woman Griffin picked up and she follows me out, shivering in the cold, which I can barely feel.

When I shut the door, Griffin speeds away, but I know he will be watching from somewhere. Grabbing the girl's arm to make it look real, I pull her over to the barriers. The water shines on the other side, deep and dark, and the moon reflects off of it. She wraps her arms around her and I sigh.

"This shouldn't take long, try not to talk too much okay?" She nods and I push her to the ground. "Huddle at my feet like you're scared, it might keep you warmer."

She curls into a ball and we wait.

Headlights flash across the empty pier, stopping in the parking lot meters away. I watch from my position, the lights nearly blinding me, as they seem to take ages to get out. For a moment I think I've forgotten something, or they somehow know it's not me, but when they get out I breathe a sigh of relief. I'm betting they are just cautious, and rightly so.

I don't look around for Griffin, not wanting to draw their attention to him. Instead, I wait with the woman at my feet as they shut off their lights and head my way. I count ten of them in total. It looks like nine bodyguards, from the way they are scanning the area and surrounding the man in the middle.

He's not what I was expecting, at all. Oh he gives me the creeps all right, but he looks old and fragile. He must be in his sixties, with short-trimmed grey hair, even a grey beard. He is almost unassuming, almost blending in with the big, muscular men around him. My eyes would skip over him in the crowd, maybe that's the point. Even the way he walks makes him look weak, but from the look in his eyes, he is anything but.

They stop meters away from me and I panic. Do they have a code word? A handshake?

"Raymond." The old man's voice is clear and strong, making me re-estimate him.

I incline my head, unsure how to greet the man before me, but I shouldn't have worried, his eyes drop to the girl at my feet and light with interest, completely ignoring me now. "What have you brought me this time?" he asks, his voice rushing in excitement.

I push the girl forward with my foot, thinking quickly on the spot. "Doc doesn't know what she is, but he mentioned fire," I blurt, and wince before schooling my expression when he looks at me.

"Fire?" He taps his chin before grinning. "Excellent. Load her up," he snaps at the men.

Two walk over to us and grab her by the arms and pull her to her feet. As they bend over, two identical necklaces slip from their shirts—a large, green glowing stone on the end of a metal clasp. Frowning, I watch as they pull her away, she starts to struggle, throwing me a look as they drag her over to the old man.

"Gag her, I hate it when they talk," the man orders, before turning back to me, the nasty look on his face disappearing in an instant.

"Your payment will be wired as usual." He nods and turns to leave, shit.

Think Dawn, think.

"Actually, we want to renegotiate," I blurt out and all the men freeze, looking between each other as the old man gives me a considering look.

"What was that?" he asks, his voice deadly, and he straightens up and my mouth drops open in shock at the power pouring from him. Holy fuck, he's a supe.

His eyes change colour, his hair turns brown, and his wrinkles disappear until a middle-aged, attractive man is standing before me. "You were saying?" he demands and the men tighten around him.

I spare them a look, noticing the same strange glowing coming from every one of their chests. The woman starts to fight, screaming at everyone.

"I'm not getting paid enough for this shit!" It cuts through the air and the man's head swivels her way, his eyes narrowing before he stomps over to her. Grabbing her head in a vice, he growls into her face as she screams.

"Paid?"

She nods, her eyes looking at me. "Dawn, he paid me."

"Dawn?" the man questions, looking over at me with confused eyes.

"Test her." He throws the woman at one of the men who touches her forehead lightly, his eyes closing as he concentrates. With a snarl he pulls away, spitting at her feet.

"Human, sir," he replies.

The no longer old man looks at me, his eyes cold. "Kill her," he orders.

One of the men pulls a gun and before I can scream a warning or move, he aims and fires, hitting Crystal right between the eyes. She falls to the ground, blood pooling around her head as I look back at the man in charge. Griffin tried to warn me, Nos as well, but I thought I could handle it. These aren't humans and they aren't messing around.

My arm starts to shake and I quickly hide it behind my back, knowing it means I need to change back soon.

"Care to explain, Ray, or should I call you Dawn?" he inquires, stepping closer, his men with him. They all look angry now, and hungry for my blood.

"We should kill the human and find another to work with," one of the men suggests, and the man in charge taps his chin before sighing.

"Maybe you are right," he mutters, sparing me a look. "He has become more trouble than he is worth. Kill him." With that, he turns and walks back to a car and gets in. It pulls away, leaving only one car and all the man's bodyguards behind.

They converge on me, their eyes excited as they move closer. My death is written across all of their faces.

I hear his wings before arms band around me, pulling me from the ground and yanking me into the air. He holds me close and I turn in his arms, burying my face in his chest as we fly higher and higher, so those on the ground below can't see us. After what feels like hours, we level out and he starts away, flying hard.

"Hold tight, we need to get far away," he screams and I nod, not trusting my voice in case the wind sweeps it away. I feel the change come over me, and I let it. I clamp my mouth shut so not to distract Griffin until I sigh, finally back to myself again. Griffin's clothes hang loose around me, so I reach down with shaking fingers, and tighten the belt on the pants to keep them up.

We don't talk as we fly away, at least for ten minutes or so, and when I peek down all I can see is the dots of the city's lights below.

Looking up, I meet his hard, angry eyes.

"What the fuck were you thinking? I knew this was a bad idea," he yells and I glare, starting to get mad. That had been close, too fucking close.

"I'm fine, I knew you had my back. That's what mates do, right?" I joke, and he turns to stone against me. His eyes glitter in the night sky, flashing down on me like lightning as he focuses his intensity on me.

"You trust me too much," he warns. "Remember, I'm an assassin. I have no loyalty."

279

"Liar," I goad. I don't know why, but I'm sick of him talking about himself and this connection like this. There is only so long you can lie to yourself and I'm tired of seeing him wallow with the pity dick in his mouth.

"I warned you, *vasculo*." He opens his arms and I scramble to keep hold of him, but it's no use. The wind pulls me away as I plummet to the city below.

He watches me, beating his wings to keep him still, looking so much like an angel watching a human fall to their death. His beauty, his anger—his everything.

In his eyes I see the truth, he is testing me. He's pushing me away because he still doesn't believe he deserves a mate. If I fail the test now, again, I will only be proving him wrong and he is wrong. I do trust him, more than he trusts himself.

He thinks he's crazy, and he is. He thinks he's nothing more than a monster, which he is, but I see something beyond all that—I see him.

I stop struggling and let the wind take me. I let myself fall, my arms and legs floating, my hair whipping around me as I keep my eyes on him while he grows smaller and smaller. I don't scream, I don't even look down. I keep my eyes up—I keep my eyes where I know my savior is.

My heart is racing. Inside I'm fighting, but on the outside—I'm calm.

The seconds pass by in a blur and I know I'm growing closer to the city below, even with my healing and strength I don't think I can survive this fall. My life is in his hands. His to take, his to save. The assassin with a choice, because if he chooses to save me, then he is choosing me. Choosing life.

I refuse to close my eyes as I feel the ground rushing up to me, but like an avenging angel, he breaks through the darkness above. He holds his wings to his chest as he spirals down to me, shooting through the air, his hands stretched out to grab me. Beaming, I hold my hands out, hoping he will get to me in time. Inside my heart leaps in happiness and I nearly purr.

He grows closer and closer, but I can see the panic and regret on his face and I know he isn't going to make it. Blinking hard, to get rid of the water from the wind, I smile sadly at him.

"It's okay," I mouth at him and he growls loudly, like thunder splitting the night, and tucks his wings in closer, diving for me.

If he doesn't pull up now, we will both hit the ground. He will be hurt, maybe even die.

"Griffin, it's okay. Pull up," I shout, but he ignores me.

His eyes glitter like stars from the determination within, his face hard and unreadable.

I stretch my hands higher as he reaches out, our fingertips brushing. I can hear car horns now, smell the ground. He screams and I close my eyes.

I feel his arms wrap around me, knocking my breath away, and my eyes fly open. Looking down, I spot the ground mere meters away and I glance back up to see his face strained as he beats his wings, trying to get us up and away from the ground. He yells, his arms tightening as we shoot upward.

He falters in the air from the strain and we drop again, but this time he turns mid-air, keeping his back to the ground I can see rushing towards us. He grunts when we hit the roof of a building, sliding slightly before stopping.

Both of us are breathing heavily, staring at each other in amazement before his expression clouds over and turns to anger.

"What the fuck, Dawn!" he yells, like I was the one who dropped me.

I snort and lean down, dropping a kiss on his parted lips. He freezes and I pull away, rolling to the roof next to him. I stare at the sky and work on slowing my heartbeat.

"Never doubted you," I joke.

He jumps to his feet with his hands in his hair as he paces, muttering to himself. I sit up and place my head on my knees. He screams and turns to me, his whole body shaking with the power and anger running through him.

"Why do you care? Why are you pushing this so much?" It sounds angry, but underneath I can hear him struggling to understand, and that's when it hits me. He probably has never experienced love, he doesn't know why or how. For him, I'm just another person in a long line waiting to hurt, betray, or use him. My poor Griffin. Jumping to my feet, I face him and lay it all out, it's the only way he's ever going to understand.

"You forget, I was alone when I died. I met death and no one cared, no one even stopped...no one noticed. So whatever the fuck this is, fate, dumb luck, even just chance, I don't give a shit. I'm going to grip it with both hands and let it warm me through, because I never want to feel the cold, dark touch of death and be alone again. I would endure any pain, any wrath. Let your rage wash over me, face your crazy and hurt, and still stand. Now, the question is, why don't you want this so much?" I ask, finally letting the hurt into my voice. I know I'm not the best mate, hell, I'm a monster, but I'm the only one they are going to get and it hurts that he keeps turning away from me so much.

"Are you really going to give up a chance of happiness, or having someone there, someone at your back, because you've been hurt before? Boo fucking hoo, shit happens. Not loving someone, or being alone doesn't stop that person from getting hurt. It just means you aren't there to see it. You've seen cities built, technology advance, and yet you're too dumb to realise the only thing we have in this fucking world is each other," I finish, my chest rising and falling quickly as I get everything out before he tries to speak.

I suck in a breath and shout, "Yes, call me all the names you want Griffin. Curse me, leave me to do whatever you want to make yourself feel better. To make sure your walls stay up and you never get hurt. In the end, it won't matter. What will is who's beside you when the end comes. Like I trusted you just then, I knew you would always catch me. You need to learn to trust me because, baby, I am never going to drop you," I promise.

The panic on his face is adorable as he watches me like a lost little boy and his wings droop behind him as he faces down his worst fear—trusting someone.

"Why, why, I need to know why!" he screams, stopping before me, his eyes filled with his own special brand of Griffin madness. I embrace that too.

Stroking the side of his face, I let him see the truth in my eyes. "I know you don't believe me, not yet, but you will. We stick together, us monsters. I will never judge you, not for your madness or your anger, and you will stand by me like you did tonight. You asked me why, it's simple. You are my mate."

It's the wrong thing to say. He growls and pulls himself away before jumping on the roof ledge, his wings spreading out. I follow him, hopping up next to him and balancing there as I grab his arm.

"No, I lied. It's not that simple. It's because even though you don't know me, you saved my life more than once. It's because of the anger I see in your eyes whenever I mention my ex-husband. It's the fucking good I see in you when you saved those women when you didn't have to. It's because of the beauty you craft with your hands and hide away so no one can see. It's because, even though you're angry and driven to madness, you take pictures to show your view of the world. Everything for you is dark, but if you let me, I will be your light," I vow.

He swallows hard and turns to face me, with the night sky and the drop to the ground to our right, and the rooftop to our left. "And if I can't?"

"What does it hurt to try?" I ask seriously. I reach out my hand and leave it in the middle, waiting for him decide. I won't force him.

My heart races and my palm turns sweaty for those agonising seconds he leaves me waiting, but he slowly places his hand in mine before using it and dragging me to him. Looking up at him from the circle of his arms, I smile.

"It doesn't mean I won't be an asshole, just not all the time," he warns and I laugh.

"I never expected anything else from you," I admit and he chuckles, and the sound makes me grin, because there is true happiness ringing there. He stops, his eyes sparkling, and I reach up on my tiptoes and kiss him gently before settling back on my feet again.

"You call that a kiss?" he scoffs.

He leans down and covers my mouth, and I part my lips and he sweeps in. Groaning, I reach up and grip his shoulders as the kiss turns hard. All fighting tongues and clashing teeth, our need exploding between us. Between both near misses and our fight, this had been brimming for a while.

He grips my ass and drags me closer before groaning into my mouth and picking me up. Wrapping my legs around his waist, I hold on to him hard, giving as good as I get. Loving the hard way he grips me, not like I'm fragile, but like I'm an equal.

I gasp and pull away from his mouth as he lifts us from the roof, his wings flapping to get us above the city until we are floating in the sky. There is no rush this time, nothing to run from or a fight to be had. Instead, I look around me in awe, loving the freeing feeling of flying.

I laugh and lean back in his arms, holding my arms out to side and letting the air flow through my fingers. Looking back at Griffin, I see him smiling softly, for once just happiness on his face.

"I have always wanted to try something," he teases, and I lean into him with a wicked grin.

"Well, come on then, do tell, wing boy," I quip.

"Why don't I show you?" he snarks back, as one of his arms stays around me, but his other snakes under my top and cups my breasts, the loose male shirt billowing around us as he untucks it. It's not like I could wear a bra in male form, so his warm palms covers my hard nipple and he starts to roll it between his fingers, making me gasp.

"Griffin," I moan, when his hand leaves my breasts and travels down my stomach, leaving fire in its wake as he touches me. He reaches the trousers, the only reason they have stayed up is the belt, which he undoes, and unzips them before slipping his hand inside. My eyes go wide as he nudges past the boxers I borrowed from him and cups my pussy.

"You can't be serious." I laugh.

"Deadly, unless you're scared?" he taunts.

Grinning, I grip his shoulders harder. "Don't drop me this time, Fallen," I order as he rubs my clit, making me moan.

He leans in and kisses me. "Never again," he whispers, as he wrings moan after moan out of me and into the night sky.

CHAPTER 53

DUME

The car stopping has me springing up in my seat. The driver looks over at his shoulder at me. "Sorry, sir, I need to visit the bathroom and get fuel." He nods at the station we are at and slides from the car.

Groaning, I slide from the car as well and stretch my body. My muscles are cramped from being in that small space for so long. Leaning back against the black car, I eye the station we have stopped at. It's busy at this time of day, with cars parked out front and at the pumps. People have pulled up on the side at a picnic area, and seem to be relaxing.

Scanning the cars, my eyes linger on a nondescript black van, but when I see the woman and man heading to it with laughter on their faces and food in their arms, I shrug it off and look away.

Night is setting, you can feel it, and with it brings a cold chill to the air, but that isn't the reason I find myself slipping back into the car. Something is off. Growling under my breath, I palm my swords and wait.

The driver eventually makes his way back to the car and he takes one look at my face before jumping inside and speeding off. Staring out the back window, checking to see if anyone is following us, I relax when I spot nothing.

Once we are a couple of miles away, I relax back into my seat

285

and look at the driver. "No more stops, we are being hunted," I order.

He nods, his hands gripping the wheel tightly. "Should I call master Carmichael?" he offers, his voice surprisingly calm.

"No, I'll handle it when they decide to make their move. Just keep your eyes on the road and get me where I need to be," I demand before sitting back, my swords ready in my lap. Waiting.

Being the hunted, the prey, doesn't sit well with me, so I am just waiting for their first move so I can flip it on them.

ASKA

I'm more relaxed now that I know the tracer is broken, even if the witches' words keep rattling around in my head. Even my dragon is on high alert, sensing an issue. I pull over when it gets dark and try to connect to Dawn, but nothing happens. Frowning, I carry on driving, planning to try again later.

Pressing down on the gas, I speed up as something urgently pushes me to reach my mate. When I pull over a couple of hours later and I still can't reach her, I start to get really worried. It's possible she is not sleeping, that she is busy, but my dragon roars inside of me. A warning, or a threat?

Grabbing the phone, I scroll through the contacts, hoping Jean Paul will have loaded some from before or kept updated numbers. When I spot the name Lucias, I grin.

Dialling, I grip the wheel as I speed through the night until the call connects.

"Who is this?" comes a heavily accented Russian voice.

"Is that anyway to greet an old friend?" I tease, and I hear him inhale.

"Aska, is dat you?" he asks, shocked.

"Yes," I say simply.

"Well, shit, if you're awake something is really fucking wrong," he laments, and I hear him moving. I can picture him now, reclining in the leather chair in his council office. I have known Lucias since he was a youngling and I watched him all my life. He grew up fast, powerful as well, until he was asked to sit on the western council. He agreed.

"Aska?" he murmurs, sounding tired.

"What is wrong, Luke?" I ask, frowning.

"Nothing, nothing, just politics," he grumbles, making me laugh.

"Well, you did choose that life, Luke," I joke.

He mutters something in Russian. "Aska, why are you calling me?" He doesn't say it harshly, more like he is curious. I made him vow to never wake me, I told him of my plans and he knew of my withdrawal from this life—so it's a valid question.

Why am I awake? Her.

"The mate call," is all I say.

"Well, shit," he chokes out.

We both go silent, my own thoughts drifting to my life before my slumber. I had been through wars with this man, he is trustworthy and good...but that was a long time ago. Has this life changed him? Is he really the Luke I fought side by side with in the crusades? Can I trust him?

"родной брат?" he prods, always impatient, just like when he was a boy and used to follow me around trying to carry my sword for me after battle.

"I have too many enemies, brother. I have been gone too long and I fear for my mate. The witches hinted at things not quite being what they seem. I have a bad feeling," I conclude, gritting my teeth and overtaking a car.

He sighs, moving around again, the seat creaking under his weight. "Your feelings are always right," he points out.

"That is what I am worried about. Could you do some digging?

Is there anything I need to know?" I inquire, knowing something is happening but unsure how to phrase it correctly.

"держать, one minute," he mutters, his English mixing with his Russian like he does when he is upset. His chair creaks again, and I hear retreating footsteps and the banging of a door before his voice comes back through the speaker.

"Aska, the world has changed, so has the council's job. We are struggling to maintain our hold over the races, they are far too spread apart and, well...losing power. This is a human's world now, not a monster's. What I know is some see us losing power as a good thing, others see it as a sign of weakness. That we are giving into the humans, letting the sheep rule us. They are unhappy," he finishes, sounding more tired now than ever.

"Unhappy, how unhappy?" I growl.

"There has been...little spurts of rebellion, I would say. Nothing much, and we have kept it under wraps, but it is happening. But, I do not see why this would affect you. I shall do some digging surrounding your new mate and her location, see what I can come up with and let you know, da?" I can hear him rubbing his head now. Just how much pressure is Luke under?

"Yes, thank you, Luke," I murmur, thinking his words through.

"Stay safe, da? I shall speak to you soon, and once you have your mate I would love to meet the woman who is going to tame the dragon," he says then laughs, cutting off the call.

Knuckling down, I stare at the signs as I speed past, my dragon clambering to leave my body. This isn't the world I left when I went away, we were gods. We were the dark, the reason humans prayed and locked their doors. Now...now we are almost being forgotten?

What does this mean for the monsters like me?

CHAPTER 54

GRIFFIN

She moans in my arms, looking so beautiful with nothing but the stars behind her. Reminding myself to keep flying, I beat my wings and grit my teeth with the need to rip off her trousers and sink into her heat. But I want to prove I can be more than just a brutal fuck, since that's what it's always been so far. I want to prove I am more, especially after she trusted me with her life earlier. Crazy bitch.

The thought makes me grin, I had let my madness take over. It whispered lies and hurt until I couldn't help it. Regret winds through me, even though she doesn't seem to care. Again and again she lets me get away with this kind of shit, maybe it's time I started to prove to her I can make a good mate too. More than just the crazy assassin she has seen. That I am hers.

Dipping my finger into her warm, wet heat, I slowly bring her to the edge before adding another finger and curling them inside of her. Grinning, I watch her eyes slip closed in pleasure as she holds on to me, her claws like a kitten cutting into my shoulders. She doesn't even know how much trust she is putting in me right now, it's astounding.

Deciding to move, I turn us flat so her back faces the ground while I fly and pleasure her. She cries out, her pussy clamping around me as she comes apart in my arms. She looks so fucking beautiful, my own mate.

She blinks open those stunning eyes, and I see that they are black. My cock is already hard, but it throbs when they lock on me. I love the soft side of her, but this? It sends me wild when her madness meets my own.

I speed up our flight, needing to get her back so I can have her. I need her screaming around my cock again. She grins and I pull my fingers from her pussy and out of her stolen pants. Watching her, I raise them to my lips and suck them clean, groaning at the delicious taste of her, which explodes on my tongue.

She moans and I wrap my other arm around her again, concentrating on flying so we can get there as fast as possible, but she catches me by surprise, something that rarely happens but only ever around her, when she reaches between us and slips her hand in my jeans, her palm wrapping around my hard cock and squeezing.

Swearing, I forget to beat my wings and we drop before I right us. She laughs, grinning at me wickedly. "Better remember to keep flying, Fallen."

From anyone else it would be an insult, in my mate's mouth she makes it seem like a compliment. Gritting my teeth, I concentrate on flying, leveling my breathing and trying to, unsuccessfully, ignore her exploring hands.

I nearly drop us three more times before I decide to fuck the flying, this isn't going to work, but I need to try something first before I set us down and fuck her senseless. Gripping those trousers, I strip them off her, letting them flutter through the air below. She grins and I yank the boxers to the side and unzip my jeans. All of it is a struggle as I juggle to keep her in my arms and fly at the same time.

She wraps her hand more securely around my cock, obviously seeing where I'm going with this. She pumps me a few times and I swear, glaring at her while she blinks innocently. I hoist her up as far as I can without dropping her, and she lines herself up with me and we work together to slowly sink into her wet pussy. She's so fucking tight that I see stars as I gnash my teeth and growl. Once I'm buried deep, I tuck my wings around us and dive bomb towards the earth.

She laughs, using her hands on my shoulders to lift herself as much as she can and drop, fucking me even as we plummet below. I'm too lost in her to control our landing, too fucking hard and turned on to concentrate.

Crazy, just like me.

When I blink my eyes open, not even realising I had closed them, I see the ground approaching, fast. Swearing, I curl my arms around her and try to slow our decent, but it's no use.

We crash into the soil of a grassy hill, skidding through it, leaving a massive hole in our wake like a meteor. Breathing heavily, I push up and look down at her in panic, but she just laughs.

I grin and look around at the soil walls on either side of us, we are in our own crater. Before I can move to check her over, she reaches down and cups my balls, dragging my gaze back to her.

"Fuck me," she orders, kicking my arse with her feet as her hands go to the joining of my wings and strokes like she stroked my cock.

Groaning, I thrust forward, her pussy still gripping me, and when I spot the blood trickling down from her hairline, I slam inside her harder, knowing I hurt her and she didn't fucking care.

"Griffin," she moans, her head arched back as she cries my name to the sky like a prayer.

"Scream my name," I gasped, before leaning down and circling her nipple with my tongue, then sucking it into my mouth. Loving the way her pussy clenches around me.

"Yes!" she screams as I slam into her harder. Lifting her leg, I use all my strength to fuck her. Knowing she can take it, take all of me.

My pace would split a human in two but she groans, her eyes dazed and her body arching beneath me, begging me for more as her mouth opens on another silent scream.

She's so close, I can feel her pussy fluttering around me, trying to push me over the edge, but I grit my teeth, needing her to come. Her eyes flutter open and she grins, and her hand slide down her body until she cups my balls and squeezes.

My thrusts stutter before turning lethal, smashing into her and sending her screaming into an orgasm. Her pussy clamps down on me and I roar my release, pumping into her. I love the way she writhes beneath me, her hands clawing at the dirt, her eyes black as night.

When we catch our breath, we start laughing, and when I look at her and see those eyes of hers dancing with amusement, I can't help myself. I lean down and kiss her hard, tangling my tongue with hers.

Dawn, Dawn, Dawn, what are you doing to me? She matches her name perfectly—like the morning, she is my new beginning, and I will fight to stay by her side even when she hates me. Even when she cringes away in fear, finally realising the extent of my depravity. I am hers now, her assassin, her monster.

The night to her morning, Dawn...you will never get away from me. I speak it like a promise into her mouth.

Pulling back, I smile softly at him and reach up to push back some of his hair. I know we should get back, I'm betting Nos is really worried by now, but I just want to take a moment to appreciate this soft side of Griffin he's letting me see. Well, as soft as Griffin ever can be.

For once his eyes aren't guarded or watching me warily, he's just staring at me. Content. It's strange. I love his madness, hell, I even love his anger, but can I love him?

My experience of loving people is twisted and messed up. My

own family didn't love me and the first man I ever said it to changed his mind a week later. Tim said he loved me, yet he hurt me. No, my own experiences in love aren't great. What if I mess this up? What if loving his emotions aren't enough, what if I can't love him?

"What are you thinking about so hard?" he asks, without that usual bite in his tone.

"I'm messed up," I blurt out, and his eyebrows raise and that mocking smile crosses his face like he can't help it.

"So?" he prompts.

"I mean it, Griffin, I'm completely and utterly messed up," I grumble, starting to get angry now that he isn't taking me seriously when I'm trying to share.

He rolls his eyes. "*Vasculo*, you don't think I know that? Fuck, we all are, even that god of yours. None of us are particularly sane or normal. Whatever you are thinking about, questioning yourself over —forget it," he says, like it's that simple.

Glaring at him, I huff, and glance over his shoulder at the sky, but he doesn't let me get away with that. He grips my chin and forces me to look at him again, and I see his eyes swirling and I can't help but lick my lips, knowing his darker side is coming back out to play. "I don't give a shit if you are fucking insane, I am too. I won't say you are my fucking light or some other fake shit, no. You are right there in the darkness with me, you're not the easily breakable light. You are the strong, constant dark at my side," he finishes, and my mouth opens in shock at his beautiful words.

"Don't get all sappy on me," he growls, looking instantly uncomfortable and I laugh, which ends in a gasp when he reaches down and cups my pussy, his cock still inside of me.

"I wonder, if I tasted you right now, would you taste like me?" he murmurs, making me moan as he presses hard, his cock moving in me slowly as he pulls out and thrusts back in.

I can feel the blood dripping from my cuts from the impact, hell, I felt at least two bones break, but I didn't care. All I could think about was Griffin, and it's the same now. He eclipses everything.

"We should get back, Nos will be worrying," I suggest, but my whole heart isn't in it.

He smirks, still fucking me shallowly. "We should."

I gasp and squeeze my eyes shut when he presses down on my clit, and drags his cock over that spot inside of me. "W-we should leave before someone comes and investigates," I try again and I look at him.

"Yes," he agrees, picking up speed.

"W-we, fuck it," I groan, wrapping my legs around him again and grinning when he laughs.

"Thank god, I was wondering how much longer you were going to go on for. I did think about shutting you up with my dick to your mouth," he replies, his dirty words making me moan. "Don't worry, you'll be doing it later. I'm sure you will do or say something to piss me off and get me all riled up," he warns and I laugh again.

"I love it when you get like that," I reply honestly and he pauses, his eyebrow arching.

"You do it on purpose?" he asks incredulously.

"Yes," I moan, rubbing against him and he growls, the sound travelling through my body, making me shiver as his wings shoot out of him on either side, blocking the sky and creating a cocoon.

"Oh, you will pay for that," he threatens, his voice deadly.

"I was betting on it." I wink.

CHAPTER 55

NOS

When I get back to Griffin's house they aren't home. Glaring at everything, I stomp around the house, trying to control my rage. I could head to the dock but by the late hour, I am betting they aren't there anymore. I just need to be patient, which with my mate's life on the line, I am finding I am not very good at.

Blowing out a breath, I force myself to sit crossed-legged and tap into the nature around me. Letting the call of the birds and the breeze soothe me. Once I had made it from fae territory, I had sprinted back to my bike and forced the change, before shooting from my cave and speeding across the forest and city to make it back here.

Cracking open my eyes, calmer than before, I search the living room for something else to distract myself with. My eyes catch on a burst of colour on the fallen's photo wall. Rising to my feet, I stalk across the room and stop before it, and a smirk curves my lips.

There, in the middle of the black and white photograph wall, is a full colour photograph of Dawn.

She's staring into the camera with her hair like a halo around her. Not a lick of makeup mars her face, just that fucking cheeky smile that drives me crazy. Her eyes are filled with laughter and a dare. She looks like innocence and sin wrapped up in one, beautiful package.

Griffin might see the rest of the world in shades of grey, but it's obvious he sees Dawn in all her splendid coloured glory. To him, the rest of the world is bland and she is his colour. Maybe he is trying to stop fighting the mate bond.

Or maybe he has finally realised trying to fight her is pointless, she will just come back stronger each time.

The door opens behind me. I was so lost in my own thoughts that I didn't even hear them pull up. Dropping my fingers away from the photograph, I turn, ready to admonish them, until I see the blood covering my mate.

Growling, my eyes turn white and I change quickly, unable to help myself. Griffin raises his eyebrow and steps to the side, and Dawn just grins.

Striding across the room, I run my finger over the blood on her head and bring it between us. "This better be someone else's," I warn.

She grabs my hand, smiling at me. "It's mine," she says sweetly.

Roaring, I pull away from her and turn to the fallen, he goes on high alert in an instant, his hands hovering over the blades strapped across his sides. I grab him and pin him to the wall.

"Griffin, no!" she yells, and I look down at the blade he plunged into my stomach. Sparing it no more than a glance, I get into his face but he stops fighting. He stares at me, frozen.

"I warned you," I growl and he nods. Anger is rioting in his eyes, but when they flicker to Dawn he sighs, not even trying to fight me.

"You did," he agrees, leaning back on the wall.

"Nos," Dawn yells, and I look over to see her arms crossed as she glares at both of us. "Put him the fuck down, or I swear to god, I will never touch your cock again," she threatens.

With my eyes on her, I smash Griffin into the wall and let go before stepping into her space. "Is that right?" I say silkily, and I watch as her eyes fill with heat, warring with her anger, and she swallows hard. I can even see the pounding of her pulse in her throat, but I'm impressed when she steps right up to me and points a finger in my face.

"This blood is mine, and not from the meeting, we both know I like to get rough. So if you're going to get angry at someone, let it be me, but you will never attack him again." She steps back when I frown, looking her over. She glares at both of us, her gaze swinging between us. "You are both my mates, you do not have to like each other, but you will never attack each other again. If you do, I'll be gone quicker than you can blink." She steps closer to us both and we step back at the menace on her face. "That's a fucking promise," she grits out, before storming between us, knocking us apart, and stomping up the stairs, muttering under her breath.

Both Griffin and I watch her go before looking at each other, properly chastised like children. Gripping the blade still protruding from my stomach, I yank it out and pass it over to him. He nods, accepts it, and wipes my blood on his shirt before sheathing it.

"She did not get hurt at the meeting?" I ask, my anger deflating as I change back. My clothes hanging in tatters on me.

"No," he answers simply, and I look at the stairs she went up.

"Then I owe you an apology, Fallen." I clasp his shoulder and he looks at me like I am crazy. "I should not have attacked you and I won't do it again unless you betray or hurt us. No matter her warning." With that I start upstairs, already planning my grovelling in my head.

"We need to speak about what we found out tonight," he calls up and I nod.

"After, let me calm our mate down before she decides to kill us both or tie us up in a sex dungeon," I joke and he laughs.

"I wouldn't be opposed to that," he retorts.

Me either.

Cracking open our bedroom door, I peer inside to find Dawn

pacing back and forth. I wince and hedge inside of the room. "Little Monster?" I murmur, and her head swivels to me, her eyes black as she advances on me.

Slipping fully inside, I shut the door and wait.

She stops meters away from me, her lips pursed in anger. "Do not 'Little Monster' me," she snaps.

I grin, unable to help myself. She is so breathtaking in her anger. "I am sorry, Little Monster, I should have waited and listened before attacking Griffin," I say calmly.

She throws her hands in the air. "Or not attacked him at all!" she yells.

I sigh. "Little Monster, we are not always going to get along. We are both strong, powerful supernaturals and we are going to butt heads and fight. It is how we get out our aggression and anger towards each other. I promise you after we will be fine with each other. But I can't promise it won't happen again, because it will."

She shakes her head, resuming her pacing. "Fucking men," she spits before looking at me, her eyes dropping to the wound on my stomach. "Are you okay?" she asks, deflating a bit.

I nod but she strides over, pushing away the tattered t-shirt so she can see the blood on my skin. When she wipes it away and finds a closed pink line, which will disappear to shortly, she nods and steps back, ignoring me again.

"Dawn," I demand and she stops, keeping her back to me with her arms wrapped around herself. Winding my arms around her, I place my head on hers. "I am sorry, I am, but I am new to this mate business and I worry. I found out some hard information and I thought I was too late, I thought I had lost you. I was so fucking worried, going out of my mind, and you come in covered in blood..." Kissing her hair, I hold her tighter.

She sighs, relaxing into my arms before turning and peering up at me, her eyes back to normal again. "Fine," she grumbles, her hands landing on my chest and stroking like she can't help herself. "I'm still not happy about the whole pinning to a wall and stabbing thing," she mutters and I grin.

Leaning down, I bend my head and kiss her gently. "I was so

worried, Little Monster," I admit, speaking my fears out loud. She kisses me again and smiles softly. "Haven't you learned by now?"

"Learned what?" I repeat, confused.

She laughs. "I don't stay dead, even if they manage to kill me." I laugh with her before kissing her again, assuring myself she is here in my arms.

"Come on, we better talk about what we found," she says, and twines our hands together and leads me downstairs.

I can't seem to stop myself from touching her, needing to know that she is here with me. When we get downstairs we find a blank-faced Griffin sitting at the table, but at the seat next to him is a cup of coffee and what looks like cookies. Obviously a peace offering for her. I snort, I can't help it.

She throws him a glare but grabs them and sits back on my lap when I sit down.

"Sorry?" he offers, the statement more of a question.

"Oh, you will be, don't you worry, Fallen," she purrs, and he cracks a grin.

He sits back in his chair, his gaze going serious again. "What did you find?" he asks, and I wrap my arms tighter around Dawn, then my mouth opens and the whole story pours out.

CHAPTER 56

DAWN

"Well, shit," I splutter, and Griffin nods his agreement. "If fae are going missing, you can bet that other supes are as well. This is so much bigger than just selling women when they find out they aren't human. They are targeting supe women, why?" he ponders.

"That's the question, isn't it," I reply, and Nos kisses my cheek.

"I agreed to go back and meet with them with Dawn. Also, I told them I would use my contacts to speak to other supernatural races and clans to check in on them. I'm impartial, so they should agree to meet me," he explains.

"We still need to find Victor and meet with him, find out what he knows, and also deal with Tim," I lament, and they both frown harder.

Picking at the cookies before me, I think through the problems ahead of us. Understandably, supes disappearing takes precedence, but with so much going on...

"Okay, Nos. Talk to your contacts, arrange meetings and dig as much as you can on the phone. It should give us some time," I muse out loud.

"Time for what?" Griffin asks.

"We have too many balls in the air," I mutter, staring at the paperwork before rubbing my head. "Okay, so let's take some out of the air. First, we need to meet with this Victor. Offer him a deal. He will want to know who in his organisation has been stealing from him, we can ask for the information we need, and if he's looking as well... we are covering more bases. Then, once we have dealt with Tim and Victor, we turn our attention to these Others. We can meet with other races, see what the fae have found, and figure out who they are and stop them."

"How do we find Victor though?" Griffin inquires.

Thinking, I search the table for an answer before I laugh. "Tim, of course. He used to go to this fucking stupid ass club every week and I never could figure out why. We go there, ask around for Victor, we'll find him."

"And Tim?" Nos questions, and I grin.

"Let me deal with that." I laugh, as a plan forms in my head. My plans have changed since I've met Nos and Griffin, but I still plan to make the bastard pay. I just have to solve these disappearances as well.

"It's the best plan we have," Nos comments, and Griffin nods.

"I don't like just wandering around, but it's the best option at the moment. Okay, we'll go tonight," Griffin suggests. "Victor, Tim, The Others, and now the fae," he mutters, shaking his head.

"You're right, it's the best plan we have so far. Nos, start contacting them today, Griffin and I will search through the paperwork, surveillance, and everything we have to see if we can find any more information on the men who are snatching supes, and Victor as well."

They both agree but Nos freezes. "What happened at the meeting? You glossed over it," he asks and he's right, his information from the fae took us by surprise and we didn't really outline what had happened last night. Shit, we really do have too much on our plate.

"Turns out that The Others are supes," Griffin snarls, and I pat Nos' arms when they tighten.

"More than that, powerful too. The man was old and decrepit when I first met him, but once he caught on to me he changed to a younger man. The bodyguards that were with him were all wearing a glowing pendant," I recall.

"He changed?" Nos repeats.

"Yep, like a younger version of the man, why?" I drawl, when they look between each other.

"For him to do that, he would have to be a skinwalker or..." Griffin trails off.

"Or?" I demand.

"Or witches are helping," Nos snarls.

"Okay, what's the deal with witches, why do you look so pissed?" I ask, confused.

"Witches are evil. Don't think Sabrina, think hellspawn. They gain their power by taking it from others, and they live on sacrifices and blood spells. They are truly fucking evil. They think they are above everyone, so for them to be working with some other kind of supernaturals..." Griffin shakes his head.

"It's unheard of," Nos adds.

"Peachy," I mutter. "So witches are working with supes, using spells and shit to change people—"

"Explains why there was no trace at the warehouse or why they are able to stay hidden. Witches' powers, especially if there is a coven, would be able to hide a whole fucking organisation." Griffin bangs his fist on the table.

"But why are supes abducting other supes?" I inquire calmly.

"Who the fucks knows? Why did they create me, why did they create other monsters?" Griffin snarls, standing and pacing.

Sighing, I rub my eyes. "Okay, the plan is still the same."

"We better get started," Nos says, kissing my head before standing. He leaves me with Griffin and heads to the living room, already dialing on his phone.

Griffin and I share a look with the paperwork between us. "I'll make more coffee," he grumbles and I nod, leaning over and spreading it all back out again.

Witches working with supes to abduct other supes, a human crime ring somehow caught in the middle of that, and an ex-husband to kill. When will shit start to make sense?

"It still looks like this club is our best bet. From what I can gather, it's a front. It's where they launder their money and a base of operations of sort." I bite into a cookie as I talk and Dawn looks up from the file she's searching through.

"Okay, so we go tonight." She nods, reaching over and grabbing a cookie from my pile.

"What are you going to do about your ex?" I ask, leaning back and taking a break. We have been at it for hours and so has Nos. I can hear him in the other room and from what I'm gathering, trying to get through to people is hard, and when he does they are reluctant to talk—even to him.

She grins, her eyes alight with mischief. "I have a plan." She winks and I snort.

"Care to share?"

"Nope." She pops the 'p,' nibbling on the cookie as she looks at me.

"Dawn," I warn and she hums, still eating.

"Don't worry so much, Griffin," she teases, and I narrow my eyes on her.

"Do I get to kill him?"

She shakes her head and her eyes go dark for a moment. "No, he's mine."

Obviously done talking, she goes back to her file and I roll my eyes, moving back to my laptop and the tedious job of searching through files and CCTV. When her foot strokes up my leg, I raise my eyebrow at her but she ignores me.

Going back to the computer, I freeze when she presses her bare foot into my semi-hard cock.

"Dawn," I growl, and she licks her lips, looking up at me.

Pushing my chair back with a crash, I mist around the table and snatch her from her chair. Kicking it away, I lay her back on the table, on top of the paperwork, and slam my lips to hers.

She groans, her hands winding in my hair, and with a teasing bite to her lower lip I pull away. I open my mouth to speak but an amused voice form behind me beats me to it.

"I leave you alone for an hour and I come back to this?" Nos laughs.

She grins beneath me and looks over my shoulder. "We were taking a break, you know, passing the time until tonight." She winks.

"And why wasn't I invited to this...break?" he inquires, and steps up next to me. Leaning back between her parted thighs, I look from her to him. Her mouth parts in a pant, her eyes light up, and I can practically smell her desire.

I've never shared a woman before, hell, I've not exactly been with many. Hardly any supes will open their legs to a fallen and humans can't handle our strength. I thought I would feel disgusted or reject the idea, but watching my mate almost pant from the thought...I find myself grinning. I look over at Nos and nod. "Touch me and die, though, and we don't cross no fucking swords," I demand and he laughs.

Turning back to Dawn, I see her eyes widen and swivel from me to Nos and back. Leaning down, I press my lips against her ear, and whisper, "I warned you I would shut you up later." She shivers against me, moaning slightly.

My cock is so hard now it's pushing uncomfortably against my jeans, pulsing with the thought of her sweet mouth wrapped around it. Stepping back with her eyes still on me, I pop the button and pull down my zip, the sound loud in the quiet room.

I pull out my cock and watch her while I stroke it, my eyes clinging to those fucking lips of hers. Nos grabs her, pulls her from the table, and places her back to his chest. "You heard the man, on your knees, Little Monster," he commands, his voice hard as he grips her hips.

She licks her lips, eyeing my cock as she drops to her knees in front of me. Groaning out loud, I watch as she crawls towards me. Her body moving so sensually that I nearly come then and there.

Nos' eyes are entranced as well, locked on her swaying ass. I don't blame him. When she reaches my feet, she sits back on her haunches and peers up at me with a coy smile as her hands trace up my legs and grip my hips.

Letting go of my cock, I reach down and grip her hair. She resists, her hand circling my cock as she strokes me from base to tip, squeezing, but not hard enough, and when I growl I know she's doing it on purpose.

I yank her to me and she relents, her hand circling my base and squeezing as her mouth opens, blowing hot breath across the tip of my cock.

"Dawn," I growl in warning.

She grins, and her tongue darts out and licks the bead of precum from the tip, and when I go to warn her again her mouth closes around me. Gripping her hair harder, I stop myself from rutting into her mouth like a fucking wild animal. She teases me, only swallowing the tip before pulling back and licking me.

Without warning, she sucks me in deep, her teeth catching on the underside of my cock and making me groan as I widen my stance and thrust forward. She doesn't gag like I expected, even when I bump the back of her throat.

She pulls back and sucks me down, faster this time, nearly making my eyes roll into the back of my head from all the pleasure assaulting me. My balls are tight, and if she doesn't slow down I'm going to explode in her mouth.

I look to Nos for help and he grins, obviously understanding me.

"Little Monster, get to your feet but keep his cock in your mouth," he orders, and she mumbles something around me, making me jerk forward with a groan.

Tipping my head back, I suck in breaths and still my movements. Looking down when I'm under control again, I watch her climb to her feet using her hand on my hip as an anchor.

Her ass is in the air, wearing only the shirt she donned earlier, and it rides up, showing off her panty-clad ass. Nos' hands massage her cheeks as she sucks me down harder in response. Motherfucker.

"Stop teasing her," I grit out, and he laughs.

"Looks like your mate is having trouble there, Little Monster." He smirks and she moans. I look up and see his fingers dipping inside her panties.

"Fuck, she's so wet. Do you like sucking his cock?" He murmurs, and when she doesn't answer, his other hand comes down hard on her ass cheek, leaving a red imprint straight away from the force of it.

She cries out around me, pulling back and panting as she looks over her shoulder at her other mate. "Yes, now fuck me," she demands, looking all sorts of beautiful with her swollen lips. She turns back to me, licking her lips while she pumps my cock a few times.

The sight has me thrusting forward, pressing my cock to her mouth as I glare at Nos. "Fucking do it," I growl.

She doesn't tease me this time, just swallows me whole, her head bobbing as she sets a punishing pace until I can't help it, I thrust forward. Holding her head still, I fuck her dirty little mouth.

Nos tears her panties and throws them away. I didn't even see him get undressed, I was that focused on her, but he's sans pants now and without warning he grabs her hips and thrusts into her, making her scream around my cock.

He pulls back and thrusts back in, pushing her farther down my cock. She braces herself on my thighs, pushing back against Nos as she sucks me. Groaning, I drop my head back and focus on not coming just yet. My cock is pulsing and I can feel my orgasm moving through me, but I grit my teeth and hold off, needing her to come first.

"Nos," I growl out.

He picks up speed and his hand leaves her hip, and when her moans become more frequent, I know she is close. I don't know what he does but she shakes, screaming around my cock as she comes.

Roaring, unable to help myself, I grab the back of her head and pound into her mouth, forcing her to take me and my rhythm as I come. Groaning, I still as my load shoots down her throat.

She sucks it down, swallowing it all until I pull back and out of her mouth, and fall into the chair behind me. She moves with me, her hands still on my hips as Nos still fucks her. Leaning her head on my thigh, pillowing her, her panting breaths blow over my cock while she gets fucked by her other mate.

I cup her head and hold her still for his thrusts, my cock already hardening again, and I groan when her tongue darts out and licks it. I lean back, watching her get fucked, more turned on by the sight than that I thought I would be.

When she cries out, Nos roars, pushing her so hard that she moves on my legs. He freezes behind her then curls over her back, both of them panting from their release.

My cock is hard again, always needing her, and I can't help it. I kick my leg out at Nos and he stumbles back into the table. He narrows his eyes on me, but I pick her up and deposit her on my lap so she's straddling me. Grabbing her hips, I line up and push inside of her.

We both groan. She's limp on me, but when I start to move she lifts her head, bobbing on my cock. Her hands come to my shoulders as I help lift and drop her, our pace picking up again as her pussy clamps around my cock.

She's so fucking tight. I groan, only realising I've said it out loud when Nos agrees.

He comes up behind her and pulls her head back, kissing her hard. I watch in fascination as they fight for control, their tongues tangling as she rides me.

Cupping her swaying breasts through the shirt, I tweak her nipples and Nos swallows her groan. She tightens around me, and I grit my teeth, using my feet on the floor to thrust up.

Her nails scratch down my chest, writhing between us as her pussy milks me, her orgasm hitting her hard until I cry out, stilling beneath her as I fill her with my cum.

Leaning back in the chair, I hold her against me as her and Nos' kiss breaks away. Snuggling into me, she holds her other mate to her and he wraps around her back, holding her between us while we all shake and shiver from the aftershocks.

"I think the break is over," I joke and she laughs, making us all groan.

CHAPTER 57

NOS

We moved into the living room after our little break, as Dawn called it. Looking over at her and the fallen now, you wouldn't think just a day or two ago they hated each other. I'm not even sure if they still don't.

She is laying back on the sofa with a file held above her head as she reads, and her feet are in Griffin's lap. He has one hand circled around them, anchoring her to him as he clicks through his laptop with a frown.

My phone rings, interrupting my thoughts, and I lean from the sofa and grab it from the coffee table, answering the call straight away.

"Yes?" I answer, my eyes still lingering on my mate.

"I have heard you have been sniffing around the packs, false god," a familiar, gravely voice growls down the line.

"Sean," I greet curtly. I had hoped to avoid the alpha of the southeast packs, but that seems to have gone out the window. I am guessing one of his alphas went straight to him. Wolves.

"You should have come to me and you know it," he scolds.

"I didn't know if I could trust you," I admit freely, and Griffin and Dawn look over at me with a frown.

"Why not?" he demands.

"You are on the council, I wanted to be sure before I presented myself to you," I point out logically.

"Fine. They said you were asking about missing wolves, why?" He is calmer now.

"Am I speaking to the southeast alpha or the fourth seat of the council?" I demand, knowing exactly how to play these games, even if I hate them. Griffin's eyebrow raises and anger burns in his gaze, so I am guessing he knows of the surly alpha.

"Alpha, always alpha," he grumbles, finally making me relax. I knew the alpha hated his seat on the council, but it was necessary to protect his people. I wanted to ensure that was still his reasoning and they had not changed the once proud wolf pup I knew.

"I visited with the fae, they have women missing. Other supes too, and I wanted to check in to see if it was the same on your front?" I ask bluntly.

He doesn't act shocked, but he is brilliant at hiding his thoughts. Usually wolves are impulsive and not very good liars because of their strong emotions, but Sean is a law all unto himself. He had a bad upbringing—very bad. I brought him over with me when I settled here, and away from his now dead family. I think that made him the way he is, cold, some call him, but underneath all that frost is lava-hot hate.

"Sean," I prompt.

"Yes," he growls, and I hear something smash, the only sign he will show of his anger. "Women are missing, four packs now. At first it was one, we thought hunters, but every day more reports are pouring in."

Sighing, I rub my forehead. "This is much bigger than hunters, my old friend, much, much worse. I will hope to have some more information in the next few days, but I assume you are conducting your own investigation, yes?"

"Yes," he sighs.

"Found anything?" I question, curious, wolves are the best trackers in the world. They pick up things that others just can't, so if they are investigating they will have visited the scenes where the disappearances occurred.

"Each disappearance was different. At first, the packs didn't link up due to them not wanting to share information and look weak. Alphas." He snorts. "When we did, some of the older scenes were too old, but we got some clues from the fresh scenes. Each one happens somewhere different, but they are always well planned and organised. This isn't sloppy, it was a snatch and grab, and they knew exactly where and when. One was at a supe club. One was at home, one on a run...I could go on and on. Point is, they have all been taken from various locations, some within pack protected land." I hear him rubbing at his skin, no doubt at the scar that mars his neck. It used to be a nervous gesture he developed as a child, but as he got older it was just what he did when he was thinking.

"We sent out wolves to track and scent mark. What they found...it makes no sense," he adds.

"Tell me, old friend," I press, sitting forward, and Griffin and Dawn lean in. Frowning, I place him on speaker and onto the table. "You are on speaker, I trust them implicitly."

He hesitates for only a moment. "Their smells were strange because there were different ones at each scene, and they were mixed. At one we smelled witches and vamps, at another...wolves."

Tapping the table, I frown. "You are saying the abductors were all different races?" I clarify.

"I am saying, old friend, races that never work together are, and they are taking our people."

"But why?" Dawn muses out loud.

"Who is that?" he demands, his voice as cool as always.

She leans in. "My name is Dawn, I am Nos' mate," she says offhandedly, and carries on like she didn't just declare her ownage and intent before us all. "We have found supes calling themselves The Others kidnapping here as well. They have been searching and forcing humans into that state."

"Mate?" he asks, his voice defrosting.

"Mate," I confirm with a smile.

"Congratulations are in order, old friend, even in these dire circumstances. I can't wait to meet her, but back to what else the fool enough of a woman willing to stick with you said, The Others?" he questions and I laugh.

"Wait until you find yours," I joke before going serious. "Yes, The Others. We found witches working with an unknown species and making deals with humans."

"What the fuck is going on?" he growls.

Rubbing at my head again, I sigh. "I wish I knew, but I plan to find out." Looking at the clock, I run my finger over the table again. "We must leave, we are chasing down a lead. Keep me in the loop and I will return the favour. Stay safe," I say.

"You too, old friend. I wish you the best of luck Nos' mate," he teases, before cutting off the call.

"Do I want to know?" She winks and I shake my head.

"Come on, Little Monster. We need to get ready to go to your human club." I stand up and offer her my hand. She leans over and kisses Griffin softly before letting me pull her to her feet.

Fae, wolves, humans...what else? How many people will go missing before we figure out what is going on?

"You look beautiful," I murmur, kissing her bare shoulder softly.

Resting my head on her shoulder, I smile at her in the mirror. The short, red dress she is wearing clings to her curves, making my mouth dry up, and I want to fling her on the bed and fuck her until she screams. Cut low in the front and back, it shows off her pale skin and ends just above her knee.

The sharp stilettos she is wearing boosts her height and she told me with a rueful smile that they double as a weapon. "Why red?" I ask, kissing her silky skin.

"It doesn't show blood as bad." She grins, winking at me through the mirror and making me laugh.

"Such a little monster," I reply, licking up her shoulder, making her shiver in delight and lean farther back into me.

The red of her outfit contrasts against the white of my shirt and the black of my pants. My shirt buttons are loosely done, and when she had looked at me and licked her lips, I knew I was going to be walking around with a hard cock all night. She said she looked like the devil to my angel. I told her that her angel is downstairs, but he isn't pure.

As if my thoughts summon him, the door bursts open, and the shadows of the stairs cling to him like a lover. "You fucking ready yet?" he snaps, but there is no real heat behind the words. Whatever happened at that meeting or after has shifted their relationship. At least now I don't have to kill him.

He looks at her from head to toe and gulps before turning pained eyes on me, and I just smirk, feeling the exact same way. He's in all black, like normal. A tight black shirt clings to his chest, and it is buttoned all the way to the top, tucked into black leather pants and boots.

She sighs, moving away from me until she can run her finger down his chest. "Hmm, you both look good enough to eat. Should have gone with red though, it's going to show the blood," she murmurs, caressing his chest.

His hands drop to her ass and pull her close. "I don't bother hiding the blood," he responds, watching her.

She laughs and looks back at me with a twinkle in her eyes. "Not a surprise. Come on, we better go before I decide to ignore our plans and fuck you both now."

With that declaration she drops a chaste kiss on his cheek and sweeps from the room, leaving us both watching after her.

"Fucking *vasuclo*," he groans, reaching down and rearranging himself.

Laughing, I follow after her with a grumbling fallen on my heels.

CHAPTER 58

DAWN

From the outside, the club looks like a low rent strip club, but when we approach the door and pay the cover charge, we are searched for weapons. I'm not sure how Griffin conceals his or where, but they don't find any on him, and when I look over at him with a raised eyebrow he winks.

We are waved inside by the vigilant bodyguards, and from the tats on their arms I'm guessing they are ex-military. Maybe even mercs. I know Tim associated with some and they meant business.

Stairs leading up and down greet us once we are through the door, and deciding to pick at random, I go down with Nos and Griffin close on my heels. I can feel the music pumping through the floor, and when we reach the bottom step, a glass partition runs along the right wall, separating the stairs from the club down here.

Running my finger along the frosted glass, I stop when we reach the opening, my eyebrow rising in shock. It isn't what I was expecting at all, I was looking for poles and scantily clad women and lots of Victor's men, but this...this is something else altogether.

A raised stage sits in the middle of the space with two walkways leading around the room. Glossy black, with stage lights surrounding it, and a red curtain behind it, it looks like an old burlesque club. Tables litter the club with booths raised to the left and right. Next to the entrance I'm standing at is a curved bar with what looks like mirrors and lights across the back of it.

Women in corsets and skirts, even a sexy suit, walk around serving, but so do half dressed men. The music is sultry, and apart from the servers and the man on stage, no one is dancing. They are drinking and enjoying the show. Moving through the opening, I spot the house band to the back of the stage as the song changes to some smooth jazz and a girl in a red dress climbs up on the stage and takes a bow.

"Nice place," Griffin comments and I nod. "I'll go left and listen for any signs of Victor. You two try and blend in," he murmurs, dropping a kiss on my lips before blending into the hustle and bustle. I blink hard, trying to see him, but it's like he just disappeared. I'm concentrating so hard that I jump when a hand lands on my waist. Looking over at Nos, I smile and he grins.

"Come on, Little Monster, let's get you a drink," he says, whispering into my ear before he leads me to the right and a free booth along the side wall.

Sliding into the black, cushioned leather seat, I throw my legs over Nos' lap and look across the club. I search for anyone I recognize or any signs of Tim's people. I don't know what Victor looks like, but I'm guessing he would be surrounded by men. When I don't spot anyone like that I sigh and sit back—maybe he isn't here yet.

"What can I get you?" comes a deep, smooth masculine voice.

Dragging my gaze from the club beyond to the server waiting at my table, I notice a white pad held in one hand. He's wearing nothing but a waistcoat and some skintight leather pants.

"Vodka, straight." I grin and he winks at me, writing down my order as he turns his attention to Nos.

"And for you, handsome?" he asks, running his eyes across Nos appreciatively. I can't blame him.

"Rum." Nos nods, his eyes going back to me.

The man writes it down and bows before leaving us alone. Nos leans in and plays with a strand of my hair. "You really are breathtaking, do you know that, Little Monster? This place could be packed, people fighting for attention, and all I would see is you. Always you. Effortlessly amazing," he whispers, leaning in. Tilting my head to give him better access, I groan when he kisses down my throat.

My eyes flutter shut, and when I open them again, they clash with Griffin's from where he stands against the bar, with a drink in hand. I watch his eyes heat as he takes us in before he salutes me with his drink and disappears into the crowd again.

"What are we going to do if Victor doesn't come here tonight?" I ask, and he lifts his head as drinks are placed on our table with a flourish.

Leaning back, he keeps his hand on my legs as he sips his rum. His eyes constantly scanning the club, yet he looks completely at ease. "We keep coming back, or we go to your husband and push him for information. Either or, we have options, Little Monster, do not fear."

"You're right." I grin before grabbing my vodka and knocking it back, signalling to a passing waiter to bring me another. The burn warms me, and usually after a few of these I would be drunk as hell, but ever since the whole dying thing it seems to take a lot more for a buzz to even start, and I haven't tried getting completely drunk yet.

We sit there for a while, watching the club and talking. More drinks flow and before I know it, I'm leaning back into Nos. "How long have we been here?" I inquire, getting frustrated. I should have known this wouldn't have been easy.

"Three hours," Griffin huffs, sliding into the booth next to me and squishing me closer to Nos.

"Anything?" I ask hopefully, and he shakes his head, throwing back my latest shot of vodka and leaning back.

"Nothing. Not even a whisper. Either he doesn't come here or he's a fucking secret," he grumbles and I lean over, placing my head on his shoulder.

He kisses my hair and relaxes against me as we run our eyes over the club. "I say we call it a bust," he mutters and I sigh, leaning away.

Nibbling on my lower lip, I think. "Let me try one more thing. If

RAGE

it doesn't work then we will come back or come up with another idea," I offer, and they both nod.

"What do you want to try, Little Monster?" Nos asks.

Smiling, I kiss them both before climbing over Griffin and slipping from the booth. "If I tell you, I will have to kill you," I joke, before turning around to face the club, as their eyes burn holes in my back.

I had watched the coming and goings in the club, and I had seen men streaming from a hidden door next to the bar all night. I had thought nothing of it until I caught a peek inside when I went to the toilet and saw an office. I'm betting we might be able to find some information in there about Victor. Or catch his attention at least.

While I stride across the club, I head straight for the door. Confidence is key, if you act like you belong, no one will question it. The door isn't even guarded, looking back at Nos and Griffin with a grin I slip inside, shutting the door behind me.

I was right—it's an office.

The left wall is made of windows looking out into the club, but you obviously can't see in since the other side looks like mirrors. A sofa is backed against the wall on the right with a small mini bar next to it, and a lamp and a side table.

A large desk is against the wall opposite the door with floor to ceiling bookcases covering the wall behind it. A laptop sits on the desk, but other than that this place is pretty bare. I'm betting they are hiding information in here somewhere. Even a hint would help us.

Deciding to get right to it, I head over to the desk and sit in the chair, wiggling the mousepad on the laptop to bring wake it. It comes up needing a password. Of course.

Rolling my eyes, I turn away knowing I won't be able to guess whatever password they use. I'm just opening the top drawer when the door opens. Shooting to my feet, I relax when Griffin and Nos come in and shut the door behind them.

"This is your idea?" Griffin asks.

I sit back in the chair and start rooting around in the drawer. "If

317

Victor comes here, then there will be some kind of hint or sign, start looking," I suggest, distracted.

The drawer is filled with nothing but stationary and some money. Sliding it shut, I open the bottom one and grin when I see all the files in there. Pulling them out randomly, I spread them on the desk and start looking through. Nos comes to my side and helps while Griffin heads to the bookcase and starts searching.

Pulling out more files, on what looks like an investigation and suspension of employees regarding money loss from the club, I freeze when I hear voices outside. Shoving the files away, I stand up quickly, and all three of us position ourselves before the desk as the door blows inward and the men crowded there take us in.

One man steps forward and the others follow him in. "What are you doing in here?" he asks, and from the black uniform, I'm guessing he's a security bodyguard.

"Looking for Victor, know him?" I counter bluntly, leaning back against the desk.

Laughter goes through the crowd of men as the first man watches me hard. I wait casually and the group splits down the middle, then another man steps forward. Some of the men circle us, going to our back and I have to choose between keeping them in my eyeline or watching the man in the middle. I chose the latter, my shoulders tensing from having them at my back.

"You have been looking for me?" comes a harsh, deep voice from the doorway. Turning, I spot the middle-age man with a scarred up face surrounded by bodyguards. I hear the men moving behind me and I force myself not to react as something covers my face and I'm pushed to my knees. I hear either Nos or Griffin growl and I know they are going to cause a fight.

"Let them." I order, I feel them hesitate before relenting.

Two bangs sound beside me and I know they have done the same to Nos and Griffin. "Don't react," I order quietly, knowing they are both about to spring into action. "It's what we wanted," I finish.

"If we are going to whisper, whisper loud enough for us all to hear," comes a snarl above me. "Now, little girl, why are you looking for me?" he asks.

"I have information." I shrug casually, the bag blocking my vision completely. Straining, I try to see through it, but it's no use.

"Information?" The man laughs and the other men in the room chuckle.

"Money has been disappearing, no? Well, I know who it is. You let me talk and I think we can make a deal," I say loudly and the laughter cuts off. I feel the tension in the room.

"If you are lying, I will kill you all," he threatens casually, and I shrug again.

"Of course, I would expect no less," I reply.

He snorts before moving away. "Tie their hands, take them out back." He turns back around. "We will take you somewhere else to speak." With that, I hear him sweep from the room as my hands are bound in front of my body with wire. I test the limits and I find that although tight, I can move my hands, and if I really wanted to, I could break free. That isn't the plan though. I need to speak to Victor, so good little captive I will play.

"Where are you taking us?" Griffin snarls, obviously sick of the silence and lack of control. We are still tied and covered in hoods after being deposited in a car of some kind and lying all together in the back as we are driven away from the club.

"Somewhere quieter, you wished to speak to Victor, did you not?" he growls.

"Yes," I reply, kicking Griffin to shut him up.

"Then be quiet," he orders, and we all shut up.

I concentrate on the turns we take and the length of the drive. We drive for over thirty minutes with ten left turns and fifteen right turns, before going off road at some point, if the bouncing and noise of the wheels is anything to go by.

The men in the car are professionals and don't speak, so I can't glean any information from them. Suddenly we stop, and the car doors open and slam shut before we are pulled from the back and forced to walk over what feels like gravel.

Stumbling a little, I hold myself upright and keep walking. Soon the ground under our feet changes into carpet as we are directed inside somewhere. From the smell of the air and the cool temperature, it's a big space, and we are pulled directly to what sounds like an elevator.

When we are pushed inside and we start moving up, I know I was right. It bings and we are pulled out again, yanked down a corridor before the sound of an opening door reaches us.

It's warmer inside the room we are pushed into, and smells like blossoms on a spring day. A man's hand pushes down on my shoulder and I fall back into something soft. A chair of some kind. From the scuffling around me, my men are pushed down as well, and when their thighs meet mine on either side, the tingling lets me know it's them.

The hood is pulled away and I blink to adjust my eyes against the light before they widen in shock. I take in the woman sitting across from me, casually watching us as she sips from a tumbler filled with orange liquid.

"Victor?" I ask, clearing my throat after not talking for a long time.

She raises her glass and a sarcastic smile curls her perfectly painted red lips. "Surprise, though, I suppose you could call me Victoria. Now, what can I do for you?" she inquires.

Victor...is a woman?

CHAPTER 59

DAWN

"From the surprise on your face, I'm guessing you were expecting a man?" she muses, leaning forward and dropping her now empty glass on the table in front of her. She's wearing a suit, a black jacket and trousers, but has no shirt on underneath and long pointy heels on her feet. She's beautiful, in a deadly looking way. Her eyes are cold and calculating, and I'm betting she is a lot smarter than people think. I also wager people underestimate her a lot. Her hair is cut short, a blonde bob, which only accentuates her model worthy face and body. She looks like she should be gracing the covers of magazines, not sitting in what looks like a meeting room as the leader of a crime ring—but here we are. Her cheeks sparkle with gold when she tilts her head, and her eyes are lined perfectly with black liner only, making their blue colour pop even more.

Standing behind her is the scarred man from the club, and his eyes are like daggers, centered on me. She leans her hand up, caressing him when she sees me looking. "I see you have met my head of security, Jedrick." She grins and I nod.

"Good, Jedrick is my right-hand man. He is also my public stand in, only a trusted few—or the damned—know who I really am. Men don't want to deal with women, they think we are weak. If only they knew the truth." She laughs and another glass appears at her side.

Without looking, she grabs it and watches me over the rim as she sips the amber liquid.

"So tell me..." She trails off, expecting me her to fill her in. She's good, manipulating me easily and playing off her gender. She obviously knows how to work a room and get she wants, but for her to be in this position there has to be more to her than just her mind. She must be ruthless and deadly. I need to make sure I tread carefully.

"Dawn, and are we the trusted or damned?" I ask casually, crossing my legs.

She grins and rests the glass in her lap, her eyes not straying from me even though Nos and Griffin sit at my side. "We shall see, I always know my enemies, yet I find myself at a loss with you. Jed said you had information for me. I deal in information, so present your case Dawn, and I will see whether you will make it out of this room alive."

"Why do you think I'm in charge?" I question, curious, and she laughs.

"It is obvious, they defer to you. I know a powerful woman when I see one and you, Dawn, are. So, let's not play games." Her voice hardens at the end and her eyes flash like ice is swirling there.

"No games." I nod. "I have come here to strike a deal, you have something I want and I have some information you need," I offer, leaning back into my men and accepting their support. Something about her unnerves me. I think it's because I don't know how to approach her and my strength or powers won't help me here. I will have to rely on my mind.

"And what do I have that you want?" she asks.

"My ex-husband," I state.

Her eyebrow raises and Jedrick moves slightly behind her. Her eyes warm slightly and a smile dances on her lips as she watches me. "I know that look on your face, you want revenge, a feeling I am very well acquainted with. Why don't you tell me a bit more and I will see what deal we can come to, Dawn."

"Huh," she says, leaning back and watching me in a new light. "Let me get this straight—one of my men forced you into a marriage you did not want, and I'm guessing from the unspoken words in your eyes it was not a good marriage," she grinds out, and I tilt my head at the anger in her eyes. At her tone, Jedrick drops a hand on her shoulder and seems to bristle. She sighs, leaning into his touch.

"From your expression, I can see you do not understand my outrage." She pats Jedrick's hand and leans forward. "Let me explain something to you, Dawn. I was not born into this business nor was I grown for it—my husband was once..." At the word, Jedrick bristles again. "Jed's brother," she adds. "We were sweethearts and I thought I loved him, we married young—too young. By the time I realised it was all a front and another side of him existed, it was too late. I was in too deep. I became his pawn and his punching bag. I was forced into meetings and other such situations, always in the background. Always listening and waiting. He was not a smart man, more like a hammer than anything else. He was a disappointment to his father and he made many mistakes. One which almost cost Jedrick and me our lives. We were taken by another family and tortured for information. My husband did not even come for us—his enforcer and wife. He left us to rot but we escaped, and when we came back, we found that he didn't care then either. He was not a good man, he did not have morals. Our law, our circle, are family and he betrayed that for money and power. It got him killed," she explains, and I grin at the fierce expression on her face, this woman is something else altogether.

"I had been by his side for years, I knew the business better than him. I was the one the other families really came to see, his father saw that. He cultivated it, made me his protégé, and I went willingly. I am good at my job, I am the leader, and that means making the tough decisions. Decisions lesser men would crumble under the weight of, but those laws—they govern us," she snarls, grabbing her drink and tossing it back. "Family always comes first, second is to never cross into another family's territory unless you want war. I do not deal in drugs or people and lastly—any crime committed against a woman or child receives the harshest sentence."

She sits back, her hand reaching out for Jedrick, and I know they are each other's weakness but it only seems to make them stronger.

"For a man of mine to have forced you into marriage—" She shakes her head. "I offer my apologies and the family will deal with it," she finishes, and it's my turn to lean forward.

"I do not want you to deal with it," I counter and she frowns. "He is mine to deal with, I have a debt to settle with him," I growl and she grins.

"I like her," Jedrick rumbles, and Victoria's grin stretches.

"As do I, it would be a shame to kill you, Dawn," she comments. "So, that is what you want in return for information. You want your ex-husband."

I nod. "I also want any information you find once I outline what I've found, it seems our paths have crossed in another way."

She watches me and confusion swirls in her eyes as she tries to read between the lines. "Do we have a deal?" I ask, knowing this woman's word is law.

"For this information, which you won't tell me, you want your ex-husband and my word that I will share any information that I find in my...investigations, that may pertain to you or what you are dealing with?" she clarifies, her wording very careful.

"Yes." I incline my head.

"Your information must be very good," she prods.

Smiling, I uncross my legs. "It is worth it and more, but why don't you make the deal and find out?"

"Very well, but know this Dawn, just because we have some hateful men in common does not mean I won't kill you if you cross me," she says casually.

"Understood, and know that if you go back on your word, I will hunt you down and wear your skin as a coat," I reply sweetly.

She laughs again. "Oh yes, I like you. Fine, we have a deal, Dawn. Now, what is your information?"

"Marco," her eyes narrow at the name, "was stealing your money under your nose and dealing in stolen women. He was also working with some other people to sell some very special women. I happened to be unfortunate enough to be taken by Marco when I approached him about Tim, my husband. It seems they were working together with some of your other men, and embezzling money and dealing in flesh without your consent." Her hands tighten into fists and every man in the room steps forward. "I, of course, do have proof." I pull the flash drive from between my breasts and pass it over. She accepts it, her eyes hard. "I had to kill Marco I'm afraid, pesky business, but he did anger my men here when he drugged and caged me. But I have everything from his phone and computer, and an address of a warehouse where the women were kept, as well as the paper trail of the money from your legitimate business, and the funneling Tim used." Sitting back, I watch the emotions play across her face before she schools it into cold indifference, but it is enough. She didn't know and she is furious.

"Is that right?" she whispers, passing over the drive to Jedrick who takes it over to a computer in the corner. We stare at each other as he boots it up, and the only sound in the room is his tapping on the computer before he smashes his fist into the table.

"She is telling the truth," he mutters.

Victoria's eyes narrow. "I see." She grips her drink and throws it back, her whole body tight and vibrating with tension. "Thank you for bringing this to my attention, I shall deal with the traitors within my family and get your husband to you. Your information is as good as you said." She nods and I can see her mind already working a mile a minute on plans and calculations. Her eyes snap up randomly, almost making me jump.

"I am curious, though, Dawn. Why did you not just take your husband?" she asks.

325

"It would have repercussions. I'm guessing you didn't like him, but he is still your man and you would, in the very least, try and come after him. No, I wanted his whole life destroyed. I want him to know he is completely alone before I kill him, like he did to me."

"Vengeful little thing." Jedrick grins.

"Very well, thank you for bringing this to my attention. I will look into it." I can still feel the anger wafting from her, knowing some of her men have betrayed her. I'm betting this city is going to feel her wrath before sunrise. "Jedrick will see you out. I will be in contact soon, but as you can imagine, I have some business to deal with." She stands and I copy her.

She reaches out her hand, and I shake it before she turns and leaves the room, as two men break away from the door and follow her. She stops at the threshold and gives me a look filled with death and violence.

"You will make him suffer before you kill him," she orders, and sweeps from the room.

I turn to Jedrick. His eyes are on the retreating form of the woman, and only when she disappears does he turn back to us and jerk his head through the door.

He leads us down the corridor and to an elevator, and when we reach the ground floor he doesn't give us time to look around before leading us from the house.

Leaving this house we were brought to—of our own accord this time, without hoods and rope—I slide into the car that Jedrick indicates. He leans in before he shuts the door.

"We will send word when we have your husband and any information." With that, he slams the door shut and steps back as the car pulls away. I watch the house and man out of the back window. There is quite a story there, and it went better than we thought. All this time and I am one step closer to my goal. Tim will be mine with no repercussions before the week is through.

Chapter 60

DUME

"Not long now, sir," the driver announces, concentrating on the dark road in front of him.

I lost sight and feel of whoever is hunting us, but I know they are out there waiting. Setting a trap. It means I'm on high alert, anticipating their move.

And move they do—right into us.

A revving car has me looking to the right, into the dense forest, but a split second too late I see the headlights switch on from where they were obviously hiding, and now what I realise is a lorry rams into the side of our car.

The sound of metal crunching on metal fills the air, as does the scent of blood as we are rammed off the road. The car flips and I hold on tight as we roll down the embankment on the side of the road. I feel my skin splitting as shattered glass from the windows cuts into me, and hear the screams of my driver before he passes out or dies—I am not sure which.

We don't stop rolling, the hill is too steep, not until we smash into some trees. One impales the front window, pinning my shoulder into the seats. Roaring, I rip at it with claws, my hands changing from the adrenaline pumping through my system. My head is ringing, my ears are stuffy, and blood is dripping into my eyes, but I ignore it all as I rip at the wood, trying to free myself before they make their way down here. But I am not fast enough. The door I am facing is ripped open and a grinning face peers in.

Snarling, I snap forward and the man pulls back until I calm down, and then he looks back in. "Well, well, well, we are going to be well paid for this capture boys. Witch, get over here and knock him out before he kills us all."

Frowning at his words, my mind sluggish from the hit, I figured it was human hunters, but that is a thought for another time. I hand myself over to my beast and he rips from my body, tearing my shoulder from the wood and shredding through muscle and skin until my arm hangs uselessly at my side.

Kicking my way out of the car, I watch the men circle me, with a cocky looking woman chanting beside him, her hands aimed towards me. Something knocks into my chest, and with a roar I realise it is a sleeping spell. If I sleep now, I will die, or worse—be captured.

Sniffing the air, I smell coyote, wolf, and vamp. I huff through my nose and stamp at the floor, and dodge another sleeping spell.

Charging at anyone I can, I rip through their masses. I ignore the pain as they tear at my body, trying to stop me. Spell after spell meets my skin until I stumble.

Shaking my head from the confusion and tiredness, I keep moving, but I am sluggish and it feels like I'm pushing through water. The world tilts sideways, but I keep fighting when three more spells rapidly hit me, sending me to my knees.

Looking up, unable to move, I glare at everyone but their shapes are blurry. "Time to sleep, beast," a woman's voice coos, before another spell slams directly into my head. I am asleep before I hit the ground.

CHAPTER 61

NOS

When we get back to Griffin's, we all just sit in silence. Tonight went well, too well. Surely it can't be that easy to earn a crime lord's trust? Victoria did seem struck by Dawn and impressed, so who knows.

For another night, we have nothing to do. No one to kill or hunt, and it is obvious by the way we all sit looking at each other that we do not know what to do. I feel like we should be moving or doing something.

"So, we just wait for her call about Tim and any information? What about The Others?" Griffin asks, obviously itching for a fight.

"We wait for these meetings with other races, and if Victoria finds something, we could hunt for them tonight, but I think we should lay low after the meeting. They obviously know someone is on to them," I suggest and Dawn nods, sitting back.

"Did you get many responses on your phone?" she inquires, leaning into Griffin. I don't think she even noticed she did it, but he looks down at her like she is breakable and awkwardly drapes his arm over her shoulder. He looks tense and I wonder if he has ever cuddled a girl before. He keeps throwing her worried looks and I can't help but soften towards him. For all his faults, he has had a hard life and he seems to want happiness but he is not sure how to have it. Like someone might just snatch it away at any time.

"You heard my talk with the wolves, and I am meeting with the fae next week. I also left a message for the vamp queen of the city and the trolls. I managed to get through to the bears and they are happy to convene. I still need to ring Rgar, who is in charge of all the other shifters in the city like rats, snakes, foxes, deer, and so on. Their numbers are low so they tend to band together." Crossing my legs, I list off as many as I can, wanting Dawn to know a bit more about this world she has found herself in.

"Wow, I guess I never realised how many there are. Okay, why don't you ring him now, and then we can settle in for the night?" she suggests, like she is forgetting something. After all this, she could use some downtime. I might offer to show her my land or the fae kingdom—of course the fallen will have to come too.

"Of course, Little Monster." I grin, grabbing my phone and scrolling through my contacts.

"I just realised, I don't have your numbers...or a phone anymore. I must have lost it in the trousers I was wearing when we flew," she mutters, her face clouding over, and I know she is thinking about the night she died and everything she lost. As selfish as it sounds, I'm glad it happened. I hate that she was hurt and betrayed, but it brought her to me.

"You can have whatever the fuck you want. Take my phone until we get you a new one phone," Griffin snaps, pushing it at her, and his panic over her being upset is clearly written on his face.

Her expression clears instantly and she laughs, tilting her head back to see him. He narrows his eyes, looking uncomfortable, but she leans up and kisses him softly. "Thank you, my fallen, but I can just borrow one of yours until I get one." She passes it back over and he nods, looking away and appearing calmer.

Hitting Rgar's number, I wait for it to ring. He lives in an old hotel on the other side of town. He owned it originally, but it only took a few reports of rats, which actually turned out to be the cleaners, and the place was shut down. Since then, it's become a hotel for the other shifters in town and people just tend to stay if they don't have people or a pack.

"The Bellhop, how may I shift your inquiries," comes a bored sounding voice.

"I need to speak with Rgar. Please inform him it is No-Cerry," I grunt and Dawn gasps. I look over and her and Griffin are both trying to hold back their laughter. I wink at her and she giggles, turning her head to Griffin and mouthing, "Cerry." He snorts, leans over, and pushes a piece of hair behind her ear. Her laughter disappears and I turn away, letting them have their moment.

"One moment." Cheery background music starts and I sit and wait until the other line clicks on.

"Cerry, is this truly you?" Rgar, the only remaining nanaue, or wereshark as people commonly call them, asks. His voice is his usual rich, deep timbre.

"Yes, it's me." I grin.

"Haven't any hunters gotten lucky and killed you yet?" he jokes, making me roll my eyes.

"Not yet, no pirates harpoon you yet?" I tease back.

"Ya old bastard, what's up, tree hugger?" he asks.

"I needed to ask, have any of your shifters disappeared?"

Silence greets me, but I know he is still there from his breathing.

"What do you know?" he questions harshly.

"Only that it is happening across the city, I wanted to know if it was every race," I reply tiredly, knowing that means they have.

He sighs. "Two kitsune, one nagual, a selkie, and coyote...all female," he finishes, and I hear the strain in his voice.

"I am sorry," I console, knowing how personally he will take this. He sees himself as their unofficial protector, so their loss will have hit him hard.

He only grunts. "Tell me you have the bastards or know who they are so I can rip them apart."

"Not yet, I only know the name they are going by, The Others, and the fact they are supes."

He snarls, muttering something before blowing out a breath. "I had wanted it not to be true, but I smelled wet dog and magic."

Rubbing my head, I nod at Dawn when she offers me a questioning look. "It seems witches are involved in this, as well as a number of other races. I am working with the humans and fae to figure out who, or at least get some information before I go to the council. Do you have anything else?" Every new disappearance seems to only add more questions and I'm at a dead end.

"Aye, I got a good bite of one of the bastards last time as he was fleeing...I also smelled him, Cerry." He lowers his voice. "It smelled like rosemary and feathers."

"Eagles?" I growl, sitting forward. There are only two eagles in this whole fucking city. One is a lackey, one sits on the council.

"Yes. I don't know which, but I know that smell," he sneers.

Mind racing a million miles a minute, I say my goodbyes, telling him to stay in touch and I will do the same.

"Eagles?" Griffin repeats, his voice cold.

"Rgar, he smelled eagle," I inform him tiredly.

"You think—"

I shrug. "I don't know, and it's no good pointing fingers. It will get us nowhere. I suggest we build a case and present it to the council. Their reaction will tell us everything."

Dawn looks between us, biting her lip in confusion. "Explain?"

"It means either our own fucking council is stealing people, or someone is doing it right under their nose," Griffin growls and I nod.

She sighs and sits back. "Huh, well at least we have some more information."

"You are calm?" I ask, confused.

She grins. "I trust no one but you two and this council is nothing to me. If they are taking our people then I will kill them like I would anyone else. Just because they hold a seat of power does not mean they can't be overthrown, and if they didn't know about it, are they really fit to rule?" she muses, dropping that bomb as a phone goes off. She must have been playing with Griffin's because she pulls it from her lap.

Dawn shoots upright. "I have a message from Victoria!" she exclaims.

"What does it say?" I ask.

She looks up and an evil grin stretches across her face as her eyes turn black. "She has Tim. She will bring him tomorrow night."

CHAPTER 62

ASKA

Speeding along the roads, getting closer and closer to my mate, I push back the sick feeling in my stomach. My dragon is pushing against me again, letting me know something is coming. I debate leaving the car and flying at least five times as fast, but I know it would not help. Only when I have her in front of me will this feeling go away.

My phone rings, cutting off my internal debate, and with a sigh I answer it. I am tired after the long, few days of travel and hardly no sleep. Even my dragon is calling for rest.

"Yes?" I answer.

"Sir?" Jean Paul replies, sounding worried.

"I am fine, just tired. What's wrong?" I ask, knowing he would only be calling if there was something to report.

"I have been doing some research and asking around to make sure everything is okay. Sir, it seems the hunters are on the move. I have humans watching them, but it seems they are all heading in the same direction you are."

Smashing my fist to the wheel, I growl. "What else?"

"There are reports emerging of some races disappearing. I am trying to find out more, but I wasn't sure it if was connected to the hunters or not, but I felt like I should inform you," he rushes out.

"Thank you, Jean Paul, I did need to know." I end the call, beyond confused and enraged. Is that what this bad feeling is? Is my mate in danger of disappearing or is it the hunters that seem to be baring down on the city she calls home? I have too many questions and not enough answers. It seems the best course of action is to keep going and hope that I get some when I find her.

Forcing myself to pull over and rest, I lean my seat back and close my eyes. I am no good to her exhausted and I am still not at a hundred percent after resting for so long. At least if I sleep I can reach out to her, it might settle my dragon as well. Happy with that, I let myself fall into the oblivion of slumber, thinking of nothing but her.

"Dawn?" I ask.

She turns, but it's like she can't see me. She searches the mist with a frown on her face. Stepping forward, I hit a barrier. It was invisible until I came into contact with it, but it's blocking her from me.

Only a witch could block all types of connection like this, and unless they are targeting me on purpose...this is a net cast over wherever my mate is.

"Get out, get out of wherever you are now," I order, slamming my hands onto the barrier again and again.

"Aska?" she calls out, looking around like I might appear before her like normal.

"Get out!" I scream, but it's no use and I am flung from her dreams like a thread is cut. A coven is blocking me—but why? Why cast a net around the whole city? What are they trying to hide? Where do the hunters and the disappearances come into play?

I wait impatiently for Victoria to reply, so it startles me when the phone rings in my hand. I answer it straight away and her silky voice comes down the line. "Dawn, I have your asshole of an ex, we have...extracted information that we needed, but don't worry, we did not break or kill him. I left that for you." She laughs and I hear screaming in the background followed by the sound of flesh hitting flesh.

"Good," I purr. "Where and when can I get him?" I almost beg, desperate for him to finally get his.

"I shall meet you in two hours, Lakes Road, you know it? Go on to the forest road and keep going, it is a dirt road, the sixth turn." I nod, knowing Nos will know how to get there.

"Oh and Dawn, you were right. The things I have learned he has done...he deserves to die. Do not let him live when you finally come to the choice, or I will clean him up myself." She ends the call and my eyebrows rise, wondering what she found.

But she has me wrong, I won't falter. He deserves to die. I'm a vengeful bitch, not a fucking hero. He won't see the sunrise, that's for sure.

I turn to Nos and Griffin and we all share a matching grin. He might be a human and evil, but we are much worse. We are monsters.

Something wakes me up. My head is foggy, and when I open my eyes they take far too long to focus, and when they do I roar, yanking myself forward only to be stopped by chains. Turning my head, I narrow my eyes on the chains binding my hands and feet to a wall. I walk forward, and test how far they let me reach and their strength. They are no ordinary chains—they are spelled.

Roaring out my anger, I let the rage take control. I will not be trapped again.

Chained.

Controlled.

Left.

Monster.

No!

The door opens and men stream in, and the next thing I know, I am knocked out again.

Waking, calmer than before, I huff through my nose, my eyes allowing me to see in the dark cell.

I can smell witches, but underneath that I smell a cloying mix of shifters and humans. What the fuck? Who the fuck hit me? I figured it was the witches wanting their revenge, but if so, then why haven't they done it yet? This isn't right.

It's that thought that has me relaxing, taking in my surroundings and calming down. No, there are not just some witches.

This is something else.

The cell door opens and a man with bodyguards behind him steps in, his head held high and a smirk curving his lips. "Hello, Dume was it?"

CHAPTER 63

NOS

W e leave the house after an hour. Dawn is antsy. It's the only word I can describe. She isn't nervous, that I can tell, but she has been waiting for this moment and now that she knows it's coming, she wants to go. We use Griffin's car and I rattle off directions, keeping my eyes on her in the backseat.

She looks out into the forest calmly, but I want to make sure she is certain of this decision. I will not think lesser of her, and if she cannot do it I will kill him for her. Hell, I would rip out each organ and make a bloody sacrifice to her if she would allow it, but I have a feeling this is a battle she needs to face herself.

"Little Monster?" I call out, once we get on the stretch of road that will lead us to the spot we are meeting Victoria.

She turns to me, blinking hard like she was a million miles away. "Are you sure this is what you want? We can turn around, or Griffin or I can do this for you?" I offer.

She smiles softly, but her eyes are as hard as steel. "He did not rape you, he did not beat you, he did not ruin your life and then kill you. No, he is mine. I've been dreaming about this. If it's my soul you're worried about, we both know I have more blood and darkness on my hands than good," she grits out, determination lacing her tone.

"It's not your soul I am worried about," I reply calmly. "I don't care if you kill him or not, I just don't want you thinking you have to."

She softens a little. "Nos, I need to do this. He needs to pay. This city is crooked and he never will otherwise. I don't give a fuck if I shouldn't be judge, jury, and executioner—I will be. He made me that, but I would appreciate you both at my back," she requests, looking worried suddenly.

Griffin snorts. "Like we will be anywhere else, *vasculo*. Not a fucking chance. I don't give a fuck if you kill this piece of shit. In fact, if you don't I plan to and I promise I will make him suffer a lot worse than you. But she's right, this is hers. She needs to do this..." He trails off, going quieter. "I know that."

I nod, turning back to the front. "Turn here," I instruct, and Griffin takes us down the dirt road. His car isn't great for the road, but we finally make it to where the forest meets the road. Waiting for us there is a car with Victoria leaned against it, looking up at the full moon.

I turn back to Dawn. "I'm with you all the way, come on, Little Monster, let's take your vengeance." I grin, letting my eyes flash white for her and she grins back.

We get out of the car and walk over to meet Victoria. She ignores us both like before, concentrating on Dawn. I should be offended but I like to disappear.

"He is a fucking weak ass pussy," she says in greeting, and Dawn laughs.

"Yes, he is." She grins.

Victoria bangs on the boot of the car and Jedrick comes around with a man bound, gagged, and blindfolded.

"He was fun to play with, though, I made sure not to break him...too much. I am still investigating, I will be in touch shortly. Have fun." Victoria laughs and Jedrick pushes over Dawn's ex to us. We all let him fall to his knees, and he screams around the gag as we all look at him in disgust.

"Griffin, grab him," Dawn orders, and when I look up to see Victoria watching us in interest, I do as I'm told without arguing.

Pulling the man to his feet, I wrinkle my nose at the smell of unwashed body odour, piss, and blood. Lovely.

Victoria grins and waves before she gets into the car. Jedrick spins it around and leaves us there, our lights hitting the trees and illuminating the area. "Grab the shovel please, Nos," she asks, her eyes locked on the man I'm holding on to. He is shorter than us, and weak, like Victoria says, but I am betting to a human woman he would be stronger and way more powerful.

That realisation comes across Dawn's face, the knowing that the reason she was so scared of him was her humanity, and it makes me want to hug her or some shit. Now, she just looks pissed as hell and all kinds of scary, especially when her eyes slide to black. It makes my cock rock-hard and I grit my teeth as I push the man forward.

Nos comes back with a shovel and none of us bother to bring lights, since we can all see in the dark. The man stumbles along next to us as we trek through the forest. Every now and again I spot Nos murmuring to something or touching a tree or flower. Fucking nature gods.

When we come to a break in the trees, Dawn stops. "Here." She nods and the man whimpers. Rolling my eyes, I push him forward, and he stumbles and falls flat on his face.

Growling, Dawn kicks him over so he faces her and rips off his blindfold. She grins down at him as he screams in terror, his eyes nearly bugging from his head.

"Hello husband, I told you I would come back for you," she purrs, and I can't help the shiver of desire it sends through me.

She turns and winks at me before grabbing the shovel from Nos, and throwing it at the man's head. "Dig a grave," she orders.

Laughter bubbles out of me and she joins in as he screams and thrashes.

Chapter 64

Dawn

Once Tim realised I was serious, I ungagged him, but when he started spouting shit I shut him up with a quick punch to the face—I may have hit him harder than I needed to, but fuck him.

Crying, he starts to dig as we all watch, circling him like prey. I'm barely keeping control, but I don't want my powers riding me when I kill him. No, I want to be fully present and human, even as he looks into the eyes of the monster he created.

"I'm sorry, okay? Please, please just stop haunting me. Do you want money?" he screams, and stops digging to look at me. Blood and sweat pour down his face.

I cross my arms where I stand at the top of the grave. "You think I'm still a ghost and you think I want money? Fuck, you really are dumb and no, you don't have any money anyway." I grin.

His face pales again. "You're not a ghost?"

"No baby, I'm all real. You should make sure that any bodies you bury stay dead," I snarl, and he falls back into the wall of the shallow grave.

"You're a zombie?" he screeches, making me roll my eyes.

"No, stupid, now keep digging," I snap.

He goes back to it, throwing us looks as he tries to plan his escape. I know he's playing weak and will try and make a break for it once he realises the nice boy act won't work. The grave is nearly done when he decides to do it—after over thirty minutes of us all ignoring his cries and pleas.

He jumps from the grave, using the shovel, and runs at me. Stupid.

I grab it mid-swing, stopping it in the air and throw it away. He stumbles back and looks around for another exit. Once he realises he has no way out, his shoulders drop before rounding. He lifts his head and sneers at me—ah, there he is. The husband I know and hate.

"Well, I'll be honest. You always were a stupid slut, couldn't even stay dead right." He laughs and I hold my hand up when I feel Griffin and Nos moving in. "What, are you going to kill me? You don't have the balls," he spits out, stepping closer.

Before, I would have cowered, maybe even crawled at his feet begging for mercy from the beating I knew was coming. Now, I am cold and filled with rage.

"Do you want to know what we did to you when you died?" he asks, grinning.

A part of me shrinks away, but I won't let him see that. There is nothing he can do to hurt me anymore and his words are just that —words.

"We fucked you real good, everybody who wanted a fucking turn in that whore body of yours," he starts, and I zone out, letting him rant. He finishes finally, looking mighty pleased with himself.

"You know what's fun?" I ask. "I made you dig your own grave." I dart forward and turn him with my hand on his head. I force him to his knees in front of it. He tries to get back up, but I push him down.

"Maybe I'll let the wolves fuck you as you die," I snarl.

When I look up, I spot all the animals in the trees, their eyes reflecting there. I don't know if any are shifters, but it doesn't matter. They are here because Nos is. Our defenders, our watches.

"I wanted you to suffer, I wanted your pain and screams, but now? I don't care, I just want you gone like a bug under my shoe. You are nothing to me, not a threat, not a worry. Just nothing," I admit honestly.

Grabbing the knife, the same one he used to kill me, from the back of my jeans, I shove it into his back before pulling out and stabbing him again. He screams and falls forward into the grave as I watch, with the knife at my side. He struggles, only making the blood flow faster. Words and spit stream from his mouth, but I ignore them all as he starts to weaken.

"Fuck...you," he gasps, and I know they will be his last words.

His eyes stay locked on mine, filled with hate and defiance, even until they are empty and lifeless. His body is pale and already turning blue as the blood seeps into the dirt below—like an offering.

I thought I would feel better with his death, but I was wrong, I just feel empty. I turn to the two men who make me feel whole. The pride and anger on their faces makes me smile.

"Let's go home." I grin.

They nod, each grabbing a hand as we make our way back through the forest to the car. I hear the animals already ripping into Tim's body and I grin.

When we reach the treeline, new lights hit us and I freeze as three cars block ours in. A door opens and booted feet hit the ground.

It's the last thing I see before magic hits me right in the center of my chest, stopping my heart. Dropping to my knees, I feel Nos and Griffin fighting next to me, but my eyes close without my permission and all there is, is the black again.

When I wake up, I'm tied to a table. My hands are bound by chains glittering with magic. The man from the meeting, no longer in the old man disguise, sits opposite me, watching me curiously. The cloying scent of feathers and rosemary hits me, making me sneeze.

K.A. KNIGHT

"I have been tracking you," he starts.

Relaxing on the table, I make sure to show nothing. I know he wouldn't have killed Nos or Griffin, he needs them alive for information.

"Ever since your little act at the meeting. Tell me, how did you do it?" He leans in, his eyes filled with excitement. "How did you change like that? Borrowed magic, spells?" he rushes out.

I say nothing and he narrows his eyes. "I will find out, but first, maybe I should introduce myself. I am Veyo, but you may call me Vey. I am a collector of sorts, of the rare and unique. You seem to know this though, of course I don't just collect for myself, but that's another story altogether and not why you are here. The council has requested your presence, and as their humble servant, of course I obliged." He grins, leaning in like we are best friends. Veyo—wasn't that the name Marco found for The Others? Wait, he works for the council? Is the council pulling his strings? "Now, tell me what I need to know about you."

I knew this man was involved in the kidnappings, but is he really the leader, and what does that mean? Does he sell them to other people? Who else does this involve and how far does it stretch? I have so many questions but I know he won't answer them.

"My name is fuck you, I like long walks and killing people, and I have imagined at least five, no wait, six ways I can kill you involving that motherfucking stupid earring in your right ear." I grin sweetly.

He sits back, frowning hard. "That is no way for a lady to talk, it's a shame really. Oh well, maybe you need some time to think this over. I shall, of course, oblige." He stands up, buttoning his suit, and nods at the men I can smell behind me.

They grab my hands, muttering under their breaths, before releasing the chain. I make my move. Darting my elbow back to the right, I hear a grunt of impact as I jump left. Before anyone can react, I rip out the throat of the guard and fly at the other. He lands on his back on the floor while I smash it into the white tile repeatedly, and blood pools around his head.

I scream when something feeling like an electricity shocks me, my whole body convulses as I fall to the side, gasping. More men

344

have entered the room and one has his hand out towards me, and a glowing pendant on his chest draws my eye. The same one I saw on the neck of the guards at the meeting.

"Oh, how I hate having to recruit new men," Veyo laments, with a twisted look of disgust at the dead bodies, he steps back to avoid the pool of blood and glares over at me. "You shall have to pay for that of course. Men, grab her. We shall throw her in cell four and please inform the council she is here." Some of them grin and I know whatever they have planned isn't good.

Even though my body is still twitching and feels weak, I fight them but it's no use. They shock me again, and as I'm convulsing they drag me from the room and down a corridor. I wait, snarling inside my head for my body to stop, before yanking forward and throwing the guards holding me of kilter. I break free, grabbing a knife from one's belt and I stab him in the heart before I'm shocked again. I go down but quickly get to my feet and fling myself at the mass of men, tearing and biting until I'm shocked three times in quick succession.

I drop like a rock and they quickly grab me, pulling me faster now.

Growling, I dart at them as they drag me from the room and down a corridor to another door.

"A little bit of time will do you well. Think about the options you have before you...if you survive it." He laughs and his men wait for us at a steel door at the end of the hall, their glowing chests lighting up the dark.

"I swear, if you have hurt my mates I will rip your fucking souls from you and kill you while wearing your own skin!" I yell, infuriated at being separated from them.

They ignore me, and when we get closer to the door, I see the outwards indentations from something heavy hitting it repeatedly. From the chains and magic surrounding it, whatever inside isn't good.

Surely, they need me alive.

They wait until I'm closer to throw open the door and I'm shoved in before I can even look inside. The door slams shut behind me and I whirl when the slat on it opens, throwing light inside the dark and damp cell.

"Good luck, skinwalker. If you live through the night, maybe I have use for you." He laughs and the slat slides shut with a bang.

Screaming, I bang on the door but a noise in the dark behind me has me freezing. The hair on the back of my neck stands on end and goosebumps erupt on my skin. Something blows warm air across me, disturbing my hair, and I hear the slink of chains and what sound like hooves on the concrete floor.

A deep, rumbling roar sounds from right behind me, making me spin and push my back against the cell door. It all goes quiet. Only the sound of my hammering heart sounds in the cell as my eyes adjust to the complete blackness.

Once they do, I gasp. My eyes lock onto it from where it stands not meters away.

A fucking minotaur.

EPILOGUE

ASKA

The city is before me, but I know I am too late. Something has happened, I can feel it thrumming down the bond that pulled me here.

My mate is in trouble, somewhere in this city. I will have to find her, and kill those that dare to hurt her.

I haven't waited a thousand years to lose her now. A pulse of pain and panic winds through my chest. When I first became close, I could feel her emotions, like a beacon, but now they are weak.

Stepping on the pedal, I weave quickly between traffic.

No one takes a mate away from a dragon, they will know my rage, and then they will know my hate.

This city will be bathed in their blood before the night is through.

It's time for the dragons to rule again and for me to don my crown.

My name is Askaliarian, first of my name, the soul eater, and I will kill them all.

Author's Note
Continued

As promised in my first note, here is the triggers featured in this book. If you feel I have missed any, please do not hesitate to reach out.

Violence is prevalent throughout this book as is bloodshed. Rape, there is a scene where the main character is raped fairly quickly into the book. It does fade to black but it does contain some graphic details. Murder, assault and graphic sex scenes are also included within this book.

About the Author

K.A Knight is an indie author trying to get all of the stories and characters out of her head. She loves reading and devours every book she can get her hands on, she also has a worrying caffeine addiction.

She leads her double life in a sleepy English town, where she spends her days at the evil day job and comes home to her fur babies.

Read more at K.A Knight's website or join her Facebook Reader Group.

Also by K.A. Knight

THEIR CHAMPION SERIES

- The Wasteland
- The Summit
- *The Cities (Coming 2019)*

- The Forgotten

DAWNBREAKER SERIES

- Voyage to Ayama
- *Dreaming of Ayama (Coming 2019)*

THE LOST COVEN SERIES

- Aurora's Coven
- *Aurora's Betrayal (Coming 2019)*

HER MONSTERS SERIES

- Rage

CO-AUTHOR PROJECTS

- Circus Save Me
- Circus Saves Christmas
- One Night Only (Featured February 2019 in the Valentine's Between The Sheets Anthology)

- The Wild Interview
- The Hero Complex
- *Shipwreck Souls (Coming June 2019)*